THE
Butterfly
Garden

SOPHIE ANDERSON

bookouture

Published by Bookouture in 2021

An imprint of Storyfire Ltd.
Carmelite House
50 Victoria Embankment
London EC4Y 0DZ

www.bookouture.com

ISBN: 978-1-80019-476-2
eBook ISBN: 978-1-80019-475-5

For my grandmother Da.

CHAPTER ONE

I had my first appointment with Dr Sham today. He has asked me to start a diary. It feels strange; I haven't written one since I was fourteen. I am not sure what he wants me to write: the fact that I didn't leave the house today, didn't even bother to get dressed? Or the fact that I had a bacon sandwich this morning for the first time in nineteen years? I had to do something radical, blow away the suffocating fog, but I just vomited violently, then sobbed on the bathroom floor. Or that I go to bed before Richard every night so that when he comes in, I can feign sleep and not have to touch the tortured soul he has become. Or that Lucas doesn't eat meals with us any more, or that I am pretending not to notice him smoking weed in the garage. Or that sometimes when everyone else is out, I go into her bedroom and get into her bed, put her pillow over my head and breathe in her sweet, sweet smell. I breathe so hard that I feel giddy. Which is a relief from the wretched weight of despair.

*

Porthteal, 2017

'Eyes Wanted', the ad read in the village shop window, below it a phone number scrawled on a scrappy piece of paper. Erin was desperate. It had rained steadily for the three weeks since she'd been back and her spirit was already crumpling under the relentless scorn of her mum. And then she'd overheard Brenda calling her a homewrecker as she scanned Mrs Talbot's groceries.

'Her poor father must be so ashamed,' she'd said. 'And now she's back without a penny to her name, living off his good nature. Such a kind man.'

So, Erin had called. Mrs Muir gave nothing away on the phone but summoned Erin to her house. 'Past the lighthouse and down the first track after the stile,' she said, but Erin knew. Everyone in Porthteal knew that house.

It was November, and the last remnants of a sunny autumn had been washed away into rivers of cold brown mud. The days were short and the fruit on the trees was rotten. The waves rolled in from beyond the fog and crashed over the sea wall with furious tenacity, filling the whole bay with a froth of white water. Icy shards of rain pricked Erin's face as she turned down the track and saw Hookes End clinging to the edge of the cliff. The house was visible for miles around but Erin had never been this close. It was tattier than she'd imagined, with greying pebble-dash and rotting windows. There was a scattering of trees with angular quiffs in front of the hostile square facade, and the beds at the front of the house were littered with dead hydrangeas, their rust-coloured heads as soggy as she felt. Erin pulled the brass knocker on the door and cowered under the shelter of the porch. There weren't any lights on, and the house was eerily still.

Then a dog barked and Erin heard footsteps, the rattling of the latch and the door eventually opened. The woman who answered had a gaunt elegance and was impossible to age. Her greying hair was scraped back into a bun at the nape of her weathered neck. She wore tinted glasses which masked her eyes. She was shorter than Erin and even scrawnier, an oversized olive cable-knit jumper hanging from her pointy shoulders. A dog with wiry brown hair and wonky ears jumped up at her legs. Erin knelt to stroke him.

'Oblonsky, down,' the woman said. Her voice was deep and husky.

'Hello, Mrs Muir, we spoke earlier about the ad,' she said with as much charm as she could rally through the wall of rain. The lady didn't respond immediately and Erin couldn't see whether she was even looking at her from behind the glasses.

'You'd best come in then.' Mrs Muir turned slowly and released her white knuckles from the door handle to grab the wall and steady herself. Then she walked with heavy feet down the hall ahead. The hollow thump of her clogs resounded on the brick floor. Erin discarded her boots and their wedge of mud in the least leaky corner of the porch and followed in her socks. It smelt musty, of wet dog and old dishcloths.

A fire was lit in the room at the end of the corridor and the glowing embers were a relief from the gale still clattering against the windows. There were no lights on and Erin had to adjust her eyes to the gloom. Mrs Muir sat down at a round table behind the sofa where Oblonsky had made himself comfortable and gestured impatiently for Erin to sit down too. It was littered with piles of paper, books and newspapers. A faded blue and white teapot with matching cups and saucers sat amid the chaos.

'Tea?' Mrs Muir asked, and without waiting for an answer lifted the pot. The lid chinked in her shaking hands.

Erin took in the books that lined the walls. Tatty paperbacks mostly, classics interspersed with detective novels and trashy romances. And lots of hardback encyclopedias and nature books: there was a whole section of the bookcase piled up with butterfly journals.

'So, what do you think I meant by the advert?' asked Mrs Muir.

'Uh, I wasn't sure.'

'Really? I was hoping it might stir up all sorts of intrigue among the villagers. Come on, "Eyes Wanted". You must have had some ideas?'

'Well, I hoped you weren't some crazy scientist who needed my eyes for an experiment.' Erin forced a laugh out.

'Nope, nothing as exciting as that, I'm afraid.' Mrs Muir stirred her tea slowly, the spoon clinking against the cup. Without lifting her eyes, she continued in the same dour tone. 'I have a brain tumour. Six months to live, maybe less. And not content with taking my life, this beast in my head is taking my eyes too. Which is why I need yours.'

'Oh!' Erin knew it was an inadequate response. 'To help with housework? Cooking?'

'God no, I don't care about that. To help me finish my book.' Mrs Muir rifled through the piles of paper on the table until she found what she was looking for. She shook some sheets at Erin. 'I thought I could do it, but I have only managed a few pages. I cannot see the words and am wasting precious time. So, I need help.'

She looked away and then picked up her teacup; the appeal for help obviously grated. Erin wondered how long it had been since Mrs Muir had had a visitor in this house. She looked down at the filth on the table. A cloud of silvery mould was sprouting from a withered satsuma next to her teacup.

'I don't really have any experience with writing,' Erin began.

'Can you read?'

'Uh, yeah.'

'Can you type?'

Erin hesitated. 'Pretty well.'

'Then that's all I need. I have already handwritten a lot of it in here.' She tapped a black leather notebook that was fraying at the edges. 'Can you start straight away?'

Unable to process the events as fast as they were occurring, Erin stuttered, 'But – but you don't know anything about me. I could be anyone.'

Mrs Muir took a sip of her tea and slowly placed the cup back on the table. 'Erin Turner, daughter of John and Debbie Turner.

John – local farmer. Debbie – sells the produce of her thriving kitchen garden. You fled to London with the artist-in-residence at the Driftwood Gallery. He obviously didn't leave his wife as promised, and so you have come back with your tail between your legs. I can't imagine the job offers are pouring in. The homewrecker harlot doesn't go down too well in these parts. But I am willing to take a chance.' She pushed her glasses to the end of her nose and examined Erin over the top of them. Her smoky irises glistened with mockery.

'How did you know?' was all Erin could muster. She was unnerved by this steely precis of her screwed-up life and the second reference to homewrecker that day, but she was quite amused by Mrs Muir's Sherlock Holmes delivery.

'People like to talk in this place. Not me, but sometimes I can't help listening. That Brenda in the shop, she had a field day when you came back. Caused quite a stir, you did. Now, do you want to help me or not?'

'I guess.' Erin shrugged; she wasn't sure, and couldn't hold her gaze. Her eyes darted around the room and she caught sight of a mass of cobwebs at the top of the window. Dead flies were suspended in its snare and fluttered in the wind that broke through the ill-fitting frame.

'Good. You can call me Maggie.'

'OK.' She didn't look like a Maggie. Her mum had called her Margaret earlier that day when she'd told her where she was going. It seemed more appropriate somehow.

Mrs Muir – Maggie – sat back in her seat. Her eyes closed as she sucked in a lengthy breath. Was she stifling pain somewhere? Erin looked up at the wall behind her which was cluttered with small butterfly paintings. Acrylics, in vibrant colours with intricate black markings like a stained-glass window. And there were more on the other side of the fireplace. They were more muted, informative-looking; you could see the tatty edges of the pages where someone had torn them out of a book. And above the fireplace was a huge cobalt-blue butterfly in an elaborate gilt frame. The wings had an iridescent sheen that flickered in the light of the fire, and it was hard to tell whether it was a painting or a photograph.

'I don't expect you have read any of my Detective Turnpike series?' Maggie said, bringing Erin's attention back from the butterflies. She shook her head and stifled a smile – so she really did have detective delusions. 'This book isn't like any of them anyway, it's a different genre altogether.' Her words were clipped, as if she needed to expel them fast, without consequence. 'And I would really appreciate it if you didn't ask questions about its content. I need you to be my eyes, nothing more.' Her head down, she gathered the pages at the table and held them out, shaking them impatiently until Erin took them.

'You want me to read this?' Erin asked.

'No, I want you to light a fire with it. Of course I want you to read it,' Maggie snapped.

'Here? Now?'

'No, you can take them home and read them tonight. It won't take you long. I haven't done much yet, which is why we need to crack on,' Maggie said. 'Is that going to be a problem?'

'Uh, no. 'Course not.' Erin fiddled with the corners of the pages.

'Well, off you go then.' Maggie shooed her away. 'Come back at eight o'clock tomorrow morning, I like to get going early.'

The rain had weakened to a gentle drizzle as Erin left the house. The sky glowed pewter and a cacophony of drips echoed from tree to tree as she set off down the hill. She knew she should be relieved that she had found a job, but she felt unsettled by it all. Maggie was rude, pretty terrifying in fact. And not much better than Brenda in the shop with that account of her affair with Simon. She really didn't relish the thought of being stuck in that dilapidated house with her all day, but what was the alternative? Her parents had made it pretty clear that she had to contribute to her living expenses now she was back, and she didn't have a penny to her name. There was no work at the pub, and no way she was going to ask Brenda for a job in the shop. And there wasn't anything else in Porthteal, apart from the gallery, of course, but that was Simon's domain and Kirstin was their only employee and she had been there for as long as Erin could remember.

No, Maggie really was the only way she was going to get enough money to get away from Porthteal. What was it her mum had called her? 'That hermit up on Lighthouse Hill'. And she was a dying hermit... Would she be expected to nurse Maggie? Surely she wasn't being paid enough for that? She was not good with bodily functions. She shivered as she recalled the smell of the house. And there was clutter everywhere. Not in a cosy way, more a dirty despondency. And what was with all the butterflies? There was barely a patch of wall that hadn't been covered with them. And it was horribly dark, with no lights on. Exactly how blind was Maggie? Erin shut her eyes and tried to imagine a life of darkness. She walked for ten paces until she tripped over a tree root and was pitched frighteningly close to the cliff edge. She peered down at the waves thrashing against the rocks below and found herself lurching forward. She had almost reached the tipping point before she pulled herself sharply back onto the path. Her heart thumped inside her chest and she staggered on wobbly legs to the other side of the path. 'Fuck,' she said.

She wouldn't have jumped – things weren't that bad. The sea roared beneath her and the spray of an especially large wave hit her face. She had a job now, she told herself, a respectable job. She rubbed her face with both hands. She was going to help write a novel. Erin took a steadying breath and turned towards her house. She broke into a run down the path and the rucksack containing Maggie's pages bounced against her back.

CHAPTER TWO

Lansdown Place, 23rd November 1986

Lucas hasn't been going to school. It has been going on since half-term, apparently. Mrs Brady called us into her office. She said she had left me a few messages, but I rarely answer the phone now: I can't bear the pity in everyone's voices, the well-wishers, the do-gooders. I didn't tell Mrs Brady that, obviously, I just shrugged my shoulders and looked bemused. She spoke to us with sickening benevolence. 'I know he has had a really hard time of it, so we have given him a lot of leniency but he is going to fail the year if he doesn't start showing up soon. And he won't get his O levels, and then he can totally forget about A levels.'

I lost her then. Her voice just started floating out of the top of her head and into the room, echoey and distant. She took my hand at the door and squeezed it tight. 'We want to help,' she said.

We had an inevitable row in the car. Richard said I was rude. He said it was all my fault, I was not taking enough interest in my son. And then he laid into Lucas when we got home and Lucas stormed out, slamming the kitchen door so that his picture of a poison dart frog that had been on the fridge for nearly a decade fluttered to the floor. I picked it up and remembered his little face squished up against the glass in the reptile house.

Lucas was just five when I took him to Jersey Zoo. He loved animals, and I had read an article in the dentist's one day all about the Durrell Zoo for endangered species and had booked it on a whim. I could still feel his little hand in mine as we walked up the gangplank onto our ferry at Poole, his lion rucksack on his back. Our hotel on the waterfront smelt of cabbage, but Lucas loved running up and down the swirly-carpeted corridors. We ate hamburgers in our bedroom both nights and slept curled up together under the apricot flannel sheets.

Orangutans, silverback gorillas, flamingos, meerkats – Lucas had never seen anything like it. But it was the poison dart frogs that really captured his attention. He was totally transfixed by the tiny, luminous creatures. Scarlet, cobalt blue, canary yellow, they clung to the jungle leaves. I read him the blurb about native Indians dipping their arrows in the poison on the frog's back before hunting, and his eyes grew so wide I thought they might pop out of his head.

I uncurled the edges of the picture that he drew in the hotel that day and stuck it back under the Tower of London fridge magnet. Richard stormed out of the house and I heard his car grumble into action in the driveway.

*

'Oh, you're home.' Erin was jolted out of her reverie by her mum, who was taking off her coat and boots in the doorway. 'How did it go? What are you reading?' She headed across the kitchen and filled the kettle before placing it on the Aga. The beads of water dripping down the side fizzed and danced on the hotplate.

'Fine.' Erin was still in Maggie's world, trying to process what she had just read.

'Well? What did she want? Is she as barking as they all say? "Eyes Wanted", I never heard the like.'

'Er, kind of,' Erin muttered, her eyes not leaving the manuscript in her lap.

'What do you mean, kind of?' Her mum retrieved an already prepared fish pie from the fridge and shooed away the cat who had jumped onto the table to sniff it.

'She's not mad, Mum, she's dying, and going blind, and she wants me to help her.'

'Who's dying?' her dad said, coming into the room and heading for the sink.

'Erin's got a job with that Margaret Muir up at Hookes End.'

'Maggie,' Erin said.

'What?'

'She doesn't call herself Margaret, she's Maggie.'

'Maggie Muir is dying?' her dad said, washing his hands in the sink, the water turning brown as it ran through his fingers.

'She has a brain tumour,' Erin said.

'Really? How sad.'

'And Erin is going to work for her,' her mum said, and her dad turned around in surprise and walked towards her. 'John! Your boots are filthy. I mopped the floor earlier.'

'Sorry, love.' He wobbled as he bent down to take them off. 'And what will you be doing for her, Erin?'

'She wants me to help her write her last book.'

'Really? How intriguing.' He pulled out the chair at the table next to Erin and leant over to have a look. Muddy water dripped from his hands onto the top page of Maggie's manuscript.

'Oh, Dad! Look what you've done.' Erin wiped the water away, smudging the print as she did so.

'I just wanted to have a look,' he said.

'I can't let you read it.'

'Why not?'

'I don't think Maggie would like that. She has given it to me to read, not my whole family.' That was an understatement; she shuddered as she imagined the wrath of Maggie if she discovered Erin's parents had read her manuscript. Quite apart from not wanting to get on the wrong side of her new boss, Erin felt an unexpected surge of protective responsibility for Maggie. She was obviously a private person, and Maggie had entrusted Erin with her words. She closed the manuscript and leant forward, crossing her arms on top of the pages.

'Suit yourself. Doesn't she write murder mysteries?' her dad asked, sitting back in his chair.

'She does, but she said this is a different genre.'

'A different genre, indeed? Wow, you sound like a writer already.'

Her mum placed two mugs of tea on the table. Her dad stroked the back of his wife's hand. 'Thanks, love,' he said.

'I'm not sure about this, Erin. I don't think you should do it.' Her mum walked back to the other side of the kitchen and took a white plastic bag out of the fridge. 'People say she's totally mad. I don't like the idea of you alone with her up in that creepy house.' She pierced a hole in the bag and forked the gelatinous contents into the dog bowl. Drops of blood from the raw meat fell onto the floor. The metallic smell and the chunks of offal turned Erin's stomach. She looked away.

'You've both been on at me to get a job, and now I have.'

'Well, yes, love. I think we're just concerned that Maggie Muir is a bit odd. You must admit, it all sounds a bit strange.'

'Strange? I thought you'd be delighted. It's better than the pub, surely? And it's not as though there are loads of other employment options around here.' She looked at both of her parents, but neither of them had an answer for this. Her dad just tapped his fingers on the side of his mug and her mum pretended to be looking for something in the fridge. Erin picked up Maggie's pages and her cup of tea. 'I'm going to finish reading this upstairs,' she said, and left the kitchen.

Erin knew she had overreacted, but she was fed up with being treated like she was a disgrace since she'd come back from London. Her mother had a permanently sour look on her face and her dad tried to pretend everything was OK, but she knew how deep his disappointment ran. Not for the first time, Erin wished she had some badly behaved brother or sister with whom she could share the focus of her parents' undiluted attention. Growing up, she had carried her loneliness around with her like a label. She would watch other kids on the beach huddled together in cahoots. Her dad would try to compensate with the biggest sandcastle, which had multiple turrets and a moat that filled with water with the incoming tide. But she'd watched the family cricket games and running races with an envy that gnawed away at her insides.

She'd had friends at school, but never a best friend. She was never in the inner circle – that was the domain of the pretty girls with high ponytails. Erin was not pretty. She was scrawny with wide hazel eyes and hair that stuck up like one of those grass potato-heads. Her parents called her 'Owly' as a baby, when her startled look was endearing. But she didn't 'grow into her eyes' like they said she would. Her hair couldn't be tamed either. She had a double crown, resulting in stubborn lumpy bits on the top of her head which refused to conform to the ponytail shackle. She finally gave up trying at fifteen and cut it all off and she'd had short spiky hair ever since.

Erin had asked her parents repeatedly why they hadn't had any more children and they came up with a myriad of responses: 'We couldn't afford it, darling'; 'You were all we needed'; 'We just never thought about it'.

Then one day her mum had snapped. Erin was thirteen and whining about Becky Rogers' sister who had passed her driving test and driven Becky into Truro to go clothes shopping, and her mum had swung round from the kitchen sink where she was peeling potatoes. 'I'm sorry you don't have a sister to take you shopping, Erin. I really am,' she hissed. 'We just didn't, OK? What's done is done. We can't go back. So please could you just leave it alone!'

Erin never asked about siblings again.

Now she could hear the muffled tones of her parents downstairs and the clattering of dishes. Her dad would be standing up for her, quietly trying to convince her mum that this job was a good idea.

The November night had drawn in, and the rain was hammering again at the bedroom window. The Turners did not believe in upstairs heating, and smoky clouds of breath puffed out of Erin's mouth. She pulled the curtains together, shutting out the darkness and the whistling draught that rattled through its leaky frame. She climbed into her bed in her clothes and pulled the duvet up over her legs. Then she picked up Maggie's manuscript and continued to read.

CHAPTER THREE

Lansdown Place, 30th November 1986

*I found Mr Gilbert on the floor in the larder this morning.
I had been having a good day; it was one of those beautifully
frosty mornings when everything sparkles. I walked the dog
and bought myself an iced bun on my way home as a reward
and settled down with it, a coffee and* Good Housekeeping. *I
cannot face the paper yet. And then I spotted his leg, poking out
from the under the larder door, and I was instantly back there,
his body lying drenched on the banks of the river. I couldn't
catch my breath and the iced bun stuck in my throat. I doubted
my sanity then: the police still had Mr Gilbert, he was their
only forensic evidence. I crawled to the larder on my hands and
knees, expecting him to disappear as I got closer, but he didn't.
I picked him up and then I realised that he was far too clean
to be Mr Gilbert, and he wasn't wearing the blue scarf that
Lucas had knitted for him at school. He was the replacement
Mr Gilbert, bought in reserve, never used. And I remembered
Skye's teddy bear picnics in the larder. I spent the rest of the day
in her bed again with Mr Gilbert. But her smell on the pillow
is fading and I don't know how to get it back.*

*

Daylight hadn't yet penetrated the heavy slate sky and it was
ominously dark when Erin left the house the next morning. Her

dad was already out on his rounds when she came downstairs and she had snuck out while her mum was in the bathroom. Tregotha Farm was down a long drive, it took a couple of minutes to walk up to the main road, and from there it was a further ten minutes into the sleeping village of Porthteal, where the street lights still flickered their amber glare. She passed the Angel pub on her left and then the Driftwood Gallery on the other side of the street. She tried to walk past without looking; she could sense the painting there and nearly made it to the end of the building before she looked back. And there it was, balanced on an easel in the bay window. The heavy oils glistened at her, the fishermen hauling in their nets against a foaming teal sea. Erin's heart lurched as she remembered Simon's calloused hands holding the brush. And the bump on the side of his finger as he traced the dimple at the bottom of her back. And then she thought of the last time she had seen him, the red lipstick and shiny black hair of the lady in his embrace, the stripy tights of the little girl, her giggles as he flung her up onto his shoulders. She swallowed down the emotion that curdled in her stomach and headed for the track behind the gallery.

The sun had peeked through the gloom by the time Erin arrived at Hookes End. Her cheeks were tingling and her bones warmed by the steep climb up the hill. She knocked on the door and when no one answered, she tried the handle.

'Hello, Maggie, are you there?' she called from the hallway.

'In here,' came a voice from the room where they had sat yesterday.

Oblonsky ran out into the hallway to greet her. Erin stroked his matted ears and followed him down the corridor. She had been too preoccupied to take it all in the day before. There were more butterflies – miniature black and white etchings, the intricate detail on their wings accentuated by the lack of colour. They were arranged haphazardly around a mirror, gold brocade peeled off the surround, the glass so tarnished and purpling that Erin's reflection was a blur. A marble Ganesh sat proudly on a rickety side table beneath it, around him piles of unopened mail, bills mostly. And keys – there must have been five different sets, nestling into the elephant's creases.

Radio Four was blasting from a room to her left. Erin poked her head in. It was the kitchen, surprisingly small given the size of the house. Toast crumbs and pools of tea littered the shabby Formica work surface. A relentless stream of drips fell from the stained ceiling into a saucepan on the cork floor. It was nearly full. Erin emptied the pan into the sink and placed it back down on the floor.

'What are you doing?' Maggie shouted.

'Nothing, just coming,' Erin replied. She shut the kitchen door and crossed the corridor into the study.

Maggie was sitting on the sofa facing the unlit fire. Oblonsky jumped up to join her and laid his head in her lap.

'I made a pot of tea, help yourself,' she said, without looking round.

'OK, do you want one?' Erin found the teapot amid the carnage of books and paper on the round table.

'I've got one, it's nettle. Do you like nettle tea?'

'I've never had it,' Erin replied. 'It smells… interesting.' She peered into the pot and gave it a stir, dredging up slimy green weeds. She poured herself a cup and sipped it. It was bitter, metallic and lukewarm. Erin looked over to see if Maggie was watching her reaction but she still had her back to her.

'Do you mind if I turn some lights on, Maggie? It's seriously dark in here.'

'I'd rather you didn't, the lights hurt my eyes.' Maggie pressed her fingers into the pressure points on the side of her head. 'And hurry up, we need to get on.'

'Right, yes, of course,' Erin said, looking around, not sure what she was supposed to be doing. She pulled the manuscript pages out of her bag and handed them to Maggie on the sofa. Maggie's brow wrinkled as she took them, obviously irritated by the watermarks and frayed edges. She turned to face Erin for the first time since she'd arrived. She wasn't wearing the tinted glasses that had shadowed her face the previous day. She looked younger than Erin remembered. She was quite striking, with her cloudy blue eyes and wide mouth.

'Did you read it?' Maggie asked.

'The diary, yes, I really liked—' Erin started.

'I don't need your literary appraisal, Erin,' Maggie interrupted. 'Just your eyes, remember.' Maggie pointed to Erin's face, her finger trembling in the air.

'Sorry.'

'And it's not a diary, it's a manuscript, for a novel.'

'Yeah, right, but—'

'No buts, Erin. Let's be getting on with it, then. You sit at the computer there. And here is my notebook, my notes for the manuscript.' Maggie laboured the words, and her point, as she handed Erin the battered black leather notebook, which had loose bits of paper stuffed inside and yellow Post-its curling around the edges of the leather. 'I need you to read out what is written in here and I will make amendments as I see fit and you will type them up. I have never done this before, not sure how it will work, but I can't see the blessed screen any more so I don't have much choice.'

Erin felt a ripple of panic as she recalled the last time she had to read aloud. It was Year 9, and they had gone round the room reading a paragraph each of *Jane Eyre*. By the time it was her turn she had whipped her nerves up into a jangling rattle. She only managed a couple of sentences before her heart started thumping with such force, she thought it might burst through her chest. She could hear her voice trembling, the words sticky with saliva. And then her classmates had started to snigger. Erin had run from the room and locked herself into a loo cubicle, refusing to come out for nearly an hour.

'Is that going to be a problem, Erin?' Maggie eyed her suspiciously.

'Er, no... of course not.'

The writing in the book was somewhat faded, but Erin was relieved to see that it was generally legible. It was big and bubbly, and reminded Erin of her art teacher's handwriting at school. So different from her own small and slanted childlike scrawl.

'Well, let's get started then. And don't mumble. I hate mumblers.' Maggie stroked Oblonsky's ears with the tips of her fingers and closed her eyes.

Erin drew in a deep breath and started to read.

Lansdown Place, 5th December 1986

Dr Sham has been asking about my childhood. I tell him that it was normal, uneventful. But he presses me harder; there must be something. And there is. The man in the woods. It comes back to me again and again, with such clarity.

And so, I tell him about the slippery leaves under our feet, the dusky shadows, the hoot of an owl echoing through the dripping branches. I was young, but old enough to be at school because we were singing songs from our Nativity. Ma had asked Sara and me to take Pip for a walk. She told us not to go as far as the woods, but we always did. Pip started barking at a tree, and a man peered out from behind it. His eyes were hidden by the shadow of his tweed cap, but there was a big livery birthmark down one side of his face. He held out a brown paper bag and asked if we would like to see some baby sparrows. I remember his voice was weirdly shrill, and he couldn't say his r's. Sara held back, but I was curious and went to look. The bag was full of pine cones. The disappointment must have shown on my face because he laughed, a high-pitched hyena laugh. And he said that the 'spawwows' were in a fallen nest on the other side of the woods, that he would take us there. Sara said no, and turned to walk back, but I grabbed her arm. I knew we shouldn't go with him, the darkness was closing in, but something willed me on – was it bravery, stupidity, anger?

He whistled as we walked. 'Nearly there,' he said, then came off the path and into the darkest part of the woods where the pine trees were crammed so close together there was no room for daylight. I wanted to run away then but I didn't dare. I pulled Sara forward, slaloming between the trees. We lost him. My eyes scanned the darkness. 'Here they are,' he said from behind a thick trunk. We edged towards the tree and there he was with his trousers down, pulling at himself. Sara screamed and we started to run. I could hear the snapping of twigs behind us as we dodged between the trees. My legs wouldn't go as fast as I wanted them to. Sara tripped on a tree root; I stumbled but stayed on my feet, pulling her up. I was too scared to look back until we got out of the woods and into the dusky light. I couldn't see him, but we carried on running, fear pounding through us. I had never known fear like that before.

I know it now, of course. It surges through your veins like lava, squeezing all the air out of your chest. Then it condenses in your head, a glacial fizzing around your skull that leaves you dizzy and disorientated. But we got away. We ran through long wet grass in the field, over the fence into our garden, through the back door and into Ma's arms in the kitchen. She called the police and we had to tell the story over and over again to Mr Bentley in his shiny buttons. They never found him, of course, and I never went into the woods again. Something died in me that day, but something else was born. The fear has flickered away deep inside of me ever since, like a pilot light just waiting to burst into flame.

*

Erin had got through it. She had stumbled over a few words and choked on the bit where he was 'pulling at himself', but she had got through it. In fact, as the extract had progressed, she had even found herself adding pauses for effect, little inflections in her voice, slowing down and speeding up. By the time she read the bit about Maggie panicking she could barely feel her own fear.

She looked over at Maggie, who was ghostly still on the sofa, with her eyes shut as if absorbing everything she had just heard with every single muscle, bone and particle of skin in her body.

'OK. Lose the last sentence,' she said eventually. 'And then type it up.'

And so the morning proceeded. With every extract Erin read and then typed, she began to feel a little less anxious. Maggie didn't make any conversation with Erin other than to change a word, lose a sentence or add a new one. When Erin asked whether to start the next extract, she would just nod her head or raise her arm in acknowledgment.

After what felt like days but in fact had only been a few hours, Maggie's trance finally broke and she said something unrelated to the book. 'Could you get me a glass of water, Erin, and pass me those pills on the table?' And Erin was brought back into the room with a thump. She walked over to the side table by the door that was laden with pill pots and potions. Some had their lids off. One had toppled over and the contents were scattered across the sticky table. Erin surveyed the chaos and wondered how on earth Maggie was monitoring her drug intake.

'Which ones?' she asked.

'The brown pot with the white lid,' Maggie said without looking round. She was holding her head so unnaturally still, Erin presumed that to move it must cause her intense pain.

'I'll just get you some water.' Erin rushed out to the kitchen.

'Hurry up,' Maggie shouted after her.

Maggie grabbed the pills and water from Erin when she returned but struggled to take the lid off with her trembling hands.

'Here, let me,' Erin said, tipping a white tablet into Maggie's hand.

'I need two, give me another.' Erin tipped the second pill into her palm and held onto the bottom of the glass as Maggie took it to her lips. Maggie closed her eyes and held her breath for a long time before letting it out slowly through pursed lips.

Erin left her on the sofa and went back to the computer, feeling quite unsettled by Maggie's pain. She looked around the room and took in the tapioca sheen that shrouded every book, picture frame and tabletop. It hadn't been as noticeable in the gloom of the previous day but was now glistening in the morning light.

Maggie sat still for a few minutes after taking the pills and then heaved herself up from the sofa. 'I think we should stop for lunch,' she said, hobbling over to the window. A shaft of sunlight lit up her profile and washed out the wrinkles from her complexion. Her cheekbones were high and defined. Maggie turned back into the shadow of the room and Erin realised it was her unsteady gait that aged her beyond her years. She probably wasn't much more than seventy. The dog jumped off the sofa and stretched his paws out in front of him before joining Maggie at the window.

'The sun is out. Shall we have a sandwich on the bench outside, Oblonsky?' Maggie walked towards the door and Erin wasn't sure whether she was meant to follow. She hadn't brought any lunch; hadn't even thought about it when she left in the dark that morning. Her stomach grumbled. 'Are you coming?' Maggie said from the doorway.

'Yes, of course.' Erin skipped towards the door a little too eagerly. 'Shall I make the sandwiches?'

'We can do it together.'

Erin was relieved when Maggie produced a tin of tuna from the cupboard. Surely anything that came in a tin couldn't have been contaminated by the bacteria rife in Maggie's kitchen. The bread was pretty stale, but Erin couldn't find any mould on it. Maggie wrapped a brightly coloured shawl around her shoulders and put on a green bobble hat and they ventured to the bench at the end of the garden, which looked out on to the sea below. Oblonsky followed at Maggie's heels, and waited until she had lowered herself onto the bench before he scampered off, the scent of something enticing him on a meandering trail under the hedgerow.

Maggie closed her eyes and tilted her face up towards the winter sun while Erin tucked into her tuna sandwich.

'Oblonsky must love this garden,' she said, and looked at Maggie for a response. But her eyes were still closed and she was completely motionless. Erin thought of her parents and their concerns about Maggie's mental health. She shifted uncomfortably on the bench. She had finished her sandwich, and Oblonsky had done at least ten laps of the garden and hedgerows before Maggie opened her eyes and looked at her again.

'Do you meditate?' Maggie said, and took a bite of her sandwich. She chewed noisily and a bit of tuna flapped at the corner of her mouth.

'Er, no. Is that what you were doing?' Maggie grunted and took another bite of the sandwich. 'Do you do that every day?' Erin tried again.

'Every day for thirty years,' Maggie said, wiping her mouth with the corner of her shawl. 'Keeps you sane. You should try it.'

'I don't think I would be very good at it. Too much stuff buzzing around my head.'

'Well, that is exactly why you should do it, Erin.'

'I guess.'

'Just look at those clouds up there.'

Erin turned to look at a line of fluffy clouds that peppered the hazy blue sky. 'Now close your eyes and picture them again.'

Erin felt foolish but did it anyway. Light rippled across her eyelids. 'Now, every time a mundane thought comes into your head, like, what am I going to have for dinner? I've got tuna stuck in my teeth. Who is this mad old bat? Just attach it to one of those clouds like a brown paper label and let it float off into the distance.'

Erin tried, but the thoughts kept coming. Would she tell her parents about this? Would Maggie realise how dreadful she was at spelling? What time would she be able to leave? I really wish she would eat with her mouth shut.

'What about your fella, then? What went wrong there?' Erin's eyes sprang open and she looked at Maggie, who was picking a bit of tuna out from between her teeth.

'He decided he didn't want to leave his wife after all.'

'So you just left, didn't put up a fight?' Maggie threw her sandwich at Oblonsky, who was chasing his tail just in front of them. He stopped and devoured it.

'What is this, the Spanish Inquisition?' Erin turned to face Maggie, suddenly irritated by the invasive turn the conversation had taken.

The corners of Maggie's mouth wrinkled into a smile. 'Just making conversation, that's all.'

Silence descended once more, and Erin regretted her curt response. Any conversation was better than none. But Maggie didn't seem to mind; the edges of her mouth had curled upwards and she breathed deeply as she looked out to sea beneath heavy eyelids.

'So, what's with all the butterflies?' Erin asked when she could bear it no longer. But Maggie didn't respond, didn't even flinch. Erin rolled her eyes and placed her hands, that were beginning to tingle with the cold, under her bottom, wiggling them around.

'The majestic monarch of the sky. Holder of universal secrets and reasons why,' Maggie said eventually with drama and poise.

'Right.' Erin scowled and bounced her legs up and down.

'Michael Levy, his poem "Touched by a Butterfly".'

'So, you just really like them then?'

'Celestial magic, he called it. Did you know that their wings are actually transparent, and those wonderful colours we see is just the light reflecting off their scales?'

'No, I didn't.'

'Well, there aren't any around now, unfortunately, their wings don't work below 55 degrees, so they can't fly in this cold weather.'

'Really? It certainly is cold out here today.' Erin stamped her feet on the ground in an attempt to bring some feeling back into her numb toes. She was relieved to see Maggie hauling herself up using the arm of the bench. 'Right, there's no time for idle chit-chat, we've got work to do.' She started to walk back towards the house and Oblonsky ran to join her.

The afternoon proceeded much in the same way as the morning had done. They worked their way through a few more pages and then Erin heard a grunt from the sofa. She didn't dare ask Maggie if she was OK, but after a while she tiptoed over and found her fast asleep, her mouth open, a trickle of saliva running down her chin. Erin finished typing up the last bit and then took the opportunity to nose a little more around the house.

There were two other rooms off the hallway downstairs. One was a dining room with a big table and eight chairs all coated in the house speciality of thick dust. And there were more butterflies on the walls. And among the butterflies were photos of women from all over the world. Indian women in fuchsia saris and chains from their noses to their ears. Muslim women with only their eyes peering out from behind their black burkas. Women with brightly coloured shawls and top hats that Erin couldn't quite place. The table – like every other surface – was covered in piles of manuscripts, journals, newspapers. Erin picked one up. It was dated 15 September 2012. Five years ago! The other room across

the hall was full of boxes but no furniture. She didn't dare go
upstairs, so she scoured the bookshelves in the study for one of
Maggie's books. She couldn't find anything by Maggie Muir and
was about to give up when she noticed a pile of hardbacks on the
floor behind the sofa by Margaret Molesworth.

Erin picked up *The Impostor* from the top of the pile. It had a
dark cover with a blurry image of a silhouette disappearing down
a dimly lit street. And beneath the title it read, *Another tantalising
mystery for Detective Turnpike*. It was one of Maggie's. She must use
a pseudonym! Erin wasn't surprised that Maggie wanted to hide
behind another name. There was something quite humble about her,
or was it secretive? Either way she didn't imagine she hankered for
the limelight. *The Assistant* was next on the pile. Its cover featured
a cigarette smoking in an ashtray. Erin took it to the armchair in
the window opposite Maggie and started to read. Turnpike was a
depraved detective who smoked Lambert & Butler and drank cheap
whisky. The book began with the poisoning of Robin Grey, attractive assistant to business tycoon Max Carter, dragging Turnpike
away from a night of poker and women. Maggie's cynical voice
shone through the cracks in the clichés, and Erin found herself
laughing out loud as Turnpike's bumbling sidekick Hopper had to
retrieve his Super from the clutches of Fanny Braddock. She was
so absorbed she didn't notice Maggie waking up.

'You've found one of my books, then?'

'Yes, sorry. I hope you don't mind.'

'Let's get back to the job in hand, shall we?'

They carried on till six o'clock when Maggie told Erin that that
was enough for today and she could go home. Maggie looked so
tired Erin was worried she wouldn't make it up the stairs. She
offered to get her some supper but Maggie said she would rustle
something up. Erin wasn't sure how. She had only spotted one
withered potato in the bottom of the fridge and a furry piece of
cheese.

Erin felt as exhausted as Maggie looked as she made her way down the hill in the pitch-blackness. She took out her phone to use as a torch, but it was out of power. Her eyes soon adjusted to the dark though and she thought about Maggie constantly acclimatising to the ever-dimming shadows.

Erin had mixed emotions about how her first day's work had gone. She had stood up to Maggie's imperious probing and she felt quite proud of that. She was definitely less daunted by the reading out loud. But she was concerned about Maggie's state of health. Was there anyone else looking out for her? The realisation that she might be all Maggie had suddenly weighed heavy in Erin's limbs as she trudged on home.

CHAPTER FOUR

Lansdown Place, 12th December 1986

I went into Skye's nursery yesterday. They left a message for me a couple of weeks ago saying they had some of her things: a pair of wellies, pieces of artwork and her learning journal. They were so kind, those ladies at the nursery, and they had written me lovely letters back in the summer and I was feeling strong, so I decided to go there. When I arrived in the car park a little girl ran in front of my car, her mother following, berating her for not looking where she was going. It was Miriam; she had come for a play date with Skye just days before we went on that dreaded holiday, and she was dressed in a white nightie with a tinsel halo. It was the Nativity.

I should have walked away but something propelled me inside. The parents were all seated on tiny chairs waiting for the Nativity to start. I hovered in the doorway and Mrs Ramsay saw me and came over. She looked flustered but spoke calmly with her head on one side just like everyone else. She asked if I would like to stay and watch. I sat down on one of the tiny chairs. Lucy Fletcher was Mary, she was Skye's best friend. She spotted me on the back row and it unsettled her. She couldn't remember her opening line. I should have left, but I didn't. I stayed to see the shepherds, little Ronnie Sullivan who lives on our road was one – the handkerchief on his head kept falling off. Then the wise men: they all murmured a song about camels except Timmy Roakes, he shouted it. And then came the angels, they sang 'Away In A Manger'. I remembered Skye singing it the year before; she was barely three yet she could remember all the words.

And then the tears came, and I couldn't stop and I knew I should leave but it was warm and cosy in there and I liked being surrounded by all the children. Mrs Ramsay came up to me and put her arm round me and I shrugged it off. I know I shouldn't have but I didn't want her to touch me. And then I got up to leave and I fell over one of the silly little chairs and everyone was looking at me. I ran outside, but I'd left my bag in there with my car key. I couldn't go back in so I just sat on the floor of the car park and sobbed. Mrs Ramsay followed me out eventually with my handbag. And she had Skye's boots and her drawing of herself with her pink spotty dress on. I don't even remember driving home.

*

Winter was a relief. The insistent rain that came with autumn paused for breath, and the chocolate rivers of mud froze into crusty peaks that crunched underfoot. The sun finally peeped through the shadows halfway through December and the pearly fields twinkled in its wake. For Erin, winter also brought a welcome reprieve from Maggie's leaking kitchen roof. The toe-curling drip, drip as it hit the steel pan on the floor was challenging her composure daily.

Maggie and Erin quickly found a pattern of work that suited them both. Erin would trudge up the hill at first light. Maggie had brewed the pot of nettle tea before she arrived. Erin suffered it initially and then, to her surprise, began to enjoy it. She lit the fire and they would get to work. Maggie sat on the sofa, Oblonsky on her lap, and Erin typed at the dusty PC on the cluttered table behind. Erin read an extract from the notebook and then Maggie would rewrite it. Or dictate some new passage inspired by what she heard. She rarely fumbled her words; they seemed to pour out of her with a natural ease, and Erin learnt to type quickly to keep up. They had lunch on the bench, and in an attempt to distract Maggie from her invasive line of questioning, Erin asked Maggie about butterflies. A subject on which she was happy to hold forth for the entire time it took Erin to wolf down a sandwich and Maggie to nibble at the corners of hers. Sometimes they took one of the heavy anthologies with them and Maggie talked Erin through the different breeds and their colourings and features. On those days when the rain drove in from the sea so hard and so relentless they were forced to eat inside, Maggie taught Erin to sketch butterflies, copying the detail on their wings from the various books and pictures on the walls. It was surprisingly therapeutic, and Erin found herself absent-mindedly doodling wings on any piece of paper, newspaper, bank statement or letter, much to her mother's despair.

After lunch Maggie took Oblonsky for a mandatory walk, whatever the weather. Erin watched her from the dining room window with a battered pair of binoculars she'd found in a drawer in the hall. She was terrified Maggie would collapse on her watch. Maggie paused every five steps to catch her breath, and Oblonsky would stop too and watch her with his wonky glare. She walked to the bench on the coastal path, where she meditated for ten minutes then walked back. On a good day, she might take a turn around the garden. Maggie then returned to the sofa and slept, her mouth open, snoring like a freight train. And while she slept, Erin worked her way through Maggie's Detective Turnpike series, all twenty-three of them. Time slowed down in the afternoon; Maggie was worn out yet determined to carry on. Erin left Maggie in front of the news at six o'clock and made her way through the velvety darkness back down to the village.

One icy morning in December Erin overslept. She was at least an hour late, and anticipating the wrath of her employer as she hurried her way along the cliff path, when her phone buzzed with a message.

Hello, stranger. It was Simon. *Do you miss me?*

*

She had first met Simon seven months earlier when she was delivering provisions to him in the cottage he rented at the other end of the village. Her mother's bounteous vegetable garden fed most of the holidaymakers in Portheal. Not the locals, of course; they weren't prepared to pay her extortionate prices. The majority of her customers came to collect their goods between nine and eleven in the morning when she was open for business, but she had the odd special punter who received daily deliveries. Simon had come into the shop a few weeks earlier, bemoaning the fact that it was only open in the mornings when the light was so much better in his studio. He would have fixed her with those dark brown eyes, and even Debbie Turner could not resist his charm. She agreed to deliver to him twice a week.

It was a gloriously sunny morning in April and Erin had been roped into helping her mother, who had a WI meeting. Erin was working in the pub in the evenings, and so she had her mornings spare. She had manned the shop for a couple of hours and then packed up the delivery boxes into the trailer which her mum pulled behind her bike. The sky was cloudless and blue when Erin left the house in just a t-shirt, but an April shower caught her unawares and by the time she had cycled the length of the village up to Simon's cottage she was soaked through. Her t-shirt clung to her body, exposing her nipples, and a droplet of rain hung from the end of her nose.

Simon had smiled at her on the doorstep and invited her in to take shelter. She refused, but the rain was pelting it down by then, and he was quite insistent. He wore low-slung jeans and a navy t-shirt which rode up when he bent down to pick up the box of vegetables. Erin caught a glimpse of olive skin above his Fred Perry boxers. He had a streak of pale pink paint in his dark hair and globules of acrylic clung to his jeans.

Erin followed him down the dark corridor of the cottage into a room at the end in which the light was almost blinding. She had walked past this house all her life but never been inside. The house was the only building on the sea side of the road. It clung precariously to the edge of the cliff and had the best views of any house in the village. Yet the curtains had been drawn for as long as Erin could remember. There was no sign of any curtains the day she met Simon, however. Floor-to-ceiling windows wrapped around the back of the house, revealing a wall of indigo sea and sky. The glass rattled in its chipped frames, letting in the roar of the waves and the screeching of the gulls beyond. The rain had weakened to a drizzle and peppered the surface of the water. A rainbow had formed over the emerald hill on the other side of the bay.

'It's pretty amazing, isn't it?' Simon said to Erin, whose mouth hung open without shame.

'I had no idea.'

'I know. The house is filthy, nothing works and there's a stubborn smell of off milk in the carpet, but when I saw this view, I couldn't resist it. A painter's paradise.' He had moved over to the tiny kitchenette in the corner of the room and was unpacking the lettuce and green beans from the box.

Erin looked around. Two giant easels faced each other. On the one nearest to her she could see the starting of an angry sea. Thick acrylic swirls of smoky blues and mossy greens. It was strong, moody, masculine, textured. The only other furniture in the room was a balding sofa in one corner and a tiny table and chair in the other. The remnants of last night's fish and chips box and an iPad sat on the table in among ketchup smears.

'I've seen you in the pub,' Simon said as he put the eggs in the tiny fridge.

'Yeah, I'm there most nights.' Erin pulled her sodden t-shirt away from her tummy, and it puffed up like a balloon. She pressed it down and hugged her arms around her chest. 'I need to get back, it's stopped raining.' She headed down the corridor towards the front door.

'OK, well, thanks for the vegetables,' Simon said, following her outside. The sun had come out again and the street was steaming. The gentle patter of dripping echoed from the trees all around. Erin had left the bike up against the fence outside. She wiped the seat down with a rag from the trailer and swung the bike round. A box of vegetables careered to the back of the trailer and a dozen eggs from the top of the box crashed to the floor.

'Shit,' Erin cursed, 'Mum'll kill me.' She bent to pick up the eggs and Simon crouched down next to her. They loaded the cracked shells back into the box and watched the canary trail of yolk run down the glistening tarmac. The seagulls circled above them.

'I'll get you my eggs,' Simon said, heading back to the house with the box of shells.

'You really don't have to do…' Erin shouted after him, but he had already gone. She was straddling her bike when he came out again with his box of eggs.

'Here,' he said, putting them in the trailer. 'Take it easy on the corners with these ones.' He brushed his thick dark fringe away from his face as he stood up, and he smeared a string of slimy egg white into it. Erin averted her eyes.

'Thanks,' she said and cycled off down the road.

Simon came into the pub that night, and the next, and every night for the next couple of weeks. He sat at the end of the bar and read his book while she worked. Occasionally he engaged in chat with one of the old boys, but never for more than a few minutes. He asked Erin probing questions about her life in between orders, always with a wry smile. She ignored him most of the time, but that seemed to amuse and encourage him further.

'What does Erin Turner do for pleasure?'

'Why did Erin Turner decide to dye her hair pink?'

'Why does Erin Turner still live with her parents?'

'What makes Erin Turner really excited?'

'What makes Erin Turner really cross?'

'You!' Erin finally snapped. 'You and your questions make me really cross!' She slammed her fist down on the bar and all the glasses rattled around them.

'Ah, she speaks,' he said, his smirk widening to a smile.

That night when she left the pub he followed her, and they kissed up against the wall of Tina's teahouse. Hungrily, desperately, he bit down on her lip and made it bleed. She ran away, saying she couldn't do this. She knew he was married, he had a kid; she wouldn't be a homewrecker. But as she licked the metallic-tasting blood on her lips walking home, she knew she wouldn't be able to stay away, not any more.

The next morning, she went to his cottage and without saying anything he took her hand and led her to the bleached studio at the end of the corridor. He undressed her slowly, peeling off the layers one by one. Then he picked her up as if she were a bird and laid her down on the balding sofa. The sun burned through the glass, drenching her naked body. He tasted of coffee; his chin was rough and scratched her as he probed her with his tongue. They made love on the sofa that morning and then every day for the next few weeks. Afterwards she would watch him work. He said she was his muse, that he was producing better work than ever before, and she believed him.

At the end of May, he went back to his family for a week, and he didn't contact her. She would go to his house and lie on the sofa, sleep in his bed, breathe in his smell. When he came back from London he told her it was over; he didn't want to see her again. But the next day he came to find her and it started up with a renewed intensity.

When his three-month residency was up, Simon asked Erin to go to London with him. He would set her up with her own apartment initially, then he would tell his wife when the time was right. Erin didn't hesitate. She told her parents. They begged her to stay, said she was ruining her life. Her mum stopped talking to her and her dad cried. They didn't even say goodbye; on the morning of her departure they left the house before she came downstairs. She got Derek, from the pub, to drive her to the station, and even he asked her if she was sure she knew what she was doing. She was leaving Porthteal, she told him. And she loved Simon: of course she was sure.

It was stifling that July when Erin arrived in London, and for at least a month she felt as though she couldn't breathe. The concrete, the glass, the bricks, it all radiated heat. Paint on the walls cracked into a desert patchwork; tarmac melted into sticky toxic pools. And the air was putrid – it gained in temperature and filth as it wafted up to Erin's top-floor flat. But the Londoners didn't seem to mind, in fact they were thriving in the heatwave, scantily clad and lazing on every balding patch of rusty grass. They spilled out of the cafés and onto the dusty pavements along with the reggae beats and the wafts of jerk chicken.

But Erin wasn't thriving, and she did mind. She minded that there was no water to swim in, no green grass to lie on, no fresh air to breathe. The Thames was nothing like the sea. Just a brown torrent that failed to look blue even on the brightest of days. And it smelt, everywhere smelt. The heat had sped up the decomposition of the rubbish to an unmanageable level and the noxious fumes from the rotting permeated everything. And then there was the noise. The unrelenting beep of horns, sirens, the thudding bass of the club at the end of the street; sounds that surfed the stagnant air all night long.

Simon had set her up in a gloomy bedsit in Dalston. It was in the loft of an Edwardian terrace on a busy road above a curry house where the mildewed walls reeked of tikka masala. At one end of the room was a tiny kitchenette and sofa, and at the other end a bed – if you could call it that. A lumpy mattress on the floor under the only Velux window, which had to be open in the insufferable heat and left them very little headspace for lovemaking. So, they did it on the floor, or the sweaty chocolate leather sofa. Or in the shower, where the plaster peeled off the walls and stuck to their backs. Erin bought a fan on her first day, which whispered a comforting hum and stirred the hot air around. Every few seconds it rattled the window blind and fluttered the crispy leaves on the spider plant in the corner.

Simon turned up three, maybe four times a week at first. After sex, they would lie naked on the mattress, waiting for the fan to breathe on their sticky bodies, and he would trace the trickle of sweat at the bottom of Erin's back with his finger. But he never stayed; she never got to fall asleep on his chest again, or watch him paint, or eat fish and chips with him in the bath. Within weeks his visits had eased off to twice a week, then once.

Erin got a job at the pub at the end of the street. But one day the landlord, Fat Trev, pinned her up against the bar after closing and stuck his thick, tobacco-fouled tongue down her throat, so she didn't go back. Simon was happy with that. He wanted her to stay in and wait for his impromptu visits. He paid her rent and threw her a few demeaning notes, but she couldn't afford to do anything.

So, she walked and walked around the city, until blisters gnawed at her toes. After a month, the heatwave ended in a mighty storm. Erin was in Regent's Park when it struck and sought sanctuary with many others under the bandstand. Huddled together, they watched as the rain pelted the brown grass and mustard rivers coursed down the paths. The thunder rumbled around the acoustics of the stand and Erin found herself consoling a frightened little boy, whose mum was busy breastfeeding his brother on the bench. A man with yellow teeth was on her other side. He spat as he talked them through the geographic timeline of the storm. It was the only interaction with people Erin had experienced in weeks, and she was reluctant to leave when the rain stopped and the crowd dispersed. It was a lonely walk back to her flat, and her sodden bed under the open window.

And then came the day, a month or so later, when she knew her time was up in London. Erin had taken to killing time in the numerous galleries around town when it was too wet to pound the streets. She had been at the V&A every day that week, enticed back by the gowns and the jewels. She was in the loos, picking the remnants of her sandwich out of her teeth in the mirror when a lady came in with her daughter. She was not beautiful exactly, but striking with dark hair and a chunky fringe. She wore denim dungarees and gold hi-top trainers. Her daughter had the same fringe and thick-rimmed glasses. She left the door open while she peed, her stripy tights round her ankles.

'Mummy, do the princesses take those gowns off when they go to the loo?'

Erin caught eyes with the mother in the mirror. She smiled back with her lips over her teeth as she reapplied her cherry lipstick.

'They probably just hitch them up, baby,' she said. Then went into the cubicle to help her daughter pull up her tights.

Erin followed them out of the loos and into the foyer. And that was when she saw him.

'There you are,' Simon said to the lady, kissing her cherry lips.

'Daddy,' shrieked the little girl and he flung her up onto his shoulders.

He saw Erin, over his wife's shoulder. His tawny eyes widened momentarily. Then he kissed his daughter once more and draped his arm around his wife's shoulders. And they walked out of the heavy doors and a gust of wind swept their fringes off their flushed faces.

He would never leave them, Erin knew that then. It took no time to gather her few belongings. She shut the door on her dingy flat, walked across London and got on a train to Cornwall. That night she found herself back in her childhood bedroom, as if it had never happened.

'Is it over?' her mother had said when she arrived at the door in the middle of the night. And Erin had nodded and collapsed into her arms, burying her head into her flannel pyjamas. Her mum had held onto her very tight and stroked the back of her head like she used to when she was a child. And then she had led her by the hand into the dark kitchen and sat her down on the armchair by the fire. The embers were still glowing in the grate. She made Erin a cup of tea and a buttered crumpet. Her dad had loitered behind, looking freezing in his nightshirt and bare legs on the icy brick floor. But when her mum had disappeared into the larder for the crumpets, he had squeezed her shoulder and said, 'It's so nice to have you home, love.'

*

She had left Simon a note in the flat saying that she was going home. She asked him not to contact her and he hadn't. For six long weeks her stomach had lurched every time her phone beeped. But he hadn't called, hadn't even texted. Until now. *Do you miss me?* A spark flickered deep inside her at his familiar arrogant tone. She wanted to hear his voice so much that it hurt. He missed her. Did that mean he still loved her? Did he have the same dreams about her and wake up with his cheeks wet with tears or his body itching with a desire so deep inside that he couldn't scratch it away, no matter how hard he tried? She needed to know. Her hand hovered over the call button. But she was late for Maggie so instead she hit reply.

Of course I do, she wrote. She was at the top of the hill and knew that in just a few steps the phone reception would disappear for the rest of that day. She deleted it. *Not really*, she typed again and hit send.

I don't believe you. His reply came back immediately, and she smiled and zipped the phone away in her pocket to stop herself answering.

She spent the rest of her walk trying to forget about Simon and practising how she would explain her lateness to Maggie. But when she arrived at the house, Maggie wasn't in the study as normal. And there was no nettle tea brewed.

'Maggie,' Erin called, but there was no response.

She peered into the kitchen and the dining room, calling as she went, but couldn't find Maggie anywhere. Oblonsky came bounding down the stairs. He rushed straight past her and up to the front door where he turned in circles, whimpering. Erin opened the door and he rushed out onto the lawn for a pee. Maggie must still be in bed.

Erin dithered. It was not really her place to go and wake her up, but what if she had fallen or was really ill? What if she had died in the night? She called again from the bottom of the stairs but still there was no reply. She went into the kitchen and turned the kettle on and clattered teacups and plates, hoping to rouse Maggie upstairs. She turned the radio on and the volume up loud. Then she went out into the garden and called to Oblonsky. Erin looked up to the windows on the first floor and the bay on the right had its curtains firmly drawn. She decided to take Maggie a cup of tea. Bruno Mars was blaring out on the radio in the kitchen so Erin didn't hear the door open. She turned towards it and walked straight into Maggie, spilling the hot tea all over her arms.

'What the hell!' Maggie cursed, and backed away from Erin, shaking the tea off her hands.

'Oh, Maggie, I'm so sorry. I was just bringing you tea. And, oh God, I've burned you. Are you alright?'

The skin on Maggie's tiny wrist was angry and already starting to blister.

'Turn that bloody radio off,' Maggie shouted.

'Of course.' Erin rushed to the other side of the kitchen and hit the off button on the radio then rushed back to Maggie. 'You need to put that under water. Or is it cling film? I saw something on TV the other day. Yes, it's cling film.' Erin started opening and shutting drawers in a desperate attempt to find cling film. But Maggie had already made her way over to the sink and was holding her arm under the running tap.

'Stop fussing, will you?'

'Oh Maggie, I'm so sorry. It's just that you weren't here when I arrived and I thought maybe you'd—'

'What, Erin? What did you think? That I'd died in the night?'

'No! God, no,' Erin said a bit too emphatically. Maggie scowled at her. She wasn't wearing her glasses and her skin was ghostly pale. Her silver hair hung limply around her shoulders. Erin had never seen Maggie with her hair down before. Her hand was shaking under the tap and she was rubbing her temples with the other hand. Her eyes were wild.

'Have you taken your pills this morning, Maggie?' Erin said, inspecting Maggie's wrist. A few white bubbles were forming on her speckled arm.

'I couldn't find them,' Maggie whispered under her breath. Erin found a tea towel and held it under the tap then wrapped it round Maggie's wrist.

'Why don't you go and sit in the study and I will find them and bring them to you?'

Maggie didn't say anything but made her way slowly out of the kitchen. She had to let go of the tea towel on her wrist to steady herself on the door frame.

'Where did you last have them, Maggie? Upstairs? Downstairs?'

'I… I'm not sure.'

'OK.' Erin did a quick scout of the kitchen and then followed Maggie into the study. They weren't on the usual side table or anywhere else in that room. Maggie lowered herself onto the sofa and gathered folds of her forehead between her fingers.

'Do you mind if I go and look in your bedroom, Maggie?' Erin asked.

But Maggie couldn't even respond; she just nodded her head. Erin ran up the stairs, two at a time. And made her way to the bedroom at the front of the house with curtains closed that she had seen from the garden. The noxious smell hit her before she opened the door. Vomit, laced with lavender, nettle tea and wet dog. The bed was unmade and muddy. Oblonsky had come back in from the garden and was covered in mud and lying in among the scrambled sheets and clothes. Dirty mugs and medicines cluttered the bedside table. A pill pot had fallen victim to a glass of water, the lid off, its contents dissolved to a milky froth.

'Shit!' Erin cursed. She went into the bathroom off the bedroom. A pair of dirty knickers was lying on the floor. As was a wet bath towel. There was a mirrored cabinet above the basin. Erin looked inside and was so relieved to find another pot of the same pills. She rushed back down the stairs with them.

'Are these the ones, Maggie?' she asked as she came into the room.

Maggie nodded and held out her hand as Erin tipped a couple of the pills into her palm. She knocked them back with a glass of water that was on the table next to the sofa. A film had formed on the top and Erin wondered how long it had been there.

Maggie closed her eyes and her shoulders dropped slowly.

'Maggie, don't you think you should maybe have someone here to look after you? Is there somebody I can call?' Erin spoke quietly and tentatively.

'No. There isn't anyone.'

'But there must be someone,' Erin started.

'There isn't. I don't need anyone.' She opened her eyes then. 'Besides, I've got *you* now, haven't I?' She turned to look at Erin and the corners of her mouth lifted almost into a smile.

'Yeah, I guess.' Erin smiled back and then looked away.

'Just give me twenty minutes for these pills to kick in and we can get going. Lots to do today,' Maggie said.

'OK, I'll just be in the kitchen.'

Erin left the study and crossed the hall into the kitchen. She splashed some cold water over her face and ran her fingers through her spiky hair. 'Fuck,' she swore under her breath. She wasn't cut out to be a nurse.

CHAPTER FIVE

Lansdown Place, 15th December 1986

Christmas is everywhere. I used to love it: the lights, the smells, the food, the family. But now it fills me with a sadness that makes it hard to breathe. And anger, too; an uncontrollable rage that fires up inside of me when I hear 'Jingle Bells' booming out of every petrol station, every supermarket, every idling car. It's hard to imagine, impossible in fact, that I might have enjoyed thirty-seven Christmases before this one.

I try to recall a time when festive cheer didn't turn my blood cold. Lucas was four and we drove down to Devon to stay with my parents. He had been revving himself up for it since the middle of November, and had reached fever pitch by the time we got in the car on Christmas Eve. The journey was less than merry, however: he vomited at Stonehenge, and then again at Lyme Regis, and at Honiton, and Ottery St Mary. We sponged him and the seats down as best we could, but by the third or fourth time I had lost the will and let Banjo lick him clean. It was nine at night by the time we bumped up the farm track. We had been in the car for seven hours. Lucas had fallen into a deep sleep, and I carried his sticky body into a bed and tried not to worry too much about the clean sheets. He woke up surprisingly happy the next day, at five o'clock, desperate to see if Father Christmas had found us down there in the depths of the West Country. By six our bed was densely populated by all the cousins and grandparents. We walked across the frosty fields to the local church, where we doubled the congregation and sang heartily along to favourite carols. And then it was back to the farmhouse for cherry brandy and presents. Pa dressed up as Father Christmas and enlisted Lucas's help to distribute the gifts to all the family. I will never forget his little face, scrubbed up clean by now; he was dressed in a Viyella checked shirt and green Christmas jumper. He had a sprinkling of freckles across his nose and a gap where his two front teeth should have been. I spent Christmas night hunched over the loo with the vomiting bug, which then took down every single member of the household one by one. We left a couple of days later with our tails between our legs. But I was happy to have had that special time with my family.

I miss them. Ma was amazing when it first happened. She came to stay for weeks on end and held me as I cried. Sara, too; she would drive all the way from Devon for a day with a freshly cooked meal and encouraging words. She asked us for Christmas of course, but I couldn't face it and I think they were relieved when we said no.

*

Christmas came later to Porthteal than the rest of the country. The Christmas lights on The Lugger, the road that ran along the harbour wall, didn't even get turned on until mid-December. The Angel waited for that signal before it put up its plastic Christmas tree dripping with tinsel in the window. Erin's parents' tree didn't emerge until Christmas Eve. She always thought it such a shame that they couldn't enjoy the glow of the fairy lights and the smell of the pine needles for longer. But the Turners were sticklers for tradition and that was what they had always done.

There was no sign of anything festive at Hookes End. Erin suggested that they pick some ivy and holly from the garden and drape it over the numerous butterfly pictures on the walls in the study, but Maggie just rolled her eyes. 'Why on earth would we do that?' she said.

'To make it feel a bit Christmassy in here.'

'I don't like Christmas, Erin.'

Erin was getting used to Maggie's belligerence and had learnt to roll her own eyes too, in response to such comments. 'Well, that's pretty obvious,' she said. 'So, what does someone who doesn't like Christmas do on Christmas Day?'

'The same thing I have done for the past thirty-five years – ignore it. It is just another day, Erin.'

'Oh Maggie, you can't do that.'

'Why not?' Erin avoided Maggie's indignant glare. 'Because it will be my last Christmas, that's what you're thinking, isn't it, Erin?'

'No!' she lied. 'Why don't you come to my parents'?' The words had come out of her mouth before she had really given them any thought.

'No, thank you,' Maggie replied tartly. 'I will be just fine here on my own.' But the thought of Maggie with only Oblonsky and a withered potato for company was too much to bear.

'Maggie, when did you last leave this house?' Maggie twisted her head round and shot her a look of pure venom, and Erin panicked that she had crossed a line and wouldn't be able to get back. 'I'm sorry, I don't mean to intrude, I just don't want you to be alone at Christmas, that's all.'

Maggie sighed and composed herself and then, much to Erin's surprise she said, 'Very well, if you must. But don't expect me to wear reindeer horns or anything.'

'Don't worry. It will be very low-key, just us and my mum and dad. Our Christmases have always been rather quiet and boring. None of that chaos you get in a big family. It will be good to have someone else there, stir it up a bit.' Erin was already working on how she was going to convince her mum that it was a good idea.

'Well, I will try not to do that,' Maggie said. 'Now, let's get on with it.'

*

Erin's Christmas Day began with a text from Simon.

Happy Christmas, beautiful. Her stomach lurched as she saw it and she couldn't help smiling. There had been several messages since that first one on the hill. It was as if he was wooing her in the pub all over again, wearing her down with his persistent banter. She hadn't replied since that first time, but her resolve was weakening with every message and she knew that he knew it. Her bedroom door opened and she hid the phone under her pillow as her mum came in with a cup of tea and festive greetings. She perched on the edge of her bed in her purple dressing gown and watched her open her stocking as she had done every Christmas morning for the last twenty-five years. It was bulging with Sellotape and highlighters, socks from the pound shop and a horrific pink lipstick, each individually wrapped, and Erin had to feign delight as she opened every parcel. Her dad was on his rounds like any other day. The sheep and cows didn't acknowledge public holidays, as he reminded them every year.

Then she took Gertie, their elderly Norfolk Terrier, for a walk while her mum was preparing the vegetables. It was a wild and blowy day. She had to lean into the wind on the cliff path to stop herself from falling over. Tears streamed from her eyes and her ears burned with the cold. She pulled her woolly hat further down and buried her neck into her scarf. Erin thought of her grandmother's story about how her parents used to put stones in her pocket when she was little to stop her from blowing away. Maggie was so frail now; she might have to weigh her down to get her as far as the car.

Maggie was still in her nightie when she arrived at her house at eleven o'clock as arranged. She was on the sofa with a blanket, Oblonsky and *The Sound of Music*.

'Happy Christmas, Maggie!' Erin said, trying to sound cheery. 'You're not dressed. We said eleven o'clock, remember?'

Maggie grunted and carried on watching the TV.

'Come on, Maggie, you don't want to spend Christmas here on your own. And Mum has already put the turkey in. She's peeling the spuds and doing whatever you do to Brussels sprouts as we speak. She is really looking forward to meeting you, they both are.' This wasn't entirely true; her mum's reaction had been less than magnanimous when Erin told her she had invited Maggie for Christmas lunch. 'The hermit on the hill, coming here?' Her dad, however, had praised Erin for her selfless invitation and insisted that Maggie must come and join them.

'It is just another day, Erin. And I don't have many of them left. At least there is good telly on today. I'm not going anywhere.' Maggie turned up Julie Andrews.

'Come on, Maggie, you promised.'

'I did no such thing.'

'OK, you didn't promise but you said you'd come, and I know you probably haven't left the house for a while.'

'Hmph,' Maggie grunted and shrugged her shoulders.

'I get it. Well, of course I don't really get it, but I can imagine it must be quite daunting if you don't get out much. But I can assure you my parents are really nice, gentle, quite boring people and we can leave whenever you want.' Maggie continued to watch the TV but her eyes flickered to the right, which gave Erin hope that she was at least considering what she said. 'I know, we could have a code! You could say something if you want to leave, that way it doesn't need to be a big deal. You could just say… Oblonsky! That's it, we'll leave him here and you could say he needs to be let out for a pee, or a walk or whatever, and I will bring you straight home as soon as you say it.' Maggie tapped her fingers on the side of the sofa and Erin held her breath waiting for her to say something, but nothing came. Erin looked around the room, not sure how to deal with this impasse. She crouched down next to Maggie and held onto her hand.

'Please, Maggie, will you do it for me? I really can't bear the thought of another Christmas with just me and Mum and Dad.' But Maggie pulled her hand away and picked at the threads on the blanket in her lap. Erin could see the emotion gathering in her mouth as she pursed her lips tight together.

'I, I'm sorry, Erin, but I've made up my mind.'

'OK,' Erin said and stood up. 'If you're really sure that's what you want.' She headed for the door. As she walked into the hallway she saw a present wrapped in green tissue paper and tied up with red gardening twine on the side table. Erin picked it up and walked back into the room.

'Who is this present for, Maggie?'

'It's nothing.' She dismissed it with a wave of her hand.

'It wasn't here yesterday. Did someone send you a present?'

'God no, it's just something… well… it's… it's for your mother.'

'You got my mother a present?'

'Not really, it's just something I had, and—'

'So you did want to come! I knew it. Right, that's it. Maggie, you invited me into your life, so I'm afraid it is your fault that I'm here, and I am not going to let you spend your last Christmas here on your own with the Von Trapps. You are coming with me, and that's that.' She strode over to the TV and turned it off. 'Now are you going to come in your nightie or are you going to get dressed?'

Maggie looked at her angrily and then the corners of her mouth wrinkled into a reluctant smile.

'Well, you've certainly found your voice.' And she heaved herself up off the sofa and towards the door, Oblonsky at her heels.

*

Erin took Maggie through the front door of her house. She never used it herself, but Maggie had made a determined beeline for it when she got out of the car and it seemed appropriate. They bypassed the kitchen and went straight into the sitting room. Her dad was sitting in the armchair next to the fire with a large whisky.

'Mrs Muir, Happy Christmas. Welcome!' he said, standing up and going to take her arm. Maggie squinted through her glasses at him but she took his hand willingly. He led her across the room and into the armchair where he had been sitting. She sat down gingerly and stroked the paisley fabric on the arm of the chair. Erin wondered how much of the room she could see. She hadn't said a word yet.

'Can I get you a drink, Mrs Muir?' her dad said.

'Maggie,' she interrupted. 'Call me Maggie. Gin and tonic, please.'

'Of course, gin and tonic coming up,' he said and limped out. He'd been thrown off a horse as a child and ever since his right food dragged slightly.

'It's not so bad, is it, Maggie? Leaving the house, I mean.' Erin sat down on the floor in front of the fire. She stroked Gertie, who was stretched out on the rug.

'Mmm,' Maggie grunted, looking around. 'Were you born here?'

'Yep, I've lived here all my life. Well, apart from my little spell in London this year. It's a bit sad, isn't it?'

'Not necessarily, Erin. Don't confuse stability with boring.' Maggie smoothed out her skirt over her legs. Erin had never seen her wear anything other than trousers and jumpers before. She had been quite taken aback when Maggie arrived downstairs in a knee-length mustard wool skirt and black polo neck, lipstick too and a long pendant necklace. She looked quite glamorous. Erin recalled her first impression of Maggie as a frail elderly woman. Over the last month she had tweaked that idea considerably. Maggie was definitely not frail. Not even that old.

'Here we are, one gin and tonic for Maggie,' her dad said, coming back into the room. Her mum followed, looking flushed.

She wiped her hands on her apron before holding one out to Maggie.

'Mrs Muir, Debbie Turner,' she said briskly.

Maggie took her hand and offered a disarming smile. 'Maggie, please,' she said.

'Maggie brought you a present, Mum,' Erin said.

'Oh, it's nothing, it's just… er.' She fumbled in her bag and brought out the present. The paper had ripped and the corner of a wooden frame poked through.

'That's very kind of you, you really didn't have to…' She unwrapped a tiny framed picture of a butterfly with silver wings. 'It's lovely, Maggie, thank you.'

'It's the Palos Verdes blue, the rarest butterfly in the world.'

'Gosh.'

'Maggie knows a lot about butterflies. She's been teaching me all about them,' Erin said.

'Erin says she's helping you to write your book, Maggie,' Erin's dad said, a little too loudly.

'Yes, that's right.' Maggie was looking up at the portrait of Uncle Harold which hung above the mantelpiece. Its dark and moody lines seemed suddenly oppressive to Erin, and its position over the fireplace arrogant. And those china dogs that sat beneath were pretty hideous, too. Erin had never even noticed them before.

'How long have you lived in Porthteal, Maggie?' her mum asked.

'Nineteen eighty-seven, I moved here. I rented old George Crossway's cottage on the Lugger for a few years. Then bought Hookes End in April Nineteen eighty-nine.'

'Did you have a connection to Porthteal before you moved here? Family or friends?'

'No one,' Maggie replied sharply. She took a sip from her gin and tonic, and the ice rattled against the glass.

Her parents exchanged uneasy glances and Erin fiddled with Gertie's ears. The fire crackled and spat out a red-hot spark which landed on the carpet next to Gertie. Erin picked it up with the tongs and flicked it back into the fire. Her dad tapped the arm of the sofa and her mum picked fluff off her apron. Maggie settled back into her chair and took another big gulp of her gin and tonic and smiled. Erin had barely ever seen Maggie smile before. Her face softened at the edges and for a moment the arched creases on her forehead disappeared. She seemed to be actually enjoying herself.

'I came on a family holiday here once,' she said, 'and had very special memories of picnicking at Tregurrick, crabbing off the pier at St Moven, rock-pooling on the beach here in the village. So, I came on a whim. It was just going to be for a while. I had to get away, you see. But then I never left.' She took another slug. 'Ha, seems pretty ridiculous when I say it out loud.' And then another slug.

'Well, it is a very special place,' her dad said. He went over to the piano in the corner of the room and poured himself another large whisky from the decanter on top.

'Have you always lived here?' Maggie asked him, draining her glass. Erin had never seen Maggie drink before. In fact, now she thought about it, she had never even seen any alcohol in the house.

'I grew up here,' he said, moving back to the sofa with his whisky. 'I moved to Exeter for a while, where I met Debbie, but I couldn't keep away and came back to run my dad's farm.'

'I met you at my publisher's in Exeter once, do you remember?' Maggie said. She swirled the ice around in the bottom of her glass and then looked John Turner directly in the eye, challenging him with her steely squint. He looked back at Maggie and wrinkled his nose. He sniffed several times. It was a tic he had, sniffing.

'What?' Erin had been quiet until now, but this revelation was too much to contain. 'You met Dad at your publisher's?'

'He was a young aspiring writer. They were really interested in him, "raw talent" my publisher said, I was pretty new to the business myself at the time.' Her dad smiled then and looked down at his fingers. He was tapping out a rhythm on the arm of the sofa again.

'Really, Dad?' Erin sat up onto her knees. 'You never told me you wrote. And you met Maggie – why didn't you say?'

'I didn't think she would remember me. It was a long time ago, and it never came to anything.'

'Debbie was expecting at the time, you told us.' Maggie interrupted him. 'You were very excited, you were late for the meeting because you had come straight from the hospital and your appointment had overrun.' Erin looked at her mum. She had not said anything during this exchange. She avoided Erin's questioning look and stood up and wiped her hands down her apron again.

'I'm just going to check on the turkey,' she said and walked out of the room.

Erin turned back to her dad. 'But Dad, you said I was born here, not Exeter. You said you moved when mum was pregnant with me.'

'We did, darling. Maggie is confused.'

'Mm, maybe.' Maggie laughed a little too loudly. 'I do get a bit confused at the moment, don't I, Erin?'

'Another drink, Maggie? G&T, or would you like to move on to wine?' He walked towards Maggie, and the whole room shook under his tread.

'Hang on a minute,' Erin said. 'I want to know more about this book, Dad. What happened? What was it about? Did it ever get published?'

Her dad rocked backwards and forwards on his wonky leg in the middle of the room as Erin and Maggie looked up at him. 'Oh Erin, it was a long time ago, feels like another life. I had a go at writing a novel. It was based on my dad's experiences as a POW in a camp in Poland, in the war. It never got published, and I didn't pursue it. We moved here, I took over the farm and there wasn't time to write. End of story. So, Maggie, another G&T?'

'Lovely.' She held her glass in the air and he took it and walked towards the door, tripping over the corner of the carpet on his way. He hovered in the doorway for a couple of seconds looking like he might say something else, but then decided against it and left the room.

Erin looked up at Maggie. 'Why didn't you tell me you had met my dad before?'

'I wasn't sure it was him until I saw him today. I had wondered over the years. I remember your parents arriving in the village. Everyone talked about it, young John taking over Old Frank's farm with his pregnant wife. That was four years after I'd met him at the publisher's.'

Maggie pulled herself up from the armchair and walked over to inspect the oil painting of a vase of flowers on the other side of the room. She seemed more agile than usual, somehow. Her movements were less creaky. Erin got up from the floor and went to join her.

'Are you telling me that my mum was pregnant four years before she had me?' Erin asked slowly.

'I'm probably confused by the timings, as your dad said.' But she didn't sound confused. Maggie moved away from Erin and towards the piano in the corner of the room. She picked up a framed photograph of Debbie and John Turner on their wedding day and pulled it up close to her face to inspect it. 'Lunch smells delicious. Shall we go and see if we can help your mum?' Maggie put the photo down and it fell flat on the top of the piano, which hummed in response. She turned for the door but misjudged how far away it was and had to steady herself on the frame as she walked through.

'I'll be there in a sec,' Erin murmured.

She walked over to the piano and picked up the photo frame. She pulled the little stand out and set the frame back down. Her mind was spinning with all the conflicting information she had just taken on board. Had her mum lost a baby? Why wouldn't she have told Erin that? Her dad was an aspiring writer in Exeter? She had thought he always wanted to run the farm. Maybe not. Maybe she had got it all wrong. And Maggie – what was she playing at? She didn't seem confused; in fact, she seemed more lucid and in control than ever.

She sat down at the piano and tapped out 'Chopsticks'. Then she drew in a long, deep breath and walked into the kitchen. Maggie was at the table nursing her second gin and tonic. Her dad stood at the other side of the table carving the absurdly large turkey. King's College carols were playing loudly on the radio and no one was speaking. Erin went to join her mum amid the steam of the vegetables at the back of the kitchen. She looked flustered. 'Erin, could you drain the carrots?' she said while struggling to open the cornflour. Erin noticed her mum's hands were shaking and she couldn't get purchase on the top of the packet.

'Sure. Here, Mum, let me do it.' Erin took the flour off her mum and pulled it open.

'It smells good,' Maggie shouted over the music. 'The last time I had a proper Christmas lunch was nineteen years ago.' She took another swig of her gin and tonic. Erin wished she could be happy that Maggie was in such high spirits, but right now she resented her and the fireball she had just sent crashing through her life. She had expected to have to guard Maggie from her mother's fierce tongue today, not the other way around.

Lunch proceeded in a similar vein. Her mum was practically silent except to offer more food or give her dad instructions on carving, while he and Maggie drank the majority of two bottles of wine. Her mum didn't seem to want to drink or eat; she just moved the food around her plate. Erin would have gladly drowned her sorrows but she had to drive Maggie home later.

'I've read a couple of your detective novels, Maggie,' her dad said over pudding. 'How did you come up with the idea for Detective Turnpike?'

'I just saw a hole in the market, John,' she slurred. 'I had a lot of time on my hands when I moved here, so I read. Don't get me wrong, I had always read, but then when my life took its – its turn,' she stammered, 'I… I stopped being able to read proper books. When I say proper books, I mean books with substance, about real life, real death… so I started reading trash, anything I could get my hands on, really. I read a lot of detective novels, a lot of shit detective novels.' Her mum winced at Maggie's profanity. 'And I thought I could do it better… and it turns out I could, twenty-three times! Twenty-three years of my life spent writing shit books!' She laughed a growly laugh and drained her glass before slamming it back on the table. It shattered on impact. 'Oh, whoops, sorry,' she said and tried to pick up a splinter of glass which pricked her finger so that a crimson trickle leaked across the table. Erin jumped up to help. She wrapped a paper napkin around Maggie's finger, which was bleeding furiously. Erin held it tight. She could feel it trembling in her grip. Then she looked at Maggie and noticed a tear spring from her eye and make its way slowly down her flushed cheek.

'Do you think we should go and let Oblonsky out, Maggie?' Erin whispered. Maggie nodded, and another tear followed in the wake of the first.

Her mum was sweeping up the glass from the table. 'I'll get your coat,' she said and rushed off.

'I'll come with you,' her dad said, and Erin smiled up at him gratefully. Debbie returned with the coat and helped Maggie into it.

'Sorry,' Maggie said, through the tears welling in her eyes, 's… sorry about the glass.'

Debbie merely nodded back at Maggie, who turned and hobbled out into the darkness.

CHAPTER SIX

Lansdown Place, 19th December 1986

My relationship with alcohol has always been precarious. When I am down it takes me away to a safer place, somewhere the restless demons aren't biting at my ankles. And when I am up it brings me back down. Somewhere my heart doesn't race and my breathing is steady. I always felt more attractive, more alive after a couple of glasses of wine. Bolder, too; I would lure Richard in with my gregarious flirting. He was disapproving on the outside but I know he liked it. But wine took too long and gave rotten hangovers, so I soon discovered spirits. I only drank in the evenings, to begin with, but afternoons dragged and went so much more quickly if I had one while Lucas was having his supper. And then Lucas no longer needed picking up and suddenly the days became very long and I rarely lasted till lunchtime.

Richard pretended he didn't notice. Until one day he came home early and found me asleep on the kitchen table, the bottle of gin beside me. He was angry, livid in fact. He smashed the bottle on the floor. I was still finding splinters of glass in between the tiles for weeks afterwards. I resolved to stop, promised him I would try, but I was so tired, and so very lonely.

Until I met Sally. She changed my life. I locked myself out of the house one day and she found me on the doorstep. I had already had a couple and it wasn't even lunchtime. I had popped next door to the chemist for some citric acid to make elderflower cordial, without my keys. I had been so excited about making the cordial for Richard, he loved it. And so, I was banging on the door to my house when Sally came along. I don't know who I was banging for, there was no one inside. Well, no one human – Banjo was barking furiously. Sally didn't try to placate me, or comment on my insane behaviour. She just joined in with the banging. Together we banged and we shouted. We got some funny looks, I'm sure; ours was a busy street with lots of people passing by. And then we collapsed on the floor in a pile of giggles. Sally invited me back to hers a few doors down. She had only moved from London a couple of weeks earlier. She was despairing of the hemp-wearing, hairy-armpitted locals she had encountered so far, thinking she would never find anyone with the sophistication of London. I am not pretending I was sophisticated, far from it, but I think she detected a kindred spirit. We drank strong black coffee and ate a box of expensive chocolate truffles. She told me she used to drink and that she discovered meditation and managed to kick it. She said she could help me. I cried that day in her basement kitchen and she held me like I was a child.

And I had kept it under control ever since, until now. Dr Sham says I am on a self-destructive mission and I know he's right, but I can't seem to stop it. I was sick last night – I didn't quite make it to the loo and vomited in the kitchen sink, all over the dinner plates. I was passed out in my clothes by the time Richard got home and discovered the evidence. He must be repelled by me. I am repelled by me.

*

The drive home was silent. Erin had to concentrate on keeping the car on the road in the buffeting wind. Leaves flew at the windscreen and the wind whistled around them, making the sides of the Land

Rover rattle. Maggie sat in the front and closed her eyes for the duration. Her dad never said a word.

When they arrived at Hookes End, Erin had to shake Maggie awake. Erin and her dad each took one of her arms and pulled her out of the car. The wind whipped at their faces and they had to hold onto Maggie tight between them to stop her blowing away. Her feet barely touched the floor as they carried her to the door and straight upstairs to her bedroom.

Erin looked at her dad to gauge his reaction as they walked into the room. The smell of sickness, the dirty clothes strewn on the floor. But he didn't seem to notice or care. Erin shooed Oblonsky off the bed and they lifted Maggie onto it. She groaned and rolled over onto her side. Erin slipped the clogs off Maggie's feet and pulled her arms out of her duffel coat. Maggie winced. 'Oh, I'm sorry, Maggie, did I hurt you?' Erin whispered. Maggie grunted and Erin pulled the duvet up over her tiny body. Oblonsky lay down on the floor next to the bed and whimpered as if to say, 'I got this.' Her dad turned the light off and he and Erin backed out of the room and down the stairs.

'Do you think I can leave her like this?' Erin asked as she got to the bottom. Her dad was still halfway up looking at a print of butterfly pencil drawings.

'What's with all the butterflies?'

'I don't know.' Erin shrugged. 'I think she just really likes them. She knows everything there is to know about every single butterfly in the world. There are piles of books, and anthol…' She stumbled over the word.

'Anthologies.'

'Yeah, that's it. And, well, you can see the butterfly art all over the house. She is quite obsessive about it.'

'Yes, I can see that.' He moved a couple of steps further down and stopped to look at the African cave drawings that hung on the wall of the lower half of the staircase.

'She really is quite eccentric, isn't she?' he said, taking a closer look at a line drawing of a tribal woman whose bosoms were exposed and hung from her emaciated body. She had huge holes in her ears and a collar round her neck. 'She must have travelled a lot.'

'Yeah, I guess. She doesn't really talk about it.'

'You should ask.'

'I will.'

'I don't imagine she's been anywhere for a while, though. She doesn't look like she'd be up for a trip to the Sahara right now.'

'Dad,' Erin said. 'Do you think she's going to be alright here tonight?'

'She'll be fine. She just needs to sleep off all that gin.' He chuckled and stroked the head of the marble Buddha at the bottom of the stairs, and then wiped off the dust on his trousers.

'But she's really ill, Dad. She shouldn't have been drinking like that. I've never seen her drink before.'

'Well, I'm sure there's a reason for that. She seemed to be quite practised at it.'

'She was really anxious about leaving the house this morning. I don't think she goes out at all. She must have been drinking to calm her nerves.'

'She didn't seem that nervous to me.'

'Yeah, well, it obviously worked, didn't it? But what if she has a really bad reaction? Or never wakes up, and I've left her?'

'I think she'll be fine. But if you like, we can stay here. I just need to call your mother.' Erin pictured her mum as they had left, leaning against the Aga fighting back the tears. They couldn't leave her alone tonight, not on Christmas Day, not after everything.

'Maybe we could just stay for half an hour or so, just so I know she isn't going to be sick or anything. Then we can go back to Mum.'

Her dad looked over at her and smiled.

'You know, your mum and I, we're very proud of you.'

'Yeah, right,' Erin said, walking into the study and turning on the lights.

'We are!'

'Oh come on, Dad, you weren't exactly proud when I ran off to London with Simon, or when I came home. And you weren't over the moon when I got the job with Maggie either.'

'I didn't say we agreed with all your decisions. But today I did feel very proud of you, and the way you were looking after Maggie. I didn't think you had it in you!' He laughed and walked over to the round table where Erin's computer sat. 'Is this where you work?' He stroked the keys on the keypad, then sat down in her seat.

'Yeah. Maggie sits over there on the sofa with Oblonsky.'

'Oblonsky?'

'The dog.'

'Ah, that stinky mutt in the bedroom.'

'Yeah.' Erin walked over to Maggie's spot on the sofa and sat down. She looked into the cold and dark fireplace and tried to imagine the warmth of the flames. Erin took a deep breath. 'Dad, did you have another baby before me?' she asked.

The silence of his response was raw. Then rudely interrupted by the carriage clock on the mantelpiece as it struck five times. Five o'clock, was that all? She felt as though a whole lifetime had passed since she'd been here this morning picking up Maggie. 'Dad?' She turned around to look at him now. He was still sitting at her desk, staring at the computer, gently tapping at the keys. 'Dad, please, I need to know.'

'Yes,' he said finally, looking up at her now. 'He was called Robert.' Erin swallowed down the acid that rose up at the back of her throat.

'What happened to him, Dad?'

'I-I can't talk about this, Erin. You need to speak to your mother.'

'What do you mean, you can't talk about the fact that I had a brother?'

'*Have.*'

'What?'

'You said had. He… he didn't die. He's still alive.'

'What? I have a brother who is still alive, and you haven't told me?' Erin started pacing up and down the rug in front of the unlit fire.

'I don't understand, Dad, what are you telling me?'

'I, I can't, Erin. Let's just go home, shall we?' He got up and walked towards the door.

'No, wait, Dad. You have to tell me.' She ran after him and grabbed his arm in the doorway. 'Where is he?' Her dad looked at her with big frightened eyes. His lips quivered.

'He, his name is Robert. He has Down's syndrome. We gave him away.'

There was a sudden thud above them which shook the ceiling. The lampshade above the table quivered and dust fell onto the computer.

'Maggie,' Erin said, and ran out of the door and up the stairs. Her father followed close behind.

Maggie was coming out of her bathroom pulling up her tights. Her skirt was abandoned on the floor behind her. Her silvery hair had escaped its bun and was hanging around her ghostlike face.

'Maggie, are you OK?' Erin said, gasping for breath.

'Why wouldn't I be? I just had a pee,' she slurred and pushed past them, then stumbled back into bed.

'What are you both doing here?' she said from behind her closed eyes.

'We were worried about you.'

'Well, you needn't. Go home,' she grunted.

'OK,' Erin said, walking towards the bedroom door. 'Shall I come and see you tomorrow?'

'Whatever,' Maggie said, shooing her away with her hand.

Erin shut the door and pushed past her dad, who was loitering outside. She ran down the stairs two at a time and out into the night. Tears were burning in her eyes and the cold wind smacked her in the face. She got into the car and gripped the steering wheel with both trembling hands, her breath gathered like smoke on the windscreen. She watched her dad through the steamed glass as he turned the lights off in Maggie's house and limped towards the car. He climbed into the passenger seat and reached for Erin's hand on the steering wheel, his gloves warm on her icy fingers. 'I'm sorry, Erin, we should have told you. We just didn't know how.' She pulled her hand away from his and turned the key. They drove home in silence.

When they arrived back, her mum was sitting at the kitchen table, nursing a glass tumbler with both hands. Erin had never seen her drink spirits before. The pudding plates were still on the table with traces of fruit sponge crusted onto them. Dirty dishes littered the work surfaces behind her. Her mum looked at them both in the doorway, questioning them with her hollow eyes.

'Why didn't you tell me, Mum?' Erin said through angry tears.

Her mum stood up and came towards them. She looked at her dad with wide, desperate eyes.

'I told her about Robert, Debbie,' her dad said gently. He and Erin were still standing in the doorway with their coats on.

'I… I…' Erin's mum tried to say something but couldn't find the words.

'How could you, Mum? How could you give him away like that?'

'Erin, I…' she started, but then looked back at her husband. 'Why, John? We agreed.'

'Agreed what?' Erin raised her voice and looked at one parent and then the other.

'I had to tell her, Debbie, she asked me outright.'

'But—' her mum started.

'But what, Mum? Were you ever going to tell me?'

'I… I don't know. I was waiting for the right time.'

'The right time! Mum, I'm twenty-five! Surely that time has been and gone.'

'Please, Erin, come in and take your coat off. Let's just talk.' She reached out to Erin, touched the furry hood of her coat. Erin dithered and then let her take the coat from her shoulders and walked further into the room.

'Erin, you have to understand. This is very difficult for your mother, she—'

'Shh, Dad, please.' Erin ran her fingers through her hair and held onto the pressure points on her head. She pressed down hard.

'Love?' Her dad was at her side. She felt giddy, as though she was bobbing up and down on a boat. Everything she had ever known was being called into question.

'I think… I just need to be on my own right now, Dad.'

'But…'

'Let her be, John,' her mum said softly with resignation. Then she sank down into one of the kitchen chairs and held onto the table edge as if she might fall off. Erin glanced at her and then walked out of the room and upstairs into her bedroom, where she collapsed onto her bed and shut her eyes. Shut out the world.

CHAPTER SEVEN

Lansdown Place, 25th December 1986

It was the church bells that woke me. And for a moment I forgot; for just a moment those bells gave me the same flutter of excitement in my belly as they had on Christmas Day for all my life. And then I remembered. Richard made me get up. He came in with a cup of tea, wearing his Christmas tree jumper. That was a shock because he had bought it with Skye the year before. He reminded me that I was supposed to be making an effort for Lucas. I told him I couldn't, not today. He said I had to. He was firm, strong. He talked to me like a child and I complied. I put on some heels and a dress and we went to church. Richard said he would stay behind and cook the lunch. He had always done that, so I didn't argue. Lucas came, though; he was making an effort too. I have taken to sitting in the empty church sometimes when I want to get out of the house. Not because I've suddenly got the faith or anything – I just like the quiet and the austerity. The seats are hard and it is always punishingly cold with a draught that rattles through even when the doors are shut. I talk to Skye in there. I know she can't hear me but it helps. You see, I have to believe that she is somewhere. And that the somewhere is better than here.

Today of course it was full of people and smelt of pine needles and candles. We had to budge up to the end of the pew so that a family of latecomers could squeeze in. I was squashed up against the dad's tweed jacket. He smelt of expensive aftershave and sang loudly. Lucas walked out halfway through the service. I still don't know what triggered it. He is not normally one to make a scene, but I guess we have all changed. I thought about following him but the family on our row had only just sat down from letting Lucas out. And my heels would get stuck in the grid in the aisle like they had on the way in, and everyone would look at me.

He wasn't outside after the service, and he wasn't at home. Richard had already tucked into the whisky, I could smell it on his breath. He shouted at me. How could I lose him? Why didn't I follow him? I shouted back and said that I couldn't get through to him. That he is fucked up. That it's no wonder he is so fucked up, because it was his fault, that night she died. Richard went grey and his eyes widened. He had seen Lucas coming in the door, standing behind me. For the second time that day Lucas bolted. This time I ran after him. I shouted that it wasn't true, that it wasn't his fault. It was mine. But he could run faster than me, and I was wearing those stupid heels. He didn't come back for presents, or lunch. Eventually we went out to look for him. I went to Simeon's house. The whole family were playing charades. Simeon hadn't seen him but he offered to come and help. I went up onto the Downs by the windmill. I know he likes it up there. Simeon went to the park and Richard had already gone to the bus station.

It was bitterly cold up on the hill and I was still in my dress with only a flimsy coat. The dusk was closing in and with it came the mist. I couldn't see more than a few feet in front of me. I shouted his name into the wind but could barely hear it myself. And then I couldn't work out which way was down. A claustrophobic panic bubbled up inside me and I walked around in circles with my arms out in front of me. I must have looked ridiculous. And then the panic gave way to a calmness inside as I imagined dying up there with just the wind and the night

*for company. I didn't die, though; a man and his dog rescued
me and escorted me back into town. By the time I got back,
Lucas was home. He had locked himself in his bedroom. So, I
sat on the floor and spoke to him through the door. I told him
I didn't mean it, but we both knew I did.*

*

Erin spent Christmas evening in her room and waited until her
parents had both gone out the following morning before she came
downstairs. Her dad was on his rounds and her mum was at the
soup kitchen in St Austell. She had been there every Boxing Day
for as long as Erin could remember. Erin scoffed at the hypocrisy
of the fraud she now knew her mother to be.

She decided to walk up to Maggie's. The storm of the day before
had broken and left a gloriously calm and crisp day in its wake.
The frost was crunchy underfoot and the sea glasslike.

Maggie was in the kitchen when she arrived. She was sticking
a knife inside the toaster, swearing under her breath.

'Maggie, what are you doing? You'll get yourself electrocuted.'
Erin turned the plug off at the wall and took the knife out of
Maggie's hands, then retrieved the raggedy bread from the toaster.

'What are you doing here?' Maggie said impatiently. 'It's Boxing
Day, haven't you got somewhere better to be?'

'Not really.' Erin shrugged and put another piece of bread in
the toaster and turned it back on at the wall. 'And I wanted to
make sure you were OK.'

'Why wouldn't I be?'

'Well, I just thought after all that gin and wine and everything.'
Smoke wafted up from the toaster and the acrid smell of burning
filled the air. 'Damn it, it's happened again,' Erin said and turned
the switch off.

'Forget it,' Maggie said and walked out of the kitchen. 'Tea
would be nice,' she shouted over her shoulder back to Erin, who

was wrestling the burnt toast out of the toaster. 'If you haven't got anywhere else to be, that is.'

Once she had retrieved the toast Erin waited for the kettle to boil. Through the open kitchen door she could see the Buddha at the bottom of the stairs and was instantly taken back to the conversation with her dad the night before. She had come to Maggie's to escape the sickening sense of unease that had haunted her from the minute she woke up. Yet the butterflies, the African women, the Buddha were all suddenly significant reminders of what had come before the revelation that turned her world upside down. Would her life for evermore be divided into before and after? Would she ever be able to live with the same carefree abandon, knowing that she had a brother out there? A brother who had been rejected by the same parents who had brought her into this horribly dull yet safe world? The kettle screeched behind her and Erin jumped, her heart racing. She shut her eyes and breathed out through puffed cheeks. And when she opened them, she saw the magnet of the Eiffel Tower on the fridge and recalled her dad's words of advice the night before.

'Maggie.' Erin hoped that Maggie couldn't hear the wobble in her voice as she carried the two mugs of steaming tea into the study. 'Can you tell me about your travels?'

'What do you want to know?'

'Anything, everything! I have barely left Porthteal. I dream about travelling to faraway exotic places.'

'And you will. But my travelling days are long gone.'

'Of course, but I'm sure it stays with you, doesn't it? The heat, the dust, the smells? What's it like?'

'Well, just as you would imagine, really. Hot, dusty, smelly.'

'What was your favourite place?'

'Oh, Erin, I don't know.'

'Surely you must have one? Did you really take all those photos? Where do those women in the top hats and stripy shawls come from?'

'Bolivia.'

'Now that is a good look. One of them even has a bird on her shoulder. She looks like a character out of a children's picture book.'

'Yes, I suppose she does.' Maggie shut her eyes and let out a long, exhausted breath.

'Are you OK, Maggie?'

'Apart from dying, you mean?' Maggie snapped.

'Sorry.'

'My head is throbbing, if you must know, but there's nothing unusual about that. Pass me some of those pills, will you?'

Erin picked the pills up off the table and passed them to Maggie on the sofa.

'I'll get you some water,' Erin said, heading back to the kitchen.

'Don't bother,' Maggie said and threw her head back to swallow them dry.

Erin walked over to the window. The sun burned through the glass and she felt the warmth on her face.

'Maggie, have you known all along that my parents had another baby before me?'

'I wasn't sure.'

Erin turned to look at Maggie. 'But you brought it up yesterday. You must have known what the fallout would be. Why did you say it?'

Maggie lifted the mug to her lips and slowly took a tiny sip of tea before putting it back down on the table next to the sofa. 'I don't have much time left,' she said finally. 'And my life is full of regrets, Erin. I didn't want this to be another one.'

'Right, so you've turned my life upside down as part of your own personal purge?' Erin couldn't hide the acerbic tone to her words. 'Sorry, I just…' She turned back to the window to hide the tears that were now stinging behind her eyes.

'No, Erin,' Maggie said slowly, 'I did what I did yesterday because I thought you should know. Secrets never help anybody, especially in families.' Oblonsky chose that moment to scamper into the room and jump up on the sofa next to Maggie. She ruffled the fur around his head and he settled down next to her, his head in her lap. 'What did happen to the baby?' Maggie asked.

'You don't know?' Erin swung round again, no longer hiding the redness of her eyes.

'All I know is that your mother was pregnant, and when they moved to Porthteal four years later she was pregnant again with you, but there was no sign of the other baby. I did ask my publisher, of course. She had been excited about your father's book, but he had changed his mind about publishing it shortly after that meeting. She had asked him how his baby was and he had said he didn't know, which she thought was a very strange response but didn't want to pry. I didn't either, so left it there. I've seen your parents in the village over the years, and they both have a sadness about them.'

'But Maggie,' Erin interrupted her. 'It wasn't your place to say it… I hardly know you. My parents don't know you at all.' Maggie looked insulted by this and she worried she had gone too far.

'Listen here, young lady,' Maggie said, pulling herself to the front of the sofa for more authority. 'Life is hard, and the truth, well, it's even harder. It hurts like hell, but in the long run it hurts a lot more if you don't know the truth. Trust me, I have a miserable life's worth of experience in this field. Challenge your parents, ask them the questions. Find out the truth now. It will be so much better in the end.' She collapsed back onto the sofa then, exhausted.

'He has Down's syndrome,' Erin said quietly. A pheasant was trotting slowly across the lawn, and it stopped to peck at something in the frozen ground. 'They gave him away.'

'Gave him away? What, to a home? Or was he adopted? Where is he?'

'I don't know. I was so upset I couldn't even talk to them about it. How could they give him away? And why didn't they tell me?'

'I don't know, Erin, but they will have had their reasons.'

Erin collapsed into the armchair by the window and the sun fell onto her lap and warmed her thighs. She watched the dust particles dance in its beam and she thought of her brother. She wondered whether he too could feel the warmth of the winter sun, wherever he was.

She stopped at the bench on the brow of the hill on her way home; it was one of the only places in the village where there was any mobile reception. She opened up Google and her fingers hovered over the keypad, unsure what to type. 'Robert Turner Down's syndrome', she tried. A paper on a rare variant of the syndrome 'Down-Turner' came up at the top of the list. Then there was a video of a Canadian guy called Rob Turner talking about his son with Down's – his voice stuttered with emotion when he said it wasn't an illness, but a gift. There was a picture of his family, two boys – one with the telltale almond eyes and one without – all four of them smiling, big, ear-to-ear joyful smiles. Then there was a medical website listing the potential health problems of children with Down's – vision, hearing, respiratory, the list went on. Then came Wikipedia, and the NHS, and a BBC article about a mother who nearly aborted her baby because of an unreliable test. Would Erin's parents have aborted their baby had they been given the choice? She rubbed at her throbbing temples as her mind began to whir with all of these unanswered questions.

She added the word 'adoption' to her search and various agencies came up, one specifically for adopting children with special needs. There were heart-warming stories about good people saving these unwanted children. Erin had always thought her parents were the good ones, but as she scoured the photos of these happy families she questioned her own, and everything she had ever taken for granted. She did an image search for Robert Turner, not sure what she was even looking for. Would he have the Turner thick hair that she had inherited from her father, or her mother's dimples?

Would she even be able to see a family resemblance through the defining features of his condition? His new family would probably have changed his name anyway.

She turned her phone off. The throbbing had crept its way around the entire circumference of her skull by then and she pressed her cold palms against her head in an attempt to numb it. She couldn't face going home, so she went to the pub.

Old Dave Taylor was propping up the bar. He had been there all day, escaping his in-laws apparently. He bought Erin several pints and a whisky chaser and they played pool. It was dark by the time she stumbled out of there. She checked the time on her phone and there was another message from Simon.

I miss you.

She had reached the bus shelter on the edge of the village. It was starting to rain, so she perched on the plastic seat under the shelter and looked at her phone. She knew that if she hadn't had the pints and the whisky she might have been able to resist. But it had been a really shitty Christmas and she just wanted to hear his voice. And so she called.

'Erin?' She recognised that faraway tone in his voice.

'Are you painting?' she asked quietly.

'How do you know?' he asked.

'Just guessed.' She sat back on the hard bench and leant against the plastic wall of the shelter.

'Do you really miss me?' she asked, closing her eyes, holding her breath for his answer.

'Of course I do.' She could breathe again. 'You just left, didn't say goodbye.'

'I saw you, I saw you with her, with your daughter.'

'What did you expect? I would run into your arms, introduce you to my family?'

'I guess.'

'Come on, Erin. You know how it is…'

There was a silence then, an impasse. They both knew there was nothing to say, nowhere to go. Beverly the cleaner from the Angel arrived in the shelter. She nodded at Erin and then sat at the other end of the bench.

'I am working on your portrait,' Simon said.

'What?' she turned away from Beverly. 'What do you mean, my portrait?'

'I've painted you, asleep on the sofa, that dimple in the bottom of your back.'

'I… I didn't know,' Erin stuttered, that familiar burning sensation bubbling up deep inside.

'It was going to be a surprise, I told you, you were my muse.' He chuckled. 'You can't see your face, of course, it's turned the other way, just your spiky hair, your gorgeous bottom, your breasts.'

'Stop, Simon,' Erin said quietly, the heat rising in her cheeks. She glanced quickly at Beverly, who was blowing her nose and stuffing the soiled tissue into her sleeve.

'Do you want to see it?'

'No… I mean, yes… oh… I… I don't know.' She got up and walked out of the shelter and up the hill leading out of town. 'Could you send me a photo?' she whispered eventually.

'I don't think so.'

'I… I can't think about this right now, Simon, I've got to go,' she hissed into the phone.

'Wait, Erin… are you OK?'

'I'm fine, Simon, I just… I'm going now.'

'Erin,' he said quickly. 'I do miss you, you know.'

'Bye, Simon.' She hung up and marched up the road. All this time he had been recreating her body, tracing its lines, shading the dimple at the bottom of her back. She was his muse after all. And he missed her, he had sounded sincere when he said that. She had heard his eyes smiling behind those words. Did he love her? She wanted to see the painting. She wanted to see him, to feel his touch; she wanted it so much that her head started to throb again, temporarily numbed by the booze. She pressed her palms into her temples and willed herself to remember the gallery, the girl in her stripy tights, her mother's cherry-red lips. 'Arrrggh!' she roared, and her voice carried across the icy air. She kicked at the muddy ground with the toe of her boot.

Her parents' bedroom light was still on when she walked down the drive towards the house and she watched it go off as she opened the front door. This infuriating routine had played out in the same way every time she'd come back late for the last decade. She knew they only did it because they cared, but she was twenty-five, not sixteen! And now this smothering that she had been subjected to all her life took on a whole different meaning. They had given away their other child, and in doing so had forfeited the right to know where he was, or what he was doing, ever again. She turned on the radio and thrashed around the kitchen, getting out the leftovers and dipping cold roast potatoes straight into the pot of mayonnaise. She knew she was being churlish, but she couldn't quite help it.

CHAPTER EIGHT

Lansdown Place, 26th December 1986

I hit Lucas once. He was always such a sweet boy, so calm. I watched other six-year-olds thrashing around the playground with sticks, rugby-tackling each other to the floor and I would count my blessings that he wasn't like that. But there was a period of time when his behaviour challenged me. I realise now he was just finding his voice, standing his ground. I should have been proud, but it was so unlike him, so far from the little boy who would have done anything just to put a smile on my face.

I picked him up from school that day and he whined the whole way home. He rejected the snacks I had bought and refused to hold my hand to cross the street. Then he insisted on scaling the railings outside the library. All pretty incidental, now I look back on it, but by the time we got home I was feeling prickly and on edge. Then he wouldn't read his schoolbook or wash his hands before dinner. And when I presented him with the Lancashire hotpot I had so lovingly prepared the night before, he just pushed it away saying 'yuck'. I took a few deep breaths — just as my mum had with me — and asked him nicely not to be so rude. I put the plate back in front of him, but he pushed it away again. He folded his skinny little arms and pursed his lips in defiance. He said he hated it and wasn't going to eat it. At this point I told him to go to his room. 'Fine!' he said, marching out the door and slamming it behind him. I watched him through the glass panels of the door into the hallway. He stopped on the second step, hovered there for a while and then turned to look at me. A wry smile crossed his face, and then he walked back towards the door to the kitchen. It creaked open and with his head held high, he marched to the kitchen table where the Lancashire hotpot sat, a crusty film forming on the surface. He picked up the plate and emptied the contents into the bin. I can still remember the rage bubbling up inside me. I stormed over and grabbed his wrists hard. He told me I was hurting him but I wrung them out harder, like a damp cloth, squeezing out every last drop of water. And then I smacked him hard on the bottom, twice, maybe three times. He was crying by then, begging me to stop. So I did, and I looked into his swollen eyes, tears falling down his freckled face. A burning nausea bubbled up from that same place as the anger. I sent him to his room and collapsed onto the kitchen table, shaking.

He cried himself to sleep that night, and I sat outside his bedroom door just as I did last night. When the whimpering finally ceased, I went in and he was curled into a ball on the bed. His starched school shirt was gathered up under his armpits, revealing his pasty belly. Strands of hair stuck to his mottled cheek and his body still flinched with leftover sobs. I knew I should take his clothes off but I was too scared to touch him. I wasn't fit to be a mother. I knew that then, and I know it now.

*

The next morning, her parents were both waiting for her in the kitchen when she came down late. Her dad was pacing impatiently and her mum was making soup, curry and meatloaf from the leftover turkey all at the same time. Her hair had gone frizzy and she had blood down the front of her apron.

'Morning,' they both said.

'Morning.' Erin picked up the kettle and took it over to the sink. Condensation had formed on the window and the grey day was blurred. Erin placed the kettle on the Aga, where it rattled and fizzed.

'Your mother and I were worried about you yesterday, Erin, where were you?' her dad asked.

'I'm sorry, I went to Maggie's and then the pub and you were in bed when I got home.' She got a piece of bread out of the bread bin and then opened the fridge for the butter.

'Do you want to talk about it?' he asked.

Erin sighed a heavy sigh. 'I don't really know what to say, Dad.' She sat down at the table with her plate.

'You must have lots of questions for us.' He raised his eyebrows at her mum, who was focused on slicing celery.

'Yes, I do, so many that I don't know where to start,' Erin said as she pasted the butter with her knife on the side of the plate, trying to soften it up.

'Well, go on then, we'll be totally honest with you, won't we, Debbie?' She didn't answer, just turned her back on them to empty the board of celery into the pot on the Aga. The kettle started to boil, and screamed its high-pitched whistle.

'OK. Why? Why did you do it? Why did you give your baby away?' She directed the question at her mother's back and watched her stiffen. But it was her dad who answered.

'You must understand, we were really young. I was twenty, your mum, she was only eighteen. And it was hard, she… we couldn't cope.' He looked to Debbie for support, but she still had her back to them, so he pulled out a chair on the opposite side of the table from Erin and sat down. 'It was a shock. You couldn't have scans like you do today, that give you some warning. And, well, in the hospital they mentioned adoption and I guess that kind of sowed the seed in our minds, and…'

'And what… and then you just decided he wasn't perfect so you'd give him away?'

'It wasn't like that, we thought long and hard.' Her mum swung round, her eyes watery, her words quiet and breathless.

'But you still did it!' Erin threw her arms in the air in disbelief. 'You're like the patron saint of Porthteal. You spend your whole life doing WI and Sunday school. You were at the homeless shelter yesterday – on Boxing Day, for God's sake! How could you be such a hypocrite?'

'That's not fair,' her mum said. The folds of skin on her chin gathered and whitened.

'Now, that's enough, Erin,' her dad interjected.

'No, it's not enough! It is nowhere near enough. And you, you're just as bad.' She pointed her finger at him. It was shaking with rage. 'You decided to give him up too. And then you both lied to me, my whole life you have lied to me! All those times I asked why you didn't have any more children. How could you do that?'

'We wanted to tell you, love. But there was never a right time. And then the years went by and the longer we didn't tell you, the harder it became, and—'

'And what? You hoped you would get away with it, that I would never find out?'

'No, no.' Her dad said it more emphatically the second time, as if convincing himself it was true.

'Yes,' her mum whispered.

'What?' Erin swung round to look at her.

'It's not a crime,' she said slowly, tentatively. 'I just, well, I hoped this day would never come.'

'You have got to be kidding. I can't believe you just admitted that!' Erin stood up and her chair screeched against the brick floor.

'I'm just trying to be honest with you.'

'I think it's a bit late for that, Mum.' She backed out of the room and got halfway up the stairs, but she couldn't leave it like that. She had to know more, so she went back down, into the room. Her dad was pacing up and down now and her mum was holding onto the work surface as if she might fall over if she let go, globules of turkey fat stuck to the backs of her chapped hands. Was it shame on their faces? Or fear? Or guilt? She really couldn't tell.

'So where is he?'

'What?' Her dad looked at her, bemused.

'Robert, of course, where is he now?' He shot her mum a panicked look, and she opened her mouth to respond but nothing came out.

'He, well, he… was adopted by another family,' her dad said finally.

'OK, so where are they?'

'I… we don't know. They used to live in Exeter but then they moved and…'

'You didn't ask for a forwarding address?'

'No!' he scoffed. 'That really wouldn't have been appropriate, Erin, once we had made our decision.'

'Appropriate!' she interrupted him. 'Well, thank God you didn't do something inappropriate, Dad!' Her voice was screeching with hostility but she didn't care. 'I don't think I can do this now,' she said and left the room again. This time she ran straight up the stairs to her bedroom.

She could feel the blood pulsing in her ears. She grabbed a rucksack from the back of her door and stuffed her pyjamas from under her pillow down inside. Then her toothbrush from the basin, her laptop from the top of the chest of drawers. Some pants, spare jeans… she had to get out of here. But where would she go? A hoodie from the floor, a couple of t-shirts. *The Catcher in the Rye* from her bedside table. Maggie had lent it to her. Maggie! She would go to Maggie's. She stuffed it all down inside the rucksack and struggled to pull the string tight enough to keep it all in.

Her parents were in the same positions when she came back downstairs. As if their stillness might halt the drama unfolding before them. But it had a momentum of its own now. They were like moored fishing boats bobbing around in the wake of the truth that had come hurtling into their sheltered harbour.

'Where are you going?' her dad said.

'To Maggie's, I'm going to stay at Maggie's for a while.'

'But Erin, you can't just go like this, we need to talk about it, we didn't mean—'

'Let her go, John,' her mum said.

Erin walked to the door and pulled her coat off the hook, then slung it over her arm and walked out of the house.

CHAPTER NINE

Lansdown Place, 29th December 1986

*Lucas left the house on Boxing Day before I had got up. Simeon's
mum called to say he was with them and that he wanted to stay
there for a while. A while? How long was a while? She didn't
say she knew what was going on, but her tone was brittle, her
words clipped. I tried to object, to ask her how he was, whether
I could talk to him – but the words got stuck in my chest and
I dropped the phone. I could hear her calling my name at the
other end but I couldn't respond. I ran upstairs, splashed cold
water on my face. I tried to remember the exercise Dr Sham
had suggested in moments like these. 'Think of your feet and
how you would describe them to an alien. It will ground you,
take your thoughts out of your head.' Pink, soft, crusty heels on
the cold floor, five tiny limbs, flecks of scarlet on rough nails. It
didn't work. I went to bed, haven't got up for two days. I heard
Lucas letting himself in yesterday when Richard was out. I hid
under the covers while he rummaged around in the room next to
mine. He was packing a bag. I heard the zip and the squeak of
his drawers. And then in the bathroom, his keys jangling on his
belt. My breath was hot under the duvet. It was claustrophobic
but I didn't move; I lay there hiding from my son, paralysed by
my own fucked-up mind. I don't think I can carry on.*

*

'What are you doing here?' Maggie was hobbling up from the bench at the bottom of the garden with Oblonsky when Erin arrived. She walked down to meet them.

'I had a fight with my parents. Can I stay for a while?'

'What? No! You can't stay here.' Maggie carried on towards the front door.

'Please, Maggie, just for a few days.' They had reached the front step and Maggie was fumbling around with the brass locust boot-pull. It clattered on the stone. Erin crouched down and held it still so Maggie could get her boot into it.

'Haven't you got anywhere else to go? What about that fella in the pub you're friendly with?' Maggie pulled her foot out of the boot and into the clog that was sitting on the step next to it.

'Derek? He lives at the pub, I can't stay there. He only has one room and a tiny single bed.' Erin guided Maggie's other boot into the locust's talons.

'Well, don't you have any other friends?'

'Please, Maggie, I'll be a real help, I promise.' Erin stood up and held Maggie's arm as she fumbled the other foot into the clog. Maggie shrugged her off.

'A help?' Maggie scoffed. 'You?'

'Yes, me! I can cook for you and shop. I could clean the house.' Erin followed Maggie inside.

'Why? What's wrong with my house?'

'Nothing, there's nothing wrong. It could just do with a bit of a spruce-up, that's all.' Maggie shuffled down the corridor and Erin hovered at her shoulder.

'I don't want anyone sprucing up my house. I like it just the way it is.'

'OK, well, just think how much more work we can get done on the manuscript. You won't have to wait for me in the mornings, I'll be here, and we can just get started straight away.' Erin could see the cogs whirring in Maggie's head as they entered the study. Maggie looked at the computer where Erin sat to type out her words.

'You would have to get up early, none of this lazing around in bed.'

'Of course!'

'Six o'clock I'm up, with the birds.'

'Right, OK, I can do that.'

'And you'll have to make your own bed. God knows where any sheets are, no one has ever stayed here.'

'Of course, that's fine, Maggie, I really don't need much.'

'Right, well, just for a few days then.'

'Oh, thank you, Maggie!' Erin rushed towards her and tried to put her arm around Maggie, who froze at her touch.

'Alright, enough of that,' she said, lowering herself into the sofa. 'Get me some tea, would you?'

'Of course.'

'Erin,' Maggie called to her as she was leaving the room. 'Was it about your brother? The row with your parents?'

'Uh, yeah.'

'A piece of toast would be nice, with the tea I mean.'

'Coming up.'

There were three other bedrooms in Maggie's house. One at the front on the other side of the hallway from Maggie's. It had the same view down the garden and out to sea. And there were another two at the back. Erin deliberated; Maggie had said she could choose her room. She wanted that view, but she wasn't sure she wanted to be so close to Maggie and all her sickness and bodily functions, so she opted for the larger of the two back rooms. It was currently housing several piles of boxes and an old exercise bike. Erin struggled to imagine Maggie ever having used an exercise bike, and sure enough, Maggie told her it had been in the house when she bought it and she had never got round to throwing it away. There was also a rocking horse in there.

'Was this yours as a child, Maggie?' Erin asked, stroking the horse's dusty head. She tried to unpick some of the tangles in the wiry mane.

'No.' Maggie shut her down. 'I think there are some sheets in the chest over there.' She pointed to it on the other side of the room and then walked out the door.

The sheets were cold, damp to the touch and smelt mildewed. Erin made up the single bed in the corner of the room. She found an old fan heater in one of the other bedrooms and turned it on in an attempt to bring some warmth into the cold walls and sheets. She pushed the boxes into one corner of the room and couldn't resist opening one to see what was inside. A stack of children's exercise books. 'Lucas Muir Maths' the top one read in a child's scrawl. The edges of the pages were curled.

Lucas! Her heart thumped in what felt like her stomach. Lucas from the story was here in this room. Erin looked behind her to see if Maggie was there, but she wasn't. Her hands were shaking as she flicked through the book. Faded ink sums in wonky writing. Lucas was Maggie's son. Maggie was the mother in the story! The thought had fluttered into Erin's mind a couple of times but she had blown it away as quickly as it arrived. Hadn't wanted to consider it, what it would have meant. That all that grief and blame was so close to home, so undeniably real. She picked up another exercise book, 'Lucas Muir English'. Her heart thumped harder, louder in her chest. It was Maggie lying in her daughter's bed, clutching Mr Gilbert, hoping her smell wouldn't fade. Maggie, drunk on the street, banging her front door down. Maggie, hitting her son and hating herself. Maggie who had lost her daughter and blamed her son? What had happened? Where was he? And Richard? How had she ended up all alone, dying in this huge house on a Cornish hilltop with only Erin for company? She looked behind her again – still no sign of Maggie. On the opening page of the English exercise book was a story about a haunted house, and a drawing of the house with a pointy roof and bats flying in from the moon. Then there was a history exercise book – tea-stained Anglo-Saxon maps fell out of the book and onto the floor. Erin was just pulling the art sketch pad out from the bottom of the pile when she heard Maggie's voice behind her.

'What are you doing?'

'I'm sorry, Maggie, I was just—'

'Being nosy, that is what you were doing. It is none of your business.' Maggie bent down and winced with pain as she picked up one of the exercise books and put it back in the box. Erin picked up the others and threw them in. She put the lid on top, but the books were in a dishevelled pile now and it didn't fit.

'I'm sorry, Maggie. I was just moving the boxes out of the way and I saw the name and I… I didn't think… I…' Erin looked at Maggie, but she refused to make eye contact. Her head was down, focusing on the books, the boxes. On Erin. Erin tried to rearrange the books into a more orderly pile and Maggie put the lid on top of the box, trapping Erin's arm inside.

'No, no, you didn't think, Erin. No… this… this is not going to work. You can't stay here.'

'What?'

'I can't… I can't have someone living in my house, not after all this time… I just can't… I'm sorry.' Her words were rattled off fast. She stood up and paced up and down the room. She pulled at her hairline with her trembling hands.

'I'm so sorry, Maggie, I know I shouldn't have looked in the box. We can just pretend it didn't happen. I didn't really see anything… not really. We can just carry on as we did before.'

'No, Erin, I can't have someone nosing around in my things.' She walked out of the room and Erin ran after her.

'Maggie, I can't go home. Not after everything. Surely you of all people understand that.' Maggie stopped at the top of the stairs and turned to face Erin. She looked like she was about to say something and then thought better of it. She walked down the stairs, holding onto the bannister gingerly. Erin waited until they had got to the bottom and then tried again.

'Maggie.' Erin held onto her arm. She could hear her voice tremble. 'I know it was wrong of me to look in that box, and I promise I won't look at anything else. And I won't get in your way, apart from when you want to work on the book.' Maggie looked at her and Erin clasped her hands together in a prayer position. 'Please,' she whispered.

'Fine.' Maggie said, and walked into the study and shut the door behind her.

Erin sat down on the bottom step and sighed. She tried to make sense of what had just happened. It felt strange that they hadn't exactly acknowledged the significance of it. Should she have challenged her about the nature of her book? Presumably Maggie now knew that she knew. But would they both have to pretend that she didn't? She thought Maggie had begun to open up and trust her. Yesterday when she had said all that stuff about family and regrets. But this scene with the boxes made her realise that the chasm between them was still so wide and full of secrets.

CHAPTER TEN

Royal Victoria Hospital, 1st January 1987

It is New Year's Day. A whole week since Christmas. Five days since I tried to kill myself. And the first time since being here that I feel strong enough to write. I remember their white coats when I came round. Their hushed tones. And the beeps and the bleeps. There was a tube up my nose. Another down my throat. I couldn't breathe. I gagged. They took it out quickly when they realised I was awake, and I remember that rush of cold air filling my lungs. I had failed. I was alive. The misery drowned me with such intensity that I wailed. Richard was there. Mum too, and Sara. But not Lucas. Richard has visited every day since but his visits are getting shorter and he can't look at me now. Mum comes too. She fusses around me, rearranging blankets and deadheading flowers. All the time twittering on. I watch her lips move without hearing the words. She doesn't expect me to respond anyway. Sara is the only one who is honest with me. Lucas won't come, she told me, he is too angry. She painted my toenails this morning, and as she held my foot I closed my eyes. It was nice to have someone touch me rather than prod me. But then I remembered painting Skye's toes on that holiday. And I was sucked back down again. Drowning.

*

Erin asked Maggie if she could borrow the Land Rover and drive into Truro to pick up some provisions. She felt quite other-worldly as she walked into Tesco's; the bright strip lights hurt her eyes and the tinny music echoed around her head. She had only been at Maggie's house for a couple of days, but she felt as though she had been out at sea. There was a tower of champagne bottles and boxes of chocolates at the front of the store and a banner which read 'New Year Offer – Two For One Chocolates and Bubbles!' It was New Year's Eve! She hadn't even realised. She was living with an old lady who would be in bed before nine o'clock. She would go to the pub. She felt in her pocket for her phone and remembered it had buzzed with messages on her way here.

There was another message from Simon. There had been at least one a day since the phone call in the bus shelter. He told her he missed her. That he was still paying rent for her flat in Dalston in the hope that she might consider coming back. He reminded her of that day when they had made love in the sand dunes at the back of the beach. And the sweltering evening in London when they had swum in the Serpentine and eaten cherries and drunk Pimm's on the bank afterwards. And every time she read a message Erin would lose herself in those memories and the same hot sensation would course through her limbs. And she wanted to reply, to call, to get on a train to London. She didn't. But she didn't tell him to stop.

I am drinking Perrier-Jouët tonight to welcome in the New Year – do you remember when we drank it in the bath?

She deleted the message and noticed there was one from her dad below.

Just checking you're ok?? Your mum and I are going to the pub tonight, fancy a pint? New year, new start??

I'm staying in with Maggie. Sorry. She typed hastily and sent the message. And then regretted it. Maggie was hardly good company. But no, she couldn't face her parents yet: she needed more time to gather her thoughts. And now she couldn't go to the pub either! Erin put two bottles of bubbly into her trolley and two boxes of chocolates. She then dashed around the rest of the supermarket, gathering milk, bread, cheese, eggs, a pile of ready meals, pizza, crisps and ice cream. And she went to the checkout with the wad of notes Maggie had thrust into her hands as she walked out the door. Erin hadn't seen where she had got them from. She imagined a suitcase of money under her bed.

When she arrived home, Maggie was on the sofa. Her eyes were bleary and her face crumpled with sleep. It was nearly eight o'clock.

'It's New Year's Eve, Maggie!' Erin announced, throwing the bags of food down on the floor. 'We must celebrate!'

'What exactly are we celebrating?' Maggie said wearily.

'Life! Or what's left of it.'

'Hmmph,' Maggie grunted and turned up *EastEnders* on the TV. But Erin was not to be deterred. She wasn't going to spend New Year's Eve on her own with a glass of milk and Jools Holland. She turned the TV off and retrieved the bottles of champagne from the bag on the floor and started to twist the wire.

'Oh no, Erin, I don't think so. Don't you remember what happened last time I had a drink?'

'I do. You were a lot more fun than you are now. And it's OK, there's only me here to insult!' She took the foil off the cork and it shot off with a bang, hitting the ceiling and landing on Oblonsky's back where he lay in front of the fire. He jumped up onto the sofa with Maggie.

'Poor Oblonsky.' Maggie chuckled softly and ruffled his neck. 'Oh, go on then, I think there are some champagne glasses in a cupboard in the dining room.' Erin grabbed the bags of shopping from the floor.

'I'll just put these in the kitchen and get the glasses.' She found some beautiful cut-glass champagne flutes in a cupboard. They were covered in a film of dust but when she rinsed them under the tap they sparkled into life.

'These ones, Maggie?'

'Oh yes, I haven't seen those for a very long time. My spinster aunt gave us those as a wedding present.' Erin poured them each a glass. She handed Maggie hers and climbed over the arm of the sofa with her glass and a bag of crisps. She pulled the blanket off Maggie's lap.

'Let me have a bit of that, will you? I'm freezing.' Maggie obliged, looking shell-shocked.

'Well, cheers, Maggie! Happy New Year!' Erin clinked her glass to Maggie's and took a big sip.

'Sorry it's not that cold,' Erin said, 'couldn't wait!'

'Mmm, that's good,' Maggie said. 'I remember the first time I tried champagne. I was fourteen and my parents had a New Year's Eve party. My sister and I were meant to be handing out the drinks but we kept sneaking sips. They were champagne cocktails – you know, with brandy and a sugar cube in the bottom?' She looked at Erin for acknowledgment but Erin had no idea what a champagne cocktail was. 'Sara...' Maggie stopped in her tracks, realising she had just said her sister's name out loud. Her eyes darted to the top corner of the room and her body stiffened.

'Your sister,' Erin prompted her quietly.

'Yes,' Maggie said with a sigh and then carried on slowly pronouncing every word with care. 'My sister, Sara, she didn't really like it. The champagne.' She looked at Erin and then smiled. 'She had to hold her nose every time she took a sip. But I loved it, the way the bubbles fizzed on the roof of your mouth, and up your nose sometimes. And that instant heady glow. Sara had to put me to bed halfway through the party, I couldn't stop giggling! She told Ma and Pa I wasn't feeling well but I'm sure they knew!'

Erin laughed, relieved that Maggie hadn't totally freaked out at the revelation she had just involuntarily made. And the mood lightened; all those unspoken truths seem to dissipate like the bubbles in the champagne. 'Mum doesn't like champagne,' Erin said. 'She says it gives her a headache, so we never have it at home. Dad's more of a whisky man. Simon liked it, though, he brought a bottle to the flat once and we drank it in the bath with salted caramel ice cream.'

'Tell me about him.'

'Who?'

'Simon. What made you fall for him?'

'I don't know.'

'Yes, you do. Come on, was it his dashing good looks? His charming wit? His encyclopedic brain? Or his other body parts?'

'Maggie!'

'Come on, tell me. I'm intrigued.'

Erin thought about it for a while. 'He was really persistent. And I guess I was flattered. No one had ever been interested in me before, not really. There had been a few spotty teenagers along the way, but he was older and wiser.'

'Quite a catch, I'm sure.'

'Yeah, he is. I mean was.'

Maggie smiled and took another sip. 'Do you love him?'

Erin pressed the cold glass against her cheek and considered her answer. 'I thought I did, but I don't know. How do you know whether it's love or just, I don't know, obsession?'

'I don't think you need to give your feelings a name, Erin.'

'I guess.' She shrugged and sipped her champagne. 'The thing is, I know he'll never be mine, but somehow knowing that makes me want him so much more. Is that bad?'

'It's not bad, Erin, it is human nature. We all want what we haven't got. And we all go after the shitty ones because when they make us feel good, it is so good.'

'Wise words from Maggie Muir. You should be a writer!'

'But you know, you shouldn't stick with the ones that make you feel bad. They are just for a bit of fun, Erin. You need to find a nice one for the long term.'

'Like Richard?' Erin asked. Maggie's head jolted round to face Erin and her eyes were wide. Then she laughed, a full-bellied laugh.

'Yes, well, maybe you shouldn't listen to me! God knows where you'll end up!' She heaved herself up off the sofa and spilled some of her champagne in the process. 'Music! We need music!' Maggie limped over to the corner of the room where there was a lamp on top of a wooden box. She put her glass down on the table next to it.

'What are you doing?' Erin asked.

'Give me a hand, will you? Hold this.' Maggie passed Erin the lamp and lifted the lid of the pine box underneath.

'This is a commode. You probably don't even know what a commode is, do you?' Erin shook her head. 'It's a lavatory! There is a big hole underneath here, see – you sit on it to do your business!' Erin peered in over Maggie's shoulder.

'Wow!' was all she could say. 'What are you looking in there for, Maggie?'

'Records. I hid them in here once and have kept them here for posterity ever since. They were a great comfort to me in the first few years when I came to Cornwall, but I haven't listened to them for years. Could you get them out for me?' she said to Erin, relieving her of the lamp. Erin pulled out Aretha Franklin, Fleetwood Mac, The Doors, the Rolling Stones, Joni Mitchell, Michael Jackson, Ella Fitzgerald. They were all shrouded in dust.

'The record player is under the table,' Maggie said, pointing at a black box that Erin would put her feet on as she typed. She hoped she hadn't damaged it with her heavy boots. But thankfully it was unscathed, and whirred into life when Erin plugged it in.

'I think Ella suits the occasion, don't you?' Maggie said, taking the vinyl disc out and placing it on the already rotating turntable.

The brass intro piped up. Maggie sauntered back across the room, swaying to the music. She picked up the bottle from the side table and shakily filled up both glasses, the bubbles frothing over the top. Then she swaggered back across the room, spilling the champagne as she moved. Erin took her glass from Maggie and had a sip. Maggie closed her eyes and swayed on the spot, rocking her heavy head from side to side.

'Haven't you been lonely living here all these years, Maggie?'

'Of course I have.'

'So why didn't you do anything about it, make some friends? See your family?'

'I was very far away from my family and they didn't want to see me. I did have a friend here once, but that didn't work out either.' She opened her eyes and found her glass and drained it. Erin's was still full, but she poured Maggie another glass. Her capacity for booze really was remarkable considering she didn't have an appetite for anything else. Erin worried that she was being irresponsible, but Maggie had never really opened up to her before and she had so many questions.

'A man friend?'

'Yes, he was a man.'

'What happened?'

'Let's just say I wasn't very good at letting anyone into my life.' Erin smiled and then regretted it. Maggie laughed. 'It's hard to believe, isn't it? Given the warm welcome I have bestowed on you!'

'Well, it's definitely beginning to warm up now,' Erin said, taking a sip of her champagne.

'Come on, let's dance.' Maggie put her glass down and grabbed Erin's hand and pulled her up to standing. Maggie wobbled on the way and Erin had to steady them both on the arm of the sofa.

'What?' She had not expected this.

'Come on, dance with an old lady on her last New Year's Eve, will you?'

'Oh Maggie, I can't,' Erin protested.

''Course you can, anyone can dance.' Maggie took Erin's glass out of her hand and placed it on the table. She grabbed her other hand and together they swayed to the music. Erin smiled through clenched teeth.

'Not me! I've got two left feet!' Maggie tried to swing her around but she was considerably shorter than Erin and a lot less stable on her feet. They ended in an awkward twist and Erin had to catch Maggie to save her careering into the side of the table.

And so the evening continued. They danced, they giggled like schoolgirls. They drank both bottles of champagne, and ate two big bags of crisps and then the two boxes of chocolates. After Ella, they moved on to Fleetwood Mac and finally Michael Jackson. Maggie had collapsed into the armchair by then and watched Erin moonwalk around the room. Oblonsky chased around her feet whimpering and jumping up at her legs. They didn't make it to midnight. Maggie's eyes were drooping by ten thirty, and Erin helped her up the stairs and into her bed.

'This is becoming a bit of a regular thing,' Maggie grunted as she laid her down on the pillow.

'Well, you've got to make the most of life, haven't you?'

'Erin.' Maggie caught Erin's hand as she pulled the duvet up over her and she looked into Erin's eyes with a desperation that she hadn't seen before.

'What is it, Maggie?'

'I haven't made the most of my life, you know.'

'I guess you're bound to have regrets at this stage.' Maggie's eyes glazed over and Erin squeezed her hand. 'Try not to think of all the things you wish you had done, think of all the wonderful things you *have* done – all the places you've been, all the adventures you've had.' Maggie nodded and curled her lips over her teeth, but didn't speak. 'Maggie, I'm sure you've led a more exciting life than most people in this village would ever dream of.'

'I haven't, I… I…'

'Shh, Maggie. It's just the booze talking. Go to sleep, and you'll feel better in the morning.' Maggie closed her eyes and took a few deep but juddering breaths. Erin sat with her a while until her breathing became smoother and her brow less furrowed. ''Night, Maggie, and Happy New Year,' she whispered as she turned off the light and tiptoed out of the room.

CHAPTER ELEVEN

Royal Victoria Hospital, 6th January 1987

I hate hospitals. The beeps of the machines and the sucking of the ventilators and the smell of disinfectant and faeces. There is an old crone in the bed next to me and she hacks up bile all day long. I think about the only other time I have ever stayed in hospital, when Lucas was born.

His birth was pretty straightforward to begin with. A thirteen-hour labour. I resisted the pethidine they were pushing on me. I wanted to feel the arrival. They laid him on my chest, his tiny wrinkled torso still scrunched into a ball. Those piercing cerulean eyes looking up at me. And then it all went wrong – I had 'retained products' that got stuck in my womb, like a lift door, they said. Instead of contracting, my uterus pumped out blood until I lost six pints. I fainted and came round to a room full of people. I could see Richard holding the baby by the window, a shaft of light creating a halo around his head. And then it went dark again and the next time I woke up I was in an operating theatre, my legs in stirrups, the heat of the surgical lamps burning my face. By then I had been stuffed full of drugs and couldn't feel anything from the waist down. I just drifted in and out of consciousness. And I felt as if I was floating above my own body, watching the bloody scene play out. I knew I should be scared but I felt eerily calm. I had to have several blood transfusions and was kept in hospital for a couple of weeks. Lucas was whisked off to a nursery and only brought back to me for feeds. We were robbed of that precious time together, those first two weeks crucial to a mother and child's bond. I look back on that time now and wonder whether things might have turned out differently had we got off to a better start.

*

It had been three weeks since Christmas, and Erin moved into Maggie's house. Neither of them mentioned the fact that it was only meant to be for a few days. Erin found herself relaxing into Maggie's pace of life and her shoulders dropped with the easiness of their uncomplicated friendship. She had even discovered a genuine interest in butterflies. And surprised herself one afternoon when she stopped on the bench for her daily trawl through Facebook to find herself searching instead for butterfly videos. There was one of kite swallowtails drinking sodium from the tears of turtles in the Amazon rainforest. Maggie had told her about the butterflies that drink from muddy puddles to satisfy their mineral and salt cravings, so she downloaded the video and showed it to Maggie that evening, who was delighted. A closeness had developed between them since New Year's Eve that Erin couldn't quite articulate. It was as though she had known Maggie for a really long time. Of course, she was learning about her life through the manuscript, but it was more than that. She had spent years trying to be somebody she wasn't, but with Maggie she didn't have to. She could be Erin Turner.

Both her parents had pestered her with daily text messages asking if she was OK, and she sent short replies saying she was. She bumped into her dad in the village shop once; his face had melted into a smile so huge she had wanted to run into his arms, but she stopped herself.

'I need to come and get some more clothes,' Erin said instead.

'Of course, any time. I miss you.'

'Yeah, well.'

'The TV won't connect to the broadband again. Could you...?' He had looked at her hopefully then and she had nearly faltered in her resolve. There were so many questions rattling away in her mind, but she didn't feel like she could ask him whether he had held Robert as a baby, in between the frozen goods and pasties. And she could feel Brenda's glare burning into the back of her head. So Erin just said she needed to get back to Maggie and turned away.

It wasn't as though she hadn't thought about Robert for the past three weeks; he was the first thing she thought of when she woke up in the morning. Where was he waking up? And then again while she was having her breakfast: what did he eat? What did he do all day? This preoccupation with his daily routine had bubbled away, underpinning her life since Christmas. She tried to snuff out these thoughts. She swallowed them down like a case of heartburn, just as her parents had done for nearly thirty years. She knew she couldn't berate them and then do the same herself, but she wasn't quite ready to go back home just yet, couldn't face another scene or her mother's stiffened reticence. Her anger with her parents was weakening, but in its place came an insecurity that was even more crippling. She delved deep into her childhood memories and turned everything over and over in her mind. Some things made more sense, like her mother's overprotective parenting. She hadn't allowed Erin to go into town on her own until a whole year later than all of her friends, and it had forged a rift between them so deep that it still made Erin angry to think of it. And her dad, he would get that glazed look on his face at times when he felt so far away that she couldn't reach him, no matter how hard she tried. It was as if a coloured filter had been laid over the top of her life, and some bits had taken on a new tinge while others sank deeper into the shadows.

And as she had left her dad in the shop that day and was mulling over the questions she wished she'd asked him about Robert, Simon had rung. His texts had persisted, but this was the first time he'd called and she answered, her mind elsewhere.

'You picked up,' he said.

'Only to tell you to leave me alone.'

'You don't mean that.'

'And you know everything that goes on inside my head, do you?'

'I know everything that goes on in your body.'

'Simon, please.'

'Come and see me.'

'I can't.'

'Yes, you can. I'll buy you a ticket. You can just hop on a train. You've got nothing else to do.'

'Actually I've got a job, people who rely on me.'

'What, at the *pub*?' He laughed and she winced at his mocking tone. 'That's not a job, Erin, it's a filler. And Derek won't mind, just tell him you're coming to see me.'

'Not at the pub. I'm helping someone.' She didn't know why but she didn't want to tell him about Maggie; she couldn't risk him mocking that sacred element of her life too. 'It doesn't matter. But I've got to go. I'm late.'

'Suit yourself.'

'Bye, Simon.' She knew she should feel proud of herself for turning him down but instead she felt horribly sad. She wanted to get on that train so much. She had hoped that with time the longing for him would subside. That she wouldn't find herself thinking about whether he would enjoy a book that she was reading or a programme she watched. That she wouldn't remember his hand in hers every time she walked on the headland or the scratch of his beard on her body as she lay awake at night. But it hadn't, and she hated herself for it.

And while Erin was busy trying to make sense of her life, Maggie had deteriorated quite dramatically. Erin could tell that her eyesight had got considerably worse: she moved about the house more gingerly, feeling her way along the walls and the furniture. And her birdlike appetite had diminished still further. She barely touched the ready meals Erin had bought at the supermarket that night. Erin's mum had tried to teach her to cook countless times over the years, but she had never been that interested in food. But watching Maggie literally waste away before her eyes gave her an incentive. She found a Delia Smith recipe book in Maggie's kitchen. It was old-fashioned but easy to follow. She cooked a cottage pie and a chicken casserole. Her mum wouldn't believe it! And Maggie ate, not huge amounts, but she ate. Erin remembered her mum talking about chicken soup and its restorative effects. 'Jewish penicillin,' she would say as she served it up to Erin when she was sick as a child. Erin found a recipe online and cooked it for Maggie. She drank it out of a cup as her hands were too shaky to hold the spoon. She gave up after a few mouthfuls but she seemed to like it, and Erin was hopeful that even those few sips had more nutritional value than the meagre sandwiches that were failing to sustain her before.

'Are you OK, Maggie?' Erin asked from her seat at the table one afternoon halfway through January.

'Fine,' Maggie said, closing her eyes.

'I think we should go out,' Erin said, turning the computer off and stretching her back out as she stood up.

'I don't want to go out, I never go out.'

'All the more reason to do it now.' Erin walked over to Maggie on the sofa and held her hand out to her. 'Come on, Maggie, I have an idea.'

'Erin, I'm too tired and I really want to finish that chapter.'

'You are too tired to work this afternoon,' Erin said assertively. 'And anyway, I'm not writing another word unless you agree to come with me on a little outing.'

'I really can't, Erin, I haven't been into the village for a very long time.'

'Well, all the more reason to go now.'

'Why?'

'Why? Maggie, you said you hadn't made the most of your life. That you had some regrets. So here is a chance to change that.'

'I meant travelling to the other side of the world, not going into the village.'

'I know.'

'You do?'

'Baby steps, Maggie. Today the village, tomorrow the world!' Maggie rolled her eyes in despair but she let Erin pull her up out of the sofa and didn't even resist when Erin took over with the buttoning up of her duffel coat when Maggie was struggling. An organic shift in power was evolving in Maggie's and Erin's relationship of which they were both aware and yet didn't dare draw attention to.

The claustrophobia of the house was beginning to suffocate Erin, and she couldn't help thinking how stifling it must be for Maggie, who had barely left it for decades as far as she could make out. She had spent many summers working at The Boathouse, and it was rare to have more than a couple of holidaymakers in at any one time, so she had been confident that on a Friday afternoon in January it would be suitably empty. But unfortunately, this was not the case. The tiny tea room was dominated by a long table of screeching women in matching sweatshirts. At the head sat a pretty blonde in a leopard print fur coat and pink veil. She looked uncomfortable and smiled apologetically at Erin and Maggie in the doorway. But there was no such humility from her friends, who were shouting over each other. Their noise shook the walls of the tea room. Erin shuddered and Maggie turned in the doorway to leave.

'Oh, no you don't,' Erin hissed, grabbing hold of her arm. 'Just think of the clotted cream.'

'I really don't want…' Maggie began to resist, but was interrupted by the surly-looking waitress coming towards them.

'Are you coming in or not? Can you shut the door, it's freezing in here,' she said, hustling them in and closing the door behind them.

'A table for two, please,' Erin said, forcing a smile. Maggie was holding onto her arm so tight it was going numb. She scoured the room for the best table and decided to sit by the door as it was furthest from the mob. She watched Maggie taking in the seafaring memorabilia that cluttered the lumpy cream walls. Ships in bottles, emerald glass buoys clad in amber netting, vintage maps and tangerine life rings.

'Have you seriously never been in here before?' Erin whispered to Maggie as she lowered her into her chair. 'You've lived in the village for thirty years.'

'And I would have happily gone to my grave having never had the pleasure,' Maggie seethed under her breath.

One of the hens stood up, clutching a bulging Primark bag. 'Listen up, ladies! I thought we could all give Becky some saucy knickers!' she shouted, and threw neon thongs at each of the squealing women while poor Becky buried her head in her hands. 'I've got some pens, so you can each draw a picture on the pants. Then the lovely bride-to-be has to guess who's whose!'

'Just think of it as research for your next book,' Erin said to Maggie while pretending to look at the laminated menu which hadn't changed for ten years.

'There isn't going to be a next book, Erin,' Maggie hissed back, her acerbic tongue wobbling slightly. She rummaged around in her pockets until she found a tissue. Her hands were shaking as she wiped her nose.

'Well, if there was, wouldn't they all be brilliantly horrid cameo characters?'

Maggie scoffed and Erin looked up at the sour face of the waitress still loitering over them, her skin was littered with angry whiteheads. She wondered if she had looked this miserable when she was working here. There was not a lot of space between the tables and so she was standing right up against the edge of theirs, Maggie's head only millimetres from the pasty expanse of her bare midriff.

'Could we have some more tea over here, please,' shrieked one of the hens. The waitress barely looked round but grunted in acknowledgment.

'What do you want?' she said to Erin.

'Two cream teas, please.'

She turned and stomped off in her DM boots. Erin could see Mrs Briskett peering at them from the kitchen as the door swung open. News of their unlikely coupling would be all over the village by supper time. Her disapproval of Erin went way back. She had caught her drinking vodka out the back with her nephew one summer, and sacked her on the spot.

Maggie was plucking at the skin on her knuckles in her lap, and Erin thought how much she had aged in the few months she had known her. Her complexion was yellowing and stretched tight over the now-bulging cheekbones. And her tinted glasses were beginning to look absurdly large, drowning her fragile features.

The door burst open as one of the ladies rushed outside with her phone. The arctic draft shuddered through Maggie. Erin looked through the net curtains at the bright, crisp day outside and marvelled at how freezing the tea room was. In the shadow of the pub across the street, it rarely warmed up, even in the height of summer.

'Maybe you should put your coat back on,' Erin suggested tentatively to Maggie.

'I'm fine,' Maggie said, her head disappearing further into the turtleneck of her jumper. She pulled her sleeves down over her fingers, and shrank a little more.

'So,' Erin said. 'I read in one of your books that butterflies are born with two mouths that they need to muddle together to form one probuscus...'

'Proboscis,' Maggie corrected her.

'Yeah, proboscis. Isn't that amazing, they literally have to join their mouths together? I found this video with one that had just hatched and was curling it and trying it out and—'

'Erin,' Maggie interrupted her. 'You really don't have to humour me any more with your new-found love of lepidopterology.'

'What's that?'

Maggie sighed. 'It doesn't matter. I'm just saying, you can stop now. I appreciate all the effort but it really isn't necessary.'

The door swung open again and bashed into the back of Erin's chair. 'I just posted that picture of you passed out in the bath, Cath!' said the hen, coming back inside. Her coral sweatshirt had ridden up over her hips, revealing blotchy folds of orange flesh oozing out of her too-tight jeans.

'You bitch!' Cath screamed, and Maggie winced. 'I can't believe you did that. Let's see!'

'Maybe we should just go home,' Maggie said. Her pleading tone unsettled Erin more than she let on.

'Oh, come on, Maggie, we're here now. Let's just have the tea,' she said gently. This benign interaction was new territory for them both. 'And for what it's worth, I'm not faking it. The butterflies, I mean.' A smile pinched at the corners of Maggie's mouth but she still looked sceptical. And at that moment, the crabby waitress appeared with a tray and threw its contents onto their table. Erin caught the jar of jam just before it toppled into Maggie's lap and rescued the pot of tea off the tray before it suffered a similar fate.

'Do you want bu'err as well as cream?' she said gruffly. Erin looked to Maggie, but she was busy rearranging the table.

'No thanks,' said Erin, and the waitress turned and brushed past Mrs Briskett, who was now standing in the doorway watching them without shame. Erin gave her a mocking salute and Mrs Briskett rolled her eyes and flounced back into the kitchen.

Erin poured the tea while Maggie wrestled with her scone. She sent one half flying across the table. Erin retrieved the scone, but knew better than to offer her help.

The cream tea was delicious, as Erin knew it would be. Maggie actually ate half her scone, which was more than she had consumed for days. So Erin was beginning to think that it wasn't such a disastrous mission after all, when the door hit the back of her chair again and a gust of chilling air shrouded them once more. Across the table Erin watched the colour drain from Maggie's face and her mouth drop shamelessly open as she stared at the figure in the doorway. It was a man in a flat cap and waxed jacket. He took off his glasses, which had steamed up, and wiped them on a red spotted handkerchief in his pocket. He didn't look at them, just strode to the back of the room where he had a conversation with the surly waitress. She disappeared and returned with a package for him. On his way back to the door, however, he saw them.

'Maggie?' He peered down at her from his great height.

'Hi, Fred,' she said quite softly, squinting up at him.

Erin stood up and held out her hand. 'Hi. I'm Erin.'

'Fred,' he said, offering her his. She took it and felt the crusted bubble of a wart on the side of his thumb. 'I'll go and pay, shall I?' Erin said, and left them staring at each other awkwardly. She watched them from the back of the room. Fred had sat down in Erin's chair and was leaning across the table and talking to Maggie quietly, his eyes never leaving her face. Maggie looked so small and vulnerable opposite him, but she smiled her beautiful wide smile and bowed her head coyly. By the time Erin came back to the table he had gone, and Maggie was watching him walk down the street through the window.

Erin helped her into her coat and took her arm to guide her out the door and down the step into the freezing cold outside. It was dark now and the road was frosting over. The glistening sheen was slippery underfoot and it took all their concentration and Erin's strength to get Maggie safely into the car parked across the road.

'Who was that, Maggie?' Erin asked as she climbed into the driver's seat and pulled the heavy door shut.

'Fred Armitage.'

'And who is Fred Armitage? An old flame?' Erin said smiling as she turned the key and the old Land Rover chugged into action.

'Just an old friend, really.'

'When did you last see him?' They were driving down the lane now and Erin had to swerve into the side of the road to avoid a tractor coming the other way. The naked branches rattled loudly as they hit the side of Maggie's window.

'Nineteen years ago last February.'

'That's a very definite timeline for just an old friend. Was he the man friend you talked about?' Erin looked at Maggie, who stared straight ahead, her mind lost in another time. 'You want to tell me about it?' Erin asked tentatively. There was a long silence before Maggie finally spoke quietly.

'We met out walking the dogs one morning. Lenin was only a puppy and had caught the scent of a rabbit and was chasing after it off under the hedgerows. I was terrified he was going to fall off the cliff edge. I was on all fours scrabbling under the bushes when Fred appeared and asked if he could help. I must have looked such a mess, I had grass seed all over my hair and sticky-weed on my back.' Maggie chuckled.

'Did he join you under the bush then?'

'Yes, he did, actually! Lenin had got himself stuck down a rabbit hole just centimetres away from the cliff edge. Fred was tall and gangly, as you saw, and he managed to pull Lenin out of the hole with his long spaghetti arms. I thanked him and went on my way.'

'But that obviously wasn't the end of it?'

'No, he came up to the house the next day to see if Lenin was OK and we had a cup of tea. After that he would pop by a couple of times a week. Not a single soul had been in the house since I arrived there eight years previously, so I was a bit out of practice when it came to hostessing.'

'Really, Maggie, I find that hard to believe.'

'Alright, yes, I know I am an antisocial old bag, but Fred didn't seem to mind. I think he was lonely and sad and just appreciated the company. He had lost his wife to cancer a couple of years previously, and then a great-aunt who he barely knew had died and left him her cottage in Porthteal. His kids were away at university, so he decided it was a perfect opportunity to start a new life, away from all his memories.' Maggie paused then, but Erin knew better than to interrupt her when she was on a roll. They were swinging into the drive when she spoke again. 'His boys came to Porthteal for the Christmas holidays and they invited me to join them for Christmas lunch. I hated Christmas since… since… you know, and declined. But he wouldn't take no for an answer and on Christmas morning he arrived in his truck and refused to leave until I agreed to go with him. Sound familiar?' She looked at Erin, smiling.

'Yeah.'

'Well, it was only the second Christmas they'd had since his wife had died and I don't think the boys were too keen on having me there. But they were very well brought up young men and were nothing but polite to me. We ate pheasant that Fred had shot, and drank a delicious Margaux from his cellar. If only we could have carried on like that. But Fred wanted more, and I… I… well, I just couldn't…' Maggie was still looking out of the windscreen ahead but her eyes were wide and her thoughts much further away.

'What happened? Did he go away?' Erin asked.

'When I told him I couldn't have a relationship with him, he packed up the cottage and moved back to Plymouth. I never heard from him again until just now.'

'He seemed pretty surprised to see you,' Erin said.

'I probably look quite different to how I did when I last saw him. His tenants have moved out and he has come to stay in the cottage for a few days while he sorts things out and puts it on the market. He was just popping in to pick up a parcel that had been left there.' She was looking at her reflection in the wing mirror now. Though Erin wasn't sure how much of it she could see.

'See what happens if you leave the house, Maggie?'

She grunted. 'I guess you're going to take all the credit for this, are you?'

'Of course! If it wasn't for me, you'd be curled up on that sofa all afternoon. Instead you've found your long-lost love.'

'Oh God, Erin, you never struck me as a sentimentalist. Now get me out of here before my legs totally seize up and I am stuck in this old banger all night.'

'Of course.' Erin jumped down onto the crunchy ground. The bitter cold wind whistled around her neck. She ran round to the other side and helped Maggie down and armed her the few steps across the frozen gravel. Maggie's sheepskin boots flailed around like she was ice-skating and Erin had to hold her under both arms to stop her falling. The walk down the corridor to the study felt longer than ever and Erin could feel Maggie wincing with every step. She had pushed her too hard.

Erin lowered Maggie onto the sofa and collected the pills and water from the side table, which Maggie washed back. Within minutes she was asleep. Erin wrapped the rug over her knees and stoked the embers in the fire. She blew on the smoky coals and they danced into life. She sat back in the armchair and watched the vitality of the flames. She had never been a believer in fate – far too cynical. But she did feel a smug sense of satisfaction for how the afternoon had panned out. She resolved to hunt Fred down in the morning.

*

But there was no need. Erin left the house early the next morning and walked into the village to buy some milk. Maggie wasn't up; in fact her early mornings were getting later every day. By the time Erin got back to the house Fred was on the doorstep, dressed in his tweed cap, waxed jacket and mustard cords. He was pacing up and down the driveway, his galoshes crunching on the gravel.

'Erin, isn't it? I – I hope you don't mind, I came to see Maggie. I rang the doorbell but she hasn't appeared and I know she is an early riser, and so…' he said.

'She is quite slow in the mornings now, she may not be up,' Erin said, walking past him and opening the front door.

'Is she ill?' he stammered in the doorway.

'She didn't tell you?'

'No, she just said she was hanging on in there.'

Erin bent down to take off her boots. She started to untie the matted laces, which she usually just slipped off, in order to buy herself some time. She placed the boots upside down on the wooden boot rack and stood up.

'She has a brain tumour. She doesn't have long.' Erin hung her coat on a hook in the hall and turned to look at Fred. He gripped the door frame a little harder, his knuckles paling to white. But he didn't seem surprised.

'I see,' he said sadly. 'Do you think I could come in and see her?' He was still hovering on the front step.

'Of course, I'm sure she would love to see you,' Erin said, smiling at him. He followed her into the hall in his galoshes, leaving waffled flakes of mud on the cherry brick floor.

Maggie was not sitting on the sofa with Oblonsky as usual, but was standing at the window. She had put her hair up for the first time in weeks and wasn't wearing her glasses. She had on her emerald cable-knit jumper that masked her emaciated body and brought out the sparkle in her eyes.

'Hi, Fred,' she said with a smile.

'Maggie.' He strode into the room towards her and took her hands.

'I'll just go and make some tea,' Erin said, backing out of the room.

She was desperate to know what they were talking about, but the soft murmur of their voices was soon drowned out by the hiss of the kettle. She realised she had never seen Maggie interact with anyone other than her parents at Christmas. And while she had read and listened to the tales of Maggie's past relationships, she found it hard to associate them with the Maggie of today.

When she came back into the room, they were sitting side by side on the sofa and Fred was telling her about his grandchildren. 'Robert has two and David has three – two boys and three girls. I can't tell you how wonderful it is to have the girls, totally different to bringing up boys, you know.' He stopped then, realising what he had said, and took her hands. 'I'm so sorry, Maggie, I wasn't thinking. I don't know what has come over me, rabbiting on like that, not thinking about—'

'It's fine, Fred. I have got much better talking about my past, haven't I, Erin?' Maggie turned to Erin, who was walking towards them with two steaming mugs of tea.

'Er, kind of,' Erin said, handing Fred his and placing Maggie's down on the table next to her. She lifted Maggie's hand and guided it gently to the handle of the mug. They had abandoned cups and saucers the week before after Maggie scalded herself. Fred watched as she lifted the mug to her mouth slowly, steadying it with her other hand.

'Erin is helping me type up my novel,' Maggie said when she had placed the mug back down on the table.

'Oh, really? You are amazing still working, Maggie.'

'Speaking of which, Erin, haven't you got some work to do? Typing up, I mean?' Maggie interjected with unusually good cheer.

'I…' Maggie shot her a look behind Fred's back. They both knew that she couldn't continue on her own, and the computer was in the room with them. 'Of course. I'll just go and type up that last bit.'

She retreated to her room and didn't dare venture back downstairs until she heard the front door close. Maggie was sitting quietly, a serene smile across her lips.

'He's gone then,' Erin asked.

'He's gone,' Maggie replied.

'But he'll be back, won't he?'

'We'll see. Shall we crack on?'

CHAPTER TWELVE

Beechwood Priory, 12th January 1987

They have moved me to a psychiatric hospital and I feel quite sane here, everyone else is so nuts. The girl next door to me is called Jacinta. She self-harms. She is only in her early twenties but she looks older. Her arms are ravaged with scars. Some have gone white, but she picks at the scabs of the more recent ones so they bleed. She draws all day long, says it keeps her stable. She draws planes. Concorde, biplanes, jumbo jets, old ones, state-of-the-art new ones. She said her dad is a pilot. He travels the world, she told me proudly. He has never been to see her. Just her grandma.

I don't want to talk. We have group therapy sessions. Individual therapy sessions. Art therapy sessions. I stay quiet, even in the one-to-ones. Jacinta opened up yesterday. She talked about how she found her mother hanging from the rafters in their mock Tudor hallway. And I started to cry. I don't know whether I was crying for Jacinta, or for Lucas, or for Skye, or for me. But everyone seemed to think it was a good thing. It didn't feel good. It felt as though I was being smothered with a pillow until I couldn't breathe. I still don't want to talk.

*

Fred did come back, twice a week to begin with and by the end of the month it was almost every day. If the weather was fine and

Maggie was feeling up to it, they would wrap up warm and amble through the garden. Fred held Maggie's arm as they walked, and she didn't brush him off or flinch at his touch. Sometimes they would sit on the bench and look out at the wintry sea.

Erin watched them from the upstairs window. She wished she knew what they were talking about. Did they regret their lost love? The time wasted? Erin knew Maggie did, but she was too stubborn to admit it. Would Erin regret leaving Simon, in years to come? There was no doubt that Fred had rekindled a spark in Maggie, given her a reason to carry on living just when she needed it. And for that Erin was hugely grateful.

The book progress slowed as a result of his visits, however. They still worked every morning, then Fred arrived just after lunch. Maggie was exhausted by the time he left and drifted in and out of sleep for the rest of the afternoon. Erin read to Maggie in her waking moments, pages of random books she picked up off the shelves. One day she would read George Orwell, the next Roald Dahl, then Dickens, or Jojo Moyes, or a rare eighteenth-century poetry anthology. And her confidence in reading aloud grew and grew until it developed a fluidity that surprised them both.

Maggie kept her eyes closed while Erin read, so it was not always easy to tell when she had drifted off into her drug-induced dreams. But when she hadn't stirred for a while and Erin was sure she was fast asleep, she would put down the book and pick up her duster. She was working her way through the house room by room. Maggie pretended not to notice; she had been resistant to Erin's suggestion about cleaning when she moved in. But one afternoon, soon after Fred's first visit, Erin took a book off the shelf and found it glazed in something sticky. Behind the book was a treacly puddle with a moth encased in it. One of its wings lay next to the carcass, ripped off in its grapple for freedom. There and then she decided that she owed it to the creatures of this house to do something about the squalor they were living in. She didn't want Fred thinking Maggie was filthy, or herself for that matter. So, while Maggie slept on the sofa, she set about taking all the books off the shelves and wiping them down.

Once she started, she couldn't stop; the clean areas just highlighted the dirty bits more shamefully. And it was unexpectedly satisfying. When she had finished the books, she moved on to the pictures on the walls. The butterflies that were shrouded in layers of dust so thick that their bodies beneath were barely a shadow. Once cleaned, the vibrant colours and intricate detail of their wings shone from the walls with a vitality that lifted her heart. And then she tackled the surfaces, the side tables, the coffee table, her own table. She cleared mountains of paper, biscuit wrappers, pill pots, shrivelled-up pieces of toast, and scrubbed away at the decades of grime.

Maggie woke up one afternoon to find Erin dragging an armchair across the floor so she could reach the mass of cobwebs at the top of the sash window. Maggie rolled her eyes and tutted before drifting back to sleep. Erin wiped the cloudy filter from the glass and light flooded into the room, flickers of dust dancing in its glare. The study came alive again as if a fairy godmother had released it from a hundred-year sleep. Maggie refused to even acknowledge her handiwork, of course, but Erin did catch her running her hand across the gleaming surface of the desk once and she smiled when she didn't think Erin was watching.

Erin was also profoundly grateful to Fred for turning up and shouldering some of the responsibility for Maggie. She hadn't realised how suffocating and lonely it had been until he came and relieved her of some of the emotional burden. There was someone else in the world who actually cared whether Maggie lived or died.

One afternoon, Erin answered the phone while Fred and Maggie were out walking around the garden. It was Maggie's oncologist at the hospital. When they got back Erin beckoned Fred into the kitchen.

'Fred, I just spoke to Maggie's doctor at the hospital. He said that since his initial diagnosis eight months ago, Maggie hasn't been to a single one of her appointments. I feel dreadful. I have thought about the fact that she hasn't seen a doctor since I've been here. I tried to ask her once, but she just shut me up in that way she does and I didn't have the balls to ask again. Oh God, I really should have…' She rubbed at her temples with the tips of her fingers.

'Erin,' he put a hand on her shoulder, 'it really isn't your responsibility. Maggie is old enough and ugly enough to make her own decisions. And it doesn't surprise me a jot that this is the approach she has taken. She has never been fond of hospitals since… well, you know.' Fred wrung his hands together and his fingers picked at the warts on his thumbs. Erin wondered how much he knew about her former life and how much Maggie had told him about the book, and what Erin therefore knew.

'I have been wondering where she gets all the pills from,' Erin said.

'I also asked her whether she had seen a doctor and how it had all come about, knowing full well she wouldn't have booked an appointment like the rest of us. She told me she had collapsed on the cliff path walking the dog one day and a young man found her and called an ambulance. She was taken into hospital and they ran lots of tests. That was how she was diagnosed.'

'Really? Oh, poor Maggie, she would have hated that.'

'Yes, she did.' Fred smiled and his kind eyes narrowed, giving way to claw-shaped creases at the corners. He took his glasses off and polished them on the edge of his jumper.

'But that was ages ago, and she is definitely getting worse. Don't you think we should make her go?'

'Mmm,' Fred said, putting his glasses back on. Erin had been hoping he might have had a more proactive response, but he was obviously as wary of interfering with Maggie's life as she was.

'Do you think you could talk to her, Fred?' Erin suggested tentatively.

'She's not going to like it.' He was now rubbing his forehead and the skin formed ripples under the pressure of his fingers. 'But yes, I'll talk to her, Erin, don't worry.' He patted Erin's shoulder awkwardly as he walked out of the kitchen.

'Bye, Maggie, see you tomorrow,' he shouted from the hallway. There was no response. She was probably asleep already.

Fred did persuade Maggie, Erin didn't know how. And he drove them to the hospital in Truro. Maggie insisted Erin accompany them. She had convinced herself that she could only leave the house if Erin was with her, and she was flattered, if reluctant. She hated hospitals. They sat in the waiting room and Erin pretended to read a magazine.

Opposite her was a young girl with no hair. Erin caught her eye and smiled. She felt as though she needed to apologise for her own well-being in that room. Erin tried not to stare at the girl's porcelain skin and the charcoal shadows under her eyes. She had headphones on and was singing tunelessly to Katy Perry. Her mother kept nudging her and telling her to be quiet under her breath. Erin wanted to shout, 'Let her sing if she wants, she's got cancer!'

When Maggie's name was called Erin kept her head down and held her breath. She only let it out when the doctor shut the door behind Maggie and Fred and she was sure she had been spared.

Left outside, Erin tried to focus on her magazine but her eyes kept drifting to the girl. She was beautiful. Her face had a purity to it, unblemished by eyebrows or a hairline. Erin found herself twiddling tufts of her own hair around her fingers and wondered what her naked scalp would feel like. A nurse appeared. She stood in front of the girl and called her name.

'Naomi, Naomi!' But her eyes were shut and her head rocking as she whispered along to the music. Her mother pulled one of the headphones away from her head and shouted her name into her ear.

'Sorry, hi,' Naomi said, taking the headphones off her head. They had left an angry red ridge across the top of her skull. She stood up and hugged the nurse as if they were old friends, then they walked off down the corridor together. Erin heard the nurse asking Naomi how her audition had gone. The mum followed silently with all the bags. Erin thought how strange it must be when this world of bright lights and antiseptic smells becomes your normal.

When Maggie came out of the doctor's room half an hour later she looked defiant but weary. She kept her head down and walked straight past Erin, steadying herself on the water cooler as she went.

'What did he say?' Erin asked as she followed.

'I just want to go home,' Maggie said. Erin looked at Fred, who shrugged his shoulders. They made their way to the multistorey car park in silence. It was only when Maggie finally fell asleep a few miles from home that Erin leant forward from her position on the back seat.

'What did the doctor say?' she whispered to Fred.

'He said she needs looking after. She has refused all treatment, of course. But he said she should have a nurse come in daily and make sure she's taking the right pain relief. And he talked about her moving into a hospice at the end,' Fred said a little too loudly, his eyes fixed on the road ahead.

'What did she say to that?'

'She said, "over my dead body".'

'What do we do? She can't carry on at home like this,' Erin said.

'I don't know, Erin. She is ridiculously stubborn. I don't think we can make her do anything if she really doesn't want to.'

When they had arrived at Hookes End, Maggie was woken by the crunch of the gravel as they swung into the drive. 'I know you were talking about me,' Maggie said, her voice still full of sleep. 'And I know you both think I should have a nurse come in, but I have spent the last thirty years of my life avoiding people. Why would I go and live my last precious months, weeks, whatever I have left, surrounded by folk I don't know fussing over me. It is bad enough having you two. And I won't die in a hospice. I hate hospitals, always have.'

She slammed her fist down on the glove compartment, then winced and shook out the pain it sent flooding into her fingers. Erin and Fred were silent. It had started to rain and the gentle patter on the windscreen was strangely comforting. Fred put his hand on top of Maggie's, and Erin reached over from the back seat and squeezed Maggie's bony shoulder. Together they watched the rain stream down the windscreen, blurring the fir trees beyond it. They had an iridescent glow to them against the dusky sky. Erin felt suddenly overwhelmed by the connection she felt towards these two elderly people who had so recently entered her life.

CHAPTER THIRTEEN

Beechwood Priory, 18th January 1987

I have a new doctor. He doesn't have Dr Sham's kind almond eyes. He has halitosis and clicks the end of his biro during our sessions. He is called Dr Dansk and he has asked me to write about my suicide attempt because I refuse to talk about it. I am not trying to be obtuse — until now there have only been blurred fragments of memory. Today, however, it came flooding back with such horrible clarity I could have been watching a movie of my own pathetic demise.

It was first thing in the morning and I was still in my nightie. Well, my first thing, which was hours after Richard had left the house. I walked into the bathroom and the floor was cold. I stubbed my toe on a chipped tile. It throbbed with pain but that felt good. So I scrunched my toe under the ridge in the tile and flicked it again and again until the knuckle began to bleed. And I watched the blood seep onto the floor, bright red droplets that trickled across the grey tiles and collected in the ridges between them. I looked up at my reflection in the mirrored cabinet above the sink. Strands of greasy hair stuck to the side of my face. I remember thinking that I used to be skinny in an enviable way. Now I just looked ill. My skin was grey and my lips were cracked. I touched my face, dragged the loose skin down over my cheekbones. It didn't bounce back. I opened the cupboard, looking for some moisturiser. It wasn't

*premeditated, you see. I have had to reiterate that fact here. I
hadn't gone into the bathroom that morning with the intention
of killing myself. I had opened the cabinet looking for something
to put on my scaly cheeks, and that was when I saw them. The
sleeping pills that Dr Sham had prescribed for those nights of
wired insomnia. Surely he shouldn't have done that? Maybe I
hadn't articulated quite how intolerable the pain in my heart
had become. But I wasn't a suicide risk. I was too responsible,
too much at stake. How ironic!*

*What was keeping me here? A son who hated me and a
husband who came home after I'd gone to bed and left before
I woke in the morning so he didn't have to talk to me. They
would be better off without me. I popped the first pill in my
mouth and then stuck my head under the tap for some water
to swallow it down. That was when I recalled this moment in
trashy movies. It wasn't just the pills. I needed something stronger
than water to wash them down with. I ran down the stairs
into the kitchen but there was nothing in the usual cupboard
under the stairs. None even in the larder, or the study. Richard
had hidden all the booze. I was about to give up when I saw
Lucas's door firmly shut at the top of the stairs. I pushed it open,
half expecting it to be locked. But it wasn't. I stepped over the
dirty laundry and a tangled mass of cables. I scoured under the
bed, but there was only old shoes and cobwebs. Then the desk
drawers – nothing apart from comics and some tobacco. I tried
the cupboard in the corner, and there it was, tucked behind a
pile of hoodies – vodka.*

*I didn't neck the whole pot at once. I swallowed each and
every pill. One, two, three. Who would find me? Four, five.
Richard wouldn't be home for hours. Six. Maybe Skye would
be there waiting on the other side. Seven, eight. Don't let it be
Lucas. Nine, ten. Would she still be in her nightie with fairies
at the hem? I tipped the rest of the pot into my hand then and*

slugged them down with the vodka. And I lay down on the cold, hard bathroom floor and waited for the gentle release. But it never came. The wooden slatted bath mat dug into my hips. I focused on the crimson trail of blood trapped between the tiles. And then came the pain. The muscles in my belly clenched and squeezed with an intensity so strong I had to hug my knees up to my chest. Bile rose up and burned the back of my throat. I swallowed it down. I couldn't be sick, I was lucid enough to realise that. I breathed in big gulps of air. But then the nausea came again and a surge so violent I couldn't contain it. It frothed at the corners of my mouth. My eyes rolled and rolled around in their sockets. And then it went dark.

*

A few days after the hospital visit Erin took Oblonsky out for a walk first thing. She had taken to doing that in the last couple of weeks. It was nine o'clock by the time she arrived back at Hookes End but the house was still dark and sleeping, which was unusual for Maggie even now. She pushed open the heavy door and heard its whining resistance echo down the corridor.

She turned on the lights in the hallway and they flickered, then hummed. Erin made her way down the corridor. The dining room door was open, which was also unusual. She poked her head round it and saw Maggie standing in the bay window at the front of the room. She was dressed only in a white cotton nightie. Her stick-thin speckled legs and feet were bare and her bunioned toes were curled and gripping onto the icy brick floor. She stood facing the window, ethereal in the gloomy morning light.

'Maggie?' Erin said tentatively from the doorway.

Maggie turned around. Her eyes scurried between the cluttered array of glasses on the sideboard to the left and the dour portrait to the right, before finally settling on Erin in the doorway. Her hair had escaped its bun and hung limply around her scrawny features.

'Are you OK, Maggie?' Erin said, moving cautiously towards her.

Maggie squinted across the room; she had to steady herself with her hand on the mahogany dining table. Her shaky fingers disturbed the layer of dust. Erin had not yet tackled the dining room.

'I, I was looking for my shoes, but I don't know where. I can't…'

Oblonsky ran to Maggie and licked her bare legs, but she barely even noticed him. Erin walked around the table and took hold of Maggie's elbow. She flinched at her touch as if surprised and then stared straight through Erin.

'It's OK, Maggie, it's me.'

'I can't, I can't find my shoes. I came into the kitchen to look for my shoes and…'

'We're in the dining room, Maggie.'

'What?'

'We're not in the kitchen, We're in the dining room.'

'Yes, right, of course. It's just, I can't…' Maggie's eyes darted to the ceiling, then the walls, twitchy and muddled. Her pupils were the colour of seaweed. 'My shoes, I must find my shoes so I can take Oblonsky for a walk.'

'I have just been out with Oblonsky. And I don't think the shoes are in here, Maggie. Let's go back to the study, shall we? You can sit down and I will look for them.' Maggie was looking through Erin like she wasn't there at all, then a flash of clarity lit up her face and she seemed to focus on her again.

'We must get to work,' Maggie said. 'I had an idea for the next section in my book. I… I… think… I…' The words came out in a flurry, and she pushed Erin out of her way and walked forward, straight into the table.

'Oh dear, I, where, which way is the door?'

'It's this way, Maggie,' Erin said as she put her arm around Maggie's waist and guided her towards the door. Maggie's feet

barely left the floor as she shuffled into the corridor. Erin stopped
at the bottom of the stairs.

'Shall we go and get you dressed?'

'What?'

'You're still in your nightie.'

'Am I?' Maggie looked down at her nightie and gathered fistfuls
of the cotton, pulling it up and exposing her knobbled knees.

'No, no, there's no time for that. We need to get going.'

'OK, well, I'll just go and get your dressing gown and slippers,
OK? It's really cold in here with no fire.' Erin helped her over to
the sofa and lowered her into it. Then she grabbed the crocheted
blanket off the armchair to wrap around her shoulders. Oblonsky
bounded up onto the sofa and curled into a ball next to her. Maggie
batted Erin away. 'Stop fussing,' she hissed.

'Sorry. I'll be back in a minute.'

Erin left her and made her way up the stairs to Maggie's
bedroom. She found the slippers under some dirty underwear on
the floor, and a brown towelling robe that was hanging on a hook
on the door. She took them back downstairs.

'Here we go,' Erin said, coming into the room. Maggie had
thrown the blanket onto the floor, so Erin draped the dressing
gown around her shoulders.

'I can do it,' Maggie snapped.

'Sorry,' Erin said, crouching down to put the slippers on the
floor. Maggie fumbled her frozen feet into them.

'It's getting worse, isn't it?' Erin said quietly, sitting at her feet.

'What?'

'Your sight, everything, it's going, isn't it? I think you need
some more help.'

'Don't be ridiculous.' Maggie had picked up the manuscript
on the sofa next to her and was rifling through the pages, as if she
could actually see them.

'Maggie, please,' Erin said, standing up and clasping her hands together in despair.

'OK, yes. It is getting worse. Are you happy now? I can't even really see you now, you are just a blur of foggy matter.' Maggie waved her hands around as she spoke.

'Maggie, do you think the time has come for you to get more help?'

'What?'

'Well, this morning, you were quite—'

'Quite what, Erin? Spit it out.'

'Quite… confused, and it scared me and I—'

'So go.'

'What?'

'If you don't want to stick around, then leave.'

'I didn't say I wanted to leave, Maggie.'

'Then don't.'

'Oh my God!' Erin stood up and paced over to the window. 'You are infuriating!'

She looked back at Maggie, who was shrinking into the dressing gown around her shoulders. She suddenly looked very small, and Erin's exasperation evaporated into shame. 'I don't want to leave, Maggie,' she whispered with humility.

'Good, well, that's settled then. Shall we crack on?'

And so they did. Erin read and typed a couple of extracts while Maggie listened on the sofa, her useless eyes closed, silent. She didn't suggest any edits or offer any new memories; she was totally still. At one point Erin had to hover really close behind her to check she was actually still breathing.

After lunch Erin sat at the window seat so she could spot Fred walking up the drive and get to him before he saw Maggie.

'Fred.' She approached him on the doorstep.

'What's happened, Erin? Is it Maggie? Is she alright?'

'Yes, I mean, no, not really. Her sight has pretty much gone, Fred. And when I came back from my walk this morning, she was in quite a state. I found her in the dining room in her nightie and she wasn't making sense. She thought she was in the kitchen.'

'Where is she now? Why didn't you call me?' He pushed past her and strode down the hallway.

'Fred, wait.' Erin chased after him and held onto his arm. 'Please, just listen to me for a sec. I've been waiting to talk to you all day. I think she needs more help. This morning obviously proves that I really don't know how to look after her properly, and…' Erin could feel tears suddenly stinging at the backs of her eyes. Fred turned to look at her and held onto her hand.

'It's OK, Erin, it's a lot for you to deal with.' He sighed heavily. 'I agree, she does need more help. She is just so goddamn stubborn.'

'I just thought that… after your wife, and everything. That maybe you might know who to call, a nurse or something.' Fred patted her hand and nodded his head slowly.

'Yes, I'm sorry, Erin. We should have done this sooner. You're right, you really shouldn't have to cope with this.'

'I don't mind, it's just…'

'I know, it isn't really in your job description.'

'Well, not really, no.' She smiled as she wiped her nose on her sleeve. 'But you weren't banking on this when you came back into her life either. And you have already been here once before.'

'Yes, I have. So I am fully equipped to deal with it now. Leave it to me.' He patted Erin's hand and walked towards the study door, where he paused. 'Maybe we won't mention this to Maggie, hey? Not until we've sorted it out?'

'But…' Erin started, then realised the sense in what he was saying. 'OK, you're right, but she's not going to like it.'

CHAPTER FOURTEEN

Beechwood Priory, 23rd February 1987

I think Richard is having an affair with that Fellowes woman next door. Or if he isn't yet, he definitely wants to. Every time he visits he talks about how she brings him lasagnes and fish pie. He hates fish pie! But when I said that he got all defensive and said he only hated my mum's fish pie because it was always really dry and you had to douse it in ketchup to make it edible. Apparently, Julie Fellowes puts prawns in hers and boiled eggs. It turned my stomach when he mentioned the eggs. He also said Lucas is going to help in their garden. Lucas, gardening! I guffawed at that, and he got really cross. He said he was worried about Lucas. He thinks he is smoking pot in the shed. I didn't tell him that he has been doing that for months. He said that Julie read about a programme where teenagers with behavioural issues were sent to work on a farm in West Wales. I reacted badly to that. I told him that Lucas wasn't a teenager with behavioural issues who you could just send away. He was a boy who had recently lost his beloved sister. One of the doctors came in then; he had heard me shouting. He asked if everything was OK and told Richard that getting me upset was not helpful for my recovery. Richard kept his head down and kicked the bottom of my bed like a naughty child being berated by a teacher. When the doctor left, I asked Richard whether he was having an affair with Julie Fellowes. He denied it, of course. But he couldn't look at me and his behaviour reeked of the Miranda Gosling episode.

I think Lucas was about two and we had decided to have another baby. It never occurred to us that it wouldn't happen straight away. But month after month went by, and no baby. It took its toll on our relationship and sex became a biological task. I went to see the doctor and he said there may have been some internal scarring after Lucas was born but that there was nothing we could do about it. A couple of times my period was late and I got excited but then it would come heavier than ever a week or so later. I wondered whether I was having miscarriages and went back to the surly doctor, but he just prescribed me some sleeping pills and berated my overactive imagination. Richard had taken over the running of the community choir, which meant he was out at least two evenings a week. I would eat with Lucas at six o'clock and leave his supper warming in the Belling. Lucas was a dreadful sleeper, so I was always tired and often in bed by the time Richard came home. Except for those crucial nights when I was ovulating. I knew when they were. I was taking my temperature daily to track it. I would wait up for Richard in my baby-doll nightie and lure him into the bedroom. He wasn't fooled by the monthly seduction, and feigned exhaustion. I invariably wept, begging him to get me pregnant. Hardly alluring behaviour; I guess it is not surprising he looked elsewhere for kicks.

It was a sticky June day and I decided to surprise Richard after school with a picnic. We used to do that a lot when I was pregnant with Lucas. We would walk up onto the Downs after work with a bottle of wine and pork pies from the butcher in town. I desperately wanted to rekindle the magic of that time. So I bought pork pies and Lucas and I made a pineapple upside-down cake. We packed our picnic into a basket and walked over to the school where I knew Richard had orchestra *practice. We passed some kids dwarfed by their cellos on the path and I worried that he might have left already. Lucas insisted on carrying the cake and it rattled in the tin as he ran. Richard wasn't there when we got to the hall. Lucas was disappointed and ran up and down the corridor shouting, 'Papa – cake.' I was hot on his heels, though not fast enough with the picnic basket over my arm. He veered off into the cupboard where they kept the instruments. Maybe he heard something, or maybe he just had an instinct. He didn't seem remotely surprised to find him there, his trousers round his ankles, nuzzling the neck of a young girl with dishevelled caramel hair. He ran in to tell Richard about his pineapple cake and I stood at the door, too stunned to stop him. I later learnt that the girl was Miranda Gosling and that she had left the school the summer before and returned to help out. Just as I had eight years earlier.*

Richard and Miranda froze in shock. Lucas ran over to them and knocked a box of recorders over in the process. He was trying to show Richard the cake. I scrambled over the pile of recorders and peeled his hands from his father's hairy leg, and Lucas dropped the cake trying to fight me off. It smashed onto the floor and crumbled on impact. He started to cry and I had to drag him bucking and screaming out of the cupboard and down the corridor, the picnic contents abandoned on the lino floor.

Richard skulked home later that evening. Lucas had finally fallen asleep, pacified by chocolate bourbons and The Magic Roundabout. *I was nursing a very large gin. He was pathetically remorseful to begin with, but when challenged he blamed his actions on my erratic behaviour and mood swings. By the end of the evening I found myself promising to be a better wife and to give up the quest for another child in return for his fidelity. I didn't really have a choice.*

But I do now. This time I told him I don't want to live with him when I get out of here. I don't think he believed me but I

*mean it. I don't know where I'll go, but somewhere different.
I would love Lucas to come with me but I know he won't.
Maybe in time he will learn to forgive me. Maybe I will be
able to forgive him.*

*

José was sent by the agency the following day. Erin couldn't
believe the speed with which it was all suddenly happening. She
felt as though she was watching her life, Maggie's life, on fast
forward and someone else had the controls. Maggie was distant.
They had worked on the book the day before but it wasn't easy
for Maggie. She wanted to rewrite an extract but her voice rasped
with every word and Erin had to really strain to hear her from
the computer on the other side of the room. Once they had
finished, Maggie lay spent on the sofa and drifted in and out of
delirious consciousness for the rest of the day. Fred had come
over in the afternoon and tried to rally her, but she could barely
look at him, let alone speak.

José was larger than life both physically and emotionally. He
sang all the time. Mostly crooners from the 1950s, despite the
fact that he was only thirty-three. His mother was from Mexico
and had come to the UK with his father before José was born. His
dad had been a 'crooked soul', he told us that first afternoon. He
died under suspicious circumstances when José was a baby, leaving
his young wife with next to nothing to live on in London. José's
mum was a seamstress and heard that there was a textiles factory
in Plymouth that needed workers. She and José had camped out
on the doorstep of the factory for three days until they gave her
a job. His mother had instilled in José a gratitude to the host
country that had saved them. And he wanted to give something
back, hence the care industry. It was refreshing, humbling and
inspiring. Within a couple of hours, he had brought life back
into Hookes End with his gallant tales and warbling. He had Fred

and Erin in stitches with his Bruce Forsyth impressions, and even went so far as to demonstrate his own version of the cha-cha-cha.

Maggie, however, was impervious to his charm. She obviously found his positivity grating and she visibly winced every time he called her 'dear'. She withdrew into herself still further. After lunch, she declared that she wanted to go to bed. She had never done that before. José insisted on carrying her up the stairs. Erin and Fred watched from the bottom step as he hauled her body, stiff with humiliation, up to the bedroom. He sang his version of 'Singin' In the Rain' all the way. She stayed there all afternoon. Erin popped her head in a couple of times to find José fussing around her and tidying the dressing table, which Erin hadn't dared to touch. Maggie was propped up against a wall of pillows in the bed pretending to be asleep while he flitted between song and story. The irony was that Erin knew Maggie would have found him highly amusing had his affections been focused on someone else. Erin finally persuaded Fred to take him to the shop in the village for some alleged provisions so that she could go and talk to Maggie.

'Can I come in, Maggie?' Erin peered round the door. José had opened the curtains and even the window. The room had a buttery glow in the setting sun and the fresh air was slowly filtering out the bad smells. Maggie's pill pots were now neatly stacked on her bedside table and the clothes from the floor had been magicked away. But Maggie was oblivious. Still resting on a wedge of cushions, she stared with cloudy eyes beyond the billowing curtains and into the distance.

'Are you warm enough, Maggie?' she asked. No response. 'I'm sorry, Maggie, I know you think this is all my fault, this – this invasion. But José is actually really funny. If you would just give him a chance, I think you might like him. And he's worked wonders in here, it's like a different room. I never knew this dressing table had a marble top.' She stroked the surface and looked at Maggie for a response, but none came. She walked over to the bed and sat down on the edge. 'Come on, Maggie. Fred and I will still be here all the time, well, as much as we can. And we can still work on the book. It's just, José is medically trained, you see, and I'm not, and—'

'Has he gone?' Maggie whispered. Her glassy eyes turned towards Erin and searched for her face.

'José? Yes, I got Fred to take him into the village to give you a break. He—'

'Well, hurry up then. Let's crack on.'

'What? Now? Are you sure, Maggie? Do you think you're up to it?'

'Yes,' she said so quietly Erin wasn't sure if she had imagined it.

CHAPTER FIFTEEN

Beechwood Priory, 8th March 1987

*I opened up to the group today. We were in one of our therapy
sessions with Dr Halitosis – that's what I call Dansk now. Not just
me, it has caught on, Jacinta says it and even Barbara. Anyway,
I was suddenly bored of everyone else's stories. Once they start
talking they don't seem to be able to stop. That mellow light that
comes with dusk was creeping into the room. And I'd had enough
of listening to Mandy's woes. So I just came out with it. I blame
my son for the death of my daughter. No one seemed shocked or
even disapproving. They just nodded their heads sympathetically
and I was congratulated for my honesty. And at that moment
the sun dipped beneath the top of the window frame and onto
my face. I wanted to hold my hand up to block it but I didn't, I
just closed my eyes. And then I seemed to be struck with the same
affliction as everyone else. I started talking and couldn't stop.*

*'Going abroad wasn't normally an option on a teacher's
salary, so we spent most of our summers in campsites in Devon
and Cornwall, but last summer we decided to go to France.
Richard had got a pay rise and I was starting to do some more
tutoring and we thought we deserved a bit of a treat. We booked
a campsite in the Dordogne for two weeks – we didn't even have
to take our own tent. It was one of those Eurocamp places where
everything was laid on for you: pots and pans, even camp beds.
Skye, my daughter, she was three and so excited. But Lucas, he*

was fifteen and was not exactly enamoured with the idea of spending two weeks with his parents in a tent, not to mention the ten hours of driving to get there.

'We listened to The Hobbit *on the way down, well, until Cognac when it stopped playing and Richard stuck a pencil into the machine and pulled out spaghetti reams of brown tape. Skye was delighted,* The Hobbit *was a bit beyond her and she now had a totally credible plea for her* "Wheels On the Bus" *singalong tape. But Richard couldn't stand it and turned it off after a couple of minutes. Skye was furious – she kicked the back of his seat again and again and the vein on his neck began to throb. I knew he was about to blow. But he sucked down his rage for another two hours until we were a couple of miles away from our destination. We were navigating this especially winding bit of road in the mountains when a lorry hurtled round the hairpin bend. The sheer drop on our side meant that we had nowhere but the grey barrier to go, and the lorry was forced up the bank where it nearly toppled over onto us. I screamed and Richard swerved onto the side of the road and stopped the car. He slammed his fist down onto the horn over and over again, then swore at us all and got out of the car and kicked the door, denting it forever.*

'So, the tension was running high when we arrived at the campsite ten minutes later. The plot we had been given was too close to the river for my liking. Skye couldn't swim yet. But Richard's sole focus was on cold beer by this time, and he had no patience for my paranoid anxieties.

'"For Christ's sakes, Maggie, she is hardly going to climb down that bank on her own, is she?" he said. And then, in a softer tone, he said, "Imagine listening to the bubbling of the river from our tent at night and being able to jump straight into the water when we wake up. This is what we came for, isn't it? That back-to-nature premise you sold me this holiday on?"'

'And so we set up camp. Half an hour later, the car was unpacked and Richard was reclining in his camping chair at the river's edge, a cold beer in his hand. Lucas was skimming stones, while Skye and I paddled in the shallows of the river. It was going to be a wonderful holiday. Amazingly, Richard did relax, more than I had seen him do for years. We rented canoes one day and we had picnics on the rocks and Lucas and Richard fished in the river. And the sun shone every day. My skin turned coffee brown and I felt attractive in a way I hadn't for years.

'I went for an early-morning swim one day and met Mike, a carpenter from Harrogate. I showed an interest in his catch and so he invited us to their pitch that evening to join them for barbecued trout. Unlike us, Mike and his wife Gilly were fully equipped campers. They had been coming to the site every summer for the past five years and reserved the best pitch a year in advance. Up on the bank above the river, under the trees so there was plenty of shade in the heat of the day, and away from the loo block, the smell of which had seeped into every pore of our tent. We ate grilled trout and tomato salad and hot chips from the café. And we washed it down with carafes of red wine. Mike had visited the local vineyard on his first day and filled up petrol cans with their vin de table, so there was an ample supply. Their girls Rosie and Natalie were ten and eight. They were delighted to have Skye – a real-life doll – to play with. They plaited her hair, put wings on her back and danced around the fire making up magical stories of fairies and elves. Skye was besotted and surprisingly obliging. Lucas, in that awkward limbo between child and adult, just hung out at the table listening to our conversations until I could bear his bored face no longer and sent him back to the tent with his Walkman. There were some other kids in the campsite about his age, and I desperately wanted him to hang out with them, *but when I had suggested it, I was met with such a bolshy attitude that I let it go.'*

*

José had been there for a week when Erin walked into the house after a walk and was greeted by the most delicious smells of lime, coriander, chilli and garlic. She followed the scent and the sound of singing to 'La Isla Bonita' playing full blast in the kitchen. José was wearing Maggie's flowery apron and every surface was covered in piles of chopped vegetables and little bowls of crushed spices. The chilli frying in the saucepan caught at the back of her throat and made her cough.

'José! What's going on?' she spluttered.

'Ah, Erin, you can come and help me. We are having fajitas, Mexican-style.'

'Wow, it smells delicious. What can I do?'

'You can grate that cheese over there.'

'OK.' José shimmied his hips as he added some diced chicken to the pan. It sizzled and spat at him. 'Does Maggie know about this, José?' Erin had to shout over the noise of the radio.

'I told her I was going to cook her a Mexican feast. She wasn't keen, but then she has never tasted Fajitas à la José Sanchez. I told her she won't be able to resist them.'

'I don't know, José, she hasn't really eaten anything for days. Don't you think it might be a bit spicy for her?'

'Don't worry, Erin, I am one step ahead of you.' He picked up a bowl on the other side of the hob with finely shredded pieces of chicken speckled with something green. 'I made her a different version with just lemon and parsley. No spice, tiny bite-size pieces.' He pinched his fingertips together and made little pincer motions as he mentioned the tiny pieces.

Erin laughed. 'You are bonkers, José. But very thoughtful.'

'My Spanish lullaby,' he sang. 'La, la, la, la, la.' His voice quivered as he hit the high notes.

'What on earth is going on here?' Fred said, coming into the kitchen. He also began to cough as he inhaled the chilli.

'José is cooking up a Mexican feast!' Erin said.

'It smells, er, delicious.' Fred didn't sound so sure. 'How is Maggie today?'

'The same as yesterday,' Erin said. 'She is asleep now, at least she was before I went for my walk.'

'I'll go and check, shall I?'

'Fred, wait.' José stopped him as he got to the door. He grabbed a pile of folded tablecloths off the table and loaded them into Fred's arms. 'Take these up with you.'

'Whatever for?'

'For our picnic. If Maggie can't come to the fiesta, we will have to take the fiesta to Maggie.' He swirled his hands in the air as he spoke and then danced back to the chicken on the hob.

'I don't think so, José,' Fred said. 'I don't think she's up to it.'

'Come on, Fred, it will be fun. And it might cheer her up a bit,' Erin said.

'Well, I'll talk to her but I'm not making any promises.'

Erin helped José put the chicken and salsa, the guacamole, cheese and sour cream all into little bowls on a tray and then she carried them upstairs to Maggie's bedroom. Fred was sitting in the chair next to the bed, reading to her from *The Quiet American*. Maggie was totally still and it was hard to work out whether she was awake or not. Erin put the tray down on the floor by the bay window and looked at Fred, questioning him silently. He shook his head demurely and carried on reading.

'I can tell you two are making faces at each other, you know,' Maggie growled.

'We aren't making faces, Maggie, I just wasn't sure if you were asleep, that's all.'

'Well, I'm still here, you know. Not dead yet.'

'And thank goodness for that,' Fred said, and leant in to grab her hand.

'So, Fred told you about José's feast then, Maggie?' Erin said brightly as she unfolded the tablecloths and laid them out on the floor between the bed and the window.

'He did.'

'It's going to be fun,' Erin said. 'A party in your bedroom!' Maggie grunted. 'He's cooking up a storm, can you smell it?'

'Thankfully not, my sense of smell disappeared along with the others. Small mercies.'

'Well, he has been so thoughtful and made you your own small portion, Maggie. He's trying really hard.'

'Yes,' Fred piped in. 'He's certainly got a lot of energy.'

Maggie grunted in agreement, or was it disdain? And José backed into the room carrying another tray with a pile of tortilla wraps and a jug of daffodils. He was still wearing the flowery apron, which was now smeared with food, and he had his baseball cap on backwards. His face was glowing with sweat and his eyes sparkled with excitement.

'Dinner is served,' he said, placing the tray on the cloths on the floor.

Erin knelt down next to him. 'It looks amazing, José.'

'Yes, it certainly is a wonderfully colourful array,' Fred said from his chair. 'You won't mind if I don't get down on the floor with you, I'm not sure I'll ever get up again.'

'Nonsense, Fred, get down there while you still can,' Maggie said from the bed.

'OK, if I must,' he said, lowering himself gingerly. Erin winced as she heard a loud crack from his knees.

'Excellent. So now you can all fill up your fajitas with a bit of everything.' José demonstrated and Fred and Erin copied. 'I'll make a very small one for you, Maggie.'

'No, I don't think so, I'm not hung—'

'Just try,' he said gently as he held the perfectly rolled parcel to Maggie's lips. She nibbled at the edges tentatively and then took a larger bite, and sour cream dribbled down her chin. José was there at the ready with a napkin and dabbed it away in less than a second.

'Mmm,' Maggie said, and went in for a second bite. Fred and Erin smiled at each other on the rug as they tucked into their fajitas. Fred had overfilled his and juice poured down his hands and into the cuffs of his Viyella shirt.

'Oh God, it's rather messy, isn't it?' he laughed.

'You need to fold in the bottom like José showed us,' Erin said smugly with her neatly tucked fajita. 'Shall I make you the next one, Fred?'

'That would be lovely, Erin, thank you. It really is rather delicious, José. How is yours, Maggie?' They all looked up at Maggie who was quietly chewing on her fajita.

'It's not bad,' Maggie said, from behind the hand that was covering her mouth full of food. José was still sitting on the edge of the chair next to her, always at the ready, and beaming from ear to ear.

'So, José, have you ever been to Mexico?' Fred asked.

'Once when I was twelve. My mother saved up for years and we went for a whole month to visit our family.'

'What was it like?' Erin tucked into her second fajita.

'Hot! Sweltering, in fact. And noisy and full of colours and smells that were so foreign and yet weirdly familiar. And so many huge insects, I already told Maggie about my butterfly experience there when I saw she loved them so much.' He turned to Maggie and placed his palm on her arm as he finished his story. Erin was amazed to see that Maggie didn't withdraw from his touch, so enraptured was she with his story. 'My family, they live up in the mountains, and in the forest outside their village there are

thousands and thousands of orange butterflies, monarchs I think.'
He looked to Maggie for confirmation and she nodded. 'I have
never seen anything like it. Swarms of them that filled the sky. They
were all over us, on our head, our arms, our legs.' He took his arm
away from Maggie and pointed to the various parts of his body as
if teaching a nursery class. 'My mother, she was a bit freaked out,
but for me it was the most magical thing I have ever experienced.
I felt as though I was being touched by God himself.' He looked
up to the sky and genuflected, a tiny flick of his fingers that was
so instinctive and yet so alien to everyone else in the room.

'Wow!' said Erin. 'That sounds pretty crazy. Are they always
there?'

'I think the butterfly population had been in decline but for
some reason, to do with the climate, I presume, they came back
that year in large numbers. They hibernate in the forest. The trees
keep them warm in the winter, all huddled together on the trunks.'

'Ten acres,' Maggie interrupted, her mouth still full of fajita.

'What's that, Maggie?' Fred asked.

They all waited as she chewed and then finally swallowed the
food in her mouth. 'The butterflies cover an area of ten acres, it
is a natural phenomenon.'

'You knew about this, Maggie, before José told you?' Erin asked.

'Anyone who knows anything about butterflies knows about
their migration to the Cerro Pelon. They go there for the milkweed.'

'And that is where your family live, José?'

'Yes, my whole family live there in a village just below the forest.'

'Well, fancy that!' Fred said, clapping his hands together. 'I
don't imagine you thought your nurse would be someone who
had experienced the great butterfly migration in Mexico, did you,
Maggie?'

Her acknowledgment was merely a shrug, but it was enough
for Fred, Erin and José, who all smiled in appreciation of this
unlikely revelation.

'Do you have a big family out there, José?' Erin asked while loading up her third fajita.

'Yes! Family is everything there, and everywhere we went there were aunts and uncles, cousins and grandparents. All my life it had only been my mother and me and suddenly there were all these people, and not just any old people – family! We were related to them all! And they touch each other all the time, smother each other in love and kisses and… and it was so unlike anything here. And yet I felt so at home.'

'Have you never been tempted to go back?' Erin asked.

'Of course!' He clapped his hands together and then held them in a prayer position under his chin. 'But my mother is here, and for various reasons she doesn't want to go back there, so I must stay here.'

'Never say never, hey?' Maggie's voice echoed from the bed and José turned to look at her and smiled.

'Never say never, Maggie.' He touched her hand and her finger curled around his and held onto it for a second before she pulled it away. He stood up. 'How about I teach you a proper Latin dance?'

'I'm not sure about that, old boy,' Fred said. 'Not sure I can even get up from the floor!'

'Come on, Fred, there's life in the old bugger yet!' Maggie said with a smile.

'Well, there's a challenge. I haven't heard Maggie so animated since I got here!' José said, and pulled Fred up to his feet. 'Come on, Erin, you too!'

'Oh God, Maggie knows how bad at dancing I am.'

'That's true, she's got two left feet!'

'Nonsense, anyone can dance,' said José.

'But we don't have any music,' said Erin.

'I'll just have to sing then!'

'God help us,' said Maggie.

José and Erin stacked up the plates and bowls put them on the dressing table, then cleared the tablecloths into a pile in a corner of the room. 'Right, you two, stand behind me and copy what I do,' José said to Fred and Erin, who shifted from one foot to the other in anticipation.

And then he started to sing. Not the cheesy crooners or pop songs they had heard before but a traditional Latino song, that began slowly. José's voice reverberated off the windows and the walls with a haunting yet beautiful tone. And while he sang he danced, slow, graceful moves, his arms out to the sides, his hips swaying as he crossed one leg over the other. And Erin and Fred lumbered behind him, unsure at first as they kicked each other and were constantly on the wrong foot. But slowly they got to grips with the rhythm, the gentle sway of the hips, the hypnotic tone of José's voice. And then he speeded up, and the room rattled under the weight of their feet and Maggie clapped with delight from her bed when Fred collapsed into Erin's arms in a heap of giggles.

'Oh dear,' he panted. 'I am definitely too old for this.'

'You are as old as you behave, Fred!' José said, and pulled Erin into a ballroom stance and led her around the room with surprising grace. 'You just have to feel the rhythm, Erin,' he said as she stamped on his foot.

'I don't have any rhythm!' And he twisted her round and flung her over his arm so her hair brushed the floor. 'Nonsense, everyone has rhythm!' She laughed and the blood pulsed in her head as he pulled her up, and she caught sight of Maggie, who was sitting more upright. Fred was on the bed next to her and holding her hand and she was smiling and tapping out a rhythm with her other hand on the blanket.

Erin collapsed onto the end of the bed, laughing. 'Oh my God, you're crazy, José. Are all Mexicans as nuts as you? I think

I would like it there. Have you been, Maggie?' The smile on Maggie's face fell.

'Er, no, I...'

'You have been to South America, though, haven't you?' José said. He had now taken to dancing on his own but still kept his arms in a ballroom stance as if he was holding a partner. 'I have seen photos of Bolivia, Peru and the Perito Moreno Glacier, that's Argentina, isn't it, or is it Chile?'

'I... I... don't remember... I...' Maggie faltered. What little colour that flushed her cheeks had disappeared and she was now sallow and grey.

'I think that's enough for today, folks, don't you?' Fred got up from the bed and started moving the plates onto a tray. 'I think we need to leave Maggie for a bit of a rest now.'

'Of course.' Erin and José both jumped up to help him.

Maggie's face, which up until a minute ago had been smooth and content, was now wrinkled into tributaries of angst. She held onto the blanket with both hands as if she might fall off if she let go. José finished gathering the plates and dishes and he and Fred carried a tray out each. Erin stayed to fold the tablecloths into a pile.

'Are you OK, Maggie?' she asked.

Her face softened. 'I'm just tired, Erin.'

'Are you sure that's all it is?'

'Yes! It was a lovely party. And you're right, José is quite a character.'

'OK, well, I'll leave you to rest.' She started to walk towards the door.

'No, wait! Erin, we need to carry on with the story.'

'But Maggie, you are so tired.'

'I have to. I need to finish it.'

CHAPTER SIXTEEN

Beechwood Priory, 8th March 1987… continued

'It was halfway through the second week of our holiday, the night that changed our lives forever. It started off so well. I had just come out of the washrooms and was still tingling from the hot shower on my sun-kissed skin. I was wearing the dress I had bought at the market earlier that day, white cotton with thin straps and scarlet flowers embroidered at the hem. The back was low and the white glowed against my chestnut tan. The muslin petticoat felt soft against my legs as I walked. Richard was sitting on the bank, and he caught my arm as I passed and drew me onto his lap, pressing his cold beer bottle into the naked small of my back. The sky was on fire with this amazing sunset; even the river glowed pink. Richard and I watched from the bank as the kids played on the little beach below our tent. Skye had made a bed for a dead crab out of grass and weeds. She was singing a made-up song about "Crabbie" as she played. And Lucas was building a tower out of pebbles next to her. They seemed so content, so utterly absorbed in their own little worlds. And I felt so happy watching them. It was as if everything had suddenly come together. Everything finally made sense.

'And then it didn't. We then wandered over to the campsite café for supper. We ate steak and chips and drank cold beer. We played Uno, or rather Lucas, Richard and I did. Skye rearranged the cards into piles and then buried them in the sand under the

table. Lucas was in a chatty mood that night, making us laugh
with tales of Simeon's antics at school. We all loved Simeon; he
had been Lucas's best friend since he started primary school,
and while his other friends had matured into cool and moody
teenagers, Simeon remained the slightly spotty prankster. I always
admired Lucas's loyalty to him, proud that he didn't abandon
him for the cooler gang. After supper Skye crawled onto my lap
and played with the ribbon that tied at the front of my dress.
She laid her head on my chest and I twisted her golden curls
around my fingers. She smelt of silt like the river and mosquito
repellent. After a while I noticed that the twiddling of the ribbon
had stopped and her breathing was heavier. I couldn't see her face
but Richard said her eyes were drooping, fighting sleep. I carried
her to our tent and took off her sandals and her dress. I found
the new nightie that we had bought from the same market stall
that morning: it was white with fairies at the hem. I pulled it
over her heavy head and laid her down on the mattress. I tucked
Mr Gilbert under her arm and she clutched onto him in her
dreams. I remember feeling an overwhelming surge of love for
her as I kissed her matted curls and breathed in her smell.

    'Mike and Gilly had joined Lucas and Richard when I got
back to the table. They had taken the girls out to supper in
the local town and had just got back. Mike was very excited
about the bottle of Calvados he had just bought and invited
us over to their tent to sample it. I was anxious about going
to the other side of the campsite and leaving Skye asleep in the
tent, but Lucas said that he was tired and would stay behind
to look after her. I presumed he was desperate to avoid another
evening listening to Mike and Richard's debating and musical
nostalgia. Richard jumped at his offer. He was in an excitable
mood and I too didn't want the glorious night to end.

    'Richard and I headed over to Mike and Gilly's plot further
up the river. Their girls were coming back from the shower block

in their pyjamas as we arrived. Gilly tucked them up into their bed in the van and then joined us. Mike poured us all healthy portions of Calvados in tin beakers. He produced a lump of hash wrapped in cling film that he had also procured in town earlier. I didn't really smoke pot, it made me feel anxious, but that night I felt invincible. I saw a shooting star and suggested we go for a skinny-dip. Since we had arrived in France I had wanted to swim naked in the river, but didn't dare during the day. I persuaded Richard to come but Mike and Gilly declined; they couldn't leave the girls.

'We had to walk further up the river, away from the campsite, in order to get to a pool deep enough to really swim in. There was this huge smooth boulder by the pool that we had picnicked on a couple of days earlier. It had been too hot to walk on then but now it was cool under our feet. I pulled my dress off over my head and left it in a crumpled pile on the rock. Richard was shocked to see I wasn't wearing knickers. I ran across the rock and bombed into the water. I remember lying in the cool water with my arms and legs stretched out like a star, looking up at the night sky and talking about how important it was to seize these magical moments so we didn't become victims of our own drudgery. About how we spend our lives being accountable for everyone, for our children, at work, even our parents. Richard joked that we had been relentlessly wiping arses now for fifteen years! We had no towels, and my dress clung to my wet body as we made our way back along the river path towards the campsite. It was dark under the trees and we stumbled over tree roots. I had to tell Richard to stifle his giggles as we neared our tent. He would wake the children… but when we got back, the tent was unzipped. And Lucas wasn't there. Skye's sandals were in the doorway but she wasn't there either. She… she…'

I couldn't carry on. The sun in the therapy room had moved from my face and down onto my chest while I spoke but I had *kept my eyes shut, lost in my own story. Until that moment when they sprang open and I found myself looking into a sea of faces, heads tilted, eyes glassy, willing me to continue. But I couldn't. I wanted to; at least I thought I did. But the words were congealed in my chest, a mass of truths caked in something hard and impenetrable. I couldn't breathe. Judy was next to me. She gathered me into the folds of her velour tracksuit and whispered comforting nothings into my neck. She had dreadful body odour and I pulled away. Dr Dansk told her to give me some space. Told me to concentrate on my breathing. Deep and slow in, deep and slow out. I wasn't ready.*

*

'Maggie?' Erin said, looking over towards the bed. The night had crept into the room now, shrouding it in a veil of darkness. Erin had just about been able to see what she was reading by the window but Maggie was merely a shadow on the other side of the room. 'Maggie, are you OK?' She walked over to the bed. Maggie was ghostly still and Erin wondered whether she had fallen asleep, but when she got closer, she could see that tears were coursing down Maggie's wrinkled cheeks. And then her mouth started to tremble under the pressure of all that gathering emotion. 'Oh, Maggie.' Erin sat on the bed next to her.

'I… I don't think I have much time…' Maggie gasped. Erin didn't know what to say, and she cringed at how ill-equipped she was to deal with this conversation. 'I need your help,' Maggie whispered, the words punctuated by rasping sobs.

'Of course. Anything.'

'I need to… finish this… I need to finish it for Lucas.' It was the first time she had ever actually said his name out loud, and the significance was not lost on Erin.

'OK.'

'He needs to read it.'

'I'll do it, don't worry. I can type it up, even after you've… I'll finish it, I promise.'

'I need you to find him.'

Maggie wiped away the tears on her cheeks with her shaking, mottled hand. Erin clasped it between her own and then Maggie let out a guttural sob that seemed to come from somewhere so deep inside that it shook the core of her frail body. And then she couldn't stop; the years of stifled grief took hold of her and she cried and she trembled and she clung to Erin and dug her fingernails into the palms of her hands.

'It's OK,' Erin said as she released her hands and put her arms around Maggie's juddering shoulders. 'Shh, it's OK, I'll find him, Maggie. I'll send him the story,' she said as Maggie's tears soaked through her shirt. Oblonsky was whimpering at Erin's feet. He turned around in circles, then tried to lie down and then to jump up. Erin knew how he felt. She was equally overwhelmed by the power of Maggie's grief, the grief that had been suppressed for so long and that had now broken through with such indomitable strength. Maggie cried and cried and Erin stroked her head and murmured meaningless pacifying phrases. And eventually the torrent of emotion ran dry and Maggie fell asleep.

Erin laid her back on the bed and pulled the blankets up around her tiny body which still shuddered with leftover sobs. Then she walked to the window and leant her face against the cold glass in an attempt to still the blood that was pulsing around her head, to numb the pain that was stirring in her heart and halt the tears that stung at the backs of her eyes. But they came anyway. Tears for Maggie, and the grief and guilt that had tormented her all that time. Tears for Lucas and for that little girl in her fairy nightie. Tears for Simon, for Robert, for the horrible mess of a life she had found herself in. She slid down the wall and sat on the floor, hugging her knees tight to her chest. The palms of her hands still stung and she looked at the red crescent scars that Maggie had left there. But they would fade in time, unlike Maggie's wounds. What had happened to Skye? And how was she going to find Lucas? Erin eventually pulled herself up to standing and walked back over to the bed. Maggie was still now, but her face was blotchy and her brow furrowed with the years of regret. Erin reached out and touched the lines between her eyes. The skin was soft and powdery and rippled under her touch. She withdrew it quickly, sickened and ashamed.

'I'm sorry, Maggie,' Erin whispered. 'I'm going to do whatever I can to help you find some kind of peace before it's too late.'

CHAPTER SEVENTEEN

Beechwood Priory, 13th March 1987

Jeremy Fellowes found Lucas on top of his daughter at the end of his garden. Richard came in to tell me. It was the first time he had visited in a while, so I knew something was up. He strode into the room with purpose but couldn't look at me. He blinked a lot and while he talked he fiddled with the bobbly cord on the window blind which rattled and twitched. Apparently, Jeremy came back early from work yesterday and went to see how Lucas was getting on digging the flower bed. But there was no sign of Lucas, just Laila's t-shirt lying in the dirt. And then he heard them in the summer house. Richard said Fellowes dragged Lucas home with a bloody nose and no trousers. On hearing this my stomach lurched as if the umbilical cord was still attached to him and was being yanked. Bile rose up into the back of my throat, and I concentrated on swallowing it back down. And Richard was talking about a boarding school in North Yorkshire. Something about re-engaging the disengaged. And then he was shouting at me, holding onto the tops of my arms and shaking me. His breath smelt sour. Lucas is sixteen. Laila is fifteen, he spat. If we don't send Lucas away Fellowes will press charges.

That was four days ago. They have kept me sedated ever since. I can hear them talking at the end of my bed. Violent outbursts. Irrational anger. In light of her suicidal tendency, they say. But I'm just too tired to respond.

*

It was mid-March, and the first signs of spring were starting to emerge. Clusters of daffodils were scattered around the bases of the apple trees and flecks of pink blossom were budding on the brittle branches. Maggie had been in bed for three weeks now, and Erin was having less and less contact with her each day. She slept most of the time and even when she was awake, it was José who saw to her needs. Erin suggested they continue working on the book, but Maggie wasn't up to it. The extract about the holiday in France had broken her. And so, as promised, Erin continued to type up Maggie's notes for the novel on her own. It felt strange, and prurient, like she was delving into her past without permission. And the rest of the time Erin dedicated to finding Lucas.

The day after Maggie's emotional breakdown, she had told Erin to fetch a photo from the drawer of her dressing table.

'It arrived in the post five years ago,' Maggie told her. 'There was no note, nothing apart from the photograph in an envelope.'

Erin opened the drawer and picked up the photo. Lines streaked the picture, evidence that it had been crumpled through over-handling. And the image was blurry, but Erin could just make out a man in a red baseball cap peering out from behind a bush. A blue butterfly was perching on the brim of his cap. The sapphire wings were the same colour as his eyes, which were narrow, the eyelids heavy. He had a mole on the side of his face.

'Is it Lucas?' Maggie nodded. 'Did he, did Lucas send it to you?'

Maggie shook her head. 'I don't think so. There was no airmail postmark, so it came from the UK, and it doesn't look very English, the photo I mean. That rubber plant?'

'No, and the butterfly.'

'It's a blue morpho – you only get them in the tropics. I think it was from my sister. It is just the sort of interfering meddling she would do.'

'Didn't you call her? Ask her whether she had sent it, whether she'd seen him?'

'I haven't spoken to her for years, thirty-two years, in fact. If she wanted to talk, she could have come. She obviously knew where I lived. She died a year later. Cancer.'

'Oh Maggie, I'm so sorry.'

'Hmph,' Maggie grunted.

'But do you know where he is? What country?'

'I know he went to Costa Rica twenty-eight years ago. And I know they have blue morpho butterflies there.'

'Is this where the butterfly obsession comes from, Maggie?'

'It's not an obsession, Erin.'

'Sorry, fascination.'

'My interest in butterflies did start at around the same time, yes.' She spoke slowly, as if only acknowledging this correlation to herself for the first time. And then her face softened. 'Lucas always loved tiny creatures, and I wonder, well, I hope, that he might have found some solace in butterflies.'

'I'm sure he has.' Erin fiddled with the tatty corners of the photo. 'It's not a lot to go on, Maggie, but I'll try.'

'I doubt you'll have much luck. I don't think he wants to be found.'

There was no internet at the house and no mobile reception, so Erin decided to go back to her parents to do her research. Her mum was sweeping the front doorstep when she arrived.

'Hi, Mum,' Erin said to her bent-over back. Her mum swung round.

'Erin,' she said brightly, a huge smile creeping onto her flushed face.

'I'm not back to stay, Mum, I just need to get online, that's all. Got to do some research for Maggie. I'll be in my room, if that's

OK?' Her mum was disappointed, obviously, but continued to smile and replied with a softness that nearly broke Erin.

'Of course, whatever you like. Shall I bring you some tea? And I was just about to make some scones.' She didn't just bake scones on a Monday afternoon, they were for special occasions. But they were also Erin's favourite, and her mum was getting to her in the only way she knew how. Erin shrugged nonchalantly and tried not to smile. 'Sure, that would be nice.'

And so every day Erin would go there for the afternoon and every day her mum would bake something different and take huge pleasure in watching Erin wolf down banana bread, millionaire's shortbread, flapjacks and brownies. And she always made extra so she could take some home to José, Fred and Maggie. After a few days Erin ventured downstairs to do her research at the kitchen table while her mum busied herself cooking and labelling for the shop. They tiptoed around each other tentatively, avoiding conversations of any significance. But on the fourth day Erin could bear the elephant in the room no longer. She watched her mum make pastry on the other side of the kitchen and decided to just come out with one of the questions that had been haunting her since Christmas. 'Did you hold him, Mum?' she asked. Her mum stopped, but didn't turn round to face her.

'Robert?' she asked eventually.

'Yes.'

There was a long pause, and then an equally long exhale from her mother before she replied. 'No, I, well, I couldn't, not at first, he was in an incubator, and then... the nurses... well, they suggested I... no. No, I didn't.'

'Not at all?' She watched the muscles stiffen in her mother's back, but she offered no response. 'That must have been hard.'

'Yes, Erin, it was all very hard. The hardest thing I have ever...' But she couldn't finish, and without turning round she walked over to the sink and ran the tap and scrubbed at the sticky dough on her fingers with a nail brush. Her hands worked hard and fast, scrubbing at her nails, her palms, the backs of her hands with a ferocity that seemed quite manic. Erin wanted to tell her to stop, that she would make her fingers bleed. She stood up and started to cross the kitchen towards her, and then the door swung open and with it came a blast of cold air followed by her dad. He shouldn't be at home at that time of day, but Erin wasn't surprised. He had pitched up the day before, too, pretending he had forgotten his flask.

Her mother's shoulders dropped with his arrival and the furious cleaning ceased and Erin, too, was relieved by the interruption.

'Hi Dad,' she said, and then as if to explain her position in the middle of the kitchen, 'I was just leaving.' She looked over at her mum who was now drying her hands on a tea towel and leaning up against the Aga, an expression of fraught relief across her face.

'That's a shame. Can I walk with you?' he asked.

'Of course.' He asked her about Maggie on their walk, and she told him about José and Fred and their fajita party in Maggie's bedroom, and they almost got to the brow of the hill before he told her how much he missed her and asked if she would come home.

As she considered her response, she realised that her anger from that night in Maggie's house had faded to a mere simmer over the past couple of months, and she missed him. But the exchange with her mum in the kitchen that afternoon had left her with a bad taste in her mouth. 'Maggie really needs me now, Dad, I don't think she's got very long left.'

'Fair enough.' He nodded with resignation and took her hand. She hadn't held her dad's hand since she was a child, when the crease between his thumb and first finger wasn't nearly as rough against the palm of her hand. 'And what is this research she's got you doing?' he asked as they turned into Maggie's drive.

'Oh, just something for the book.'

'Cryptic as ever, Erin.'

'OK, I'll give you a little spoiler – it's about Costa Rica. Maggie is setting some of the book there and wants me to research some facts about places and customs and food and…' It was only partially untrue, yet she cringed with the deceit.

'Costa Rica, hey? Fascinating!' They reached the top of the drive. 'Well, I guess we're here. I'll see you tomorrow?' He held onto her hand for a little longer than necessary and then let it go.

'Yeah, bye, Dad.'

In fact, progress on her hunt for Lucas in Costa Rica was painfully slow. She googled him and was amazed at how many Lucas Muirs there were in the world, but none who looked remotely like the man in the photo. She looked for him on Facebook, Twitter and Instagram but there was nothing that resembled a forty-six-year-old man who may or may not live in Costa Rica. And that was all she had to go on. So she started trawling through pictures and articles, blogs and travel guides of the country. She read over and over about the biodiversity of which the nation is so proud. The fact that it has no standing army and is said to be one of the happiest places to live in the world. She read that monkeys are its most common mammal and that ten per cent of the world's butterflies live there.

And butterflies were the only other lead, so she searched and read about the hundreds of butterfly farms all over the country. They weren't concentrated in any one area but seemed to crop up everywhere in all shapes and sizes. The biggest one was in a hangar-sized cage and featured five waterfalls and observation decks. And there were smaller ones on farms, in wildlife sanctuaries, in people's back gardens.

After a week, she was beginning to lose hope and was about to pack up her laptop and set off back to Maggie's when she came across the blog of a traveller and butterfly enthusiast. And there in among his ravings about zebra longwings and banded peacocks was Lucas's photo. The same picture that Maggie had. Erin yelped with excitement and her mum came rushing out of the larder.

'Are you alright, love?'

'Yes, I'm fine, I'm more than fine. I just… never mind.'

'I thought you might have hurt yourself, you screamed so loudly. What is it?'

'Sorry, Mum, I just found something, that's all. Just give me a minute, will you.' She reread the blog. It didn't say anything about the photo or where it was taken but there was an email address at the bottom. She sent NatureLoverDale a message and rushed out of the house and up the hill towards Hookes End. She couldn't wait to tell Maggie that she had a lead on the photo. But as she rounded the corner, she saw that there was an ambulance in the driveway.

'Maggie,' she called, running towards it. José was standing on the front doorstep, propping the door open with his back. 'José, what's happened? Where's Maggie?' She pushed past him and ran into the hall where she met a burly paramedic in a reflective jacket. He was carrying a stretcher behind him. Maggie was lying on it under a blanket. She was trying to hold her head up to see where she was going but her eyes were useless and wide with fear.

'Maggie.' Erin grabbed Maggie's hand, which was hanging off the edge of the stretcher.

'Erin, I don't want… I don't want to go,' Maggie whispered.

'Maggie is going to the hospice, Erin,' José said and Erin felt the weight of his hand on her shoulder.

'José, she doesn't want to go.' Erin was still gripping onto Maggie's hand as the paramedics carried her out into the cold. 'You said she could stay here if we had you to help.'

José's grip on Erin's shoulder tightened as he tried to pull her away. She let go of Maggie's hand reluctantly. 'Erin,' he said under his breath, 'she can't stay at home any more. She had a seizure in the night. She needs doctors looking after now, not just me.'

'A seizure? But… but I told her that if you came, she could stay at home, that she could die here.'

'I'm sorry,' he said, shaking his head with infuriating sincerity.

Erin turned her back on him and climbed up into the ambulance. Maggie had been transferred to the bed inside. Her knuckles were white as she gripped onto the blanket over her legs.

'I'm sorry, Maggie, I know you don't want to leave the house,' Erin said, conscious of the flutter in her voice. 'But it's the best thing for you now. We can't look after you here anymore.'

'Erin, I haven't finished…' Maggie said, her cold hand grabbing Erin's arm.

'I know, Maggie, I'm typing it up for you. And I've got a lead on Lucas.'

'What? What do you mean?' Maggie gripped tighter onto her arm.

'I found your photo online. I've emailed the guy who took it.'

'Right, off you go now, missie, we need to get Maggie out of here.' It was a skinny guy with glasses, who Erin had barely even noticed carrying the other end of Maggie's stretcher. He had a sing-song Scottish accent and a long fringe that flopped in front of his eyes.

'I'm going,' she said, not hiding the irritation in her voice. Then she turned to Maggie and whispered, 'I'll come to the hospice later, with Fred.' Erin turned to go but Maggie didn't let go of her arm.

'Wait,' Maggie's eyes flickered from side to side as she searched for Erin's face. 'Upstairs, in the drawer under my bed, there's a letter.'

'OK, I'll find it,' she said and climbed out of the back of the ambulance. The burly one got in the front and started the engine while the Scot closed the doors in the back.

Oblonsky barked and chased the ambulance, all the way down the drive and out onto the road. 'Oblonsky, come back!' Erin shouted, running after him. He was halfway down the lane when she finally reached him, still barking and jumping around in circles. José arrived a few seconds later, red-faced and panting.

Erin knelt down and ruffled the fur on Oblonsky's head. 'Come on, boy, she's gone now,' she said to him and hooked a finger under his collar and led him back to the house.

'It's quite normal, you know,' José said when he had finally got his breath back. 'The seizure, I mean, at this final stage. But I couldn't look after her on my own any more, Erin, she needs round-the-clock care now until the end.' Erin was too numb to respond. The end, the end, he kept saying it. 'And I can't be with her twenty-four-seven, which is what she needs. If she was to have a seizure when I wasn't with her, well, she could fall, bite her tongue, bang her head. It's just not safe.'

'Safe! José, she's dying of a brain tumour, of course she's not safe! She just wanted to die at home, and you said she could. Maybe it would be better if she fell out of bed and died of a bang on the head anyway!'

'Do you want that to be your call, Erin?' José shouted after her as she went into the house and ran up the stairs, two at a time. She knew Maggie wanted to die at home more than anything. But he was right, infuriatingly right. It wasn't her call to make.

Oblonsky followed her into Maggie's bedroom. The duvet had been pulled back on the bed, revealing a stained incontinence sheet on top. Erin knelt down next to it, and the stench of ammonia caught at the back of her throat. She pulled out one of the drawers. There was something wedged in the top and she had to force it open. But there was only a load of blankets inside, no letter. The drawer on the other side slid open easily. It contained a shoebox. She took the lid off and found two toy rabbits. One was balding, it was missing a leg and its neck was saggy, causing the head to flop to one side. And the other was a newer, less loved version of the same. Underneath the rabbit was a child's painting, a face with wonky eyes and yellow hair. It had a triangle for a dress with pink spots on. 'Skye' was scribbled at the top of the piece of paper. Beneath it was a little tin containing a hospital tag. It said

Baby girl Muir 11/02/1983. Underneath the tag was some kind of crusty stem with a plastic peg. She picked it up. It took her a few moments to realise that it was a withered umbilical cord with the clamp still attached. She threw it back in the tin. There was also a lock of hair, a caramel curl that was so soft she put it to her lip. And underneath the tin at the bottom of the box was a letter addressed to Lucas Muir.

CHAPTER EIGHTEEN

Beechwood Priory, 17th March 1987

I was scared of Lucas by the time we finally took him home from the hospital as a baby. I was scared of my baby. He cried relentlessly for three months. Reflux, they said, or was it colic? I can still see his knotted, cherry-red face and crinkled limbs. That shrill howl reverberated through me, shattering my nerves. I fed him until my nipples bled and then paced up and down the room for hours at a time. He would finally fall asleep, suckered to my breast or curled on my chest like a little frog, and I would hold my breath waiting for it to start up again. Richard was never there. He had a week off work when Lucas was first born, but we were still in hospital then, with nurses to help change the nappies and rock him to sleep. He charmed them all, of course. I found him once in the nursery with a group of five ladies hanging on his every word as he told them how he had got his students to recite poetry to cows.

He went back to the school as soon as we got home and worked suspiciously long days. He couldn't cope with the tears; when he finally came home in the evening he would shout at me to do something, to make him stop. Ma came for a week, and that was nice. She would take Lucas off for walks in the pram. And I would try to sleep, but couldn't. I was too wired. I fainted once, I had just fed him and hadn't eaten breakfast and I walked to the chemist. It was only a few doors down. I went to get some lanolin for my bleeding nipples. The pavement started to swim in front of me and the cracks between the stones seemed to rise up towards me. The next thing I knew I was lying on the floor. There was blood trickling down the side of my face and some man was fanning me with his newspaper.

After that I was terrified I was going to faint again so I rarely left the house. Ma went home. And the visitors dried up. I was on my own with only my deranged thoughts for company. It should have been such a happy time. Then at twelve weeks the screaming stopped, just like that. I took Lucas to the doctor, terrified by his apathy. But he had expelled all his fury in those first few months, and from that point on he was rarely ruffled. He seemed to just take whatever shit life threw at him. While I was thrashing and screaming, he was calm, possibly simmering under the surface, but calm.

*

'Erin! Erin, are you up there?' It was Fred coming up the stairs. Fred! He didn't know about Maggie. She stuffed the letter into her pocket and then the box back in the drawer. She was on her knees closing the drawer under the bed when he came into the room.

'Erin? What are you doing?' he said, coming towards her. 'I saw José downstairs. He told me about Maggie.'

'Just, er, looking for things to take to her,' Erin said looking around the room. She picked up a nightie from the floor and started opening and shutting drawers, cupboards, not sure what she was looking for.

'Are you alright, Erin? It's for the best, you know, she couldn't stay here any longer,' Fred said.

'Er, yeah. I'm OK.' Erin threw the nightie on the bed and marched over to the window – she couldn't bear the stench in the room any longer, and she heaved it open, letting in a welcome gust of salty air.

'Erin.' He put his hand on her arm.

'I just feel so bad, Fred, she looked so frightened, and we had promised her she could stay at home.'

'We always knew this would probably happen. These last two weeks have been really hard. She needs more help than we can give her at the end.'

'Stop saying "the end", Fred! José keeps saying it too.'

'Well, it is the end. We have to be realistic.' She looked out of the window. A cluster of starlings were diving through a hole in the roof of the dilapidated shed at the bottom of the garden. 'Come on, let's take Oblonsky for a walk and go and see Maggie at the hospice. José can clear up in here.'

When they reached the top of the hill Erin took her phone out and checked her emails. He had replied, NatureLoverDale – he was happy to help and he told her he had taken that photo at The Butterfly Garden in Puerto Viejo on the Caribbean side of Costa Rica. He thought the guy in the picture was the manager at the farm; it was tiny, and he was the only person working there on the day he had visited.

'Fred, I just need to write an email, do you mind if I stay here?'

'OK. I'll come to the house in an hour and we can go to see Maggie.' Erin sat down on the bench. A cool breeze wrapped itself around her neck and she pulled her hood over her head.

'Great,' Erin said, her head down. She was already googling The Butterfly Garden. The Tripadvisor review came up first. It only had two stars and some pretty shoddy reviews. Someone said they had gone all the way there only to find it closed and deserted. Others said it was tired and shabby and there were not enough butterflies. One of them made a reference to a 'surly' manager who made them feel most unwelcome. But there was the odd one that said it was 'charming' and 'delightfully unpretentious' and 'away from the tourist trail'. There weren't any official photos on there, just visitors' pics. Mostly close-ups of blue morpho butterflies like the ones in Maggie's painting on the wall.

There were photos of various visitors in their sun hats online. She scrolled down through the sweaty faces. There was one of a little blonde girl smiling and covered in butterflies. And there was a picture of the entrance and a big colourful banner that said BUTTERFLY GARDEN – COME AND SEE OUR MAGICAL CREATURES. It was hanging up between two huge palm trees. Erin clicked on the link to the actual website. It was incredibly dated and Erin winced at the spelling mistake on the home page: 'See the butterflies in their natural habitait'. There was a form to fill in on the contact page but no email address, no phone number. Her fingers hovered over the keys. Would he even read it? There didn't seem to be another way, so she filled out her details and then wrote: 'I am looking for Lucas Muir. It is to do with his mother. Please can you ask him to contact me ASAP either by email or phone.'

She hesitated for a moment and then hit send. Then she went back to Google and searched for pictures of Lucas. She only found one other. He wasn't in the foreground, he was hiding behind a group of Japanese tourists. He was wearing the same faded red baseball cap. He had Maggie's smoky-blue eyes. He looked serious, troubled. She recalled Maggie's stories of this charming little boy with freckles on his nose, who loved encyclopedias and tiny frogs and who sang to his baby sister. What sort of a life had he led on the other side of the world?

Erin looked down at the clump of daffodils that had sprouted next to the bench and picked some, she would take them to Maggie.

'I'm just going to have a word with the manager, she knew my wife,' Fred said to Erin after they had registered with the receptionist at the hospice.

'Don't you want to see Maggie first?'

'You go on ahead, I won't be long.'

'But Fred…'

'Go on, you'll be fine. She's down there, room number three, the lady on the front desk said.' He pointed in the direction of some double doors and then disappeared down a corridor on the other side of the hall.

Erin pushed through the doors and walked down the corridor. It was ghostly quiet, not at all like the hectic hospital. She peered through the glass into the first room on the right, but it was just a waiting room with chintzy armchairs. An elderly man was reading the paper. The next room was full of beds and patients. She couldn't see a room number, so she opened the door and stuck her head round.

'Can I help?' A man in a blue nurse uniform came to the door.

'I'm looking for Maggie Muir,' Erin said. 'She came here this morning.'

'Ah yes, Maggie – next room on the left, you can go straight in.' He had a round, kind face. Erin wondered whether everyone working in this death industry had big, kind faces. It really wouldn't help to have someone with scrawny features and alarming eyes like herself.

The door to Maggie's room was open. She hovered in the doorway for a minute before plucking up the courage to go in. There were heavy paisley curtains and watercolours of Cornish landscapes on the walls, cursory attempts to make it feel less clinical. But it still had the same antiseptic smell of the hospital. And the four beds had rails and levers attached. Two of them were empty and Erin was pleased to see that Maggie was by the window.

The woman in the bed opposite Maggie was lying flat like a corpse, with her eyes shut and her mouth open. A lady sat in a chair next to her. She glared at Erin over the top of her glasses then went back to the book in her lap. Erin's boots squeaked as she walked across the room. She smiled an apology and tiptoed the rest of the way. There was a nurse with a clipboard bustling around Maggie. She felt her pulse and scribbled notes, and all the while she hummed. 'Greensleeves'; there had been a caretaker at school who did the same thing. Maybe there was a whole movement of people out there who hummed that insidious tune.

'I've come to see Maggie,' Erin said, but the words got caught at the back of her throat and came out all croaky.

'She's sleeping, luvvie. We gave her something to help her relax when she first came in as she was a bit distressed. So don't expect much,' the nurse said in a broad Cornish accent.

'Right, OK,' Erin said and looked around for somewhere to put the daffodils she had picked at the top of the hill.

'Shall I put those in a vase for you?' she said, and made her way round Maggie's bed to take the flowers. She had trainers on, but they seemed to make as much noise on the floor as Erin's boots. They should all wear slippers, Erin thought. She wanted to share that with Maggie and looked at her hopefully for some kind of acknowledgment, but there was nothing. The nurse hummed as she left the room and all the way down the corridor. Erin sat in the armchair next to Maggie's bed. There was so much she wanted to talk to her about, but she felt self-conscious with that woman there pretending to read her book.

'Maggie,' she whispered. 'Maggie.' Nothing. 'It's OK. You don't have to talk. You must be so tired. I just wanted to say I'm sorry. I know you wanted to stay at home until, well, you know. And I just want you to know that I really tried to make that happen.' Erin could feel the afternoon sun burning through the window and onto her back. It lit up the bump of Maggie's legs under the turquoise blanket. 'It was José, you see. He said you couldn't stay at home. And I know it was my fault that José came at all, and you didn't like him, or maybe you did. Well, anyway, I'm just so sorry, Maggie. Maybe you would have been better off if I hadn't moved in, if you hadn't even met me…'

'Hmph.' Maggie was clearing her throat. Erin leant forward and took her hand. It was cool, despite the suffocating warmth of the room.

'Maggie, can you hear me? It's Erin.' Her voice picked up in volume and pitch. Maggie croaked again but no words came out.

'It's OK, Maggie, you don't have to talk. Is it sore?' Maggie had gone still again and Erin thought she was losing her. She leant forward from her chair and words tumbled out of her mouth in panic. 'I found your letter to Lucas, and guess what, Maggie. I think I've found him!'

Maggie opened her eyes then; very slowly she peeled her lids back to reveal her smoky irises. Her pupils darted from side to side trying to focus. 'I'm here, Maggie,' Erin said.

'Lucas,' she whispered breathlessly.

'Yes! I've found his butterfly garden in Costa Rica, and another picture of him. I've sent him a message.'

'Can you take it to him… the letter?' Maggie spoke so quietly that Erin wasn't sure if she had heard her right.

'No, Maggie, he's in Costa Rica. I can post it to him.'

'Go.' It was more of a grunt than a word.

'Go where? To Costa Rica?'

'Ye…' she whispered.

'What? I can't go there. I haven't got any money, I… I… I've never been on a plane. Never been further than France. Costa Rica! That's on the other side of the world. I don't think I ca—'

Maggie looked like she was going to say something else then, but a gurgling rattle sounded instead. She reared her head up off the pillow. Her eyes were bursting with fear.

'Maggie? Are you OK? Maggie. Nurse!' Erin ran to the doorway 'Nurse. Can someone help? *Nurse.*' She was shouting now. The large nurse bustled out of a room down the corridor with her clipboard.

'What is it?' she called to Erin.

'It's Maggie, she can't breathe.' Erin looked back at Maggie on the bed. Her chest was arched and the same croaking, rasping noises were coming out of her open mouth. The nurse arrived in the room and made her way over to Maggie surprisingly quickly, then gathered Maggie up from behind and lifted her shoulders off the bed so that she was propped up on her enormous bosom. Maggie took a loud, rasping breath, clearing whatever was gurgling in her throat. A few more whining croaks and then her breathing calmed to a slower rattle.

'There, there,' the nurse said softly, 'you're OK, love.' She lowered Maggie's head back onto the pillow and she closed her eyes again.

'She's OK. Just had a little trouble breathing, that's all. It happens. You OK?' Erin looked down at her shaking hands. She collapsed into the chair by Maggie's bed.

'Yeah,' Erin said, trying to catch her own breath. 'It was scary, I thought she was going to…' The nurse looked at Erin from behind her glasses and her eyes smiled kindly.

'I know, luvvie.' She squeezed Erin's shoulder, and then delicately moved a strand of Maggie's hair that had fallen across her face and tucked it behind her cheek. Then she picked up Maggie's hand which was hanging off the bed and placed it by her side, checking her pulse as she did so. 'There's a kitchen down the hall if you want to make a cup of tea,' the nurse said as she moved around to the end of the bed and picked up the clipboard and scribbled something on it.

'Thanks, I might later.'

'OK, well, give us a shout if you need me.' She bustled out of the room. Erin shut her eyes and took a couple of long breaths in an attempt to calm her heart, which was hammering so hard and so fast in her chest.

'You alright?' A deep and growly voice came from the other side of the room.

'Yeah, thanks.' Erin swung round to look at the woman sitting next to the lady in the bed opposite. Her narrow eyes were glaring at Erin over the top of her glasses.

'You family?'

'Uh, no. Just a friend.'

'Really?' Her tone was mocking and made the hairs on the back of Erin's neck prickle.

'I live… well, I have been living with her for a while.'

'You don't have to explain yourself to me.' She pushed the glasses up her nose and went back to her book, signalling that the conversation was over. But Erin was unsettled by her, by what had just happened. Maybe she shouldn't be there. Maybe she just wasn't up to it. She crossed her arms tight over her chest and her fingers pinched at the damp patches under her armpits. She looked at Maggie, whose breathing was still punctuated by little gasps, not unlike when she had cried herself to sleep only a few weeks ago. She was so thin now; her cheeks were sunken hollows in the sides of her face. The skin around them fell back towards her ears with nothing to hold onto. Her collarbones protruded like rusty nails out of the top of her nightie. She looked so vulnerable, her whole body ravaged by this ferocious disease. 'I'm sorry, Maggie.' She stood up and her chair screeched back against the floor. 'I can't do this.' She strode across the room, her head down, trying not to run until she reached the corridor. And then she ran, bursting through the double doors at the end and straight into Fred coming through from the other side.

'Erin, are you OK? What's happened? Is it Maggie?'

'I'm sorry, Fred, I can't…' Erin pushed past Fred and nearly collided with a lady in an apron with a trolley of food. 'Sorry,' she mumbled and headed for the main door. But she couldn't open it; there was a big brass door handle which just rattled around in her hand.

'Here, Erin, let me do it.' Fred twisted the handle and the door swung open and Erin rushed out into the car park, where she stopped and shut her stinging eyes. Fred followed her and put his arm around her shoulders.

'There was this woman in there – she obviously didn't think I should be here. I don't think I can…' Erin said, leaning into his scratchy jumper. It smelt of sheep.

'It's OK, Erin. I'm sorry, I should have come with you. I wanted you to have some time on your own with Maggie,' Fred said. He led her across the car park and onto the soft, dewy lawn. There was a bench at the far end near the cliff edge. They sat on it and watched the flecks of white bubble up from the indigo sea. The waves crashed on the rocks below them and the seagulls squawked above their heads.

'Maggie asked me to go to Costa Rica to find Lucas. At least, I think she did,' Erin said eventually, her gaze fixed on the horizon. 'I think she wants me to show him the manuscript, and she's written him this letter. I think she needs to tell him something, Fred. But I panicked. I've never been abroad before – well, to France, but not anywhere far, not like her. I know she has travelled the world, and been to all these exotic places, but I haven't. No one in my family has, and I was scared and I said I couldn't, and then she couldn't breathe, and…' She wiped away the tears with the sleeve of her hoodie.

'Here.' Fred handed her a red and white spotted hankie from his pocket. 'You know, Maggie hasn't really been to all those places, Erin.'

'What do you mean?'

'She isn't who you think she is, the adventurous traveller, I mean.'

'But all the photos, all those things she has collected from her travels.' She looked at Fred, who shook his head and curled his fists into balls.

'I... I... think she wants to be that person so much,' he stuttered. 'But... but... she's scared, just like you.'

Erin thought about Maggie at their Mexican feast in her bedroom. How her mood had changed so definitively when she had asked her questions about her travels. It seemed so obvious now. Maggie had barely left the house for years, had got herself into a total spin about going into the village for tea. Of course she hadn't travelled the world. Otherwise she would have gone to find Lucas herself. 'It's a big ask, Erin,' Fred continued. 'I don't think Maggie can expect you to go all the way to Costa Rica. I'm sure we could just post the letter...'

'But she did ask,' Erin said quietly. She looked out at the cold expanse of water and tried to imagine a place on the other side of the world where the sea was warm and full of tropical fish. There would be monkeys and the jungle and white sand and blue morpho butterflies. The sun peeked through a gap in the clouds and the silvery sea turned to blue. 'Why did I say no, Fred?' She turned to face him on the bench. 'What's to keep me here?' A smile had crept onto her sticky face. 'I should go, shouldn't I?'

The creases at the corners of Fred's eyes wrinkled. 'I don't know,' he said, half laughing. 'It's your call.'

Erin knew what she had to do. Maggie was rescuing her, giving her an opportunity to get away. It was what she had wanted all along; she was just too blind to see it. 'I'm going to go to Costa Rica.' She stood up from the bench and planted her feet firmly on the freshly mown lawn. 'If Maggie thinks I can do this, then I can do it.'

Erin marched back across the lawn and her feet crunched across the driveway. She stomped the loose grass off her boots on the front step and went inside. As she strode over to Maggie's bed, Erin glanced briefly at the woman opposite. She was reading a paper now, and she raised her eyebrow at Erin over the top of her glasses. But Erin held her head high and pulled the turquoise synthetic curtain that hung from a track on the ceiling around Maggie's bed. They were alone.

Maggie looked more peaceful now; she wasn't holding her face so tight. Her breathing was slower and heavier. Erin was pleased but realised this meant she was deeper into her dreams than before and she might not be able to rouse her.

'Maggie,' she whispered at first, but then raised her voice. 'Maggie, it's Erin, I'm back.' Nothing. 'Maggie, I'm sorry I said I couldn't go, I have had a think and I will do it. I will go to Costa Rica, I will find Lucas, show him the manuscript and give him the letter.' She looked at Maggie hopefully, willing her to give her a sign, any sign that she had heard, but none came. She sat back in the chair. She would wait.

She had no idea how long she sat there waiting. She picked up an OK magazine from a table in a corner of the room and flicked through the pages, barely registering the pictures, let alone the words. And then her eyelids became heavy and her head jerked forward, then back. She succumbed to sleep, and her dreams were fitful – dreams of jungles and butterflies and monkeys and Maggie. When she woke it was dark, and Fred was reading the paper in the chair on the other side of the bed.

'Hello, sleepyhead,' he said.

'Hi,' Erin said, yawning. She shook the sleep out of her body and looked at Maggie, who was lying perfectly still. 'Has she?'

'No, she's been asleep all this time,' he said. 'Do you want a coffee?'

'Yeah, please.'

Fred heaved himself up from his chair and walked out of the cocoon of curtains. Erin heard him offer the woman visitor a coffee too, and she accepted with a much warmer tone in her voice.

'Maggie,' Erin whispered when Fred's footsteps ceased to squeak as he met the carpet of the corridor. 'Maggie, can you hear me?' Erin leant back into the chair again, disheartened. She shut her eyes and tried to take herself back to the jungle.

'Erin.' It was Maggie. Her voice was crumpled. Erin's eyes burst open and she leant forward and grabbed Maggie's hand.

'Maggie,' she said, 'you're awake.' Her eyes were open and staring in the direction of Erin but over the top of her head.

'Barely,' she whispered, and Erin could have almost cried with happiness: she had made a joke.

'I'm so sorry, Maggie, that I told you I wouldn't go to Costa Rica, it was just such a shock. But I've been thinking, dreaming, and of course I'll go. I can't wait.' She was delighted to realise that she actually meant it.

The corners of Maggie's mouth tilted and she smiled. 'There's money… for your ticket… in a box in my wardrobe.'

'OK,' Erin said, smiling. She had always wondered whether she might have a box of cash hidden somewhere.

'Tell him…' Maggie's fingers curled around Erin's hand. 'Tell him… I'm sorry,' she whispered.

'Of course I will, Maggie,' Erin said, the enormity of what she was taking on beginning to dawn on her. A tear trickled down her cheek and hung precariously from the bottom of her chin. Maggie closed her eyes again. Erin kept holding onto her hand, but more and more tears followed and she soon had to release it to grab the box of tissues so tactfully placed on the table next to the bed. She was blowing her nose noisily when Fred came back into the room. He saw Erin's face and his eyes immediately darted to Maggie, but her chest was still rising and falling with her breath.

'Erin?' he said.

'She woke up.' Erin smiled at him through the tears. 'I told her.'

Fred smiled back at her. 'I'm glad,' he said and sat down, taking hold of Maggie's other hand.

'I guess I need to go and sort it out, then. Shit, where do I even start? I need a ticket. I will have to tell my parents.' She breathed out a long breath through rounded lips.

'They'll understand. Go and have an adventure.'

CHAPTER NINETEEN

Beechwood Priory, 2nd April 1987

So, they've sent Lucas away, some boarding school up north where they keep you permanently cold and feed you a diet of gruel to toughen you up. He doesn't need toughening, he needs loving, and he needs to be told that it's OK. Apparently he went quietly and calmly. Richard said he didn't utter a word for the entire six-hour journey. I can imagine his brooding resignation as he stared out of the window. He used to do it as a child; it drove me mad, I wanted to shake a response out of him. But I have learnt to stay quiet here, too, otherwise they dope me up with drugs to silence me. I am having to swallow down the injustice and the anger that makes me want to scream and eats away at my insides, creating so much acid that everything I put in my mouth burns its way down into my stomach. But I've got to get better for Lucas's sake. I've got to get out of here and tell him I didn't mean it. The doctors are actually impressed with my recent progress; they say I am more motivated. Even my mum said I was beginning to get a sparkle back in my eye. I want to tell her that the only sparkle is a delight in deceiving them all.

*

Erin stepped off the plane and the wall of heat hit her. She felt instantly overdressed and uncomfortable in her leggings and trainers. Her feet had swelled and pinched at the sides of her shoes. She walked across the steaming tarmac into an airless grey room where the queue snaked around and around. Erin watched the families with young children and the elderly being ushered to the front. She thought of Maggie and wished they could have made this trip together. She joined the back of the queue and fanned herself with her passport. She turned on her phone and there was a message from Simon.

I've finished the painting. Thinking about delivering it in person. Her heart leapt then sank at the same time. For months she had longed for such a message. Had dreamt that he might chase after her, come and knock on her door in Cornwall rather than summon her to London. And now that moment had come and she was on the other side of the world.

I'm in Costa Rica! She hit send.

Yeah right.

No really I am.

Seriously?!!!! WTF??!! She laughed out loud and then covered her mouth and looked up. She was nearly at the front of the queue.

Gotta go. Will message you when I get back. She put her phone back in her bag, and couldn't contain the huge grin that had made its way across her face. She had the upper hand for the first time ever in their relationship, and it felt great.

'Bienvenida a Costa Rica,' the lady said behind the desk.

By the time she had collected her bag from the carousel and emerged into the Arrivals hall, the smile had faded somewhat and Erin was feeling giddy and overwhelmed by the heat, the smells, the shouting. There were throngs of people, five-deep, holding up boards with names.

'Taxi, ma'am.' A man with rotten teeth and a baseball cap approached her. 'Where you wanna go?' He tried to take Erin's rucksack off her shoulder. She snatched it back and hugged it to her chest.

'No, thanks.' She shouldn't be blowing her money on a taxi at this stage. She looked around for a sign for the bus station but everything was in Spanish. Three more drivers approached her.

'Taxi, ma'am.'

'Very cheap, very safe taxi, ma'am.'

'I am air-condition taxi.' That was tempting, but the driver had sweat dripping down his forehead and a creepy glint in his eye. She turned back to the first guy in the baseball cap.

'I am very cheap taxi, ma'am. Wherever you want to go – hostel, bus station, the beach. I am no rip-off martian.' His eyes glistened and his mouth widened to a gummy smile. Erin noticed that in among the brown teeth was one gold one that sparkled incongruously amid the rot.

Erin grinned. 'OK. How much to the bus station?' she asked.

'Fifteen dollar, ma'am. Good price. Let's go, ma'am!' He tried to take the rucksack but she was reluctant to let go. So they moved across the airport like a crab, holding a strap each.

Erin longed for her sunglasses as soon as they left the building and the intensity of the light hit her. But there was no stopping the taxi driver as they weaved their way through the crowds. The sun burned down on the top of her head as they crossed the car park and she felt quite breathless by the time they reached his battered grey Escort. There was no reprieve inside the car, just tobacco fumes and fetid air. The seat was covered in brightly coloured beads which pinched the skin on her arms. She wound the window down as they drove off and closed her eyes as the warm air blew across her face.

When she opened them again, they were speeding down a highway which was lined with palm trees and stalls selling fruit and vegetables, mobile phone cases and large knickers. Every time the traffic stopped a vendor stuck his head through the window and brandished his wares. After the fifth time of smiling politely and saying 'No thank you', Erin wound the window up.

'First time in Costa Rica?' The driver looked at her in his rear-view mirror.

'Yes.'

'Ah, beautiful country. Where you go on the bus?'

'Puerto Viejo de Talamanca,' she said slowly, labouring every alien sound.

'Caribbean side?' He sounded surprised, which alarmed Erin momentarily until he turned round and fixed her with another toothy grin. 'Pura Vida,' he said. She wasn't sure what it meant but it sounded good, so she nodded and smiled.

He dropped her at the bus station and waited while she bought her ticket for a mere twelve dollars. She was so delighted he hadn't kidnapped her or stolen her bags that she gave him another five dollars. At which he grinned so wide another sparkling tooth was revealed. He bade her farewell and pinched his index and pinky fingers together on both hands while saying 'Pura Vida' again.

'Pura Vida!' she replied. She had to put her bags down to replicate his hand thing. He laughed and left.

The bus station was a huge concrete hangar with no walls so the buses could drive straight into the bays. The roof was lined with a blue metal grid and strips lights that fizzed. Despite being open to the elements it was stifling, and there were so many people. No one seemed to be in a hurry to go anywhere; so unlike the bustling London stations where everyone moved with purpose. Here they sat around on piles of luggage.

The bus to Puerto Viejo wasn't for another two hours. Erin looked for somewhere to pass the time. There was a café selling greasy empanadas, but no spare tables. She bought herself a bottle of water and a warm Twix that was covered in white spots – a sure sign that it had melted and re-formed several times – and sat down on her rucksack on the pavement. The sun was setting now. It was half past five; that was half past midnight back home. She had been travelling for twenty-one hours and felt sick with exhaustion. For the umpteenth time that day she doubted her impetuous decision to come to the other side of the world on her own. She had always dreamt of going on an epic adventure, but in those dreams she had someone to share it with. Someone to help navigate the maps and read the foreign signs. Someone to help her make the decisions about whether to splash out on a taxi; someone's lap to lie on while she waited for the bus. She thought of her parents, and the anxious look on their faces as they dropped her at the airport. After the initial and inevitable row when she told them what she was doing, they had been unnervingly supportive. Her mum had helped her pack and twittered on about the last time they had done that when she went on a school geography trip ten years earlier. And her dad had thrust a large wad of US dollars into her bag and kept telling her not to eat the ice or talk to strangers. She hadn't told them that she hadn't actually made contact with Lucas, or that she wasn't exactly sure where she was going to find him. Three days had passed since she'd messaged The Butterfly Garden and she had sent another two messages a day since then, but there had been no replies. She had asked NatureLoverDale if he could tell her anything else about The Butterfly Garden and he gave her very vague directions about how to get there from the town, but it was three years ago when he went and he couldn't even be sure it was still open. And now she had come all this way. Her exhausted body fizzed with anxiety. What if she never found him?

A family took up camp next to her on the pavement. The grandmother was given an upturned plastic crate to sit on. She flapped a flannel back and forth over her shoulders; Erin wasn't sure whether she was batting away flies or the heat, but either way she was so close that every other swipe would catch Erin's shoulder. But she couldn't move any further away or she would be in the overflowing bin on the other side. Next to Grandma sat Mama with her enormous bosom bursting out of her too-small tank top. And on her lap was a pretty little girl, no older than two, with glittery studs in her ears. She was staring intently at Erin and her melted Twix. Erin offered her the end of her second stick and she took it slowly. She didn't smile and her brown eyes never left Erin. The mother scolded her and handed it back to Erin, but by now it had melted beyond recognition and lost its appeal. Erin put it on the top of the overflowing bin. The dad was on the other side of them. He shouted into a mobile phone. And while he was shouting he clipped the back of his son's head over and over again. The boy didn't seem to be doing anything wrong. He just stood there, his eyes also fixed on Erin.

By the time the bus finally pulled in half an hour later than it was supposed to, both the kids were asleep on top of the mother and Erin was struggling to keep her own eyes open. She climbed into the blissfully cool air-conditioned bus and found a seat halfway down. Then she rested her head against the condensation on the window and was unconscious before they had even pulled out of the terminal. It was a fitful sleep, her heavy head jolting her awake as it veered towards her chest or the window. Her dreams were permeated by bleating horns and Bruce Willis speaking in Spanish. *Die Hard* was on a loop on the TV at the front of the bus. They stopped at a petrol station in the middle of the night and everyone had to get off the bus. They piled into a harshly lit canteen serving rice and beans with egg. Sour-faced ladies spooned out the slop onto plates. The smell of the egg turned Erin's stomach. She bought a coffee and a bread roll that came out of the fridge and was hard.

It was 4 a.m. by the time they were allowed back on the bus, and Erin felt wired with coffee and anticipation. She put her headphones in and closed her eyes. When the dawn emerged a while later, the jungle had thinned and Erin caught her first glimpse of the Caribbean Sea through a gap in the silhouetted palm trees. The amber glow of the morning sun glistened on its silvery surface. She picked up the Lonely Planet guidebook and familiarised herself with the location of the Coco Loco guest house she had booked, and read up on the different eateries in Puerto Viejo. The best place for eggs, fresh juice, pizza, tacos. Her stomach began to rumble; she had barely eaten anything in the last twenty-four hours. On one page, there was a picture of a surfer walking into the sea at dawn, a dark figure against the cherry-streaked sky. Erin had grown up surfing; it was a rite of passage for a Cornish child. She had dreamt about surfing the tropical waves of the Caribbean Sea where you didn't have to wear a wetsuit, gloves and booties.

It was 5.30 a.m. when the bus pulled into Puerto Viejo. The shutters were still down, but dogs roamed the empty streets and there was the odd person walking or cycling past. The day obviously started early here. She found her rucksack, which had been thrown onto the dusty ground, and waved away the couple of taxi drivers who approached her and set off on foot. A couple of guys with dreadlocks down to their bums carrying surfboards crossed the road in front of her. And a motorbike whizzed past with an entire family on board. A toddler sat in front of the dad, who drove, and behind him was the mum with a baby in a sling on her back.

Coco Loco was less than a kilometre out of town but in the thick of the jungle. She had emailed ahead and was told that someone would be there to meet her, even at that hour in the morning, yet the reception was shut and padlocked. Erin hammered on the door and eventually a girl came out with tousled hair and eyes puffy with sleep. She took her to her bamboo hut across a wooden walkway over a carpet of parakeet-green moss which gave way to an ominous black mud that might suck you in and never let you out. Palm trees with leaves so big they looked like they had been fed a growing potion swamped the bungalow. Dragged down by their own weight, the ends were curled and crisping. The lush green trees reached high into the sky and were covered in hairy creepers. Tarzan-like ropes hung from the great heights of the canopy. And the noise, the intoxicating cacophony of rattling, buzzing, screeching and tweeting was like nothing Erin had ever heard before. Thankfully the girl was still there when a Neolithic roar reverberated around the jungle. She scanned the trees for the perpetrator and the girl laughed.

'It's a howler monkey,' she said as Erin clutched onto the handrail of the balcony.

'A monkey? A monkey makes that noise?'

'It's crazy, huh? They have an enlarged neck-bone, which is why they make such a loud noise. Apparently they used it as a sound effect in the *Jurassic Park* movies.' She had opened the door of the hut now and was turning on the fan and opening the shutters.

'It does sound like a dinosaur. How big is it?' Erin followed her into the room and took in its sparseness. A lone bed sat in the middle with a purple mosquito net and there was a shelf in the corner with a safe on top.

'I guess the adults are about the size of a dog,' the girl said unconvincingly, with no further explanation as to whether it was a chihuahua or a Newfoundland. 'There is a bathroom in here.' Erin followed her into the room at the back where a mosquito was buzzing around the mouldy shower.

'I suggest you put your stuff in the safe.' She pointed to it. 'And don't leave that window open if you go out. Breakfast doesn't start till seven thirty. Enjoy your stay.' And with that she walked out of the room and left Erin alone and feeling very far away from home. She lay down on the hard, damp mattress and fell into a deep sleep.

She woke with a start, disorientated. The rattle of the fan sounded like a creature scuttling across the floor. She jumped off the bed and her head swam with dizziness. She had to hold onto the bamboo strut of the wall to balance herself. She stood under the pitiful, cold trickle of water in the shower. The sand-coloured tiles on the walls and floor were chipped and flaking. A cluster of brown hair nestled in the plughole, preventing any of the water from draining out. She thought about Lucas; she knew all about his childhood, that he liked tiny animals, encyclopedias and *The Magic Roundabout*. And about the teenager who was blamed by his mother for the death of his sister, who smoked pot in the garage and was caught with a girl at the end of the garden. But nothing about the forty-six-year-old man living in Costa Rica. Erin shivered despite the searing heat. And was Maggie hoping that she might bring Lucas back with her? To be reunited with her son before she dies? This thought had popped into Erin's mind again and again since that day in the hospice. And with every appearance it took root further and further into her subconscious until she had become convinced that this was in fact Maggie's driving motive.

Erin turned off the shower and the mosquito landed on her shoulder and pinched at her skin. She slapped it, too late, and looked at the red smear of her own blood against her pale skin. 'Fuck,' she whispered, suddenly overwhelmed by the magnitude of her mission in this place so very far from home.

She stepped out of the shower and looked for the towel; there was none. She tiptoed across the room, drenching the floor in her wake and rifled through her rucksack to find a sarong to dry herself. Her stomach rumbled; it was a long time since she had nibbled at the concrete bread roll at the petrol station. She looked at her watch. It was 10 o'clock – she had been asleep for three and a half hours. She imagined breakfast was over, so she decided to head down to the beach in search of a café.

She could hear the roar of the sea from outside her hut. She followed the sound across the road and down a path littered with hairy coconuts. And then she saw it, cerulean and sparkling. The sand was so bright it burned her eyes. And it was insanely hot. She had taken her flip-flops off in the shade at the back of the beach, anticipating her barefoot skip down to the sea. But her feet were scorched instantly and she struggled to get them back on. The sun beat down on her head and back with a burning intensity she had never experienced before. She could feel her pale, freckled shoulders bubbling under its fire and wrapped her sarong around them.

The sea was amazingly warm, foam-like bubbles frothing at her feet as the waves pounded in. This ocean felt familiar yet so alien at the same time. The beach stretched for miles, a gracious arc of biscuit sand flanked by emerald forest and turquoise water. There were smatterings of people up and down the shore. Children were playing in the shallows. She could hear their squeals of delight and terror as they jumped over the waves. Further out, the surfers sat on their boards, looking to the horizon for their ride. She scanned up and down the beach for a café, but there was none. She remembered all she had read about Costa Rica's pioneering ecotourism; they were strict about buildings on the beach, and while her head and environmental conscience applauded this, her stomach was disappointed. She had imagined a beach bar playing Bob Marley tunes, serving banana lassi and pancakes.

She headed back to the road and found a stall with empanadas and cold bottles of Coke. Not exactly what she had in mind, but she was ravenous and the hot pastry wrapped around spicy minced meat and beans was so delicious she went back for a second. A man with a baseball cap and hair in a ponytail crossed the road in front of her and she wondered whether it could be Lucas. She found herself scouring his bare back for a birthmark, but couldn't see one.

A girl came up to the empanada stall and ordered one. She was still wet from the sea. Erin stared enviously at her gleaming caramel skin. She felt conspicuous with her sarong still wrapped around her luminously white shoulders. The girl caught her staring and she averted her eyes, embarrassed.

'You just arrived?' she asked, smiling. She had a lilting Spanish accent with an American twang.

'Is it that obvious?'

'Kinda! Where are you staying?'

'Coco Loco.' The girl's wet brown hair hung down to her waist. She had a tattooed lily around the bottom of her back. It curled its way round to her stomach.

'Right. You surf?'

'A bit back home, but not for a while.'

'I help out at Mickey's, just across the road there.' She pointed to the ramshackle pile of surfboards propped up against the palm trees. Mickey, presumably, was asleep with his feet up on a pile of boogie boards. 'Swing by if you wanna rent a board.' She headed back towards him.

'Wait,' Erin called after her and ran across the road. 'Do you know a butterfly farm around here?' she asked. She breathed in the cloud of weed that was wafting up from the semi-conscious Mickey.

'Mickey.' The girl kicked the boards out from under his feet. 'This is, er…' She looked to Erin.

'Erin.'

'Right. Erin was asking about a butterfly farm. Isn't there one out at Punta Uva?'

Mickey opened one eye to glance at Erin and then shut it again. 'Yeah, man, The Butterfly Garden.'

'That's it!' Erin couldn't believe it was that easy. 'Do you know how I get there? How far is it?' Erin waited for Mickey to respond, but he was done. She looked to the girl who was sitting on a fallen branch eating her empanada.

'About two Ks that way.' She pointed down the road. 'You can hire a bike in town.'

'Great, thanks. And I might take you up on that board later,' Erin said, backing away.

'Sure, whatever.'

*

Erin made her way into Puerto Viejo, which had woken up considerably since she was there earlier that morning. Stalls selling jewellery, brightly coloured sarongs and t-shirts were lined up along the back of the beach. Every other building was a café with tables spilling out onto the dusty street or a shop selling touristy trinkets. Smells of barbecued meat and exotic fruit engulfed her as she went in search of the bike hire shop. Lola was a larger-than-life Israeli who wore layers of ethnic skirts and waistcoats, with long feather earrings and piercings in her nose, eyebrow, lip and cheek. She was a one-stop shop offering canopy tours, horse riding, internet access, henna tattoos, massage, eyebrow threading and bicycle hire. She pushed them all on Erin who left with some joss sticks, a pipe for Derek, a bottle of overpriced factor fifty sunblock and an orange bike. She headed off in the direction of Punta Uva and The Butterfly Garden.

CHAPTER TWENTY

Train heading north, 16th May 1987

I'm out! Only on day release – I still have to go back and punch in like a criminal on remand. But they have let me out to visit Lucas. I am on a train watching the world that has carried on turning without me in it for these past few months. The missing front teeth of the little girl sitting opposite me that must have fallen out while I have been living in that other world of shiny floors and brightly lit corridors. The tree which must have been bare when the ambulance carried me into hospital covered in my own vomit and faeces, but which now has pert green buds forming on its brittle branches. My nerves are on edge and my senses heightened. Every time the tannoy announces its arrival at a station I flinch as if a lion has roared behind me. I nibble at the corner of a croissant that I have dreamt about for months but it sticks in my throat and curdles in my stomach. My letters have come back unopened, so he might refuse to see me. If I could just touch him, just bring him into my chest like I used to when he was a child. He never could stay cross for long; I would mimic his grumpy face and the downturned corners of his mouth would slowly lift to a smile. Then we would belly-laugh. Sometimes we lay on the floor and took it in turns to lie on each other's stomachs and see how long we could keep a straight face while the other one laughed and their stomach wobbled the head of the other. If only today was about laughing. If only

*today wasn't about the gritty truth from which we have been
hiding for way too long.*

*

The Butterfly Garden wasn't as easy to find as she'd hoped, and
Erin spent a couple of very hot and sweaty hours riding up and
down the road between Puerto Viejo and Punta Uva. She turned
down numerous tracks, as directed by Mickey; she swore he had
said to turn left off the main road, but all the ones on the south
side eventually led to the sea, so she presumed it must be on the
other side of the road. There were several guest houses there, not
dissimilar to Coco Loco and a much plusher one with a pool and
swanky-looking huts. One of the tracks led to a sloth sanctuary,
but it was closed, so she couldn't ask for help, and a couple of the
roads meandered their way deep into the rainforest and eventually
petered out as the jungle became impenetrable.

When she ran out of water she decided to give up for the day.
Fed up and too exhausted to ride in a straight line, she was slaloming across the road with heavy legs when she spotted a rickety sign,
half hidden by a giant palm leaf on the side of the road. THE
BUTTERFLY GARDEN, it read, each letter on the splintered
plank of wood painted a different colour, and in the corner a big
blue butterfly. This was it. She swallowed down the lump in her
dry throat and turned onto the dusty track beyond the sign. Half
a mile or so later she found herself in a clearing in the jungle where
a dilapidated truck was parked. Erin propped her bike against
a tree and looked around. She flinched at a rustling in a bush
behind her and turned around to see a brown mole-like creature
with longer legs scamper across the clearing. It had a snubbed,
elongated nose, like an anteater, which clung to the forest floor as
he scuttled around. It didn't appear to be remotely interested in
Erin, so she followed it round the back of the truck where there
was a path. There were no more signs and not another soul to be

seen. She had anticipated a thriving tourist attraction with tickets and hordes of travellers. Erin checked the manuscript was in her bag, despite the fact that she could feel the plastic edges of the binder digging into her back, and set off down the path. It was lined with bright red and orange flowers with pink pointy stamens. The petals had a glossy coating that make them look almost plastic. She remembered seeing something similar through the window of an office building in London. It was a flower arrangement on a reception desk which had caught her attention because its hard lines were so harsh, ugly even. Yet here in their natural habitat the flowers made perfect sense.

At the end of the path was a concrete tunnel that led towards a netted dome. The tunnel was eerily dark despite a couple of tiny windows with metal bars. It was cool, damp and claustrophobic. She picked up her pace and tried not to think about the fact that no one in the world knew where she was right now. The metal door at the end was so heavy she had to lean on it with her shoulder and it whined with resistance. But once open, she was enveloped in a warm light and the sweet aroma of flowers and fresh fruit. A giant blue butterfly flew at her face. The door slammed behind her.

The dome was made up of a series of metal arches with a dark netting shrouded over the top. The sun beamed down through the holes in the netting and the silhouette of the jungle canopy loomed above it. Inside the dome the trees were smaller, tamer but no less vibrant. There were palms, ferns and flowers of fuchsia, lapis and gold. And through them meandered a path of emerald-green moss. A crumbling stone fountain stood in the middle, a cherub holding a vase on her shoulder that was empty and dry. One of her arms was missing and a vine wove its way around her middle and up the back of her neck, its tendrils collapsing around her face. Rickety wooden tables were dotted throughout the plants. Each table had a plate on it with halved oranges and flower heads. And there were butterflies everywhere. They clung to the netted walls and ceiling. They hovered on the fresh fruit spoiling in the heat and on the petals of the flowers. Their wings of blue, black and orange fluttered through the air. Within seconds they attached themselves to Erin's shoulders, her hair, her rucksack. She thought of José and the hundreds of butterflies in the forest in Mexico, and of Maggie – how she would love this!

There were more blue morphos than any other kind of butterfly. They were so much bigger than Erin had imagined. When they were still, their closed wings were a tawny mocha, with inky black eyes and white fringing, but the minute they took flight the electric blue of their wings was revealed, almost iridescent as they sparkled in the dappled sunlight. They were like the peacock and peahen all in one body.

A smile crept across Erin's face as she took in the magic of this ramshackle place. She walked down the narrow brick path towards one of the feeding tables and crouched to examine the extraordinarily intricate markings of the butterflies.

'Their wings aren't actually blue, you know.' It was a male voice that startled her. She jumped up and knocked the table over with her rucksack in the process.

'Oh shit, sorry, I – I didn't see you there.' She picked up the hollowed-out oranges and put them back on the plate, they were covered in dust and their sticky residue clung to her fingers.

'It's an illusion. The way the sun shines on them makes them look blue. One of nature's own magic tricks.' He was next to her now and picking up the flowers and putting them back on the plates next to the oranges. She tried to help but her hands were shaking. She rubbed them on her shorts. He was so close to her she could hear his laboured breathing, smell his smell – it was musty, of tobacco and earth. She knew it, that fact about the wings, but her heart was thumping too hard in her chest to find the words to tell him. 'How did you get in here? Did you buy a ticket?' he asked.

Erin dared to look up at him. 'Um, no, there wasn't anywhere,' she said. He was dressed in a faded grey vest and khaki shorts, his hair long under the red baseball cap. Tanned, tattooed shoulders were crumpled with years of sunning. He had a beard that was starting to go grey and piercing blue eyes. Maggie's eyes.

He seemed to be unnerved by her stare and so she looked to the ground while he walked away with one of the oranges caked in mud and threw it in a bin in the corner of the dome. 'Well, you were supposed to buy a ticket at the sloth sanctuary down the road,' he said, unloading some leaves from a wheelbarrow in a corner of the dome.

'But the sloth sanctuary is shut, I went there.'

'It's only open in the mornings.'

'Right. How… how would I know that, to get a ticket there, I mean?' she asked.

'It says so on the sign. You can go and get one tomorrow,' he said, and with that he wheeled the empty barrow out of the heavy green door and into the tunnel.

She stood up on wobbly legs and shook them out. 'Wait,' she called after him, and picked up her rucksack which was covered with a layer of orange dust from the floor. He hadn't waited, and was out in the forest by the time she emerged from the tunnel.

'Wait,' she called again, running after him. 'It's Lucas, isn't it?'

He stopped with his wheelbarrow and looked at her then, fixing her with his cloudy glare.

'Yeah, how do you know my name?'

Erin moved towards him. He was not on the path so she trod tentatively in her flip-flops. She tried to avoid a stream of ants and in doing so tripped over a gnarled branch on the forest floor.

'The guys at the surf place on the beach told me.'

'You're a surfer, are you?' He was gathering leaves off the forest floor and loading them into his wheelbarrow.

'Well, I do a bit back home, but I'm pretty rubbish really. I just arrived here in Costa Rica.'

'And what brings you to Puerto Viejo? Most people go to the west coast. Especially surfers. We've got quite a bad rep over here for the surf. Suits me. Keeps the hordes away.'

'I, I didn't know that.' Erin looked down at her feet. Her little toe throbbed where she had stubbed it on the branch and she could feel the ants biting her feet.

'You're not a surfer, and you don't look like you're a rainforest enthusiast.' She was hopping up and down now trying to flick the ants off. 'So, what brings you here?'

'Uh, well, actually… you do.'

He stopped shovelling and looked up at her. 'Sorry, do I know you?'

'Not exactly, no. I'm here about your mum.'

He stopped what he was doing and looked at her. 'What?'

'Your mum. Maggie Muir. She sent me.'

He smiled and shook his head and snapped a branch over his knee.

'No, you must have got it wrong. I haven't seen my mother for a very long time.'

'Yes, I know. And, well, I'm really sorry to have to tell you this but, well… she's dying. And… she asked me to find you.' Lucas stood upright and looked Erin directly in the eye. Then he laughed. A deep belly laugh, with his head thrown back and his mouth open, revealing his metal fillings. It startled Erin; the forest too. Birds screeched and flapped through the trees, making them rattle. 'That is typical,' he said, then picked up the wheelbarrow and wheeled it past Erin and over to another part of the forest, where he began to pick up more wood from the forest floor at a more manic speed than before. Erin followed. He muttered and cursed under his breath as he snapped sticks over his knee and threw them in the wheelbarrow. 'Unbelievable, unbe-fucking-lievable.'

'I tried to send you a message, on the website. Several, in fact, before I came.'

'I don't really check that very often. Sorry, how did you say you knew my mum?'

'I didn't, but I work for her. I'm helping her write her book.' He shook his head in disbelief.

'And how, how did you find me?'

'Someone sent your mum a picture of you. She thinks it might have been her sister.'

'Auntie Sara?'

'Yeah, and I trawled the internet and eventually found that same picture on a blog, and the blogger told me where it was from and…' Lucas shook his head and sighed heavily. 'Look, I know you haven't seen each other for a while.'

'A while? I don't know how well you know my deluded mother, or what lies she has fed you, Ellen.'

'Erin.'

'Right, whatever. But we haven't had any contact for thirty years.'

'Yes, I know. And that's why she sent me.'

'She *sent* you? From England?' He stopped what he was doing briefly to shake his head with disbelief. 'Wow, she doesn't change. She always was a manipulative bitch.' He was quite red in the face now, and sweat was dripping off his forehead as he bent down to pick up another branch.

'What? No! She hasn't manipulated me. She's got a brain tumour. Only weeks, maybe days to live. She asked me to help, and I… I wanted to help her.'

'She really has got to you.'

'What? No, she hasn't. She's my friend.'

'Yeah, right.' He picked up another branch, broke it and threw it into the wheelbarrow, which toppled over under the weight. He sighed and pulled the barrow back up.

'Look, I don't know what she was like thirty years ago. But right now she is just a lady in a hospital bed who can barely breathe. And this was her last wish. She wanted me to give you something.' Erin pulled her rucksack off her shoulder and started to fiddle with the clasp, but her hands were shaking and she couldn't get a grip on it.

'I don't want to know,' Lucas said. 'I didn't want to know thirty-five years ago, and I certainly don't want to know now.'

'But, could you just—'

'No, I couldn't *just* anything, Erin. You have no idea what this is all about, and if you did, you wouldn't be here. So why don't you just fuck off back to good old Blighty and leave me alone?' He wheeled the overloaded wheelbarrow past Erin and back onto the path towards the dome. She followed him.

'But don't you want to know what she says? Aren't you curious about what happened to her?' Erin could hear her words becoming increasingly screechy, but she didn't care. She had travelled across the world for this meeting, and she was not going to go home without fighting Maggie's cause. Lucas stopped pushing the wheelbarrow and turned around to face her. Sweat was beading down his cheek and a vein above his eye was throbbing. He glared at Erin, breathing heavily, and pointed a finger at her.

'No, no, I don't want to know. I couldn't give a shit what happened to her. And do you know why I couldn't give a shit? It's because she couldn't give a shit what happened to me. She left me – I was sixteen, *sixteen*! – when she left me in that hellhole. So no, she gave up the right to be any part of my life back in 1987. And I have no desire whatsoever to know what happened to her.' He turned away then and stormed back down the tunnel and into the dome, slamming the heavy green door. Its chime reverberated around the forest.

Erin stood on the path for a minute, gathering her thoughts. She was tempted to go back to her bike and get the hell out of there. But she hadn't given him the manuscript and letter, and she had come all this way. What would she tell Maggie? Besides, she really wanted to know what had happened to Skye. Erin walked down the tunnel and pushed open the creaking green door. She crept through the small gap. Lucas was at the other end of the dome. He had tipped the wood into a pile and was distributing the leaves around the edges of the dome with a broom.

Erin walked down the twisted path; an orange butterfly with tiger stripes landed on her shoulder and clung onto her bra strap. Lucas carried on with his work, not looking up.

'You're still here?'

'Yeah.'

Erin wrestled with the clasp on her rucksack and pulled the manuscript of the diary out of her bag along with the letter. 'She asked me to tell you that she's sorry,' Erin began quietly. 'So very, very sorry. The book I am helping her with, well, it's her story, and so it's your story too. And she obviously wants you to read it. She has written you a letter as well. I'm going to leave it here.' She placed the manuscript and the letter down on the mossy brick path. 'It's up to you whether you read it, but I made a promise to Maggie and I would never forgive myself if I didn't at least try to keep it.' He didn't look up, just carried on distributing leaves. He stopped to rub the sweat off his forehead with his t-shirt. 'OK, well, I'm going to go now.' She buckled up the straps on her bag and walked back to the metal door. She paused and looked back at him; he had stopped sweeping and was looking at the manuscript and letter, but when he saw her watching him he turned his back on her and picked up the wheelbarrow again. So she opened the door and made her way through the tunnel, all the way along the path back to the clearing. She got on her bike and pedalled fast down the track and then onto the road. And as she picked up speed, she screamed into the wind. 'Fuck,' she yelled, not noticing a young boy walking down the other side of the road. He giggled into his hand.

Erin called Fred when she got back to her hut. Maggie had had another seizure that morning, but she was stable. She was asleep most of the time now, dosed up on morphine. She told Fred about her meeting with Lucas and he didn't seem surprised. She asked him not to tell Maggie and he agreed she didn't need to know right now. But what was she going to do? Would she have to tell Maggie that Lucas didn't want anything to do with her? Maybe she could just make up some elaborate tale about how he forgave her, but couldn't leave. Or she could just pretend she'd never found him. She imagined delivering any one of these options to Maggie in her bed in the hospice, and felt sick with sadness.

CHAPTER TWENTY-ONE

Beechwood Priory, 17th May 1987

Lucas wouldn't see me. I think I caught a glimpse of him at an upstairs window as I got back into my taxi, but he hid behind the curtain as soon as I looked up. It was a dinosaur of a teacher who came to tell me that he wasn't coming down. He had dark, bushy eyebrows and peered at me over the top of his glasses with small bloodshot eyes. He wore a gown like something out of a movie and it billowed under his arms as he strode into the room. He told me not to bother coming again. That Lucas has made it perfectly clear that he won't change his mind. He wants nothing to do with me, ever. He seemed to be enjoying the drama of it, with his booming voice slowly pronouncing every syllable as if he might be performing a soliloquy to a darkened audience. He ushered me out of the room, holding onto my arm as if I was an old lady. And then I was on the doorstep and the cold wind whipped around my neck and pinched at my cheeks. It was late by the time I got back to the hospital and one of the nurses undressed me like a child. Then she popped a sleeping pill into my open mouth and left me to my misery. I woke up this morning groggy and subdued. Richard visited and couldn't hide his satisfaction at the outcome of my wasted trip. He had warned me not to go, of course. It suddenly dawned on me that Richard might have called ahead, told them not to let me see Lucas. He denied it,

*of course, mocked my deluded imagination, but his blinking
gave it away. He has never been very good at lying.*

*

The howler monkeys woke Erin at dawn the next morning. Their
roar was so loud she assumed there must be a whole tribe on her
balcony. Yet when she tiptoed out there were none to be seen. But
the sweet-smelling fruit in the trees and the fizzing and screeching
of the waking jungle were intoxicating. She wanted to breathe it
all in and record it in her mind forever. She couldn't possibly go
back to sleep, so she put on her bikini and crossed the road to
the beach. The sun was just coming up and the sea was bathed
in a misty light. There was one surfer out beyond the break, his
silhouette dark against the orange sky. Erin ran into the sea and
dived under a wave. She came up and looked back at the long
swathe of pearly sand, interrupted only by abandoned driftwood
and coconuts. And beyond it the rainforest encroached with a
furious charge, as if halted in its tracks by the sight of the vast
ocean. Its tangled mass of foliage looked dense and uninhabitable,
yet she knew her hut was not far away.

Breakfast at Coco Loco was a feast of mango, guava, pineapple
and tiny bananas that were sweet and crunchy, followed by
pancakes and strong, bitter coffee. Afterwards she went to find
Mickey and hired a surfboard. She headed to a spot further down
the beach which he recommended for less experienced surfers. As
she was propping her bike up against a gnarled tree trunk at the
back of the beach, a local kid shouted at her. He called her over
and pointed at a tree above.

'Slot,' he said as she approached. 'Two-toe slot.'

Erin scanned the trees and her gaze settled on a dark shadowy
lump that could have been a cluster of coconuts or a nest. She
walked around to the other side of the tree and there she saw its
face. With eyes set apart, almost on each side of its head. They were

half closed, with dark patches around them which dipped down to where ears should be. But there weren't any. Its mouth peaked at the corners as if smiling. And the boy was right: it was clinging onto the tree with big furry paws and two scissor-hand claws. It peeled its head up from its arm and turned in slow motion to balance it on the arm on the other side of the branch. She willed it to move again or to come down, but it settled into that pose and didn't look like it was going to move for a while.

'Thank you,' she beamed at the boy, who was now sucking at a mango. The juice dribbled down his chin and hands.

She spent the whole morning in the sea. Surfing was almost like riding a bike, and her basic muscle memory from surf school as a child on the northern beaches of Cornwall came back to her. But her adult body was clumsier, and her mind more tinged with fear. Nevertheless, within an hour she was catching some of the smaller waves, and by the end of the second hour she was actually riding them onto the beach. The warm water meant that she lasted a lot longer than she would have back home. When every muscle in her arms and shoulders ached, and the rash from the board across her belly became too much to bear, she retreated to the back of the beach and dozed under the coconut palms.

And that was how she spent the next couple of days. Riding her bike out to the different isolated beaches along that stretch of the Caribbean coast. They were all different. Some were long and windswept, with big surf, and others were more protected coves where the jungle came right down to the calmer turquoise waters and she swam with the brightly coloured fish she had read about in storybooks as a little girl. Every evening she would call Fred and was heartened by the fact that Maggie hadn't got any worse. She was holding on in there. Erin couldn't help but wonder whether she was keeping her alive with false hope.

After she had recovered from the emotional meeting in The Butterfly Garden, she began to appreciate how much of a shock her arrival must have been for Lucas. He hadn't read any of her messages, and so had no warning before she rocked up and told him his mum was dying and dredged up all of those traumatic memories. Maybe it wasn't so surprising that he had reacted as he did. She hoped that given time to reflect he would calm down, maybe even read the manuscript. She was always on the lookout for him, her heart in her stomach every time she spotted a guy in a cap. She constantly scanned the beach, the surf, the restaurants.

After a couple of days without spotting him, she figured he probably kept to himself and rarely ventured to the beach or the few cafés she had discovered, and her heart settled into a more comfortable rhythm. Las Chiquitas was her favourite. It was a little shack with a cluster of wooden tables painted in rainbow stripes and a sandy floor which served delicious fish tacos that reminded her of José. They were doused in avocado and a tomato salsa with heaps of coriander and lime. And the guy who ran it was gorgeous. He had a shaved head and intensely green eyes. A tattoo of a serpent ran across the tops of his shoulder blades, and like everyone else he was nut brown. He had a girlfriend, of course, who was equally beautiful, and a little boy with an afro and those same eyes. He had a surfboard that was bigger than him. Erin had watched it bobbing down the beach towards the water that first day. He was so small that when he was on the other side of the board it seemed to move of its own accord.

It was four days after her first encounter with Lucas that Erin saw him again. She had just left the beach as the sun was disappearing into the sea and the sky was streaked with pink. Her skin was crispy with salt and her face tingled and felt tight from the sun. She headed to Las Chiquitas and ordered a beer and some nachos at the bar. The little boy was baiting a puppy on the floor with a piece of rope. Erin knelt down to stroke the dog, which rolled onto its back and wrapped its paws around her arms.

'An animal lover as well as an envoy for dying old ladies. Is there no end to your charms?'

'Oh, hi.' She looked up at Lucas and then went back to the puppy. He had caught her unawares, and she wasn't sure how to react.

'I'm sorry, Erin, I know I was out of order the other day.' He crouched down next to her and the puppy turned its attention to him and nibbled his toes. 'Can we start again, please?'

'I guess. Look, I'm sorry. I shouldn't have just arrived like that, it must have been a shock.'

'Just slightly. Come on, I'll buy you a beer.'

'Thanks, but I've already got one.' She stood up and retrieved her bottle off the bar.

'Then I'll buy you the next one. Hey, Chaz, will you bring us a couple of Imperials?' he shouted to the barman, then looked over at Erin and the corners of his mouth lifted into a wry smile. 'And two tequila shots.' Erin felt her stomach grumble and willed her nachos to come before the shots.

He walked over to one of the stripy tables and sat down and Erin followed. She sat opposite him and leant back in her chair. She took a big gulp of beer to calm her thumping heart. She had to tread carefully this time.

'I wasn't sure if I'd see you again,' she said.

'I wasn't sure you'd still be here.' He took a cigarette out of the pack and lit it and inhaled deeply.

'It took me two days to get here. I wasn't just going to turn around and go home again.'

'Fair enough.' Lucas took his baseball cap off to reveal an oily slick of hair plastered to his scalp. He smoothed it down with his hand and tightened his ponytail before placing the cap back on his head.

'So, what do you make of Costa Rica? Pura Vida?' he said to Erin, the cigarette hanging out of the side of his mouth. He clasped his index fingers and thumbs together on both hands, just as the taxi man had done on that first day.

'What does that even mean?'

'Literally it means "Pure Life". But it's more than that. I guess it's a mentality here.' He was leaning back in his chair trying to look relaxed, but his eyes kept flitting over to the bar.

'And is it?'

'What?'

'Pura Vida, here? Your life?'

'It's had its moments, but give me this over the cold and grey of England any day.'

'It's not grey where I live, actually. It is lush and green. And the sea is bright blue just like here.'

'You live by the sea?'

'Yeah, in Cornwall, near Mag… your mum.'

Chaz arrived at their table carrying a tray with the two tequila shots on it and a couple of beers. Erin hated tequila. She had been horribly sick on it once and had never been able to stomach it since. There wasn't even any salt and lemon to wash it down with. Lucas pushed one of the shots across the table towards Erin, and he held his up.

'Pura Vida,' he said and downed it.

'Pura Vida,' she said, and did the same. The liquor caught at the back of her throat and brought tears to her eyes. She tried not to cough. Lucas barely flinched and moved on to his beer. He seemed calmer now, with the bottle in his hand.

'Tell me about it – where you live, I mean,' he said.

'You really wanna know?' Erin twisted the beer bottle around between her fingers and kept her eyes down. He laid his arms on the table and leant in towards her, and she could smell the beer and cigarettes on his breath. 'Come on,' he said more softly. 'Tell me about it. I want to know where you live. Where she lives.'

Erin looked up at him. His expression had softened. He had the same wrinkles at the sides of his eyes as Maggie. 'It's a small fishing village on a peninsula on the south coast of Cornwall. There is a pub and one shop, a tea room and a gallery. We live just outside the village, on a farm.' He didn't say anything so she continued. 'Maggie lives on the other side of the village on the headland. Her house has the most amazing views across the bay. Her garden runs down to the cliff edge. She has a bench where she likes to sit and meditate.'

'Meditate?' Lucas grunted and took a swig of beer. 'My mother, are you sure?'

Erin shot him a warning glance. 'You wanted to start again.'

'I'm sorry, but really? My mum meditates?'

'Yeah, she does it every day. Well, not now, but until only a few weeks ago. She says it saved her.'

'What?' Lucas rolled his eyes.

'She is really quite spiritual, your mum.'

'Nah, you must have the wrong person.'

'No really, she is! It freaked me out at first. I thought she was a bit witchy, but as I got to know her better, I began to understand her way of thinking. She says that there are some things in life that are totally out of our control. And she has obviously experienced more than her fair share of hardship.' Lucas took another swig of his beer and looked away. 'She says meditation has helped her to calm her mind, which she never had any control over before. She is quite kooky about what she puts into her body too. She even got me drinking nettle tea!' Erin took a sip of her beer and looked down and fiddled with her bracelets. 'I guess it's ironic, really, when you think of how badly it is failing her now, her body I mean.' He didn't answer and she was worried she had gone too far, said too much.

'Her body certainly wasn't a temple when I knew her!' Lucas said eventually.

'Yeah, I gathered that. So, what was she like back then?'

'Well, you've read the manuscript.'

'So, you read it too?'

'Yeah.'

'And do you still hate her?'

He shrugged his shoulders and looked down. The silence lingered around them. Erin shifted in her seat, but Lucas was still.

'What was she like as a mum, before… all that?'

He flicked at the edges of the label on the bottle and Erin worried that she had lost him. 'Well, she was a rubbish cook,' he said finally. 'And totally chaotic. The house was always a tip.'

'I can imagine that!'

'She was faddish, she would suddenly get into some new craze. Like making jewellery or bottling elderflower cordial, and she would do it all the time. Covering the house in tiny gems or flower heads, and then she would abandon it and move on to the next thing. That was when she was on an up. But then she would go down. She would take to her bed for days on end and the house would reach whole new levels of carnage. Dad would finally realise no one else was going to clear it up so he would do it, but it pissed him off. She was erratic. Her moods would flip really suddenly. One minute she was smothering you with so much love you could hardly breathe, and then she'd just get morose or angry. You never really knew where you were with her. She just needed a bit of Pura Vida!' He gulped down the remaining dregs of his beer. 'Hey, Chaz, another beer, or…' He looked at Erin, who hadn't even started her second, 'Yeah, just one more, mate.'

'OK, mate,' Chaz shouted from behind the bar.

'Wow, she's nothing like that now.'

'Really? People don't change.'

'Do you believe that? Are you still the same boy that came here all those years ago?'

'What do you know about that?' His head snapped round quickly, a fire in his eyes that hadn't been there before.

'Nothing really, well, apart from what's in the book. She hasn't talked to me about any of it.'

Lucas sat back in the chair and his eyes flitted around the bar. He bit down on his lip, making it go red.

'So, what's your mum like?' he said eventually.

'My mum? Well, I guess she is pretty different to Maggie. In fact, you could almost say she's the opposite of Maggie. They met once, and they didn't exactly hit it off.'

'Why?'

'Maggie got pissed. Mum didn't approve.'

'Now that sounds more like the Maggie I knew. Is she a bit of a prude, then, your mum?'

'Not exactly. She just never really shows any emotion.' Erin picked a shard of wax off the side of the candle and broke it up into tiny pieces with her thumbnail. She looked up at Lucas, who was staring at her intently.

'They all fuck us up one way or another.' He downed the rest of his beer.

'Maybe.'

'So, tell me, what have you been doing the last couple of days?'

She was relieved at the change in conversation. 'I've just been checking out all the different beaches. I rented a board off Mickey and have been trying to surf.'

'Great! How was it?'

'Well, I'm pretty crap, and my shoulders hurt like hell. But I really love it.'

'You'll never want to leave.'

Chaz arrived at the table with her plate of nachos. 'Here we go, guys,' he said, putting them down.

'Thank God, I'm starving,' Erin said. 'Do you want some?'

'No thanks.'

She carried on talking as she ate. 'I used to surf with my dad up at the northern beaches – there isn't any surf on the south coast, you see. But it was always cold and I was so skinny I really felt it. But here, here you can stay in the water for hours. It's amazing. Do you surf?' The nacho cracked in her hand and everything dribbled down her wrist. There wasn't a napkin, so she licked the side of her hand.

'Of course. You couldn't live here and not surf, you'd be a laughing stock! How the hell do you stay so skinny when you eat like that?' Lucas was smiling at her.

'I didn't have lunch,' Erin said, wiping the sour cream from the corner of her mouth on her sarong.

'Mum was like you, she could just eat and eat and never get fat. Nervous energy, she called it.'

'Yeah. Although she's too skinny now.' She looked down at the plate of demolished nachos and pushed it away. She suddenly felt full and sick.

'Do you want to get out of here?' Lucas said.

'What do you mean?'

'There's a party at the other end of the beach tonight, nothing fancy. Just some old friends chilling around a fire, some music.'

'I don't know.'

'Come on, it'll be fun.'

'Are you going to shout at me again?'

'I promise I won't shout, and there will be other people there so you won't be alone with me, if that's what you're worried about.' She felt her cheeks redden as that was exactly what she had been thinking. She delved under the table for her bag to hide her blushing.

'OK,' she said as she came up, and flung her bag over her shoulder. 'My bike's just outside.'

'Leave it here, we can take mine.' Chaz had arrived at their table and was clearing the plate and beer bottles. 'Put it all on my tab, mate, will you.'

'Alright, mate. Might be nice if you pay the tab sometime soon, hey?' Chaz was smiling as he cleared the table, but Erin could sense an edge to his words.

'Will do, Chaz. Soon, soon.'

CHAPTER TWENTY-TWO

Beechwood Priory, 18th June 1987

They are discharging me next week, despite my relapse after my trip up north. I pulled myself together after a few days and Dr Dansk said he was impressed with the way I dealt with the rejection. That it showed how far I'd come. How much better I was. I want to tell him that I am still broken inside, that I still feel so utterly weighed down by this thick cloud of misery that I can't imagine ever seeing the light again. But I don't; I tell him that I am trying to look forward, not back. And that I have decided to move to Cornwall. I told Richard too and he laughed, and said I hated that holiday we had there. That I was miserable and cold, that I found the sea oppressive, the sand infuriating, the cider flat. But I don't remember it like that. It's true the weather was terrible, but it didn't matter. We went rock-pooling, and crabbing off the pier. We ate Cornish pasties out of brown paper bags on the beach for lunch and beans on toast in the caravan for supper. And every day Lucas and Richard would jump off the jetty at high tide. You could see the rocks that clung to its wall at low tide and it was quite incomprehensible to me that there should be enough water to jump into just hours later. Lucas wasn't the bravest child, and he cowered and shivered up there on the jetty for ages that first time. Richard tried to talk him round but soon ran out of patience, so eventually he grabbed his hand and pulled him in with him as he jumped. I held my breath waiting for him to surface and was amazed when he came up smiling. After that he went again and again, we couldn't stop him. Richard was so proud. He took us all for a cream tea afterwards; we had scones and clotted cream with strawberry jam.

*

Lucas's bike was a battered-up Harley. Erin climbed on behind him and its roar reverberated through her whole body. There was no mention of a helmet, so she held on tight as Lucas pulled the bike into the street. They sped up the hill and out of town. The hot air blew in her face and ruffled her hair. Lucas's ribcage was hard under her hands. Strands of his hair escaped his ponytail and whipped her cheeks. He smelt ripe, of sweat and beer. They drove for fifteen minutes or so, dodging tourists on bikes and trucks full of coconuts and bananas. And then the road became darker and they didn't see anyone. He pulled off onto a track down towards the beach. The bike skidded on the sand and Erin had to grip Lucas's t-shirt in order to stay on the back. He turned off the ignition and it was pitch-black in the clearing behind the beach. Erin climbed off the bike. Her legs felt wobbly as she put her feet down on the sand. Her face felt tight and she knew her hair would be sticking up on end. She damped it down with her hands and looked around, her eyes adjusting slowly to the darkness. She didn't think she recognised the clearing, but they all looked pretty similar.

'You alright?' Lucas asked as he opened up the box on the back of the bike and took out a four-pack of beers.

'Yeah, great!' Erin said a little too eagerly, and she followed him through the jungle towards the crash of the waves.

There was a fire on the beach and twelve or so people sitting around it. A guy with long grey hair and tattoos all over his chest was strumming a guitar. A much younger girl in a bikini top and shorts was sitting next to him playing a bongo between her legs.

'Lucas!' another girl with long dark hair waved and called out as they neared.

'Hi guys, this is Erin. She's a… a friend of mine,' he stuttered, 'from England.'

'Hi, Erin,' a chorus of voices responded.

'Hi,' she said. A couple of guys on the nearside of the fire budged up to make room for her and Lucas and they sat down in the gap. Lucas handed her one of the cans of beer. She cracked it open and had a sip. It was warm and sandy from the lid, but the bike ride had sucked all the moisture out of her mouth so she gulped it down.

The guy next to Erin was young, probably the same sort of age as her. He had fair skin and a downy beard. 'Hi, I'm Stefan,' he said to Erin. His voice was soft, but his accent brittle. Scandinavian, possibly. 'And this is Doug.' His hand rested on the knee of the guy sitting next to him. He was older than Stefan with a mop of grey curls and a beard. He wore a brightly coloured floral shirt that was open and revealed a hairy belly that bulged over the top of his shorts.

'Hi, Erin.' Doug leant across Stefan and clasped Erin's hand between his own. They were sticky, and he held on for a bit too long.

'You want some of this?' Stefan handed her a joint.

'Sure,' she said, and scanned the circle while she inhaled the smoke down. The girl with long hair who had first greeted Lucas had a child asleep in her lap – a mass of salty blond curls and bronzed limbs curled up in her skirt. On the other side of the circle was Mickey, who she had rented her surfboard from. And in between his legs sat the girl with the lily tattoo who she had met at the empanada stall on her first day.

'Erin, how is your surfing going?' she called across the fire.

'Getting better, I think. I'm loving the warm water.'

'Yeah, I bet. I can't imagine surfing in cold water.'

'Yeah.' Lucas hadn't spoken since they'd sat down, and his gravelly voice next to Erin was surprising. 'Man, we used to go on holidays to English beaches when I was a child, and my dad was always making me jump into that fucking freezing water. I hated it so much.'

Erin knew about those holidays, and Lucas knew she knew. She looked at him over her shoulder and he held her gaze intently for a few seconds before looking away. He seemed to be enjoying these mind games. She looked around at the darkness beyond the fire. She could hear the waves crashing on the shore but couldn't see them. The smoke blurred everything beyond the circle. She leant back on her elbows and watched the amber ashes dancing in the sky above. She could hear a medley of different languages and accents around the circle. And beyond that was the relentless buzz of the rainforest. She suddenly felt very far away from home. Lucas handed her another spliff. She hesitated, then took it and sucked on it hard.

'Well, this is a cosy gathering.' A voice came from behind them. Erin looked round to see a guy in jeans with a suede waistcoat over a bare chest sauntering across the sand towards them.

'Oh Christ, Don Juan is here,' Doug said a little too loudly. 'Watch out, Erin, he's always on the prowl for fresh bait.'

'Lucas! Fancy seeing you out and about,' he said, slapping Lucas on the back as he arrived at the circle.

'Alright, Geoff,' Lucas said without looking round.

'And who is this gorgeous thing I haven't met before?' he said, crouching down behind Erin.

'What did I tell you?' Doug smirked.

Geoff was probably a similar age to Lucas. He had brown greasy hair down to his shoulders and a cowboy hat. He was overly tanned and the muscles on his chest were tight underneath the waistcoat. He smelt like the floor of the pub after a busy night.

'This is Erin, Lucas's friend from England,' Stefan said.

'Lucas has a friend in England! Well, I'll be damned. Hi, princess, pleased to meet you.'

He picked up Erin's hand and kissed it. His stubble grazed her fingers.

'Hi,' Erin said and took another drag of the spliff and passed it to him.

'Cheers.' Geoff took a drag and then blew out smoke over Erin's face. She sidled up to Lucas and Geoff nuzzled his way into the circle between her and Stefan.

'So, Erin, what brings you to our little spot of paradise?'

'I came to see Lucas.'

'Oh, right. Have you known each other long?'

Erin looked at Lucas for help, but he was facing the other way and pretending not to listen. 'Not exactly.'

He didn't push her for more information, but he asked her about what she had been doing since she arrived. He was sitting very close and looked at her with such intensity that she couldn't look back at him. She kept her head down and fiddled with her bangles. He was really drunk and not much time had passed before he was draping his arm around her shoulders and sticking his nose in her ear as he talked. His breath stank and the hair on his armpits brushed up against her shoulders. She pulled away from him and edged closer towards Lucas, who thankfully twisted round as he felt her proximity.

'Hey, Geoff mate, back off, will you,' Lucas said, pushing Geoff's arm off the back of Erin's shoulders. 'The poor girl doesn't need you slobbering all over her. Nobody needs that.'

'Ooh, Lucas, I'm so sorry.' His words were slurred and mocking. 'You should have told me she was spoken for. I didn't know.' He staggered to his feet. 'Lucas has got a girl from England. I don't fucking believe it!' He stumbled his way around the edge of the circle. 'Hey Juno, darling. Where have you been all my life?' Geoff said as he sat down next to the girl with the child asleep in her lap. She rolled her eyes and turned her back on him.

'Thanks,' Erin whispered to Lucas.

'No worries,' he said and passed her a bottle of rum.

Time melted the rest of the night away. Some people sang, some danced, the guitar and drums hummed a constant melody and beat. Lucas was mostly quiet. Stefan ranted at Erin about the devastating effects of Western capitalism while Doug buried Stefan's feet in the sand and drew circles around them with his fingertips. Erin was fascinated by this unlikely couple. While Stefan looked young enough to be his son, it was Doug who fidgeted around him like a small child. Erin mumbled in agreement with Stefan and made sympathetic noises in the right places, but she was having trouble focusing on his face. She had another beer and the bottle of rum came round again. As did the spliff. She was struggling to keep her eyelids apart, and her head became so heavy. And then came a surge of nausea that rushed over her like the wave she couldn't catch on the beach. She got up and staggered to the trees, thinking she might be sick.

'You OK?' Lucas had followed her.

'Yeah.' She took a deep breath and ran her fingers through her hair. 'Shit, how embarrassing.'

'It's OK. This weed, it's pretty strong. I should have warned you.'

'Yeah, maybe.' Erin breathed in and out deeply through her mouth. 'I'm not normally such a lightweight. I think maybe I've had too much sun and not enough sleep and… well.'

'Come on, I'll take you home.'

'No, I'll be fine,' she said but she was unbalanced by another surge of dizziness and had to hold onto a tree.

'Yeah, right, come on.' Lucas put his arm around her waist and started to guide her towards the bike.

'No, wait, I don't want to go home. Fresh air is good.' She took another deep breath. 'My bag, I think I've got some water.'

'I'll go get it.' He ran over to the circle, giving Erin a moment to compose herself. The nausea was passing and she felt a bit clearer in her head.

'Here you go.' Lucas ran back from the fire with her bag and passed her the water. 'Shall we walk down the beach?'

'Sure.'

They headed towards the sea where the sand was harder. The air was warm and still. It was calmer here than the beach where she had surfed earlier in the day. The waves broke with a gentle splash and the warm water frothed around their feet. Erin looked out at the reflection of the moon glistening on the inky surface.

'Isn't it strange to think that it's the same moon you look at back home,' Lucas said, breaking the silence.

'Yeah, I guess.'

'When I first got here I was so miserable I used to come and sit on the beach at night and stare at the moon just to feel closer to home.'

'Really? So, it wasn't your choice to come here?'

'I didn't say that.'

'What happened? How did you end up on the other side of the world?'

'So many questions, Erin. Why are you so interested in my family?' She didn't know how to answer that.

'I wasn't,' she said defensively. 'It was Maggie who needed me, remember? She gave me the job. And I guess your screwed-up family was a welcome distraction from my own.'

'Fair enough.' She looked at him out of the corner of her eye and could see a smile. It spurred her on.

'Come on then, you can tell me, why did you come here?' He picked up a stone and skimmed it across the water. It bounced four, five, six times.

'Alright,' he said eventually. 'I was pretty screwed-up, my parents had sent me to this hellhole school and I was miserable. Then this lady came to talk to us in our final term about a conservation project. She must have thought she had landed on the moon. God knows who asked her to come, everyone there was a fucking dinosaur. Anyway, the project was here, well, not here exactly, it was on the Pacific Coast. She was all about protecting the rainforest and saving turtles and for the first time in… well, a long time, there was something that actually sparked an interest in me. I fucked up my exams and was told I couldn't go to university or anything and I couldn't go home, so I contacted her when I left school and went to see her in London. She lived in this massive house near Hyde Park. Her dad was funding the project and when she heard my sob story she convinced him to pay my airfare and sponsor me to come out here and work on the project. She saved my life, she did.' Erin was still having trouble focusing on his face, but she was determined to remember this crucial conversation. She blinked hard to bring him back into focus.

'Wow, and have you ever been back to England?'

'No, why would I, when I've got this?' He waved his hand out towards the sea. They carried on walking, Erin digging her toes into the sand with each step. She liked the sensation of the cold sand solidifying on her feet before the wave came and softened it again.

'But you were homesick at first?'

'I guess it was all just new and different. And I was pretty fucked up at the time.'

'Have you not seen either of your parents since?'

'Dad came out once.'

'Really? When?' Erin was desperate to know what had happened to Richard.

'I'd been here about eighteen months. He was on his way to Australia.'

'Australia?'

'Yeah, he moved there with his new missus.'

'Oh right, so he got married again?'

'Yeah, she was an Aussie, much younger than him. He got her knocked up and that was that, had to do the honourable thing. Moved to the back of beyond in Western Australia and had two more kids. I never saw him again.'

'Well, never say never…'

'Actually yeah, he died ten years ago. Some heavy farm machinery fell on him. Killed him there and then.'

'Shit, Lucas, I'm so sorry. I didn't know.'

'I probably wouldn't have seen him again anyway. He had his new life, a new family. He wasn't any more of a dad to me than Mum was a mum. Not in the end, anyway…'

Erin didn't know what to say. She thought of her own parents and their anxious faces at the airport. Lucas hadn't seen his parents for nearly ten years by the time he was her age.

Lucas broke the silence eventually. 'You know there's phosphorescence out there?'

'No way, I've read about it, but never seen it.'

'Come on, then.' He stopped walking and looked at her with a mischievous smile.

'What now?'

'Well, they're not around in the daytime, you know,' he said, pulling his vest over his head.

'I know that, but I don't have a towel or anything.'

'Where's your sense of adventure, Erin? Come on.' He took his shorts off and ran into the sea in his pants. He had a tattoo of what looked like a scorpion on his right bicep. He dived into the water and came up shouting, 'Come on, it's beautiful in here.'

Erin dithered on the shore. She looked around her and then stepped out of her shorts and took off her t-shirt. She was still wearing her bikini from the beach, thankfully. She ran into the water and sparks of light flushed at her legs.

'Oh wow.' She moved her arms and glittery ripples dispersed through the inky blackness.

'It's amazing, isn't it?' He swam over to her and the water shimmered with light all around him.

Erin spun around in circles. 'I've never seen anything like it. It's like we're in space.'

She rolled over onto her back and lay suspended in the salty water with the dazzling light show above and beneath her. Lucas did it too. Neither of them spoke, lost in their own reverie.

'Come on. I'll race you to that boat,' he said eventually and pointed out to sea. Erin looked but couldn't see a boat. And then he disappeared under the water leaving nothing but ripples on the surface. Erin continued to swim in the direction she thought he had gone but he didn't surface. All around her it was dark. She could see the flicker of the fire miles down the beach and hear the drums and guitar in the distance, but in the water it was quiet.

'Lucas, Lucas, where are you?' she shouted and continued to turn in circles, scanning the darkness. She put her legs down to touch the bottom but it was too deep. 'Lucas! Please come back. I don't like it. Where are you?' She could see a dark shadow off to the right; it could have been a boat. She started to swim towards it and in her haste swallowed a big mouthful of salty water. She coughed and spluttered. And then his hands were round her waist, but she still couldn't see him. Erin screamed and swallowed another mouthful. Lucas came up laughing.

'You bastard!' Erin spluttered, and Lucas laughed.

'I'm sorry.'

Erin struggled to get her breath back. She kicked her legs trying to stay above the surface of the water. Lucas put his arms around her waist.

'Hey, it's OK, I'm sorry. Here, hold onto me.' She put her arms around his shoulders.

'I didn't know where you were. You really freaked me out,' she said between gasps.

'It was just a joke. Hold onto my back while we swim to the shore.' She put her hands on his shoulders. He was a strong swimmer and she could feel his muscles working under her palms. When they got back to the shallower water he stopped swimming and put his feet down on the bottom.

'Are you OK?' he asked. 'I'm sorry if I freaked you out.'

'You did, you fucker.'

'It's quite easy to wind you up, isn't it?'

'No.'

'Really? I seem to be doing a pretty good job so far.'

Erin scowled at him. 'Yeah, well, you obviously have form for pissing people off.'

'That's true. I'm good at making up, though.'

'Not what I've heard.'

'So how can I make it up to you?'

'You can't.'

'Really?' She still had her arms on his shoulders and he was close to her and smiling, and she wondered for a minute whether he was going to kiss her and she wasn't sure whether she wanted him to or not. He started to pull away and then changed his mind and kissed her hard on the mouth.

'Lucas, I can't,' she said between breaths, but she didn't pull away. She let him kiss her shoulder. And then her neck. And then her mouth again. And she kissed him back. He pulled her close to him. Her breasts squashed against his chest. He moved his leg between hers and she wrapped her legs around his body. And out of the corner of her eye Erin could see a halo of light sparkling around them as their bodies moved through the water.

CHAPTER TWENTY-THREE

Lansdown Place, 25th June 1987

They have let me out. For real this time. Richard had to pretend to the doctors that he was going to look after me, which we both knew was a lie. I had barely walked in the door before he said he was leaving. I presumed he was going to move in with Julie Fellowes, but he said that was over. That he had rented a flat on the coast. It has two bedrooms, apparently, so that Lucas can stay there in the holidays. I didn't object. I looked around at my house. The kitchen table, the four chairs, Lucas's picture of the poison dart frog still there on the fridge. The photo of Skye as a baby lying on a sheepskin rug holding onto her feet still tucked into the frame of the mirror. I knew I should be happy to be home, but it had been easier to hide from the truth in hospital. I walked over to the sink and looked out of the window. Richard was behind me, still talking about his flat which backed on to a pub garden, and he was worried about the noise, but the view of the sea more than made up for it. And as he talked, I held onto the cold, hard edges of the sink.

It was such a surprise when I found out I was pregnant with Skye, I was thirty-seven and Lucas was nearly twelve! It had been years since we stopped trying and the hope of another baby had faded from a raging obsession that consumed my every thought to a tiny flicker buried deep at the back of my mind. I didn't tell Richard or Lucas for weeks, months. Terrified it would be tempting fate. I was sick as a dog, but I didn't care; it just further compounded the reality of it all. When the bulge in my belly could no longer be hidden, I told them both. Lucas's face lit up instantly and I realised how desperately he must have wanted a sibling all these years. Richard's reaction was harder to gauge. I think he was shocked and possibly frightened about the financial implications – he certainly didn't whoop for joy. A couple of times over the next few days, however, I found him quietly smiling to himself. Then a week or so later he came up to me here in the kitchen, while I was washing up, and he closed his arms around me from behind, and placing his hands upon my stomach, he kissed my neck with a tenderness that took me right back to those early days and our flat above the launderette. I remember thinking that everything was going to be alright.

*

The sun woke Erin. She felt its warmth on her toes. And the familiar click-clicking of the fan that had permeated her dreams became a conscious reality. Every few seconds its breeze blew her hair across her face and the sheet billowed against her back as it passed. Her mouth was dry and her head pounded in her skull. She opened her eyes and looked down. She was still wearing her shorts and t-shirt. She sat up and looked around. She struggled to bring her eyes into focus through the mottled gauze of the mosquito net. She was in a bamboo hut, not dissimilar to the one she was paying a pittance for at Coco Loco. But this one was more cluttered. There was a guitar propped up against the wall and next to it was a pile of empty beer bottles. Beyond the bottles was a chest with clothes spilling out of the open drawers. On top were some notes and coins, a lighter and a pack of Rizla. On the other side of the room was a turntable and some records with Horace Andy on top of the pile. Next to it was a small bookshelf with a few faded paperbacks. Erin recognised the covers of Maggie's

Detective Turnpike novels. She shook her head in an attempt to rattle her memories of the night before. The fire, the spliff, the rum, the phosphorescence, the kiss. She stroked her arms, her torso as if tracing the touch of someone else's hands.

Erin muddled her way through the opening in the mosquito net. There were Tibetan prayer flags hanging above the open door. Through it came the cacophony of the jungle outside. She walked onto the balcony.

'Lucas,' she called and looked around her. The hut was on stilts, about twenty feet above the ground. She looked ahead at the sandy path that led through the trees ahead of them. She could just see the shimmering of the turquoise ocean at the bottom. The gentle lull of the waves sounded beneath the deafening screech of the rainforest. A hummingbird hovered in the air in front of her. Its wings fluttered so fast they became a hazy blur, then it flew away into the jumble of palms and reeds. Erin wondered how it could fly so fast yet navigate the tangle of trees so adeptly. Her stomach churned and the throbbing continued at her temples.

Unlike her hut, Lucas's balcony circled the entire building. She called for him again as she walked round. At the back of the hut the jungle was so thick the sun barely penetrated the canopy and the buzzing and screeching was even more intense. She picked up her pace and came back to the front. There was another room off the bedroom, a tiny kitchen. It had just one small netted window with a hole in it and a mosquito was buzzing and banging against the inside of the net. There were two hobs, a mini fridge and a rickety wooden table with brightly coloured butterflies painted all over it. There was a coffee cup on the table that was still warm. He couldn't have been gone long. She found a bottle of Coke in the fridge and put it to her lips. It was flat but deliciously cold. She drained it and looked for something to eat. There was only half a black and mouldy avocado and a few cans of beer in the fridge. Just like Maggie! She found a bag of crisps on a shelf by the door which she opened and carried with her back to the bedroom. They were hard to swallow, and her crunching reverberated around her head as if it were on loudspeaker. The bathroom was also off the bedroom and had the same damp smell as hers at Coco Loco. She sat on the loo and watched as a gecko scuttled up the wall and out of a gap in the ceiling.

Back in the bedroom, she flicked through Lucas's record collection. She found Ella Fitzgerald and The Carpenters; he obviously wasn't beyond nostalgia. There was a lot of reggae – predictable given the location – and then a whole host of heavy metal: Metallica, Faith No More, Jane's Addiction.

On the top of his chest of drawers was a pile of documents – a diving certificate, a letter from the local authority about The Butterfly Farm. And underneath the letters was a wooden box with an ethnic aboriginal pattern on the lid. Erin opened it up. There was a scrap of pale blue knitted fabric that was unravelling at the ends. Erin picked it up and underneath was Maggie's letter to Lucas. It was open, he had read it. She turned the envelope over in her hands and fiddled with the edges. She started to pull it out of the envelope. She could see Maggie's familiar bubbly writing on the page, and she saw the name Skye. And then she heard the heavy tread of someone climbing up the steps to the hut. She stuffed the letter back into the envelope and then into the box and snapped the lid shut just as Lucas walked into the hut holding two cups of orange juice.

'You're up, you were totally dead to the world when I left,' he said, handing her one of the cups of juice.

'Er, yeah.'

'How's your head?'

'Sore,' she said, and had a sip of the orange juice. It was fresh and delicious. Bits of pith got stuck in the end of the straw. She was horribly thirsty and drained the entire cup. Lucas had gone into the kitchen and Erin followed.

'You OK?' He looked around at her as he put some milk and a big bottle of water into the fridge.

'Yeah.' She ran her fingers through her hair. 'I just, well, there seems to be a bit of a blank in my mind about last night.'

'Really?' He smiled as he went over to the bin and hauled out an overflowing bag of rubbish. 'Which bits do you remember?'

'Well, the beach, obviously, and the phosphorescence, and then you disappearing and freaking me out, and then…'

'And then what?' She shrugged. He smiled and carried the bag of rubbish out to the front of the hut and chucked it to the bottom of the steps. Erin followed; he was clearly enjoying this, and wasn't going to make it easier for her.

'Lucas, please.'

He laughed. 'I can't believe you've forgotten the best bit. That doesn't reflect too well on me.'

'So we did…?'

'Did what, Erin?'

'Oh, for fuck's sake, Lucas, did we shag?'

'And I thought you were such a lady!' Erin rolled her eyes in exasperation and Lucas laughed.

'I'm sorry, but it's so easy to wind you up, and I can't resist it.' She scowled at him. 'I'm sorry. OK, we kissed in the sea – you remember that?' She nodded. 'And then we went back onto the beach to get our clothes and I had to help you into your shorts.' Erin could feel her cheeks flush with shame. He smiled. 'And then we walked, or stumbled, back to the bike, and I had high hopes for the rest of the night, but you passed out on the back of the bike.'

'Oh…' Her stomach gurgled noisily and she hugged herself tight to silence it.

'I drove to Coco Loco but had no idea which hut you were in, and you were so unconscious I couldn't just leave you there.'

'So, we didn't…?'

'Didn't what?'

'Lucas!'

'No, Erin, I am not in the habit of taking advantage of young girls, despite what you may have read.' Erin felt her eyes widening at this reference, and she looked away to avoid his glare. He laughed. 'You slept in the bed and I spent the night in the hammock on the balcony. Got eaten alive, in fact.' He lifted up his arm to show a mass of swollen blisters down the side of his body. He walked past her and back into the bedroom. 'Shall I take you out for breakfast?' he called over his shoulder. 'You must be feeling rough. I know this place that serves a mean huevos rancheros.'

'I don't know, I think I might just go back to Coco Loco.'

'Come on, you must be starving. I swear their eggs cure any hangover.' On cue her stomach gurgled so loudly she couldn't mask it. Heat flushed back into her cheeks again. 'Well, your stomach wants eggs even if your head doesn't.' He laughed. 'Come on, I'll take you back to Coco Loco after.'

Erin swallowed her discomfort and put the queasy feeling in her stomach down to her hangover and they went to Lucas's favourite café for breakfast, where the huevos rancheros were better than anything Erin had ever tasted. After that she didn't go back to her hut, but Lucas took her to his favourite surfing spot. He taught her how to spot the best wave and how to catch it at exactly the right time. And after that, they went on to a bar which served the best empanadas, the best mojito.

The next couple of days proceeded in the same vein. He took her to his favourite place to snorkel where the fish were so abundant and so bright they didn't seem real. And then to a remote headland where you could spot dolphins jumping out of the water. And to an animal rescue centre where baby monkeys wearing nappies climbed on her head. And every day Erin's shoulders dropped a little further, and she became more and more enchanted by the Pura Vida that the country had to offer. And every day Lucas softened a little more, as if seeing his world through Erin's eyes was melting away the brittle edges.

Simon had continued to message her every few days, asking when she was coming back, and each time she had replied saying she didn't know. It was true. As was the fact that he no longer dominated her every waking thought, and that for the first time in so long she was enjoying experiences for their own worth without having to imagine him being there. The thousands of miles between them had created a distance in her heart which surprised and empowered her. She was loath to admit that it had anything to do with Lucas. Or with the fact that he hadn't kissed her again, and that she was increasingly preoccupied with whether he might and whether she wanted him to. He was twenty years older than her, and she had resolved never to go for an older man again. And she knew way too much about his screwed-up past. But there was something about the way he looked at her, with those narrow blue eyes. About the way he held onto her hips on the surfboard, guiding her onto the wave. About the way the muscles in his back rippled under his skin as he dived under a wave, that made her stomach flip into her heart.

'That first day, before I met you, I looked for a birthmark on the back of every guy I passed on the beach.' Erin was sitting on her towel and Lucas lay face down on the sand next to her under the trees at the back of the beach. The dappled sunshine flickered on his back.

'Really? My own little stalker.' His voice was muffled.

'Yeah, it was weird, I knew all these snippets about you. What books you read as a child, your favourite food, your family Christmases, your holiday in my home town.'

'God, I hated that holiday.'

'Why did you hate it so much?'

He rolled over and propped himself up on his elbows. 'Well, the sea was freezing, for a start. And everyone sat on the beach in their jumpers, eating revolting pasties with towels wrapped round their knees, pretending to enjoy themselves.'

'Hang on a minute, I love pasties! And it isn't always cold. And you have to admit it rivals here for beauty.'

He lifted his head and looked around him. 'Nah. There's no contest, I'm afraid,' he said and lay back down.

'What?' She slapped his back.

'You've got to get out of there, you know, before you turn into one of those purple-rinsed old ladies twitching at their net curtains.'

'Yeah, I know. I have tried – went to London last year but it didn't go so well.'

'You should stay here.' He sat up and looked at her with a sincerity she hadn't seen before.

'Yeah, that would be nice.' She rolled her eyes and looked around.

'I'm serious.'

'Oh, come on, Lucas, what would I do? Where would I live? How would I survive?'

'Well, you would live in a hut just back from the beach in among the coconut palms. You would work at any number of chilled-out cafés in town – you've worked in pubs and the tea room, right?' She nodded. 'And as far as surviving is concerned, if I could do it as a fucked-up eighteen-year-old, then anyone can.'

'Pura Vida,' she said, burying her feet in the sand.

'Pura Vida, baby,' he said and flicked some sand at her with his feet.

She looked around at the white beach, the glistening sea, the deep green of the jungle on the other side of the bay. And then she thought about her own bay at home, sometimes blue, sometimes green. And Maggie meditating on the bench at the end of her garden.

'Not everyone turns into one of those purple-rinsed curtain-twitchers, you know. Your mum hasn't. She just kept to herself.'

'Yeah, I bet she still knew what was going on with everyone, though.'

Erin thought back to the first time she met Maggie, and how unnerved she had been by the steely precis of her life. And then there was Christmas. 'Maybe. She definitely knew more about me than she first let on.'

'See, I knew it.' This sparked his interest. He sat up and looked at her, eager for more.

'Not in a gossipy way. She wanted to help. She kind of revealed some family secrets.'

'What?'

'Yeah, it all came up at Christmas.'

'When she got pissed?'

'Yeah.'

'So that's why your mum hates her.'

'I didn't say she hated her.'

'Whatever. So, what happened?'

'Maggie had met my dad years ago at her publisher's. Dad had written a book which I never knew about. Anyway, they got chatting. Mum was pregnant at the time. Maggie revealed all this after a couple of gin and tonics on Christmas Day. And, well, one thing led to another and I found out I have a brother.'

'What?'

'Yeah! My parents had a baby boy four years before me. He had Down's syndrome, and Mum freaked out and gave him away.' She hugged her knees to her chest and burrowed her feet further into the sand.

'Shit.'

'Yeah, shit.' She piled more sand onto her feet with her palms.
'Have you met him?'

'No, this only happened at Christmas. And I was so pissed at
my parents for keeping it from me that I moved in with Maggie.
And then she got really ill and I guess I was distracted and, well,
now I'm here, and…'

'What are you gonna do?'

'I dunno.' She shrugged, then looked at him. 'What do you
think I should do?'

He looked as though he was seriously considering his
answer for a while, and then dismissed it. 'Don't ask me, I fuck
everything up.'

'Oh come on, Lucas. You can't always play the fucked-up card,
you know.' She tried to hold his gaze, but he looked away and
reached for his packet of cigarettes on the towel. Erin sensed this
was a moment she had to seize. She looked out to sea and tried
to ignore the fluttering in the pit of her belly. 'It's not too late for
you and Maggie, you know.' He didn't answer, but she was not
going to give up. 'Do you want to tell me about it?'

He lit his cigarette. 'About what?'

'About the night that Skye… you know.'

He inhaled deeply and then exhaled before he spoke. 'You read
the manuscript.'

'Yeah, but she didn't finish her story.'

'Well, maybe there's a reason for that. Maybe the past is just…
best left alone.'

'Maybe. Or maybe not. I don't think Maggie wanted to leave
it alone, otherwise she wouldn't be writing this book.'

'Well, maybe I do. Maybe she doesn't get to decide when to tell
my story. Maybe I can actually be in charge of my own fucking life
at the grand old age of forty-six.' He took his cap off and threw
it down on the sand and ran his sandy fingers through his hair.

'I'm sorry, Lucas, I didn't want to upset you. I just thought it might help. To say it out loud, I mean. Have you ever talked to anyone about what happened that night?'

Lucas shrugged and looked down. He took a long, deep drag of his cigarette. 'I was pissed off,' he said while exhaling a tube of smoke.

'What?'

'That night. I was a teenager, I wanted to be the one getting fucked up and having fun.' He took another drag and then spoke with a clenched jaw as he inhaled deeply. 'I was shit at it though, meeting new people I mean. Mum had tried to get me to talk to the other kids on the campsite the day before, but they were German and Dutch and they seemed to all know each other and I couldn't really talk to them. Then those same kids walked past the tent that night while I was sitting there feeling sorry for myself. They had a bottle of vodka and they asked me to go with them down the river.' He had another drag and spoke while holding onto the smoke, his voice strangled. 'I had given up, you know, hadn't smoked for nearly six months before you turned up.' He exhaled.

'Sorry.'

'Yeah, right you are…'

'Look, you don't have to do this.'

'It's OK, there's not much more to tell.'

'Did you go with them?'

'Yeah, I went with them. Bad, huh?'

'Well, I mean…'

'It's OK. You can say it. I fucked up. I left my little sister asleep in the tent while I went to drink booze with these kids I didn't even know.' He stubbed the cigarette out in the sand and buried it down deep. 'It was my fault, I never should have—'

'What happened to her, Lucas?'

'I… I… could hear them shouting her name from where we were drinking. So, I ran back and Mum was… she was wading into the river… I can still hear her screams, they kept coming back at you again and again as they echoed off the rocks. She was holding Skye's bunny, clutching it to her chest while she screamed. And Dad was also in the river and he kept diving under the water. And every time he came up for air his eyes would be bulging with fear. And then more and more people came, other campers, people from the café, the guy who sold the croissants in the morning. They were in the river and on the banks. I remember their torchlights bouncing around in the trees.'

'Oh, God. I'm so sorry.' Erin touched his arm and he flinched.

'Yeah. Fuck, it was horrible. I just stood there on the bank, watching this scene play out like a horror movie. Someone carried Mum out of the water at one point – I think it was that guy they were drinking with, the one with the Calvados. And that was when she saw me. She ran at me and held onto my arms, shaking me. "Lucas, where were you? You were meant to be looking after her," she said. I don't really remember what happened after that. It was two days before they found her body, a few kilometres downriver. There was a lot of police questioning, in their broken English. Mum had to be sedated. We checked into a hotel and she slept a lot. When she wasn't sleeping, she was wandering around in a trance. She couldn't look at me. Dad tried, he would put his arm around me and call me buddy and ask if I was OK. But he couldn't look me in the eye either. We all knew it was my fault.'

'But you weren't to know. You were young. You…' He turned to face her, his eyes suddenly fiery.

'But she did blame me. You read it, you typed it up… it's there in black and white. "I blame my son for the death of my daughter".'

'But I think she regrets saying that, Lucas. She wanted to say sorry.'

'She hates me. I ruined her life.'

'No, no. She loves you and she wants to say sorry for ruining yours.' Erin put her arm around his shoulders; they were hot and gritty with sand. He continued to stare out at the sea with glassy eyes. She squeezed his shoulder and leant into him. And then he turned towards her and their faces were so close that their noses were nearly touching. And she could feel his breath, hot and smoky on her face. And he leant in and kissed her on the mouth. He grabbed the back of her neck with his sandy hands and pulled her closer. And their teeth clashed, his stubble was rough on her chin, his face sticky against hers. She opened her eyes and saw his tears. She held his face in her hands and kissed his salty cheeks. She pulled him closer and he held on tight, burying his head into her neck, his whole body writhing with sobs.

CHAPTER TWENTY-FOUR

Lansdown Place, 28th June 1987

Richard has gone, and I feel nothing. No emotion whatsoever as I watched him pack his life into our car and drive away. His guitar was on the roof, just like when we arrived here twelve years ago. I expected nostalgia, regret, remorse – but there was nothing. I pinched my arm. I dug my fingernails into the skin on my wrists and rubbed at the dents that were left behind. Was I dead inside?

I went into Skye's room. I looked at her red towelling dressing gown on the back of the door, the My Little Ponys lined up in a row on top of the chest of drawers, the duvet cover with pink bunnies and her name in a fluffy cloud at the top. I hugged her pillow tight, just as I had in those early days. But there is no smell now. She is trying to fade away but I won't let her. I must remember everything.

Her birth – it was straightforward. She came fast, like a thunderbolt. We nearly didn't get to the hospital in time: Richard stopped for petrol on the way and I thought she was going to arrive in the car. But I managed to hold on and she was born within minutes of getting there. It was intense, there was no build-up to the pain like with Lucas. I got third-degree tears and had to sit on a rubber ring for weeks. Her arrival was indicative of the way she was. A bundle of determined energy. She thrashed her tiny wrinkled limbs around and barely ever slept. In those early days a twenty-minute kip could fuel her for hours. I felt delirious from lack of sleep and worried that the anxiety would find its way back to haunt me. There were bad days, but every time the darkness started to seep in I just held onto her really tight, I breathed in that heady smell and nuzzled my nose into the soft, powdery folds of her neck. And I blessed the stars that had given me this treasure.

Richard was besotted. He would cradle her in his arms, singing Simon and Garfunkel songs as he paced up and down the house with her. Lucas, too. Sometimes when she woke in the night he would go to her and the tears would cease immediately. I would find him in her room the next morning. Asleep on the floor, holding her little hand through the bars of the cot. I was jealous of the love that they shared. I knew she needed me; she would cry angry tears until I picked her up and then she would squeeze her chubby limbs around me like a monkey holding on tight. But when Lucas walked into the room, her cherry-red lips would break into a gummy smile and those big blue eyes would sparkle. She learnt to say 'Ucas' long before Mummy or Daddy.

Skye had a confidence and an inner beauty that charmed everyone she met. Lucas had always hidden behind my skirt, too shy to look anyone in the eye or call them by their name. But Skye had no such modesty. She never stopped talking. To the shopkeeper, the postman, the teachers at Lucas's school. She had huge indigo eyes and a round, open face. Her nose was slightly snubbed at the end revealing perfectly round nostrils. Her hair was like silk, soft golden tendrils collapsed around her face. It fell in front of her eyes, so I would twist it into a little bun on the top of her head. Candyfloss dreadlocks formed at the back and stuck out like a bantam chicken's crown. She had bubblegum cheeks, pink and smooth. Her pearly belly swelled out like a doughy ball. Her bottom wobbled when she ran naked around the house. She never stopped moving; there was *a fire bubbling away inside her which only stilled in sleep. She giggled, she belly-laughed, she howled, she shouted. There was so much life bursting out of her – until the flames went out forever.*

*

A few mornings later, they were in the butterfly dome. Erin had come to love the ramshackle magic of it. The sweet smell of mangoes and passion flowers, the dappled light and the warm air filled with the flutter of wings. She was chopping oranges when a small crowd of tourists gathered around Lucas. Erin peered over their backs. He was crouching on the floor and held a tawny butterfly between his fingers with one hand and in the other he was cutting out a tiny section of its wing. Erin held her breath as she watched his fingers move with such precision and delicacy. Then he released the butterfly to fly away.

'The broken wing was stopping it from flying,' he said, 'so I cut the other one into the same shape. Now they are symmetrical and it can fly again.'

'Wow,' the group murmured. He folded the scissors into his penknife and put it in his pocket.

'Doesn't it hurt?' asked a young girl at the front.

'No,' he smiled, 'it's just like having your hair cut. That doesn't hurt, does it?'

The small crowd dispersed and Erin followed Lucas over to the other side of the dome where he began to load a bucket with rotten fruit. Flies hovered around him, and clouds of grey dust puffed up as the fruit hit the plastic on the bottom of the bucket.

'Quite the Dr Dolittle, aren't you?' she said. Lucas looked up at her and smiled. 'Your mum said you were fascinated with tiny animals, even when you were young.'

'Well, she would know,' he said. 'I'm nearly done here. And then I want to take you somewhere.' He placed a lid on the bucket and stood up.

'Really? Where are we going today?' She wrapped her arms around his waist and smiled up at him.

'Wait and see.' He kissed the top of her head and Erin felt her phone vibrate with a message in her bag. She pulled away from him and found the phone. It was Fred. *Erin. Please could you call me.*

He had never messaged her before. It was four days since she'd called him. Four of the best days. But now that sweet pleasure was curdling in the pit of her stomach. 'I have to make a call,' she said, and walked outside the dome and up the path through the jungle.

'Fred?'

'Oh Erin, hi. I'm sorry to bother you,' he shouted into the phone.

'I'm so sorry I haven't called, Fred. I…'

'It's OK, Erin. I didn't expect…'

'Is it Maggie? Is she… is she?'

'No, not yet. But she's got worse overnight. I don't think she has much time.'

'Oh, God.'

'I'm sorry, but I thought you would want to know.'

'Yes of course… I…'

'It's OK, you said your goodbye.'

'But she wanted to see Lucas, I know she was hoping I'd bring him back.'

'It's OK, Erin. I don't think she expected…'

'No, Fred, it's not OK. I promised.' She swallowed down the bubble that was rising at the back of her throat. 'How long? How long does she have, Fred?'

'I don't know, Erin, maybe a couple of days. Maybe less.'

'Oh, God.'

'The doctor is here, Erin, I have to go.'

'OK… OK… wait, Fred…' But he had gone.

Lucas came up behind her. 'Who was that?'

'It was Fred.' She followed him up the path into the clearing at the end where the bike gleamed in the midday sun.

'Who's Fred?'

'I told you about him, he's Maggie's friend. He's with her at the hospice.'

'Oh yeah,' he said, climbing onto the bike. 'Are you coming?'

'She hasn't got much time, Lucas. She's dying, like, in the next day or so.' He put the key in the ignition and readjusted the baseball cap on his head. 'Well, you knew she was dying when you came out here.'

'Yeah, I know, but it's happening like, now, and it's a bit of a shock… and, well, I hoped…'

'What?' he looked at her. 'What did you hope?'

'Well, that you might come back with me… to say goodbye.'

He shook his head and looked down, smiling. 'Oh, man, are you for real?'

'Why not, Lucas? You could lay it all to rest. It would mean so much to her. To you.'

'Is that why you came? Is that what all this has been about?'

'No! Well, I mean, I guess I…'

'Man, I'm such a dick…' He turned the key and the bike growled beneath him. He revved the engine and Erin jumped back.

'What are you doing?' she shouted over the noise of the engine. But he couldn't look at her. 'Wait! Lucas, can you just turn the engine off?' she shouted, and edged closer to him, but he revved the engine with the pedal and she backed away.

'I've got to go, Erin.'

'Where have you got to go? A minute ago you were going to take me somewhere. We could still go. Let's just talk about this…' But he shook his head.

'I can't.' He swung the bike round and dirt sprayed from the wheels and flew at Erin's face, sticking to her cheeks and stinging her eyes. And he drove off down the track and disappeared into the cloud of dust.

'Fuck!' Erin kicked at the ground. She couldn't believe he had driven off and left her there. 'You bastard!' she shouted after him.

Lucas's hut was only a twenty-minute walk from the dome; hers was the other side of town. At least forty minutes. She dithered at the end of the drive and then turned right towards his hut. In the heat of the middle of the day the walk felt longer. She hugged the edge of the road where there was shade under the trees. But when she rounded the corner it was flanked only by low shrubs and the tarmac shimmered in the heat. She picked up her pace but her legs felt heavy and she could feel her shoulders bubbling under the sun. By the time she arrived at his hut, her clothes were stuck to her body with sweat and she felt quite giddy.

He wasn't even there! She wasn't that surprised. She didn't know where he would go, but it would definitely be somewhere she wouldn't find him. Erin considered going back to her hut, but she was hot and exhausted and it was back past the dome and beyond, and she couldn't face doing that walk again. She would wait; he had to come home eventually.

She found the key under the Buddha on the balcony and let herself in. She turned the fan on in the bedroom and stood in front of it for a few minutes. She shut her eyes and let the cold air blow over her face. Then she found her phone and called the airline. There was a flight from San José in the morning. She booked herself a seat, and willed Maggie to hold on just a bit longer. She kicked off her shoes and lay down on the bed. She looked up at the net; it was tied into a knot and swayed in the breeze. Only a few hours earlier she had watched it moving back and forth with her head on Lucas's chest. How could he just drive off and leave her there? Erin rolled over onto her side and hugged herself tight. Why was he so angry? The aboriginal box was in her line of sight.

She swung her legs off the bed and walked over to it. She traced the dots on the lid with the tips of her fingers and then lifted it up.

The blue knitted fabric lay on top of the letters. Erin picked it up and put it to her lips, just as she had done a few weeks earlier with the identity bracelet in the box under Maggie's bed. She remembered the umbilical cord, the drawings, the bunny. There was a screech outside the hut and then a rustling of leaves. She rushed to the door and peered out. 'Lucas?' she called. But there was no sign of him. She looked down at the wool in her hands. Mr Gilbert was the bunny in Maggie's box; she talked about it in her diary, how she'd found it on the larder floor. Except it wasn't Mr Gilbert, and she knew that because it wasn't wearing the blue knitted scarf. Was this the scarf? Lucas had said that Maggie was holding the bunny that night in the river – he said she was clutching it as she waded in and out screaming for Skye. But why was the scarf here in Lucas's box? Erin scrunched it in the palm of her hand and picked up the letter. Her heart thumped in her chest as she pulled it out of the envelope.

Dear Lucas,

Your dad told me you had gone to Costa Rica, after school. I should have come to find you then but I didn't think you would want to see me. Give it some time, let the wounds heal, I told myself. And then the months rolled into years, years into decades. And all that time I have imagined what I would say if I was to meet you. How you would dodge my gaze and scuff the floor with your feet. Would you blink a lot like your dad does when things become uncomfortable? Maybe you would shout at me, tell me I had ruined your life?

I have finally accepted the fact that I will never know. I have a brain tumour, and that dream of reconciliation that I have stupidly held onto for the last thirty-five years is dying with me.

And so I thought I'd write. Over and over I wrote this letter. Pages and pages of reasons why and excuses for everything, but they all ended up as ashes in the bottom of the fire grate. For there are no excuses. And no justifiable reasons why I behaved as I did. I just need to say sorry.

Sorry for letting the nurses take you away in those early days, and for questioning my love for you. Sorry that you had to put me to bed that afternoon when I had drunk too many vodkas before lunchtime. Sorry that I was always so consumed with my own misery that I didn't have space in my heart for you. Sorry for all those times that I shouted. Sorry that I didn't believe you about Laila Fellowes. Sorry that I hit you for not eating the lamb casserole. Sorry that I didn't protect you from Jeremy Fellowes. Sorry that it was your vodka that I drank to wash down the pills. Sorry that I didn't follow you out of church on Christmas Day. Sorry that I let you cry yourself to sleep after I hit you because I was too ashamed to face you. Sorry that you had to find me on the bathroom floor. Sorry that I let them send you to that awful place. Sorry that I didn't come and rescue you. Sorry that I blamed you for Skye. Sorry that I couldn't forgive you for the lie that you told. And sorry that I never told you that I knew about the lie you told. That I knew what you did that night. That I have worked it out over the years – your wet clothes, Mr Gilbert, his scarf, the coroner's report, Celeste. None of it made sense, until it did. And then it screamed at me like crashing symbols, like a car alarm that refused to be silenced, like a—

'Erin.' She swung round. Lucas was striding into the room. 'What the fuck are you doing?' He snatched the letter out of her hand and stuffed it into the back pocket of his shorts. Erin flinched and backed away. There was a fire burning in his eyes.

'I'm so sorry, Lucas, I know I shouldn't have… but… I saw it and… I…' She was struggling to comprehend what she had just read, or what she had not read. Her mind whirred and the palms of her hands were wet with sweat.

'I don't fucking believe it.' He strode right up to her and pointed his finger in her face. Saliva frothed at the sides of his mouth, making the words sticky. 'Have you no shame?' He spat as he spoke. Then he turned and strode out of the room. The wooden hut rattled as he paced up and down the balcony, cursing with every step. Erin wiped her face and looked down at the scarf in her hands. They were shaking. She wrapped the frayed wool around her finger until it was so tight she could feel the blood pulsing in the tip. Lucas stopped pacing outside and she heard the flick of a lighter, and then a waft of smoke drifted in through the door and caught at the back of her throat. She composed herself and followed him out onto the balcony.

'I'm sorry, Lucas, I know I shouldn't have read your letter.' He didn't say anything, just pulled hard on his cigarette and stared out into the jungle. 'I didn't come here with the intention of reading it. But when I got here you weren't here, and then I saw it and… What did she mean? Your mum? What does she know?'

'You read the letter, Erin.' He spat the words at her with venom.

'No, you came back… I didn't finish.'

He laughed a manic laugh. 'Well, I guess you'll never know then.'

'Please, Lucas.' She edged towards him but he turned quickly, the fire still burning in his eyes.

'What, Erin?'

'I know it was out of order. I just thought that maybe there was something you weren't telling me, and—'

'When will you get it into your head that this is none of your fucking business?'

'But Maggie, your mother – she has made it my business! She employed me to type up her wretched manuscript and then she sent me to the other side of the world to find you. And now she's back there, dying, and... she's all alone... and you're here. And yes, I want to know why. Is it really that surprising?' He didn't respond, just carried on smoking and staring.

'Why do you have this scarf?'

'What?' He turned to look at her and then down at her hands. She held it out to him on her palm. He went to pick it up and then stopped himself. He flicked his cigarette into the bushes and then picked the scarf up with a delicacy that was surprising given his mood. He stretched the wool out between his two hands.

'It's Mr Gilbert's scarf, isn't it? Skye's bunny?'

'Yes.'

'But you said Maggie was holding the bunny when you came back to the river that night.'

'So?'

'So, why do you have the scarf?' He shrugged his shoulders and looked away.

'Lucas.' She touched his arm gently.

'I just wanted something to remember her by, is that so hard to understand?'

'No, no, of course not.' He leant over the balcony and pulled at the threads at the end of the scarf, rubbing them between his thumb and forefinger. It was habitual and absent-minded, and Erin realised he must have been pulling at the threads of that scarf between his fingers for a long time. She recalled the satin seam of a blanket that she had slept with as a child, and the calm sensation it had brought her as she rubbed it across her top lip every night. But something told her that this scarf was not a comfort to Lucas. His fingers were jittery and his breathing laboured as if it were more of a penance, a constant reminder of his guilt.

'You never said you were going back to see her,' Lucas said quietly, snapping her out of her reverie.

'What?'

'You lied to me. You said you wanted to stay here.'

'Is that what this is all about?' He shrugged. 'Oh God, Lucas. Of course part of me would love to stay, it's paradise here, but—'

'But what?' He turned to face her.

'It's not real.'

'Don't patronise me, Erin, this is my life. And you just waltzed on in with your short shorts and your big eyes, messing with my head. Do you know where I was taking you today?'

'Where?'

'To a house on the beach, just like you wanted. Except you don't.' She closed her eyes and took in a long, deep breath, gathering resolve. Then she looked him in the eye with as much sincerity as she could muster.

'I… I'm sorry, Lucas, I don't really know what I want… But right now, I know that your mum doesn't have long left, and I want to see her before she dies.'

'Did she set you up to it?'

'What?'

'Mum, did she send you out here to lure me back?'

'No. Well, she never asked me to do that, but I figured it's probably what she wants.'

'She's totally manipulated you. How can you not see it? All that shit about your brother. You don't think it was a mistake, do you, her reveal? She will have done her research, she's good at that. Found this young, naive, insecure girl, desperate to get out of her home town. You've got form for older men. Ha, that's why she will have sent you to me. I've got form, too, but you know all about that.'

'What? What are you saying? Why are you being like this?'

'Can't you see? We're both just pawns in her fucking games.'

'This is ridiculous, you are being ridiculous.'

'Well, now you see me.' He held up his arms and opened his chest as if bearing his soul. The scarf dangled from his fingers.

'I'm sorry you feel like that. You're wrong, you know. About a lot of things. But most of all about Maggie. Sure, she fucked up, but now she's just trying to make it right.' He shook his head in disbelief and kicked at the wooden struts on the balcony. 'Look, I'm booked on a flight in the morning. There's still time. You could come too.' She touched his elbow with her finger, but he flinched and moved away.

'I can't.' He said it quietly, his jaw clenched tight with years of emotion.

'OK,' she whispered, and walked back into the hut to pick up her shoes and bag. He hadn't moved when she came out. 'I'm going to go back to Coco Loco and pack.' She hovered there for a moment, hoping he might at least offer to drive her there, but he just stared out into the jungle, fiddling with the scarf. 'OK, well, I guess that's it then. It was nice knowing you, briefly.'

And then she was back on that hot road again. As wound up and even more confused than she had been an hour earlier. But this time the walk was even further. She was sweating before she'd started. After ten minutes of walking, she heard a bike behind her. It slowed as it drew up by her side. Thank God! She tried to curb her smile as she turned to face him. But it wasn't Lucas, it was Geoff, the letch from the beach.

'Hey, princess, you look hot. You wanna ride?' The disappointment hit her like a punch in the belly.

'I'm fine, thanks.' She walked on and the bike growled along next to her.

'Oh, come on, it's scorching out here. Where are you heading?'

'Coco Loco.'

'What? That's the other end of town. Where's Lucas? Does he know you're out here on your own?' She didn't answer. She could feel a trickle of sweat making its way down her back between her shoulder blades.

'OK, suit yourself.' He looked over his shoulder to pull out onto the road.

'Wait!' Erin could hear the screech in her voice. 'Geoff.' She ran towards the bike and for an awful moment she thought he hadn't heard her. But it stopped and waited. When she was level with it, Geoff turned and fixed her with a grin. A bit of food was hanging off the corner of his moustache.

'Changed your mind, princess?'

'If you could just drop me in town.'

'Sure, hop on.' She climbed onto the back of the bike and held onto the seat but Geoff jumped on the accelerator and drove the bike off at such speed that she was forced to wrap her arms around his waist. 'Hold on, princess!' he shouted, and his hair whipped in her face behind him. He didn't stop in town as she had asked; he drove straight through at speed, nearly taking out several people on the road. Each time someone jumped out of his way, he would laugh. Erin shouted, asked him to stop, but he just laughed louder. He roared up the drive to Coco Loco and the bike skidded and nearly landed on its side as he ground to a halt. He was still laughing. Erin was covered in dust and her nerves were shattered. She climbed off the back of the bike and her legs were shaking as her feet hit the ground.

'I asked you to take me to town,' she said, and started to walk away, but he grabbed her wrist.

'Hey, that's no way to speak to someone who has just given you a lift.' He was still smiling and his eyes were small and mocking, his face covered in a layer of orange dust.

'Let go of me, Geoff.' She tried to pull her hand away but he tightened his grip and her skin twisted and burned under his touch.

'Come on, princess, aren't you going to ask me in? It's the least you could do after I drove you all the way here.' He swung his leg over the back of his bike while still holding onto her wrist.

'You're hurting me.' She tried to pull away from him, but he pulled her towards him and wrapped his arm around her waist. His breath was sour and the piece of food was still clinging onto the edge of his moustache. It fluttered every time he exhaled.

'Geoff, please, let me go.'

'I'm not holding you here, princess.' He smiled and pulled her closer towards him and twisted the skin on her wrist a little harder. And then there was the sound of an engine.

'Hey, Geoff, what the fuck?' It was Lucas, getting off his bike. Geoff let go of Erin and she staggered away from him. 'What's going on?'

'Nothing, man.' He held his hands high in surrender. 'I just found your lady friend here alone on that road in the heat of the day and I gave her a lift home, didn't I, princess?'

Erin didn't answer. She rubbed her wrist that was still burning from his touch.

'Are you alright, Erin?' Lucas walked towards her and put his hand on her shoulder. She nodded and wiped the dust from her face, trying not to cry.

'You'd better not have fucking touched her, man.' Lucas strode towards him and Geoff backed away.

'Lucas, chill out, you're the one who left her to cook on the side of the road.' He laughed and climbed onto his bike.

'Just fuck off, Geoff.'

'Hey, Pura Vida, man, remember?' He did the sign with his fingers and laughed as he kick-started his bike and drove off.

Erin turned and ran into her hut. She grabbed her rucksack from under the bed and began throwing things in. Lucas followed her inside.

'Erin, are you OK? Did he hurt you?'

'No,' she muttered. She could feel the tears stinging the backs of her eyes. She kept her head down and went into the bathroom where she crammed bottles into her washbag. He followed her and leant against the doorway.

'Look, I'm sorry, I should have given you a lift. I was just so cross about the letter, and...'

'It's fine,' she said without conviction, her voice trembling.

'Hey.' He caught her by the arm as she tried to push past him back into the bedroom. He drew her into his chest and held her tight, and for a few seconds she relaxed into his arms and her tears soaked into his vest. But then she stiffened.

'I'm OK, really,' she said, wiping her eyes. She pulled away from him but he grabbed her wrist, the same wrist that Geoff had held, and she winced.

'Shit, man, did he do that to you?' He picked up her arm and ran his finger down the angry streaks that lined her skin.

'It doesn't matter.' She snatched it back and strode over to the safe where she typed in the code.

'Of course it matters, he's a wanker.' Lucas followed her and stood close behind her. She could feel his breath hot on her neck. The safe beeped an error message. She tried the code again but it beeped again.

'Fuck,' she said and tried it a third time. It opened and she pulled out her passport and hugged it to her chest.

'Erin.' She turned around to face him. 'I'm sorry I got so angry, I just, it was a pretty fucked-up time, and...' He took his cap off and ran his fingers through his hair. He blinked repeatedly, just as Maggie said he would. Then he pulled the letter out of his back pocket and handed it to her.

'Here,' he said.

'Are you sure?' She looked up into his eyes. He nodded and she reached for the letter. Her finger grazed his and for a moment they were both holding onto either side of the envelope until Lucas let go. She turned it over and over in her hands.

'Not now, though. You can read it after you've gone. When's your flight?' he asked.

'Tomorrow morning. But there's a bus to San José in...' She looked at her watch. 'Shit, twenty minutes.'

'I'll take you, here, let me help.' She stuffed the letter into her back pocket and together they threw the rest of her things into her rucksack. He carried it out to his bike and she paused at the door and looked back at the dishevelled bed and the sandy floor. She would miss this hut and all the geckos that inhabited it. After the first few nights when she had jumped at every alien sound, she had come to love the buzzing and screeching of the jungle that permeated its flimsy walls. Even the freezing, mildewed shower had become a pleasure. She had changed from the pasty, wide-eyed girl who had arrived ten days ago. Her skin was tanned, her hair lighter, and she felt older, braver, more alive. She blew a kiss at the gecko and followed Lucas down the steps.

The bus was already loaded when they arrived, the engine chugging out plumes of charcoal smoke.

'I guess this is it,' she said to Lucas from the step at the door of the bus.

'I guess so. It's been fun.'

'Yeah,' she said, nodding slowly. 'I'll tell her you said hi, Maggie, I mean.'

He couldn't reply; he looked away and then back at her and nodded his head.

'See you then.' Erin took the next step up into the bus but Lucas grabbed her hand.

'Erin, please don't think badly of me, when you read the letter, I mean.'

She didn't know how to answer that; she had no idea what she was going to read. His brow was furrowed and his eyes pleading.

He had lost his earlier fire and now looked strangely lost. She squeezed his hand and smiled what she hoped was a reassuring smile and turned into the bus.

CHAPTER TWENTY-FIVE

—and then it screamed at me like crashing symbols, like a car alarm that refused to be silenced, like someone had turned the floodlights on.

Celeste hung back that night, when you said you didn't want to leave Skye and the others walked on down the river. She stayed and batted those huge brown eyes at you, and flicked her long chocolate-brown hair, and I'm not surprised you were besotted. The two of you chatted in the porch. God knows how, your French was dreadful and I don't think she could speak much English, but with words or giggles or maybe something more, you woke Skye from her dreams. You heard the zip of the tent and she crawled out of the gap in her white nightie with the fairies at the hem. Her hair was still in a topknot, but ruffled from sleep. She rubbed her eyes with Mr Gilbert tucked under her arm. 'Ucas,' she said. You must have been cross at the intrusion, but I know you didn't shoo her away. You were patient and calm. You talked to her and then sent her back to bed, but she wanted stories and songs and she was fully awake by then and excited by all the late-night activity. And so, you told Celeste that it could take some time. You sent her down the river, said you would follow when Skye had gone back to sleep. You see, I know you tried to do the right thing. But when you read her Peter Rabbit, *she wanted another story and then another and when you sang 'Hush*

Little Baby' she wanted it again and again. And all the time you were thinking about beautiful Celeste by the river and you got more and more impatient. And more and more cross with us: you were missing out on potentially the most exciting night of your life while your parents were getting drunk with their new hippy friends.

And so you left, you kidded yourself that she would go back to sleep quickly. And you told her that you would be just outside. Or maybe you didn't; maybe you told her you were going down the river but that you would be back soon. Either way, you left. You knew she was awake and you left her there. You went down the river to find Celeste. Except Skye followed. Of course she did, she was frightened on her own. You walked along the river path, but you had a torch to guide your way. Skye didn't, she felt her way through the darkness, tripping on the tree roots, the rusty pine needles pricking her bare feet. And all the time she clung to Mr Gilbert under her arm. And then the path dipped down to the water's edge to avoid a fallen tree and she had to scramble over the trunk. I had walked it myself earlier that day and thought how unfortunate it was that the tree had fallen at the point where the water ran fastest. Where it deepened to an inky blue and the current swirled away from the banks and into the middle of the rushing river. She fell, you heard the splash, you heard her scream. You ran back with the torch and shone it on her body fighting to keep her head above the water. Her white nightie ballooned around her face, her beautiful blue eyes wide with fear.

You jumped into the river, but she was drifting away, the current taking her fast, she was on her front now, her face down. Then her body was stopped by a boulder; it thrashed against the granite rock and stayed there. You caught up with her and then flipped her over. She didn't move. Her eyes were still open, still wide with fear. You shook her, you called her name. You dragged her to the bank and pulled her out of the water. You gave her mouth-to-mouth, you pumped her chest. You cried. Your whole body writhed with sobs. But it was too late. And then... and this is the bit that has haunted me the most all these years. Then you threw her lifeless body back in the river. You were panicking, you were out of your mind with guilt and shame and the realisation that this was all your fault. But what if you were wrong? What if it wasn't too late? Did you hesitate? Did you change your mind and chase her body, rushing down the river? Did you sit on the riverbank and sob? At what point did you decide to retrace your steps back to the tent? And where did you find Mr Gilbert? In the river? Or on the bank where she fell?

You see, Lucas, I have pieced it all together over the years. I overheard you arguing with Celeste the day after we found her body. I heard you begging her not to tell the police. After you left, Celeste broke down and told me that Skye had woken up when you were both at the tent. She told me what had happened, and the rest I figured out over time. I found your wet clothes in the boot of the car a few days later – why didn't you throw them away? And the coroner's report said she had broken ribs, I presumed it was from the rocks and so did they. But it was because you had tried to resuscitate her. And when I found Mr Gilbert on the riverbank, he was missing his scarf. Did you just want something to remember her by? You knitted that scarf as part of a school project. I can still see the delight on her face when she tied it around Mr Gilbert's neck. Do you still have it?

All these years I have kidded myself that I didn't tell you I knew because I wanted to protect you. But now I know I was wrong. You haven't escaped the guilt, you've just had no one to

*share it with. I hope in time you will learn to forgive me as I
have now forgiven you.*
    I'm sorry, my darling.

I love you, now and always.
Mum

*

The light was fading as Erin finished the letter. She looked up and
out of the window, and through the gaps of the leaning palms she
could just make out the silhouettes of fishermen holding up their
nets against a blushing sky. She thought of the fear and pleading
in Lucas's eyes just minutes earlier and she wished she could run
back and hold him. Tell him that she didn't think badly of him.
That she just felt as though somebody had ripped out her insides
and left them lying in the middle of the road to be run over again
and again and again. That he must have felt like that every day
of his life for the past thirty years. That she wished there was
something she could do to take away his pain, Maggie's pain, the
pain of that poor little girl in her fairy nightie as she struggled to
breathe in the river.

She had a few hours at the airport at San José where she tried
to sleep with her head on her rucksack. And then a three-hour
stopover in New York when she called Fred. Maggie was hanging
in there. Fred had told her that Erin was coming and she had
rallied slightly. She hadn't asked about Lucas, and Erin dreaded
having to arrive without him and telling her that he wouldn't
come. She also called her parents to let them know she was on
her way home, and her dad insisted on coming all the way to
Heathrow to collect her. She was so pleased to see him when
she came through Arrivals at the airport. She collapsed into his
arms. He smelt familiar, of grass cuttings and engine oil. His olive
jumper scratched at her cheek.

'You look fantastic, Erin,' he said when she pulled away. 'You're so tanned, and your hair.' He ruffled her head. 'It's grown, and the pink has faded. It's more of a rose gold now.'

'Yeah, I'm thinking of growing it out.'

'Really?' He tried to curb the smile that was stretching across his face.

'Or shave it all off.'

'What?'

'Just kidding, Dad.' She nudged him in the ribs.

'I think I'm beyond surprise with you.'

He tried to quiz her in the car, but she was so exhausted she was asleep with her head squashed up against the window before they had even hit the motorway. She woke briefly at Exeter Services for a pee and a coffee, but even the caffeine failed to rouse her and she slept again the whole way to Porthteal.

'Could you take me straight to the hospice, Dad?' she said, wiping the sleep from her eyes as they drove into the village.

'Really? Are you sure?'

'I have to, Dad. I may already be too late.'

'OK.'

It must have been nearly midnight when they pulled up in front of the hospice, and Erin could barely remember the last time she had slept in a bed. She breathed in the salty air as she got out of the car and could hear the tinkling of the boats bobbing around in the harbour below them.

'Thanks for coming to get me, Dad,' she said to him through the open window.

'That's alright. I don't think you could have sleepwalked your way here.'

'Don't wait, I don't know how long I'll be.'

'OK, well, call me and I'll come and pick you up.'

She walked across the gravel drive and tried the handle on the door. It swung round in her hand and she remembered the last time she was here. So much had happened since then, it was hard to believe that only a couple of weeks had passed. Eventually it opened and she made her way down the corridor which was lit only by emergency lights. Her trainers squeaked on the floor. The door to Maggie's room was ajar. She peered through the gap and she could see Fred sitting in a chair under the window. There was a lamp on behind him and he had a book in his lap. His lips were moving. She wasn't too late. Relief flooded through Erin and she released the breath she hadn't realised she had been holding. She could only see the bump of Maggie's body under the turquoise blanket. She pushed the door open and crept into the room. Erin was relieved to see the empty bed opposite, but then flinched with guilt as she realised that it meant the poor lady had probably passed away.

Fred looked up at her and smiled. He walked around the bed towards her.

'Erin.'

'Is she…?'

'No, she's still here.' He put his hands on Erin's shoulders and kissed her on both cheeks. He looked tired. His wispy white hair was ruffled and there were smudges on his glasses.

'She will be so pleased,' Fred said.

Erin dared to look at Maggie for the first time. Her eyes were closed and her head dipped back into the pillow. She looked smaller than before. Her cheeks were more sunken, her eye sockets more hollow. Her bony chest rose and fell irregularly with every rasping breath. Erin walked over to the bed.

'Hi, Maggie,' she said, and crouched down next to her.

'Here, Erin, sit here.' Fred pushed the chair underneath her and Erin perched on the edge.

'Can she hear me?'

'It depends. She drifts in and out of consciousness. She spoke to me a couple of hours ago when I said you were coming.'

'Really? What did she say?'

'She said you shouldn't bother. She hoped you would stay in Costa Rica.'

'Oh, great. I'm so glad I just traipsed across the world then.'

'I think she hoped you would find the life you wanted out there.'

'Yeah, well, there's still problems in paradise.'

'Did you… did you see him?'

'Yeah. Yeah, I saw him.'

'You don't have to tell me, Erin. I'm going to go for a walk. Stretch these old pins.'

'OK. Thanks, Fred.'

When he had walked out of the room, Erin picked up Maggie's hand. It was cold and felt smaller, frailer than ever.

'Maggie. Maggie, can you hear me?'

Nothing.

'So I went, Maggie. I've been to Costa Rica. I found Lucas. I told him. I told him you were sorry and gave him the manuscript and the letter.' Erin looked down at her hand clasping Maggie's. 'Can you hear me, Maggie? It's me, Erin.' Nothing. She had raced across the world to get back here in time but Maggie wouldn't even know she had been.

'You were right, Maggie, about me needing to get out of here and see the world. I couldn't get over how different it was over there. I hadn't realised quite how sheltered my life is, my parents' lives, most people in Porthteal's lives. It's all so different – the smells, the heat, the mosquitoes, the food. Not necessarily for the best, definitely not the mosquitoes – look, I got bitten so badly at the bus station yesterday.' She pulled her jumper down to reveal a band of crimson spots all the way round her shoulder. 'I can't believe that was only yesterday – it feels like a whole world away. They have this saying over there, "Pura Vida". Everyone says it all the time with this funny hand gesture.' She did it to Maggie and looked down, willing her to respond, but there was nothing.

'Anyway, it's on every t-shirt, every baseball cap. I guess it's their mantra. But it seems to work – everyone is pretty chilled out, and they are really big on looking after the planet. I think you'd approve, apart from this one wanker called Geoff. He…' Maggie opened her eyes then and stared up at the ceiling. Erin leapt off the chair. 'Maggie, I'm here. It's Erin. Can you hear me?' She leant over Maggie so close that she could smell her fetid breath. But Maggie's haunted eyes looked straight through her as she drew in a rasping breath and then closed them again. 'Oh shit,' Erin said, and slumped back into the chair. 'Maybe it's best you don't know I'm here, it's not as if I've brought the prodigal son home with me.' She looked out of the window. She could see the moon; it was nearly full and casting shadows into the room. She closed her eyes and remembered the sunset on the bus the evening before. She tried to work out the time difference and exactly how many hours it had been since then.

'Erin,' a voice croaked from the bed.

'Maggie?' Her eyes were open as before, and while she wasn't focusing on anything, Erin could tell that she was more present somehow. Her head was turned slightly towards Erin.

'Are you there?' she croaked.

'Yes, hi, Maggie.' She leant forward and grabbed Maggie's hand; her fingers closed around Erin's and the crusty corners of Maggie's mouth lifted into a smile.

'Did… did you?'

'Did I see Lucas?'

'Mm,' she grunted.

'Yes, Maggie. I saw him. And I told him you were sorry. I gave him your letter and the manuscript.'

'Did he…' She stumbled on the words; they got stuck at the back of her throat amid the phlegm and she struggled to breathe.

'Shall I get someone, Maggie?'

'N… no.' She held up her hand.

'He forgives you, Maggie,' Erin whispered when the fluttering had subsided. 'I'm sorry he didn't come. He wanted to, but I don't think he could leave Costa Rica. I don't think he even has a passport. And after everything, he just wouldn't, I mean couldn't…' Erin felt the back of her neck flush with heat as she stumbled over her words.

'Face me…?'

'No, no, it's not that. He totally forgives you.' Maggie's hand clenched in hers.

'Did… he… tell you?'

'About what? About Skye?' Maggie nodded. 'Yes, he told me about that night and, well, he showed me your letter.' Maggie flinched when she said it and she wondered whether she shouldn't have told her that. 'I'm sorry, Maggie, maybe you didn't want me to know what happened.'

Maggie opened her mouth and looked like she was about to say something and then her face softened. 'Tell me, what is he like?'

'What's he like? Well, he's handsome, he has the same laughter lines around his eyes as you. And the birthmark between his shoulder blades, well, that's obviously still there. And that mole above his lip. He's gentle and kind and he's amazing with the butterflies. There was this one blue morpho that had a broken wing, and I watched as he cut the other wing with a pair of scissors to make it the same so that it could fly again. He has a great life out there. It's so beautiful, Maggie. The water is so clear and so blue. And the rainforest comes right down to the beach, and you wouldn't believe how loud it is. There are these howler monkeys…' Erin looked down at Maggie and saw tears streaming down her cheeks. 'Oh, Maggie, I'm sorry, I didn't mean to upset you.'

'Don't stop.'

'Well, the howler monkeys, they are so loud. I thought they were a dinosaur at first, but they're actually quite small. And there are sloths in the trees, they are amazing. And Lucas took me to all these remote beaches on his bike, and…'

'Did you and he…?'

'Did we what?' Maggie smiled and Erin dithered; she hadn't prepared herself for this question.

'Well, er, kind of, for a bit, but it wouldn't work. He's too old for me, Maggie. I know I've gone for older guys before, but… We got on well, though.' Erin could feel her palms getting clammy. She pulled her hand away from Maggie's and wiped it on the blanket. She was trapped between the truth and lies so definitively she no longer knew which was which. 'I'm so sorry I couldn't get him to come, Maggie. I did try.'

'I didn't want him to come.'

'But I thought that was why you sent me?' Maggie didn't respond. Her eyelids closed over her watery eyes. Erin leant forward. 'Maggie?' she said, and her voice croaked with emotion. She went to sit on the side of Maggie's bed and took her hand again. She felt it tighten in hers around her fingers. And she heard Maggie whisper ever so quietly.

'I… hoped…'

Maggie's eyes rolled to the back of her head then and she struggled to breathe. She coughed. Erin moved behind her and lifted her up under her arms just as she had watched the nurse do a couple of weeks before. Maggie's pointy shoulder blades dug into Erin's chest as she spluttered, and her whole body heaved with the effort. Eventually the coughing subsided and Maggie's breathing returned to its irregular wheeze. Erin started to wriggle her body out from behind her, but Maggie stopped her and held onto her leg.

'Stay,' she rasped. Erin stayed on the bed, sitting behind Maggie with her tiny body propped up against her chest.

'I know he forgives you, Maggie, I just don't think he can forgive himself,' Erin lied, and felt Maggie's body relax in her arms.

'Thank you,' Maggie croaked. Erin hugged her tight. A tear trickled down her cheek and landed on Maggie's white hair.

'He still loves you, Maggie,' she whispered, and Maggie's breathing deepened as she drifted away into her dreams. Erin continued to sit behind Maggie and felt her tiny body rise and fall against her chest with every wheezy breath. Dusky shadows crept into the room, and it was surprisingly peaceful. She was still there when Fred came back into the room a while later. He squinted at Erin through his glasses.

'Are you OK?' he whispered.

'Yeah,' she whispered back.

'Shall I take over?'

'Yeah, my arm has gone dead.' Erin eased herself out from underneath Maggie and Fred took her place, propped up against the back of the bed. Maggie barely stirred, but while the manoeuvre took place her rasping breathing ceased. Fred lowered her onto his chest and she breathed again.

'I might go for a walk too, I've got pins and needles.'

'OK.'

Erin crept out through the gap in the curtain but couldn't bring herself to leave entirely. She hovered in the doorway. And then Fred started to sing. His voice was soft and lilting like the waves. It was the 'Mingulay Boat Song'. The familiarity of the sea shanty made Erin feel warm inside, yet a shiver coursed down her spine. Her dad always cried at the May Day regatta as the lifeboat choir sang that song while their boat was launched into the water. Erin peered back through the curtain. Fred's fingers were tracing patterns over the backs of Maggie's mottled hands as he sang. Erin backed away, ashamed of her nosiness and tiptoed out of the room.

Erin walked across the grass and the dew seeped through the frayed stitching on her trainers, wetting her socks. The water was glasslike and silvery in the light of the moon. She sat down on the bench and hummed the 'Mingulay Boat Song'. She had learnt it at school. The girls did the first verse, about the wives waiting on the shore. Then the boys sang the next one about the men hauling the boat out to sea. She remembered the year the boys' voices had started to break and how strongly their growling tones had resonated. They had all giggled at the time, but the potency of the moment had stayed with her.

She thought of Maggie and of Lucas. She thought about the grief that both of them had lived with for thirty-five years. She wondered whether there was anything beyond this out there for Maggie, somewhere the guilt didn't gnaw away at your soul so relentlessly and the pain didn't hurt so much. She fixed her gaze ahead and a cloud moved slowly across the moon, obscuring the glimmering shaft of water beneath it. Erin held her breath in that moment of dark calm until the cloud passed by and the silver sheen emerged once more.

When Erin went back inside a while later, she found Maggie had died. Fred was in the chair next to the bed. He turned to look at Erin as she walked in and she knew the minute she saw the pain in his swollen eyes, the single tear that trickled down his weathered cheek. She opened her mouth to speak but couldn't find the words. She squeezed his shoulder and walked around to the other side of the bed. Maggie lay on her back, her head tilted to the sky. She was still, silent. The skin on her face had fallen back into the pillow, leaving her cheekbones exposed and her lips pulled tight. A blanket had been pulled up over her. She wondered whether Fred had covered her with the blanket and closed her eyes, or if he had called for help. Had she struggled in those last moments, or had it been a peaceful release? Erin picked up Maggie's hand and put it to her lips – it was powdery-soft and cool. There were no words. They stayed with her, frozen in their own emotions, until the dawn crept into the room. And the birds began to sing in the world that carried on outside the window.

CHAPTER TWENTY-SIX

Lansdown Place, 1st July 1987

Skye found a dying bird under the apple tree at the bottom of our tiny garden once. She was not yet three, but she picked it up with a tenderness way beyond her years. She brought it into the house and laid it on a cushion on the rocking chair in the kitchen. She filled up her dolly's bottle with water and fed the bird tiny sips. She sang to it, the song I sang to her in the darkness of her bedroom: 'Little baby, little baby, oh my darling, my sweetheart, little baby, little baby, oh my darling baby girl'. She didn't revive the little bird; within an hour it had passed away into endless sleep, but Skye had made its last few moments on this earth precious and peaceful.

*

The sky was cloudless on the day of the funeral, but the air still felt fresh. It was May and Porthteal was green and bursting with life. Speckled wood butterflies fluttered around the ripening hedgerows, and watery ditches filled with jellylike spawn. Outside St Mary's Church, the gravestones emerged from a carpet of bluebells glistening with dew and blossom fell from the trees above them like confetti.

There were just five people seated inside – Erin, Fred, José and Erin's parents. Fred was the only one who had known Maggie for longer than a few months. Erin looked around at the open door, still hoping Lucas might appear. She had sent him a text after she read the letter, saying that she understood what he'd done. And then another when Maggie died, and another a few days later, telling him when the funeral would be, but he never replied to any of them. Fred had also found a number for Maggie's niece, Sara's daughter, but she lived in America. She did say she would tell her brothers, but no one had made contact.

Despite the warmth of the day outside, the church was draughty and the seat cushions were damp under their legs. The only sunlight that penetrated the narrow stained-glass windows fell on the silver curls of Patricia Knox, who was hammering out 'Morning Has Broken' on the organ in the corner.

All morning Erin had been fighting the sensation of moving underwater. She had been waking up at four o'clock since she got back from Costa Rica, her head swimming with all the conflicting emotions that Lucas, Maggie and her parents had brought to her in the past few months. She counted the pews for distraction. There were only ten. A couple of starlings flew in through the door and dived between the wooden rafters in the ceiling. They had probably made a nest there, Erin thought. Maggie would have liked that. She looked at the coffin in front of the altar, a single white lily lying on top. Behind it was a synthetic blue curtain which was at odds with the ancient wood and stone that surrounded it. And above the curtain was a crimson banner with 'Jesus for Life' sewn in an arc of patchwork letters. One corner had been bleached salmon where it had caught the light from the window. Erin wondered what Maggie would have thought about 'Jesus for Life'. She wasn't a believer, yet she had wanted a burial rather than a cremation. 'An irrational fear of fire,' Maggie had said months ago, plus she liked the view from the graveyard. She was right there – the church was stuck out on a promontory, so the ocean was on three sides. You could see all the way to Ships Rock one way and over the village to Penruth on the other.

Erin heard her mum muttering to her dad in the pew behind. 'They could have gone easy on the bleach, my poor hyacinths don't stand a chance.' She had done a flower arrangement which sat on the plinth in the corner. Her mum had been an active member of the church for as long as Erin could remember; her mugshot was on the noticeboard by the door along with the rest of the Church Council. Erin had spent every Sunday morning as a child in the vestry assisting her mother with Sunday school. The smell of bleach and damp was oddly familiar, comforting even, though she hadn't been back for years.

The Reverend closed the door behind them and strode down the aisle towards the eagle lectern as Patricia thumped out a final chord. Erin held her breath. 'Maggie was a beloved mother, wife and friend,' he began. Erin looked at Fred to see if he would acknowledge the irony of this, but his eyes were closed and he was nodding his head slowly as he listened. Fred had told Erin that the vicar had been to see him a few days ago to ask questions about Maggie. He now held his hand up as if under oath and told them that he had never met Maggie Muir, she liked to keep herself to herself, but he was a fan of her novels. He threw his words to the back of the church as if he was preaching to a crowd, not the five of them huddled together in the front row. And then he proceeded to analyse the complexity of Maggie's books and Detective Turnpike's depth of character with a sincerity that made Erin grind her teeth together in frustration. He made a casual reference to her two children, Skye and Lucas, without acknowledging their absence. And then he praised Maggie's efforts as a mentor. Erin looked at Fred again, but his focus was on the lectern now. She had never thought of Maggie as her mentor before, but she couldn't imagine her having played that role in anyone else's life. He moved swiftly on to God and the garden of life at that point, and lost Erin to her thoughts. She tried to imagine Maggie's reaction to this eulogy delivered by a man who she had never met. She would have made some dry snipe about his lisp and hook nose. But Erin couldn't help thinking that she would have been disappointed at how inadequately her seven decades were being represented.

After the address, they sang 'All Things Bright and Beautiful' accompanied by Patricia on the organ. Her dad and Fred's deep church voices resonated. While José sang an octave above and added little twiddles at the end of each line, Erin and her mum barely mouthed the words. Had Maggie requested this? Was she watching Erin cringe from up there?

They went to the graveyard after the church and it was only as she watched Maggie's coffin being lowered into the hole in the ground that the tears rolled down Erin's cheeks. With the warmth of the sun on her back she looked out at the blue of the sea that Maggie had loved, feared and revered all at once. And she was suddenly overwhelmed with sadness at her friend's lonely demise. She looked around at the pitiful gathering and decided she owed it to Maggie to say something. She took a deep breath and tried to clear the emotion from the back of her throat with a cough.

'I'd like to say something.' She coughed again and didn't dare look up at the faces that she knew were all focused on her.

'Of course,' the vicar said.

Erin looked down at the heap of earth that was piled on top of Maggie. 'I just wanted to say,' she began quietly. Her heart thumped in her chest and she could hear her voice trembling. She swallowed. She hadn't planned this, and for an awful moment she didn't know what to say. And then she did. 'That Maggie was a really special friend to me. And I didn't know her for very long, but in just a few months she taught me so much. She taught me how to meditate, and all about butterflies, and she introduced me to lots of different books. But, more than that, she taught me about what is important.' She dared to look up at her parents then; they were on the other side of the grave and holding onto each other's hands. They both smiled with encouragement at her.

'And what is not. And she taught me how to be brave, and how to be me. And I will really miss her.'

There was a long pause, and Erin realised they didn't know whether she had finished or not. 'That's it,' she added, and everyone sighed as if they had been holding their breath for the duration of her speech.

'Thank you, Erin, for those lovely words,' the Reverend said, and she felt Fred's hand squeezing her shoulder. 'She would be very proud of you,' he whispered.

'Thanks.' She closed her eyes and listened to the gulls and the sound of the waves breaking on the rocks beneath them. And she hoped that Maggie could hear them too from beneath that pile of earth.

After the funeral, the five of them headed back to Hookes End for a cup of tea. Erin hadn't been there since the day that Maggie was taken to the hospice, and it felt strange being among Maggie's things without her. It was probably the biggest gathering that Hookes End had hosted for over three decades. They were an unlikely party: José was predictably cheery and treating her parents to stories about his childhood and his mother, who still refused to speak a word of English in the thirty-five years she had lived in this country. Erin had heard it all before. Fred rolled his eyes at her and she smiled secretly back. He had bought a ginger cake from the village shop which he sliced into chunky pieces. Erin handed the cake out on Maggie's china plates. Her mum pretended to listen to José, but Erin could see her critiquing the room. She had visibly winced as she sat down on the sofa and a cloud of dust and dog hair had wafted into the air. And now she was looking for somewhere to put her teacup down, but the table next to the sofa was piled high with books and newspapers. Erin watched her mother raise her eyebrows in disdain and she prickled with rage. They had no business having tea in Maggie's house; she would hate them being there with all their scrutiny and false bonhomie. She couldn't stand it any longer.

'I'm just going to take Oblonsky for a run around,' Erin said, standing up. 'Come on, boy.' But the dog's allegiance had transferred to Fred while she had been away, and he sat firmly on his master's feet. Erin had to pull him by his collar to make her not-so-speedy exit from the room while everybody clinked their teacups awkwardly. She walked out of the front of the house and took a welcome breath of fresh air. It smelt different inside, without Maggie. Even more fetid, as if the whole house was rotting away in mourning. Erin realised she actually missed the bitter aroma of nettle tea that she had found so repellent when she first arrived.

Oblonsky clung to her heel. 'Go on, boy.' Erin encouraged him to run ahead, but he didn't move, he just looked up at her with his big sad eyes. And so Erin started to run herself. 'Come on, Oblonsky, if I can do it, you can,' she said between breaths. But he just walked along behind her with his head hung low. She ran to the end of the garden and collapsed onto the bench with her heart racing. She looked up at the sky and tried to dismiss her thoughts as passing clouds, but there was a heavy black one that wouldn't budge no matter how deeply she breathed. She felt so incredibly sad that Maggie's life had ended without the reconciliation she so desperately wanted. And angry, too, with both Maggie and Lucas for all their lies and their wasted lives. How could they not see that everything would have worked out better for both of them if they had been honest with each other from the start?

Unable to find the peace of mind she craved, Erin got up and headed along the cliff path with Oblonsky following. It was the first time she had been on the hill since returning from Costa Rica, and everything felt more intense somehow. The thrashing of the foam-crested waves against the rocks beneath her. The vibrancy of the green hills that were speckled with white sheep on the other side of the bay. The lush abundance of the hedgerows thick with cow parsley and wild garlic. Oblonsky trampled over the foliage, releasing the spicy odour of the garlic and the sweeter smell of the bluebells as they walked under the dappled light of the trees. How could Lucas say it wasn't beautiful here? Erin had laughed at the time, but now she understood that all of his childhood memories were so tainted with sadness that he had become blind to that beauty.

As she came out of the trees and up the hill her phone vibrated in her pocket. Could it be Lucas? *Do you like it?* It was Simon. He had messaged her while she was at the airport on her way home, asking again when he could come with the painting. But she was so devastated by Maggie's letter, and by leaving Lucas, that she hadn't replied. And then she had got home and hadn't known how to reply. She had typed various responses in the days since Maggie's death but had deleted them before sending every time. Her body still yearned for him, and part of her heart, too. But she felt different since she had been to Costa Rica, since Lucas. And now it was too late; he had given up on her and sent the painting instead. Was it here in the village already? She stopped in her tracks and looked up the path towards Maggie's house. She knew she should head back, but the thought of the musty room and forced conversation turned her stomach. 'Sod it!' she said. 'Come on, boy.'

She went to the gallery first, but they hadn't seen the painting, so she headed home, where a large brown paper package was propped up against the back door. Erin picked it up and carried it through and into the kitchen. Oblonsky pushed past her into the room, leaving a trail of wet mud in his wake. Gertie was asleep in her bed at the other end of the room, but her head pricked up the moment they entered. Oblonsky was more animated than she had seen him all day as he rushed over to her, wagging his tail. But Gertie snarled at him, baring her teeth, and he backed away.

'Oblonsky!' Erin said, chasing after him and grabbing his collar. 'Gertie, this is Oblonsky, he's my friend.' Gertie looked at him warily and he bowed his head and retreated to the other end of the kitchen.

Erin went back to the painting and ripped the paper off. She stood back from the canvas to get some perspective. A naked body in light acrylics. Pinks, greys, blues – the colours of the apartment she knew so well. A bottom, her bottom, was at the forefront, textured and pink. She was lying on her side, one leg tucked up underneath her and the other stretched out behind. Her long back stretched up the canvas; there were dusky shadows over each vertebra. Her unmistakable head of cropped pink hair sank into a pillow at the other end. And the dimple, it was there at the base of her back with a glimmer of sweat in its dip. Erin wrapped her arms around her chest instinctively: she felt exposed. There was a piece of paper on the floor and on it, Simon's familiar scrawl. *'Hope you like it. The Driftwood want it. Could you take it over there for me when you get a chance. S x'*

Erin carried the painting up to her bedroom. She didn't want her parents to see it. She propped it against the doll's house under the window and lay down on her bed to look at it properly. He had captured the brightness, the mesmerising light of his studio. Blurred sea and sky were visible beyond the body. Her body. It was skinny, and the edges were sharp. Her bony shoulder blades pointed to the sky. She could recall the light bearing down on her, the noise of the gulls, the smell of sex and paint. She was back there in that room lying on the sofa, the heat of the sun through the glass on her body that still tingled from his touch, asking herself whether this was love. The heat that coursed through her veins and muddled her thoughts – was it love? And was it love that made her go back for more day after day, and convinced her to follow him to London? Was it love that blinded her as to what was right or wrong? Or was it love that she had witnessed that day in the gallery? The very same love that she had been willing to destroy? What was it that he had felt for her? Was it his love that put her up in that shabby apartment? Was it love in his relentless messages since she left? Or was it love that swung his daughter onto his shoulders and kissed his wife's cherry-red lips? She knew the answer. It was there in front of her in swirled acrylics. She hadn't known he was painting her. He told her she was his muse, but was she just his prey? And what about Lucas? Was he driven by the same conflicting desires? She remembered that look of desperation in his eyes as she left him on the bus. Was that the look of love? Or of guilt? Or maybe it was just relief that she was leaving after dredging up his past and messing with his head? Erin shut her eyes in an attempt to quieten her thoughts, and though her mind raced, her exhausted body fell into a deep sleep.

She woke with a start as she heard her parents coming home downstairs. 'What the hell has happened here?' She heard her mother gasp. 'Erin!' she shouted up the stairs. Erin jumped off the bed and had to steady herself as the room spun. She stumbled her way down to the kitchen. There were little pieces of brown paper and bubble wrap all over the floor and Oblonsky lay there in the mess, looking guilty.

'Oh, Oblonsky, what have you done?' Erin crouched down on the floor and started picking up the bits of paper.

'Where is all this paper from?' Her mum slammed the cupboard door as she retrieved the brush and dustpan.

'Oh, just a parcel.'

'What was in it?'

'It was just some… stuff I ordered. I'm sorry, I shouldn't have left Oblonsky down here.'

'No, you shouldn't, Erin. Where have you been? You left and never came back. And you took the dog. He can't stay here. We'll have to take him back to Fred.'

'Yeah, I'm sorry, Mum. I'll take him back. I just had to get out of there. It felt weird being in Maggie's house, with all her stuff. I guess I kind of freaked out. I meant to come back but I just started walking and—'

'It's alright, love, you've had a big day,' her dad said as he sat down in the armchair by the unlit wood burner and stroked Oblonsky's head. 'What have you been up to, you naughty mutt? Did she forget about you?'

'No, it's not alright, John. You have to start taking more responsibility for your actions, Erin.'

'Sorry. I know I shouldn't have left.'

'No, you shouldn't! We felt ridiculous without you. José just rabbited on, and poor Fred obviously didn't want us there. And the whole thing was incredibly awkward.'

'I'm sorry, Mum. I'm sorry if I made you feel *awkward*.' Erin emphasised the word.

'Erin, we know how you felt about Maggie, and we're truly sorry that she died,' her mum said in a more conciliatory tone. 'And what you said at the grave, well, it was very moving.'

'We were very proud of you, love,' her dad interjected.

'Yes, we were, very proud. But you should have been there at Maggie's. You… you…' She stumbled over the words.

'I think your mum is trying to say that you were the common denominator in what was rather an odd group of people.'

'You were! And I just don't understand why you abandoned us all.'

'Abandoned! That's a strong word,' Erin said as she gathered up the bits of brown paper in her dress and carried them over to the bin. And then the momentum of the day's events seemed to build and overwhelm her. The funeral, the painting, and now this. She emptied the paper from her skirt into the bin and slammed down the lid. 'While we are on the subject of abandoning…' she said slowly.

'Erin,' her dad said in a warning tone.

'What, Dad?' She swung round. 'It's been months since I found out I have a brother and we still haven't talked about it.'

'We did try, Erin,' her mum said as she washed her hands in the sink. 'If you remember, you didn't want to talk, and stormed off to live with Maggie.'

'Fair enough, but you didn't try very hard.'

'You've barely been in this house since! First you were at Maggie's, and then in Costa Rica.'

'OK, I know I left. And maybe I was running away from it all.' Erin sat down on the edge of the armchair. 'But I want to talk now. I have had a lot of time to think recently, and if there's one thing that all this Maggie and Lucas stuff has made me realise, it's that secrets don't help anyone. Not in the long run.'

'You're right, love, you deserve to know. Right, Debbie?'

Erin looked up at her mum, who was drying her hands. She twisted the towel around her wrists and her brow wrinkled into worried peaks. 'OK,' she whispered eventually.

'I'll make a pot of tea, shall I? And we could go and sit out at the front of the house. The sun's still there and the cherry blossom looks amazing.' Her dad took charge and Erin and her mum let him usher them out to the rickety bench where they sat down. He disappeared back into the house and they waited in silence for him to reappear with the tea.

'So, what do you want to know?' he said as he handed Erin a mug.

'Everything, I want to know everything. I want to know about his birth. About how you made the decision to give him away. About where he went and where he is now.'

There was a silence which her dad presumably hoped her mum would fill, but Erin could feel her stiffening on the bench next to her and she pursed her lips firmly closed.

'Well, where to start,' he began awkwardly. 'It was a November evening. You could hear fireworks going off all around. I remember going outside to take the rubbish out and smelling the gunpowder in the air. And that was when I heard your mum scream from inside. Her waters had broken. We packed a bag and drove to the hospital in Exeter.' His tone up until this point had been abrupt, just stating facts. But then his face softened and the smile lines at the corners of his eyes creased. 'There was a kid with a burnt hand going into A and E as we pulled up. I remember that was the moment I really thought about what was going to happen, that I was going to be a father and that this little person would be my responsibility for ever after. And that was pretty terrifying.' He grabbed Mum's hand and her fingers closed around his. 'Anyway, thankfully there wasn't much time to think about things. The birth started out straightforward. Slow, but no dramas. Your mum was amazing. But then the baby's heart rate dropped and everyone was speaking in hushed tones and making notes. They told us the cord was wrapped around its neck. And they prepped your mum for an emergency C-section.' He stroked the back of mum's hand with his thumb and looked at her, willing her to speak, but she just stared ahead into the cherry blossom.

'Go on, Dad,' Erin encouraged him gently.

'Well, I didn't think they were going to let me in the operating theatre but then they gave me these scrubs to put on and a mask. It was a teaching hospital, you see, very forward-thinking. So I was actually there when they pulled him out. I saw this shock of jet-black hair. And I heard him cry. And then… well…' He shook his head as if trying to rattle his memories into shape. 'I'm sorry, it's all a bit of a blur.'

'Did they tell you then?' Erin asked.

'No… no… they told us he was a boy, didn't they, love?' He looked at his wife, but she just shrugged her shoulders silently.

'I guess you wouldn't remember, you were drugged up to the eyeballs! But then they whisked him away before we, well, your mum, had a chance to hold him. And it felt like hours, didn't it?

Before anyone came back to us. They stitched your mum up and we kept asking where they had taken our baby, and some nurse said they were just doing some tests, and we would see him soon. They were very reassuring, and I don't think we imagined anything was wrong at that point.' Erin and her dad both looked at her mum, but she had closed her eyes now and was alarmingly still. Erin resisted the urge to shake her. She wriggled her hands under her legs and smiled encouragement at her dad. 'Then we were taken out of the theatre and put into a private room,' he continued. 'I guess that should have raised some alarm bells, but it didn't. And then eventually the doctor came in, and, well, he told us that our baby had Down's syndrome.'

'No, he didn't,' her mum's croaky voice interjected and her eyes sprang open.

'What, love?'

'He didn't call it that, he said he was a mongol.'

'What?' Erin said. 'He actually said that?'

'No, love, that was the nurse, not the doctor. We overheard her chatting to some other nurses, she didn't say it to our faces,' her dad said.

'That's horrendous. Neither a nurse nor a doctor should ever say things like that.'

'Erin, you have to remember things were different back then.'

'I was sick,' her mum said. 'The shock of it on top of all those drugs, I vomited on his shiny shoes.'

'Oh Mum,' Erin said, and grabbed her other hand.

'They couldn't bring him to us because he was in an incubator in intensive care,' her mum continued, staring into the blossom. 'So they took me in a wheelchair and I looked through the glass at his tiny body. He was so covered in tubes that he didn't look any different from the other babies in there. I kept hoping that maybe they had made a mistake.' Her voice faltered then and Erin was almost relieved to hear the emotion.

'Go on, Mum,' she whispered.

'You asked me whether I held him.' Erin nodded. 'Well, it was three days before they said I could hold him, but by then one of the nurses had already mentioned adoption and I had decided I couldn't touch him. I think I was terrified of falling in love with him.' A tear escaped her eye and she released her hands from Erin and John to wipe it away. He tried to take it back but she resisted and clasped her hands together in her lap. 'If someone, anyone, had just said to me you can do this, you can love this child and raise him and be happy. But they didn't.' She spoke so quietly, but Erin could hear the resentment behind every word she spat out.

'Oh, love, that's not fair. I did say…' Her dad tried to speak, but her mum held up her hand to silence him.

'Let her finish, Dad,' Erin whispered.

She continued. 'We left the hospital a few days after he was born, without him. He was still in intensive care. I remember sitting on the floor of the nursery that we had made for him at home and sobbing that he would never see it. So I had already started thinking that he wasn't going to come home. I visited him in the hospital every day and then a week after that they told us he couldn't stay there any more, he was well enough to leave. I panicked. I still hadn't even held him. And no one, not the staff at the hospital, not my mum, my friends, not even your dad, no one encouraged me to take him home. They arranged for him to go into foster care. I just had to sign the form. I was in shock. And I felt so alone. My friends just melted away. No one knew what to say to me. Even my mother didn't come to visit after that first time in the hospital.' Her dad buried his head in his hands and then dug his fingers into the sides of his temples with so much pressure they left white dents.

'How long did he stay in foster care?' Erin asked.

'Eight months. I went to visit every week. It was a lovely couple in their fifties who had fostered loads of kids over the years. They were so calm, so unfazed by him. I always left feeling inadequate and useless. And then an agency called to say that there was a lady who had already adopted three children with Down's and she wanted to adopt Robert. It was the foster parents who called him that. I wasn't sure at first – I didn't want him being just another piece in her collection. But then I met her, and she was the kindest lady I had ever met. She didn't hate me for wanting to give away my child, in fact she said I would be giving her the greatest gift. She had adopted her other children when they were older and she desperately wanted a baby. She didn't want a child without Down's. She talked about how loving and generous they are. And how she wanted all her children to be the same so they didn't feel different. I felt it was meant to be.'

'But didn't you ever consider keeping him? Bringing him up yourself?' Erin asked.

Her mum swung round and looked at her then for the first time, and there was spirit in her glassy eyes. 'Of course I did, Erin. Part of me wanted to, so much. But I was scared, and so young, younger than you are now. And, well, I had seen a girl with Down's walking along the street holding her mother's hand. Not just one – I seemed to see them everywhere. But it was this one girl that stuck with me. You see, she was old, older than me, in her thirties probably. And at the time it felt like a life sentence. The fact that he would never leave home. And I just, I just didn't think I could do it. Of course now…' She scrubbed at the sticky tears on her face with trembling hands. 'Now… now I know I could.' She succumbed to her sadness then and her body shook with wretched sobs, the same way it had that day when Erin had watched from the doorway. This time Erin put her arms around her mother, who clung to her and soaked Erin's dress with her tears as the years of bottled emotions came flooding out.

CHAPTER TWENTY-SEVEN

Porthteal, 15th November 1987

I haven't written for a while. I just wanted to leave everything behind, the doctors and psychiatrists and hospitals, and pretend that I could be normal. That I could reinvent myself here in Cornwall where no one knows my story. The cottage is tiny and there is no central heating, which was fine for the first few months when the weather was balmy, but the last month has been hard. There was ice on the inside of the windows this week, and when the wind picks up the whole building rattles and creaks like we are on a ship. I can see the sea from my bedroom window and am constantly overwhelmed by its magnitude, its strength, its grace. I can't quite believe that after everything that has happened, I have ended up living by water. It is both a comfort and a constant reminder of how it all went so wrong. I have forced myself to swim in the icy water every day since I arrived. It began as a penance; pains would shoot into my feet and my chest would tighten and squeeze out all the air. It would subside after a minute and I'd swim out into the bay, tingling and elated. But then came the fear, the sometimes crippling panic about those shadows looming underneath. Ridiculous, really, I know what is there, it is revealed to us shamelessly twice a day when the water withdraws and the rocks and sand bed are exposed. Yet despite the pain and the panic I cannot miss a day. And I feel more alive than I have in years – apparently the cold water releases some endorphins, or something. Well, I can feel it. Not just the fizzing, tingling sensation when you get out of the cold water, but a healthy glow that keeps me going through the darker moments of my mind.

*

The following morning Erin carried Simon's painting down the stairs and into the kitchen, where her parents were having breakfast. The three of them had made a solid vow after the tears on the bench the previous evening that there would be no more secrets. So the painting was Erin's proof of that promise.

'Morning, love, what's that?' her dad said, looking up from his newspaper.

'It's me.'

'Well, I can see that.' She was almost relieved to hear the sarcasm in her mother's voice after her breakdown the day before.

'Simon painted it. I… I didn't know he was doing it. And, well, it's pretty revealing, and he wants me to take it to the Driftwood where the whole village will see it, and I just…'

'It's beautiful,' her mother said quietly.

'What?'

'It's a beautiful painting, you should be proud.'

'But, Mum, I'm naked. You can see my bum, my boobs, well, just one boob, actually. I thought you would…'

'What?'

'I thought you would be ashamed of me.'

'Oh, come on, Erin, I am not that un-sophisticated that I can't recognise good art when I see it.'

'It's very nice, dear.' Her dad's reaction was more on the level than Erin had expected. He couldn't quite bring himself to look at it, just buried his head in the newspaper and mumbled into his cornflakes.

'Oh, John, look at it. It's not *nice*. It's our daughter, naked on a bed, painted by a married man she was having an affair with.'

This was more like it. 'It's not *nice*, it's stunning. Look at the light, look at her beautiful body. Look at the way he has captured her character even while she's asleep. It's a masterpiece.'

'Wow, I really didn't think you could surprise me again, Mum.'

'Life is full of surprises, Erin.'

'I'm beginning to realise that. So what do you think I should do?'

'Take it to the Driftwood, of course.'

'But won't you care about what all those curtain-twitchers will have to say?'

'Let them talk. I'm tired of worrying about what anyone else thinks.' And with that, she got up from the breakfast table and disappeared out of the room.

'Is she alright, Dad?'

He had been looking quite bemused throughout this whole exchange, but then he smiled. 'I think she's more than alright, Erin. I think she's better than I've seen her in years!'

'Is she in shock? After yesterday and everything. I mean, she is behaving quite strangely.'

'I think she's relieved, Erin. She's spent the whole of your life waiting for yesterday, and now it's done and she can move on.'

Her mum walked back into the room carrying a cardboard box, battered and curling at the edges. She put it on the kitchen table in front of her dad.

'While we're all being honest, I wanted to show you both something.'

'What is it?' Erin asked, peering at the closed box.

'These are scrapbooks of Robert's life,' her mum said, taking the lid off to reveal piles of exercise books, not dissimilar to the ones at Maggie's house.

'What?' her dad said, standing up and taking one of the books out of the box. 'You've been in touch with her?'

'Since the beginning.'

'But, what… why didn't you tell me?' He turned the pages of the books and a photograph of Robert dressed as Spider-Man fell onto the floor. He bent down to pick it up and held onto it with both hands so tight that Erin thought he might pull it apart.

'You were despairing of me,' Debbie said. 'You wanted me to move on, stop moping around. I knew you wouldn't want me to stay in touch, you'd think it was damaging, that I was brooding… but I couldn't not. And Angela, well, she thought it was a good idea, and so once a year I wrote her a letter telling her about both of you, and every year, just after Robert's birthday, she sent a scrapbook full of photos and some of the drawings he had done that year.' Erin pulled one of the scrapbooks out of the box and sat down at the table.

There was a picture of Robert blowing out the candles on a Thomas the Tank Engine cake. Above the picture it said 'Robert is 4!' And then there was a picture of him gazing into a fish tank at an aquarium, and on the opposite page a picture of him with his own goldfish in a plastic bag. He was beaming from ear to ear. There was one of him in his red school sweatshirt and grey shorts. He was standing on the front doorstep with all of his brothers and sisters around him. Erin looked up at a similar picture of her which had been pinned to the chalkboard in the kitchen all these years. She was also standing on the front doorstep, in her grey pinafore dress with pulled-up white socks, her hair in plaits with blue bows. She was alone and looked anxious.

'I can't believe it, Mum. All this time, you've known where he is. Have you never gone to see him?'

'No. Well, actually, I did a few times in those early days. I hung out in the park near her house. I only went on Fridays because I knew that was when Angela's mum looked after him and she wouldn't recognise me. I used to sit on a bench just outside the playground and pretend to read a book and watch them. He loved the swings and the slide. But then they moved and there was no park nearby and his granny got ill and couldn't look after him any more. So I haven't seen him since.'

'But you know where he is?'

'I have an address where I send the letters.'

'And you have never thought to go there?'

'Of course I've thought about it. A couple of times I have even got in the car and headed up the A30, but I always turn back. We had an agreement, you see, me and Angela, that I wouldn't just turn up on her doorstep.'

John hadn't said anything for a while. He had closed the book and was turning the photograph of Robert as Spider-Man over and over again in his hands.

'You never said a word,' he said, so quietly.

'I'm sorry, love. I've wanted to tell you all these years. But then I would have had to admit to the lies, and I just couldn't do it.'

'Well, you've told us now, Mum,' Erin said. 'And we can have a good look at these books, can't we, Dad?'

'Maybe later, love. I've got to see to the sheep.'

John heaved his weary body up from the table and limped out of the room with his leg dragging behind him.

Erin turned to her mum, who was sitting at the table. She looked oddly serene. The lines on her face seemed to have faded and she was almost smiling.

'Is there anything else you want to tell me, Mum?'

'No, that's it, love. I'm all out of secrets.' She got up from the table and kissed the top of Erin's head before she stacked the breakfast plates and carried them over to the dishwasher.

Erin spent the rest of that day at the kitchen table poring her way through Angela's scrapbooks. They were mostly photos with very few words. And in almost every shot Robert was smiling a big, gummy smile. He was often being cuddled by an older sibling in the early years, and even as he grew up into a teenager he always had his arm around someone or some animal. There were guinea pigs, dogs, fish, cats, even a donkey. There was one picture of him in a hospital gown, but even then he was smiling and holding the hand of a nurse. Angela had thankfully written on that page that he was having his tonsils out so that they knew it was nothing too serious. There were pictures of him starting secondary school. Again on the front doorstep in his blazer and tie, still smiling. Erin flinched as she recalled a boy with Down's syndrome at her school, and the grief that Boyd Fletcher and Jason Vernon used to give him. She wondered how real a portrayal of his life these pictures were. 'Doesn't he look handsome in his uniform?' her mum said, peering over her shoulder.

'Yeah,' Erin replied. Debbie had made several such comments as Erin worked her way through the scrapbooks, sometimes from the other side of the kitchen. She could tell what page Erin was looking at from the colour of the scrapbook and the layout of the photos. Erin imagined her spending hours looking at them while her dad was on the farm and she was at school. Did she sit here at the kitchen table, or had she hidden away somewhere for fear of being caught?

There was a picture of Robert at a fun run. He wore a sweatband around his head and a running vest with DSA – Down's Syndrome Association – stapled to his front. He was sweaty and flushed but still smiling. And then there was one of him in a Tesco uniform. He was pushing a stack of trolleys into the trolley park.

'Does he work at Tesco then, Mum?' Erin asked her mother, who was on the other side of the kitchen bagging up salad to sell.

'I guess so. I don't ask Angela questions. She tells me what she wants me to know through the pictures. It has always been that way.'

'But don't you want to know more?'

'I gave up that right a long time ago, Erin.'

'But I didn't.'

'What do you mean?'

'I would like to know more even if you don't.'

'OK.'

'I want to go and meet him.' Debbie didn't even turn around when Erin suggested this; she just carried on stuffing the lettuce leaves into plastic bags.

'Mum.' Erin got up and walked across the room. 'Did you hear what I just said?'

'Yes,' she said, closing a bag with a plastic tie.

'And?'

'Well, I presumed you would.' She stuck one of her 'Tregotha Farm' labels on the side of the bag and put it with the rest in the box on the floor.

'Really, so you don't mind?'

'I don't know how well you'll be received, but I can't stop you.' Debbie picked up the box of bags of salad and carried it over to the back door. Her bike with the cart on it was parked up outside. Erin followed her as she put the box on the cart.

'OK, so I think I'll go tomorrow.'

'Tomorrow?' Debbie swung round. She looked quite pale and her eyes were wide with alarm. 'You can't just turn up like that. You need to write to Angela, give her some warning.'

'But then she might say no and I couldn't bear that.'

'You can't just turn up, Erin, it's not fair on her.' Debbie went back into the kitchen and started pulling jars of mayonnaise out of the fridge and loading them into another box on the floor.

'Not fair? Mum, I've just found out that I have a brother and that you've known where he is all along.' Debbie slammed the fridge door and the contents inside rattled. Then she carried the box of mayonnaise jars out to the bike cart. Erin followed. 'I can't wait any longer, Mum. I'm going tomorrow. Do you want to come?' Debbie looked up at her.

'I can't do that, Erin, I promised.'

'But you didn't promise I wouldn't go.'
'No, no I didn't.'

And so Erin set off the following morning in the rain. She dropped Simon's painting at the Driftwood on her way. Then she typed him a message saying she had delivered the package and asked him not to call her again. She hit send before she could change her mind and felt the familiar butterflies in her tummy and rush of blood to the head as it went. And then she waited for the regret to seep in, but it didn't. Not even as she climbed the hill to Bodmin Moor, where the sky was so thick and gloomy that she could only see a few metres in front of her. It was a relief to dip down into the valley where the air cleared and she no longer had to grip onto the steering wheel with sweaty hands. And she was surprised to feel a sense of relief in her heart, too.

Robert lived in Exeter on an estate on the far side of the city. There was a pub near his house, and Erin was desperate for a pee, so she pulled up outside. The White Lion was a dull concrete building with one boarded-up window on the ground floor and a pile of fag butts outside the front door. She skulked past a group of bulky guys propping up the bar and into the loo at the back. As she breathed in the strong smell of piss and read the words 'motherfucking cunt' scribbled on the back of the loo door, she suddenly doubted Angela's cheery scrapbooks. What if she was just putting her mum off the scent, and in actual fact Robert's life had been one struggle after another? What was she doing here, stirring up the blissful ignorance her mum had enjoyed all these years? She was tempted to get back in her car and drive home. And then she thought of Maggie and Lucas and their constant denial of the truth. She could do this. She strode out of the loo with confidence and avoided eye contact with the barman who shouted after her, 'This is not a public lav, you know!'

Robert's street was a cul-de-sac opposite the pub. There were three boys kicking a football around in the middle of the road. Above them hung a pair of discoloured trainers on an electricity cable. Erin remembered a gang of boys at her school trying to claim their turf in such a way. But the wire was at an angle, and the shoes had just slipped down behind the maths block where they couldn't be seen. In front of the first house on the corner was a toddler with a full nappy and no trousers sitting on a stained mattress. He was picking up empty beer cans with his toy bulldozer and tipping them off the edge of the mattress into a bed of stinging nettles. Erin scanned the front door, hoping it wouldn't be number 34. There was a number 3 there, but just an arrangement of holes where the second digit should have been. She dodged the football that came flying at her head and the kids sniggered as she chased it under the purple Fiat parked up outside the next-door house. Before she kicked the ball back she spotted the number 34 on a metal postbox that was dug into an overgrown lawn. She braced herself and walked up to the front door. There was a window box with pansies in it; the soil was cracked and the flowers were wilting but her heart was lifted by them. She peered into the front window and through the gap down the side of the net curtain she saw a girl sitting on the arm of a sofa. The girl swung round and Erin jumped back, embarrassed to have been caught spying. She took a deep breath to calm her racing heart, but before she had time to ring the bell, the door swung open.

'Why were you looking at me?' It was the girl from the sofa. She looked about ten, with bunches and a unicorn sweatshirt. She had Down's syndrome.

'Sorry. I just... is your mum in?' Erin said as warmly as she could.

'She's not my mum,' the girl said with a lisp.

'Oh, OK, Angela, is she here?'

'Yeah,' the girl said but she didn't move. 'Why is your hair pink?'

''Cos I dyed it, do you like it?'

'It's pretty,' she said and pulled at her bunches.

'Is someone at the door, Trish?' Erin heard a voice coming down the stairs.

'Yeah. She's got pink hair,' Trish shouted behind her.

'Oh, hi, sorry about that.' A lady appeared, wiping her hands on her floral trousers. 'I was upstairs, didn't hear the door.' She had dark hair with grey roots that came down to her shoulders and a fringe that framed her round face. She wore a white t-shirt which clung to her bulges. There was a yellow stain just above her right boob.

'That's OK. Are you Angela?'

'Yes.' She wore thick glasses that magnified her eyes. Her forehead wrinkled into an arch as she frowned at Erin.

'I'm Erin. Debbie's daughter. I hope you don't mind me coming.' Erin could feel the heat flushing to her cheeks. And her words were sticky in her mouth. But Angela obviously didn't have a clue who Debbie was, and continued to wipe her hands on her trousers absent-mindedly.

Erin blundered on. 'I'm sorry, I shouldn't have just turned up like this, but Mum didn't have a number for you, just this address, and I only found out she had it yesterday and I just couldn't wait. You see, I'm an only child, well, I thought I was, and I guess, I hoped I could meet Robert.'

Angela stopped rubbing her hands on her trousers at this point and her palms hung in front of her like a rag doll. Her big eyes glared at Erin.

'What?'

'I'm, er, Robert's sister. I was hoping I could meet him.' Erin whispered the words slowly, afraid of the effect they might have.

'Oh…' Angela took her glasses off and rubbed her face. Her hands were still slightly wet and left a sheen on her skin.

'I'm really sorry, I can come back another time.' Erin started to back away.

'No, it's OK. It's just, well, it's a bit of a shock after all these years. I… Come in, come in.' She walked down the corridor towards the stairs and then turned right into a living room. Erin followed and so did Trish.

CBeebies was playing on the TV, the volume on loud. Angela turned it off and started picking up various items of clothing from the floor, and an upturned plate with some toast which she had to peel off the thick-ply carpet.

'Have a seat,' she said, pointing at the sofa while she disappeared out of the room with the plate of toast and clothes under her arm. Trish sat down next to Erin.

'I'd like to have pink hair,' she said. 'Will you help me?'

'I don't know if your mum would approve.'

'I told you, she's not my mum.'

'Oh yeah, sorry.'

'Does your mum approve?'

'Not really,' Erin said as Angela came back into the room.

'Robert's not here. He's at work,' she said as she sat down in the armchair opposite Erin.

'At Tesco's?' Erin asked.

'What?'

'In the picture that you sent Mum he was wearing a Tesco uniform.'

'Oh right, yeah, that was a while ago now. It didn't work out at Tesco, so he's at McDonald's now.' She took her glasses off and cleaned them with the bottom of her white t-shirt, revealing folds of pasty flesh underneath.

'Oh right, does he like it?'

'Well,' Angela shrugged and put the glasses back on. 'He likes burgers, so…'

'Don't we all!' Erin said a little too enthusiastically. Then the silence hung in the air like a bad smell. She looked around the room. The carpet was grey and fluffy and the sofa was black leather, or maybe plastic. It squeaked as she shifted in her seat. Trish picked up a My Little Pony from the floor and started brushing its tail with a miniature brush.

'Look, her hair is the same colour as yours,' she said to Erin.

'So it is.'

'Trish, could you go and get me and Erin some of those cookies from the kitchen? You know, the ones in the tin.'

'But I'm brushing Pinkie Pie's hair.'

'You can take Pinkie Pie with you if you like,' Angela said. Her tone wasn't entirely soft; there was an abrupt edge to it that made the hairs prick at the back of Erin's neck.

'Alright,' Trish sighed, and reluctantly left the room.

'I'm sorry, but what exactly do you want with Robert?' Angela turned to Erin the minute the door closed.

'Oh, I don't want anything, really. I would just like to meet him, that's all.'

'But why, after all these years? Why now?'

'Well, I've only just found out about him.'

'Really? You never knew, all this time? Did she, did your mum tell you?'

'Eventually, but only because she had to. Someone else let it slip that she was pregnant before me.'

Angela seemed to relax a bit on hearing this. 'Oh right,' she said, and sat back in the armchair. 'She didn't tell you so you could come and take him back?'

'Oh God, no. She said she had promised she would never come. But I couldn't not come once I knew about him, you see.'

'But you're not going to try to take him away?' She clasped her hands together as she said this and squeezed them really tight. Erin began to realise that what she had read as hostility in Angela was in fact extreme anxiety. Her impromptu visit had obviously sent her into a total spin, as her mum had predicted.

'Look, Angela, I'm so sorry. I realise now that I shouldn't have just turned up like this. Mum tried to make me write, to give you some warning, but once I had decided to come I had to do it right away. I guess I was scared I might bottle it. I just wanted to see where Robert has lived all this time and to meet you for myself. Mum said you are the kindest person she has ever met. And I'm sure she's right. She has always been a good judge of character.'

'I don't know about that,' Angela said, flicking her hair in front of her eyes, but she smiled nevertheless.

'Well, you must be, taking all these kids in and giving them a happy home and everything. Obviously I haven't met any of the others, but Trish is lovely.'

'Oh, I haven't adopted Trish, we're just looking after her until a family comes up. I haven't adopted another child since Robert.' Trish came back into the room with a round tin. The My Little Pony was standing on top and she was taking tiny steps, her eyes focusing intently on the toy, willing it not to fall.

'Well done, Trish, you found the biscuits.' Trish lowered the tin very slowly onto the carpet and then removed the pony and took off the lid and handed Erin a Maryland Cookie.

'Here you are.'

'Maybe Erin would like to take her own biscuit,' Angela said, and Erin looked down at Trish's hands which were covered in blue pen.

'Thank you, Trish, my favourite,' Erin said and accepted the cookie. The chocolate chunks had started to melt and left smudges on both of their hands.

'He won't be back till later. Four o'clock, his shift finishes.'

'Maybe I could come back then,' Erin said, not sure what to do with her sticky hands. She didn't really want to lick them, as Trish was.

'I was going to take him to the funfair this evening. It's on the green on the other side of the estate. He's been watching them set it up for days.'

'We're going to the funfair!' Trish clapped her hands together in excitement. 'Do you like funfairs?' She turned to Erin.

'Um, yes, of course.'

'Can she come to the funfair with us, Angela, please, please.' Trish put her hands in a prayer position and smiled a big gummy smile at Angela.

'Oh no, don't worry,' Erin mumbled.

'Please, Angela, please please please please,' Trish begged, and with every please she got a little louder and squeakier.

'I'm sure Erin has got to get back, Trish,' Angela said.

'Well, not really. I mean, I'm not in a rush or anything.' Erin looked at Angela, who was biting her lip, clearly in a quandary.

'Please, Angela, please let her come. Do you like the spinning teacups? They have them, and a waltzer, and…' Now Angela had taken her glasses off and was wiping them on the edge of her t-shirt.

'You know what, Trish, I think you guys should just go to the fair and maybe I'll come back another time.'

'Not fair.' Trish bowed her head and started kicking at the bottom of the sofa where Erin was sitting.

'Maybe we could just play with your ponies. Can I brush her hair?' Erin knelt down on the floor next to Trish and picked up Pinkie Pie and started brushing her tail. Trish stopped kicking the sofa and picked up a purple pony from the floor.

'Here, you can brush Twilight Sparkle.'

'OK, you have Pinkie Pie then.' They swapped ponies and Trish smiled. Erin was thankful for the distraction of the ponies. The silence that followed made her toes scrunch into the carpet.

'I guess it couldn't hurt,' Angela eventually said from her armchair.

'She can come?' Trish looked up excitedly.

'If Erin would like to come?'

'I would love to.' Erin smiled at her.

'Yes!' Trish crawled over to Angela and hugged her legs.

'I have to go out now, though.' Angela stood up. 'I have to take Trish to the optician today, and then we have to pick up Jeremy from the care centre and then Robert.'

'OK,' Erin said, also getting to her feet. 'So, I could come back and meet you here later, then?'

'We won't be back till four thirty. That's three hours away. What will you do?'

'I don't know, are there any cafés or anything?'

'Cafés? Well, there's Greggs on the high street. Or the White Lion across the road.'

'Oh right, yeah, I'll go there. I'll see you later, Trish.'

'OK! Can we go on the merry-go-round?'

'Sure. I love merry-go-rounds.'

'Yes.' Trish punched the air with her fist and then launched herself at Erin with a force that pushed her back against the wall as she wrapped her arms around her waist and aimed her head into her chest.

'Oh, Trish, leave her be,' Angela said, peeling Trish's arms from Erin. 'Now go and put your shoes on or we'll be late.' Trish ran upstairs and Angela followed Erin to the door.

'You won't tell Robert who you are though, will you?' she said as they reached the doorway.

'No, not if you don't want me to.'

'He wouldn't understand, you see. He thinks I'm his mum. He already has brothers and sisters.'

Erin swallowed down the lump in her throat. 'Of course, and he's very lucky. I'll see you later.'

CHAPTER TWENTY-EIGHT

Porthteal, 23rd December 1987

I have got a dog, a mongrel from the farmer in the village who no one wanted – his siblings were drowned at birth. And the dog needs exercise, and so I walk. Sometimes I walk all day along the cliff paths. The ever-changing vista never ceases to amaze me. The same location can look so utterly different on a calm and sunny day in August when the sea is glasslike and the sky is a rich blue. And then this morning when the grey waves rolled in from afar and the whole bay was filled with white water. And the wind was so strong I could barely walk forward and the rain pierced my cheeks like needles. Yet I have never felt so alive, so vulnerable, so completely at the mercy of the elements.

I have started writing again – I am working on a detective novel. Richard calls occasionally. He has hooked up with some Australian bird, another young newly qualified teacher. And Lucas has gone to him for Christmas. There was no mention of me joining them, and I realised I was slightly relieved when the subject didn't come up. I don't think I could leave the village. I feel safe here, something I haven't felt for a long time. Ma came to visit. She fussed around the cottage, dusting and complaining about the draught. She couldn't bear the cold and only stayed one night, and I was so relieved when she left. I found it really hard sharing my space and having to adapt my routine to accommodate someone else. Sara hasn't been; she says she will but I don't believe her. She is really cross with me that I let Richard send Lucas to that school. Not that I had any input on that decision. She has been to visit him, and keeps telling me how unhappy he is, how they make them run through the freezing river in tiny shorts and eat boiled cabbage. She doesn't understand why I won't go and rescue him. I told her I tried, but she says not hard enough. She hung up on me a couple of weeks ago and I unplugged the phone. I'm not sure I will plug it in again.

*

Erin didn't dare go back to the White Lion, so she set out on foot in search of Greggs and the high street. With the help of her phone she navigated her way across the estate. On the far edge was a small park with a concrete playground at one end, and she could see the funfair gearing up for action at the other. A waltzer and a big wheel stood proudly in the middle and a circle of brightly coloured stalls and rides surrounded it. Clusters of people wearing money belts tugged hard on their cigarettes. The sweet smell of onions and burgers wafted over and twisted the anxious knots in Erin's stomach tighter. She crossed the park and found Greggs on the high street and ordered herself a cup of tea and a cheese and onion pasty.

She wished she had brought a book with her. Someone had left a copy of the *Daily Mail* on the next-door table, so she flicked through the pages but found it hard to concentrate on the words as her mind whirred with the enormity of what was about to happen. At least she didn't have to talk to Robert about who she was. And thank goodness for Trish: if the worst came to the worst they could just chat about My Little Ponys and pink hair.

After a painfully long three hours, several cups of strong tea and numerous laps of the park, Erin knocked on number 34 again, her heart in her stomach. She could hear the heavy thud of footsteps pounding down the corridor.

'Robert, she's here, she's here!' Trish shouted from the other side of the door before she opened it.

'Hi, Trish, are you ready to go to the fair?'

'Yes, I am. Come on, Robert,' she shouted over her shoulder.

Robert sidled his way slowly down the stairs. He leant on the bannister which seemed to bow under his weight. He was big, much bigger than anyone else in their family. He had a wide face and broad shoulders that pulled the yellow Simpsons t-shirt tight across his chest. He was smiling, not the huge smile she had seen in all the pictures but a shyer smile, his head tilted forward. He couldn't quite lift his almond eyes to look at her.

'Hi, Robert, I'm Erin,' she said, still standing in the doorway. 'Are you ready for the funfair?'

He had reached the bottom of the stairs by then and dared to look her directly in the eye. 'Do you like rides?' he said, not quite rolling the r so it sounded like 'wides'.

'I love them,' she said.

'Me too,' he said, and beamed at her with so much delight it made her stomach lurch.

'Oh, Erin, you're here. I didn't hear the bell.' Angela was coming down the corridor behind Trish and Robert.

'Yes, hi, Angela. Trish let me in.'

'So, you've met Robert, then?'

'I have.' It was becoming quite cramped in the dark, narrow hallway, half of which was taken up by piles of shoes and bags. Erin backed out of the open front door, welcoming the fresh air that wafted over her shoulders.

'They're both very excited. Shall we get going?'

Trish and Robert had followed her outside. Robert bounced a little on the spot, bursting with excitement. Angela locked the door and they set off down the hill towards the park.

'What's your favourite ride, Robert?' He had his head down and was skipping with every other step next to her. He was avoiding the lines on the pavement just as she had done as a child.

'I like the waltzers, and those ones that swing round in the air.' His tongue sounded thick in his mouth.

'Oh, I know, I think it's called the Paratrooper,' Erin said.

'Yeah, the Paratrooper, I love that!' he said.

'I like the teacups best,' Trish said on her other side. She put her hand into Erin's. It was clammy and soft.

'Oh yes, I haven't been on the teacups for years,' Erin said. 'I like the dodgems.'

'Me too,' Trish said. She was skipping now, too and Erin was having to walk fast to keep up with their pace. 'And I like the ones where you throw balls at the cans to knock them down.'

'Oh yes, I know,' Erin said, 'although I'm really bad at throwing.'

'Me too!' Robert said, nearly walking into a lamp post, he was so focused on the floor.

They could hear the fairground before they rounded the corner and saw it. The twinkling accordions of the merry-go-round fighting for airspace with the techno from the newer rides. The clanking of the machinery and the children screaming with delight – or was it terror?

Erin remembered the fair that came to Truro once a year. Her mum hated it, so she went with her dad. He loved the waltzer, his hair stuck up on end and all the blood rushed into his face as he howled, a noise she had never heard him make at any other time. He kept that blood-tinged glow and crazy hair for hours afterwards.

Robert headed straight for the Paratrooper ride. He had paid his money and slid into his seat before the others even got through the gate.

'Do you want to go on, Angela?' Erin asked tentatively.

'God no, those rides do funny things to my insides. I'll watch you all from here.'

So Erin and Trish joined Robert in the carriage. Erin sat in the middle and they both grabbed her hands as the whir of the machine started and they were slowly lifted into the air. Trish went pale and Erin panicked that she was going to freak out. But she started to laugh, a high-pitched, hysterical laugh, and they plummeted to the ground and all screamed and held onto each other tight. And then they were soaring up again and spinning around and Robert howled just like her father. Erin's eyes watered as they spun and tears streamed down her flushed cheeks as they were thrown from side to side and up and down. When the whir of the machines finally ceased and they came to stillness, Erin wanted to stay sitting in the carriage with both of them gripping onto her hands, their cheeks glowing and their eyes glassy. But the guy lifted the bar and Robert and Trish rushed out of their seat, off to find their next thrill.

As they walked past the High Striker, Trish begged Robert to have a go and win her a fluffy snake on a pole. He needed little encouragement and puffed out his chest as he swung the hammer down on the bell with great enthusiasm, but to little effect. The puck only climbed halfway up the tower. He had another go and missed the bell entirely. At this point Trish stamped her foot in a rage. Erin looked back at Angela for guidance, but she had bumped into someone she knew and was deep in conversation.

'Just look at the bell, Robert,' Erin said, gently but firmly. 'Keep your eye on it, that's it, and now slam the hammer down as hard as you possibly can.' Robert gritted his teeth and stared at the bell so hard he nearly went cross-eyed. Then he threw the hammer down hard and let out a roar so loud that several people nearby turned to look. And the bell at the top chimed with glory.

'You did it! You did it, Robert!' Trish threw herself into his arms and he beamed with triumph, a bead of sweat trickling down his forehead. The man on the stall handed him the fluffy snake which he gave to Trish, and she swished it through the air and ran to show Angela, who beamed with pride when she heard that Robert had won it.

Angela suggested she and Trish go on the merry-go-round together while Robert and Erin went on the big wheel, which only had seats for two. Erin was conscious of Angela conspiring to give her some quality time with Robert and she smiled gratefully at her as they joined the queue.

'You've had a very happy life, Robert, haven't you?' Erin said after they had buckled themselves in and were waiting for the wheel to start. Robert wrinkled his nose but didn't answer, and she realised her question was either too loaded or too abstract for him to comprehend. 'Have you been to this fair with your brothers and sisters?' She tried again.

'Yeah, but Shelley doesn't like the rides. She always throws up.'

'Poor Shelley. What are your other brothers and sisters called?'

'There's Johnnie, Paula, Brian, Shelley and me, Robert.' He patted his bulging belly as he said his name.

'You're lucky, having so many people in your house.'

'Do you have brothers and sisters?' he asked.

'No, it's just me and my parents. It's a bit quiet.'

'It's not quiet at all in my house, Johnnie shouts a lot and Paula sings all the time. Shelley's quiet though, she keeps her headphones on most of the time.'

'And what about Angela, your mum?'

'What about Mum?'

'Well…' Erin fumbled for the words. 'What is she like?'

'She's the best mum in the whole wide world. She makes me toad-in-the-hole with gravy and chocolate cake with sprinkles if I'm sad. It my favourite.'

'Do you get sad a lot?'

'Not really, only if someone is mean.'

'Are lots of people mean?'

He shrugged his shoulders. 'Mum says people are only mean 'cos they are sad themselves. She says you just have to smile at them to make them happy.'

'Does that work?'

'Sometimes.' He shrugged as they were slowly lifted into the air and his eyes grew wide with excitement.

'Look, we can see Trish and Mum on their horses. They're waving.' He waved back with so much enthusiasm that it rocked their carriage. And as the wheel spun and they climbed higher, the noise of the funfair became more distant and the air cooler and calmer. Robert slid towards Erin and the weight of his shoulder pressed into hers, and she was overwhelmed with a feeling so strong she had to hold onto the bar to steady herself.

After the big wheel they went on the dodgems and the waltzer and then the Paratrooper again. And they ate burgers and candy-floss, and they shot at bottles and threw hoops over poles. When she realised that Erin wasn't going to run away with her children, Angela took up residence on a bench at the edge of the park and left them to it. But as the dusk drew in and the lights shone brighter, the techno was turned up and the fair took on an edgier tone.

'I think we should be heading home now.' Angela appeared out of the darkness as they left the dodgems for the second time. Trish and Robert whined with resistance, but Angela was firm and they quickly recovered their good humour and spent the walk home regaling her with animated stories of each ride.

'You'll be wanting to get going now, won't you, Erin?' Angela said when they reached the doorstep of number 34. 'It must be quite a drive.' And Erin's bubble was burst. She wasn't going to be invited in for hot chocolate and *The X Factor* as they had discussed on the dodgems.

'Yeah, an hour and a half or so,' she said.

Trish flung her arms around Erin. 'Bye, Erin,' she said, and then to Angela, 'Has *X Factor* started?'

'Only just,' Angela called as Trish ran inside without so much as another glance at Erin.

'Yes!' Robert pulled his hands into fists and turned towards the music now blaring from the TV in the front room.

'Robert,' Angela said sternly. 'What do you say to Erin?'

He turned back and rushed at Erin. 'Goodbye, Erin.' He put his arms around her. He was wide and soft and smelt of candyfloss and gherkins. She held onto his broad back before he pulled away and rushed towards the sitting room.

'Sorry,' Angela said. 'He really loves *X Factor*.'

'No, don't be silly, it's fine. I had such a great time. Robert is a really lovely boy, I mean, man... I...' Heat flushed to Erin's cheeks as she backed out of the front door. 'Thanks for letting me tag along.' She turned and started to walk down the path. She could feel the familiar stinging sensation at the backs of her eyes and hurried down the steps and past the Fiat.

'Erin!' Angela called after her. She turned and blinked, and hoped that Angela couldn't see the tear that was making its way down her cheek. 'If you want to come back and see him again, I'm sure he'd like it.'

Erin nodded. 'I'd really like that, Angela, thank you,' she said and turned, unable to stop the tears that now drenched her cheeks, and made her way back to her car.

CHAPTER TWENTY-NINE

Porthteal, 15th October 2017

Some say dying is like going home, and I wonder which of my homes I will be going to – before or after? I have had a life of two halves, and the latter has not been entirely wretched. I have been alone but not lonely. I have Oblonsky for company, and before him there was Lenin. And I have my books. I am richer and more successful than I could have possibly conceived of in my before life.

But I have so many regrets, and it is only now in life's final phase that I can concede to them. I always wanted to swim to Ships Rock. I tried once and got halfway there, but the sea suddenly darkened like onyx, and those gloomy shadows swirled beneath me, so I retreated. I wish I had learnt to like goat's cheese, and baked more bread; changed the awful curtains in my bedroom and mended the leaking kitchen roof. And I am sorry I never learnt to play the guitar, or joined a choir. I sing sometimes out on the cliff, and the way that my voice sails out to sea warms my soul.

Of course, all these other regrets fade into insignificance up against the 'big one'. If only there was a way to turn back the dial to that summer of 1982 when the air was full of hope. To that morning when the tent glowed in the honeyed light of dawn and the reflection of the river danced on its walls. Every day since I have counted one hundred ticks of the clock and remembered the gentle wheeze of my family around me before I dared to open my eyes to the dark reality of the day. This morning it was a fog of black and white shadows. I waited for the sleep to clear and the clarity to come, but it never does now. The edges are blurred and the colours are fading. I have started counting my paces in preparation for the blindness. There are eleven from my bed to the bathroom. Sixteen from the front door to the study. Forty-two from the porch to the bench at the bottom of the garden. And I am filing away images in my mind: the cerulean wings of the butterfly painting in the study, the view of the lighthouse from my bedroom window, the tawny stripe on Oblonsky's belly.

I am not scared of dying; more intrigued about how this world transcends into the next. Will it be a writhing struggle or a gentle release? Will I be alone? At home? Will she be there waiting for me in her white cotton nightie with fairies on the hem? Will there be scars that tell her story? Weeds from the river and bruises on her peachy skin? Perhaps she is a grown woman in an alternative world. Perhaps I will never know.

*

Erin could feel the sun trying to burn through the clouds as she trudged up the hill to the cemetery. The ground was mostly dry except for the patches of path under the trees which were soggy with mud. The seasons had been kinder to them this year. There was the odd defiant leaf clinging to a branch, and withered fruit on the ground, not yet washed away by the winter's advance. She approached Maggie's headstone. A jar with crisp violet hydrangea heads had been knocked over on the grass in front. That must be Fred, Erin thought as she picked them up and wedged them securely into the ground.

'Hi, Maggie,' she said, then paused to catch her breath. 'God, I'm unfit. I haven't done that walk in a while. I've become a slave to my desk, can you believe it, Maggie, I work in an office? I took your manuscript to your editor, Cressida, like you told me to. And she asked me to help her finish it. She asked me about Lucas, and I told her everything about Costa Rica and his side of the story while she typed. It was strange being on the other side. It took a few weeks, and we had a laugh – she's quite eccentric, isn't she? And then she offered me a job! Of course I am just a lowly pen-pusher, but that's fine. I get to read some of the manuscripts on the slush pile, as they call it. I found one with potential last month, showed it to someone and they said I have a good eye. All those months of reading to you, that's what did it!

'And I have got out of Porthteal – finally! I am living in Exeter in my own flat. Well, I share it with three other girls, found it on Gumtree. I was quite nervous about living with other people, but then I figured I lived with you, so surely I can live with anyone! One of the girls is Spanish, she is teaching me some so I can surprise Lucas when he comes. He is actually coming here, Maggie, next month. It's going to be so cold in December, he'll hate it. I told him to wait till spring, but he said he wants to come now. I don't know how I feel about it, really.

'We did have a fling in Costa Rica as you guessed. And I know I wasn't going to go for an older guy again, not after Simon. But Lucas is different somehow, he is kind, and not married, and he has been through so much. But then he got so angry with me for reading your letter, and it freaked me out, he had this crazed look in his eye and we had a huge row and then I left and didn't hear anything from him.

'I presumed he didn't want anything to do with me, that I was too much of a reminder of you, of his past. And that was OK, in fact I thought it was probably for the best. But then he called! A few weeks ago, says he's changed. He's given up drinking, smoking too. I'll believe that when I see it. He said he was sorry. He actually asked me to go back to Costa Rica. But I can't do that! I have a life here now, a job, a house and Robert. I have found Robert! I guess it's thanks to you. I see him every week. He doesn't know I'm his sister, but that's fine. I take him to watch a movie or to the zoo – he loves animals. And he's just around the corner.'

Erin felt warmth on her back and the flecks of graphite in the headstone suddenly sparkled as the sun broke through the clouds.

'I've got to go now, Maggie, I'm popping in to see Fred and Oblonsky before heading back to Exeter. But I'll be back soon, and I'll bring Lucas to see you, I promise.' Erin kissed her finger and then traced the inscription on the stone with it. *Maggie Muir, Beloved Mother and Friend.* She stood up and peered over the edge of the cliff at the waves thrashing against the rocks below, the sun giving the foam a silvery sheen. And then something fluttered past her ear: it was a red admiral butterfly, charcoal in colour with fiery stripes and white spots. It landed on Maggie's headstone momentarily and closed its wings as if in salute before flying off. And as it disappeared, so did the sun, and the water became dark once more.

A LETTER FROM SOPHIE

Dear reader,

I want to say a huge thank you for choosing to read *The Butterfly Garden*. If you enjoyed it, and want to keep up to date with all my latest releases, just sign up at the following link. Your email address will never be shared and you can unsubscribe at any time.

www.bookouture.com/sophie-anderson

I hope you loved *The Butterfly Garden*, and if you did I would be very grateful if you could write a review. I'd love to hear what you think, and it makes such a difference helping new readers to discover one of my books for the first time.

I love hearing from my readers – you can get in touch on my Facebook page, through Twitter, Goodreads or my website.

Thanks,
Sophie Anderson

sophieandersonfiction
@MSophieanderson
www.sophieanderson.co.uk

ACKNOWLEDGEMENTS

Thank you to all the wonderful people in my life who have helped me to make this dream a reality. To my agent Madeleine Milburn, who took a leap of faith in me on a dark day in March 2020 when the whole world was fraught with uncertainty, and who has continued to be a perceptive force of wisdom and support ever since. To my editor at Bookouture, Lydia Vassar-Smith, who also saw the potential in this story and has guided me through the process with a brilliantly instinctive and nurturing hand. And to everyone else on the Bookouture team who have worked their magic behind the scenes.

To my inspirational tutors at the Creative Writing Programme, Beth Miller and Susannah Waters, who taught me everything there is to know about writing a book. To my writing group, we began this roller coaster ride together and you have been there with me every step of the way.

To my early readers Debby and Neach, for their enthusiasm and gentle prompts, and to my mum, who dedicated her entire holiday to combing my manuscript for errors from the beach. To fellow authors Lulah and Emily, and their sage advice in our freezing-cold studio. To Jo and John and their girls for locking down with us and sharing the workload so I could write.

To all my wonderful friends who believed in me – there are too many to name. And finally to my amazing family: my parents Charlie and Fenella and my brother Marcus for their never-ending love and support.

To my children, Jago, Albie, Arlo and Delphi, for their relentless capacity to distract and inspire.

And last but by no means least, to Myles, for loving me and making me believe that anything is possible.

Printed in Great Britain
by Amazon